WHEN AN ELEVEN-YEAR-OLD, WHISKY
DRINKING, PIANO PRODIGY ENCOUNTERS A
WEALTHY FAMILY POSSESSING
SUPERNATURAL BEAUTY, HER ENSUING
OBSESSION UNLEASHES FAMILY SECRETS AND
A CATACLYSMIC PLAGUE OF CICADAS.

The summer of 1956, a brood of cicadas descends upon
Providence, Georgia, a natural event with supernatural
repercussions, unhinging the life of Analeise Newell, an
eleven-year-old piano prodigy. Amidst this emergence, dark
obsessions are stirred, uncanny gifts provoked, and secrets
unearthed.

During a visit to Mistletoe, a plantation owned by the
wealthy Mayfield family, Analeise encounters Cordelia
Mayfield and her daughter Marlissa, both of whom possess an
otherworldly beauty, a lineal trait regarded as that *Mayfield
Shine*. A whisper and an act of violence perpetrated during
this visit by Mrs. Mayfield all converge to kindle Analeise's
fascination with the Mayfields.

Analeise's burgeoning obsession with the Mayfield family
overshadows her own seemingly, ordinary life, culminating in
dangerous games and manipulation, setting off a chain of
cataclysmic events with life-altering consequences—all of it
unfolding to the maddening whir of a cicada song.

What People are Saying about THE CICADA TREE

"Following in the magnificent footsteps of Carson McCullers and Harper Lee, Robert Gwaltney creates a wonderful snapshot of the friendship that forms between Analeise and Etta Mae, two eleven-year-old girls in '50s small town Georgia... This is a book to love and remember, and every book club in America would be wise to snap it up."— **Robert Goolrick, #1** *New York Times* **bestselling author**

"The gothic beauty of a relentless Georgia summer is brought to life through Gwaltney's deliberate details and exquisite imagery, while all the while evil lurks beneath the surface; from where or what the reader does not know but is as convinced by Gwaltney's expert storytelling as he is."—**Zoe Fishman, bestselling author of** *Invisible Air* **and Georgia Author of the Year 2020**

"This is Southern Gothic with a vengeance—a dark blast of family secrets, strained loyalties, and bitter betrayals. We follow young Analeise Newell with fear and hope, dreading what may happen to her even as we turn the pages. Robert Gwaltney is a writer to watch."—**Christopher Swann, author of** *A Fire In The Night*

"Gwaltney's Southern Gothic, THE CICADA TREE mesmerizes and seduces, the language redolent and deadly, the characters steeped in secrets and madness, and the whole of it an enthralling and perfect read. Easily my favorite book of the year."—**Kim Taylor Blakemore, bestselling author of** *After Alice Fell*

"In his novel, Gwaltney assembles some classic ingredients of the Southern gothic tradition, with Analeise's world being haunted by death, madness, the past, and the supernatural...the eerie tone is well orchestrated for those who appreciate a sinister frisson."–*Kirkus Reviews*

THE CICADA TREE

Robert Gwaltney

Moonshine Cove Publishing, LLC
Abbeville, South Carolina U.S.A.
First Moonshine Cove Edition January
2022

ISBN: 9781952439247

Library of Congress LCCN: 2021925751

Cover and interior design by Moonshine Cove staff, cover image by Ebook Launch.

To Mama and all my ghosts

And Timothy, always.

About the Author

Raised alongside three feral, younger brothers in the rash-inducing, subtropical climate of Cairo, Georgia, Robert Gwaltney is a lifelong resident of the South—a circumstance that has left an indelible mark upon his voice as a writer,

A graduate of Florida State University, Robert Gwaltney resides in Atlanta, Georgia. By day, he serves as Vice President of Easter Seals North Georgia, Inc., a non-profit organization that strengthens children and their families during the most critical times in their development. Through his non-profit work, he is a champion for early childhood literacy. Robert also serves as Fiction Editor for *The Blue Mountain Review*. In all the hours between, he writes. *The Cicada Tree* is his debut novel. Please visit him at:

www.robertlgwaltney.com.

Acknowledgment

There are many who contributed support to the making of *The Cicada Tree*. Without my critique group: Jef Blocker, Mickey Dubrow, and Marissa McNamara, I am uncertain I would have ever found my way to the end of the thing. Thank you for your friendship and the great care you took with my novel and me. Love y'all to the shimmery moon and back.

A special thank you to my literary agent, Mark Gottlieb, for believing in me and giving me the courage to call myself a writer. And to my publicist, Ann-Marie Nieves, I could not make my way out into the world without you.

To Gene Robinson and Moonshine Cove Publishing, I am honored to have worked with you on my debut novel. You have turned it beautiful, and I am forever grateful.

Thank you to my partner, Timothy, for dreaming alongside me and reading every word. And much gratitude to my oldest and dearest friends: Christine Brazill, Tom Eaton, and Zane Shelfer. You thought I could do this crazy thing when I did not. And a special thank you Leigh Harwell, for all the dinners, birthday cakes, and loving support of me and my writing career. Jon Esther, your book trailer is a revelation.

The Southern Collective Experience: Charles Clifford Brooks, Hunter Carl, Rebecca Evans, and Zach Riggs, thank you for cheering me across the finish line.

Claire Fullerton, my crocodile, thank you for your sisterly guidance in this peculiar and wonderous world of publication. You are dear to me. I remain forever grateful of your introduction to the incomparable Kathy L. Murphy and gang at The International Pulpwood Queens and Timber Guys Book Club. Mandy Haynes, I love you and how we both sometimes walk the wrong way home.

Kim Taylor Blakemore and the Novelitics crew, thank you for allowing me into the fold. Tonya Murphy Mitchell and Jacqueline Vick, so glad to have your friendship and talent in my corner.

To my fur babies: Georgie and Templeton. And to the two we lost along the way: Bently and Logan. Thank you for the unconditional, never-ending fountain of puppy dog love.

Mama, Daddy, Chris, Benji, and Chance—love you all.

And to that summer all those years ago. There would be no novel at all without the cicadas and the secrets they keep.

The Cicada Tree

Come away, O human child!
To the waters and the wild
With a faery, hand in hand,
For the world's more full of weeping than you
can understand.

—W.B Yeats, The Stolen Child

Chapter 1
Providence, Georgia - 1956

A storm was coming.

Way off in the distance, its inky edges began to spoil the late morning sky. A low roll of thunder grumbled from the ground tickling the bottom of my bare feet.

"How many more?" Etta Mae said, holding the front of her dress out before her like a basket.

"A bushel or two." I plucked another cicada shell from the bark of a pine that grew in the far corner of Mama's old Thinking Spot.

Etta Mae giggled. "I love you a bushel and a peck," she sang, her voice holding a sort of magic that shot clean through, like winter static— through anyone who listened.

I smiled, the corners of my mouth pulling back from the lovely sound. "A bushel and a peck?" I laid the shell gently to rest with the others.

Etta Mae blinked down into the mound of casings. "Where did they come from?"

I spooled a length of my hair around my finger. "From the ground," I said, pulling my finger free, leaving a perfect curl down the front of my blouse. "That's what your granny says." I stood tall, placing my hands on my hips, speaking deep in my best Miss Wessie voice. "They needs room to grow." Etta Mae squinted her eyes and giggled.

Thirteen years had passed. Thirteen long years since the cicadas last came, years before Etta Mae and I were born. Now, they returned, digging loose from the earth, attaching themselves to trees, leaving behind a fragile crop of amber-tinted shells.

It was the cicada's singing I remember best—their courting song. It was this frenetic beckoning for the affection of another that stirred the humid air to reckless speeds that summer, the summer I turned eleven.

The earth grumbled again. "Sure must be a dark lonely place down there," Etta Mae said.

"I reckon so." I eyed a shell big as a ping-pong ball. Etta Mae hummed slow and sad, the quality of it, a drape blocking away the happy. I knew then, before she would speak, of whom she was thinking.

"Poor sweet, Mama," she said, looking down at the ground. "Dark and lonely."

"Analeise Newell. Etta Mae Johnston." Miss Wessie yelled from the back porch. "Get your little fannies back on in this house."

"Shhh." I touched my finger to Etta Mae's lips. That had been a game of ours, evading Miss Wessie, our warden that summer and three before. Our mamas knew one another from packing pickles into jars at the Mayfield Pickle Company, my Mama at the white table, and Etta Mae's at the colored.

"You've got 'til I drop these biscuits to dumplings," Miss Wessie said. "Then I'm breaking off a switch."

"Then I'm breaking off a switch," I mimicked, puffing up my chest, grabbing hold of my hips, hoping to bring Etta Mae back from thoughts of her poor, dead mama. To dissolve the sadness she sang into the air.

A gust of wind swept across the old garden, dozens of husks blowing free from Etta Mae's apron. "Best hurry."

"Get on over to the bench." I motioned to the rickety seat. Etta Mae settled herself on the splitting wood, mindful of the delicate cargo gathered up in the front of her dress. "I wish you didn't have to go."

"Me neither," she said, smiling, but I knew it was only half true. I was certain it was singing she loved best, even more than me. Even if it was singing at a stranger's funeral. "I'm ready."

I nodded, glancing off into the horizon, a swirl of smoky clouds moving across a perfect plain of blue. I still held the enormous shell I pulled last from the tree. "This one first." I positioned the prickly appendages into a course plait atop the center of her head. I made busy placing several more.

"How's it looking?"

I stepped back to regard my work. "Just one more."

"Girls," Mama hollered from the house. "The last dumplin's been dropped."

Etta Mae took in a quick breath of air. I tucked the cicada shell into the pocket of my dress. "You look beautiful." I admired the crown I made. "Miss Cicada Bug—1956." I kissed her cheek.

"We best get." Etta Mae touched her hand to her face. "Granny's done dropped the last . . ." She hopped from the bench, letting loose the hem of her dress, our work released to the rising wind. "Come on," she said, grabbing hold of my hand. A whirl of storm blew my hair about my face. Etta Mae pulled at me, but I held firm, my toes pinching the ground. An errant shell clung to strands of my hair. I watched as it bucked in the gale, until it let loose at last, lifted by the current, sucked away into the newly darkened sky.

A shiver shot up my back. Only then did I loosen my toes from the earth letting Etta Mae untether me from the spot. Only once did I turn back, just long enough to watch the first lightning strike, that moment the sky caught fire.

* * *

The sky boomed, rattling the walls of our clapboard house, jostling the windows in their shoddy frames. Etta Mae and I passed the hour at Daddy's old upright, attempting to rehearse the stranger's funeral song. Etta's Mae's gift was singing, and mine, the piano—each of us the perfect accompaniment to the other. Though I never played it before,

"Stormy Weather" was the only song my heart could remember—as though it were the only song that ever was.

I always knew how to play, where my fingers should go, an instinct planted way down deep, just as easy as breathing. Daddy thought it had been he who taught me, but I knew long before, back before I first opened my eyes to the world. It was easy pretending, just a little lie, a reason to be close—if just for a spell. But that was when he loved us, Mama, and me. Before he drank all the good away.

"Sure is pretty," Miss Wessie hollered from the kitchen. "The two of you could coax an angel right down from heaven."

"Don't it make you sad?" I said. "Singing for dead folks?"

She sucked in her bottom lip, then let it loose. "No, not really." She cast her green flecked eyes down at her hands, running them the length of her fingers. But I knew the truth of it. Somewhere in that deep down spot where the music lived and swirled, I knew when she sang, she sang for her poor, sweet mama.

Percussion rolled above us, vibrating the floorboards. Piano keys shivered. Everywhere was music, even in the clink of Mama's jelly jar vase.

"Wish I could go with you." My voice sounded peculiar amidst the storm's refrain.

"Me, too." Etta Mae sat down next to me on the piano bench, leaning her head against my shoulder. "But you get to go to the Mayfield's." She feathered her fingers across my arm. "Folks say the whole town could fit right inside their house.

"I guess." I contemplated the size of such a place, the place Mama went on Saturdays to earn extra money. "Must take a long time to clean."

"Maybe you could play with Marlissa."

Marlissa. Such a pretty name. I poked gently at the cicada shell hidden inside my pocket. In truth, I knew very little of the Mayfields or their daughter, Marlissa. Mama never spoke of them, and I had yet to see one up close and in the flesh—only the passing of their long black car through town, the world caught and reflected in the sheen of its darkened windows.

"One more time," Miss Wessie said from the kitchen. "Then its dressing time."

The rain dissipated, the weight of Miss Wessie's feet across the floorboards audible once more. Etta Mae lifted her head from my shoulder. The cicada shell shifted in my pocket, the sharp tips of its legs sticking into my skin, grabbing hold around my finger. I flicked at the thing until it turned loose, my fingers finding their place on the keys.

Etta Mae did not wait for my music, finding the song within her without the help of a single note of mine. I pulled my hands from the piano and listened, sorrow seeping from the perfect pitch of her soprano. I sat, eyes shut, letting her enchantment settle over me, feeling a tingle just under my skin, the weight of the thing growing until it sat heavy, pressing against my insides, until there was nothing left for me to do but cry.

Rain fell against the tin—at first a smattering, the tempo gaining speed, the force greater until there was no other sound. Nothing left of the music but a deafening whir, and the vinegary taste of sadness on my tongue.

Chapter 2

I leaned forward looking up through the truck's windshield at a two-story brick building, my eyes following the loops and flourishes of the iron scrollwork. "Mistletoe," I said, reading the letters at the top of the enormous iron gate. Before Mama could knock or toot the horn, I spoke again. "Looks like nobody's home,"

"That's not the house."

"Plenty big enough to be a house. What is it then?"

The building, a place large as any home I ever saw, was bigger than the one my best friend, Jane Fenton, lived in on Broad Street with her hateful, twin sister, Virginia. I tugged at the end of my ponytail. Mama and I sat, regarding the place. The old Ford pickup rattled and hummed, the ruckus sending vibrations through the seat. My stomach, already sour from the taste of Etta Mae's sorrow, did not take kindly to the whole affair. Never had I tasted music, and the occurrence left me unsettled and wanting to go home.

"It's the gatehouse," Mama said, staring straight ahead, her words holding a rhythm in harmony with the truck's thrum. Her hand pressed into the horn—three quick honks. She cranked down the window, the glass wobbling and vanishing into the door. "Halbert!" Mama yelled. "Halbert."

"Who you hollering at?"

"The gatekeeper." Mama pushed at the truck door. "You stay put." Mama walked toward the gate's archway, a space cutting clear through the middle of the building. Hands firm upon her tiny hips, she yelled his name again. I watched her grey eyes drift up above the building, gazing into the mottled sky, scratching at the old snake bite scar on her arm.

I pushed at my door. The old rattletrap refused to budge. I slid myself across the seat to the steering wheel and hopped down onto the ground. "Mama?"

"Get on back up in the truck. Before you muss yourself." She walked toward the gate, smoothing her floral, cotton dress and pushed at the right side of the gate. It relented, the sound of iron and hinges playing an unsettling chord, pimpling my ankles clean all the way up my back. I tugged at the hem of my yellow gingham dress trying to pull it to my knees. My legs, refusing to cooperate, had grown longer since Mama sewed it for me at the start of spring.

A man spoke from behind, startling me. "Miss Grace?" I spun about, my shabby brogans wedging into the rain softened earth, tipping me off balance.

"Halbert! Sweet Lord Jesus. Where've you been?"

My eyes ran the length of the man, stopping at the scar blossoming from the collar of his shirt, growing wider up his neck, and gobbling up his ear.

He stared back at me when he answered, one eye blinking quicker than the other—a pair of broken baby doll eyes. "Been around," he said, turning away his bad side from view. "Who's this here?"

I wanted to take a step backwards, to lay space between us. Mama moved toward me, the sound of gravel crunching beneath her saddle-brown ballet pumps. "This here is my daughter, Analeise." She rested her hands on my shoulders.

"Miss Analeise," he said, contemplating the name. "You look a bit like your Mama." One of his eyes clicked shut and then the other. "But it's the eyes that's different." He took a step forward, showing the whole of his misshapen face. "I might have seen them eyes before. Whose eyes is it you got?"

"I reckon' they're my eyes." Mama squeezed my shoulders.

"How's ole' Claxton Newell these days?" Halbert glanced at Mama that time. "Still raising hell down on that river?" The old man chuckled, his face more gruesome with a smile, his scar pulling his right eye down to his cheek.

"Claxton is as drunk and sorry as ever," Mama said. "Of course, you know that. Everybody does."

The sound of her words shocked me. Hard and deliberate. Ugly. Mama never spoke ill of Daddy in my presence. That was Miss Wessie's way, not Mama's. Mama was all whispers and door latches. I tried to turn to Mama, to look up into her face, but she held my back firm against her.

Halbert nodded at Mama, his awful smile put away. Awkwardness strung together the length of silence until the old man spoke. "They done come back." He cupped his hand to his disfigured hear. "Can't you hear them?"

"Who's come back?" Mama said, her voice weary, the edges dipped in annoyance.

"Them ole' locusts" he said. He took another step closer. "They got secrets they keep. Things they know and keep buried down in the ground with them—until they have the mind to come back. To sing out what they know."

"What kind of secrets?" I said.

"Just listen," he said, lifting his chin.

The drone of cicadas rose up around us, stirring fear around my insides like a spoon in a tea glass.

"Enough of that nonsense," Mama said. "You open up that gate." Halbert nodded, his eyes out of sync with the movement of his head. Mama nudged me forward. "Get back on up on in the truck. And roll up that window."

"Mind your secrets," Halbert said. "Keep em' close." Mama eased the truck forward. I took my time rolling up the window, wanting to hear more. He walked along side the truck laughing, his fingers poking in and wiggling at the top of my window, pulling them free just as the glass rolled shut. Above the engine's commotion and the drone of cicadas, he spoke louder. "Just listen," he said, drumming his hands against the side of the truck. "Listen . . ."

"Pay him no mind," Mama said. "He's not right in the head."

The road beyond the gatehouse wound into what I thought must be a forest, one tree twisting into another, fighting for skinny slices of light creeping through the foliage.

"What is this place?"

The song on the radio turned to static. Mama leaned closer to the wheel, squinting into the artificial dusk, "Mayfield Wood." She twisted at the radio knob until the fizzle was gone.

Stifled by the heat, I cranked down the window, letting in a *whoosh* of cooler air and cicada screech. I yelled above the racket. "Why can't I go with Etta Mae?" Any place seemed better than there in the choke of greedy trees and heat, and that creepy old gatekeep.

"We've been over and over that, and you know I don't mind one bit. But other folks do. Now, what is it I done told you time and time before?"

I curled the ends of my yellow hair ribbon around my finger. "A colored church is no place for a white girl-child." I leaned back into the ripped upholstery, the jagged edges poking at my spine. "Why do you have to work on Saturday anyway?"

"Because your daddy drinks all our money away." Mama rarely spoke ill of Daddy, and in a matter of minutes, she disparaged him twice. But she was right. I knew the truth of the thing, had stuck my fingers into my ears to keep from hearing, humming to myself until I fell off to sleep at night. "I hate him," I said, not so much because I really did, but because I needed to hate something right then and there.

"Mind yourself." Mama accelerated the truck. "You can help me with the chores. How about that?" The sudden draw of air tugged at my hair ribbon, fluttering loose bits of hair to tickle my face.

"I don't want to help." I recalled Etta Mae's suggestion. "Maybe I can play with Marlissa."

I sat upright, leaning away from the window and looked at Mama. Her hair, the same color as my own, was pulled from her face into a twist, her forehead crinkled up and busy thinking. "The Mayfields won't be there. They spend Saturdays over in Tallahassee at the Country Club." Nothing about the day was going my way. "Besides."

Mama bit at her lip. "Mrs. Mayfield wouldn't take to you playing with Miss Marlissa."

Her matter-of-fact tone did not diminish the blow. "Why? What's wrong with me?"

"Baby, nothing's wrong with you." Mama softened her words. "Little girls who live in little houses can't play with little girls who live in big ones. That's all."

I knew that could not be entirely true. After all, I played with Jane Fenton, and she and her family lived in a home much bigger and finer than ours. And I played with Etta Mae, and their little house only had one room with no indoor plumbing. "Then how come I can play with Etta Mae."

"That's different."

"How so?" The cab of the truck brightened, the tangle of quarreling trees finding forgiveness and turning loose, letting in the sky. I stared through the cracked windshield, a vista of oaks sprawling before us. It was then I saw it, a goliath of column and brick. I leaned forward placing my hands on the dash. The gravel of the driveway churned and slid beneath the jalopy's slick tires. Never had I seen anything like it. "That's a house?"

"That's Mistletoe."

Mama and I stood at the rear portico. She tugged at the hem of my skirt. "When did you get taller?"

"Miss Wessie said I'm shooting up quicker than a corn stalk."

"Nothing left to let out. Guess it's Etta Mae's now."

"Good. Will you make me a blue one?" I spoke halfheartedly, distracted by the enormity of the wooden door before us and what might lay beyond.

"Fabric's not free." Mama pinched at my chin, tilting my face up to meet her own. It was the tired in her eyes that struck me, bluish-black rings below her lashes accentuating her dark gray irises—setting her eyes off in a beautifully peculiar way.

"Daddy drinks all the money away," I whispered.

Mama squeezed her eyes shut. "Analeise . . ." Her eyes opened and drifted to my collar. She leaned in closer, inspecting the tiny daisies embroidered at the edges with her fingers. Though Mama was brilliant with a needle and thread, it was her ability to read the future in her own sewing that was the true gift, an ability as a part of her as the music inside me. This knack, never discussed in the Christian company of others, was hardly a secret. Such goings-on could hardly be contained within the weak seams of a place like Providence.

"What do you see, Mama?" The cicadas drifted to quiet, then riled up again.

She shook her head and turned me loose. "Just a pretty girl." She pulled my ponytail over my shoulder, fanning the end of it across my collar, covering up the daisies. "We best get on about the day." She took a few steps toward the door then turned back to me. "Stay close to Mama. Don't want you getting lost."

"Yes ma'am." I tossed back my hair, running a finger across Mama's embroidery. Mama pounded her fist against the enormous door—the sound, a faint, hollow thud. She stepped back, and I leaned my head in to listen for any signs of a stir. Nothing could be heard except for the rising cicada buzz, a sound so fierce, the vibrations caused my skin to tingle. "Maybe nobody's home." I hoped that time it was not true. More than anything, more than I wanted to be with Etta Mae, I wanted to be there at Mistletoe. To see inside.

Mama knocked again, then pushed at the door until there was ample space for her to fit her face through the crack. "Mercy?" Mama sometimes spoke of Mercy, the Mayfield maid. The familiar name was a comfort there in the strangeness. Mama pushed at the door again, and I followed close behind peering around her slow-moving hips.

We entered through the kitchen, an expansive, good smelling place with gleaming edges. It was not the impressive size of the place, or the glossy black and white checkerboard floor that held fascination. Across the room, a fireplace roared. "It's summertime," I whispered, perplexed by the queer nature of the thing.

"Mrs. Mayfield has peculiar ways. Now, you stay here." She pointed to a table and ten chairs. "I'm going to see about Mercy."

I tugged at the hem of my skirt watching Mama pass through the archway, wondering how long a girl's legs could grow in a day. The heat from the fireplace grew more oppressive, a slick of perspiration forming at the nape of my neck beneath the weight of my ponytail.

Alone there with the fire, a terrible anxiousness rattled from my temples all the way down through my right foot. I watched and listened to my worn loafer tap a paradiddle on the floor. I slowed the beat and lowered myself to my knees, finding my reflection in a white, glassy square. The floor was cooler than expected, the sensation welcoming. I pulled off my shoes and socks acquainting my sweaty feet to the well-tended floor.

I contemplated the black and white squares and thought of Etta Mae and the fun we could have there together. I set myself hopping across the floor in an elaborate array of hopscotch patterns, my feet slapping out a lively tempo. The shear fun of it took hold, giggles spilling out and bouncing about the kitchen walls. Before I knew it, I ran out of floor, standing beneath the archway through which Mama had passed. I whispered out into the passage. "Mama? Mercy?" I pulled at the hem of my skirt and waited.

Nothing. I lifted my right foot and poked my toes across the threshold and then my left. Before I knew it, I was creeping through the place with my fast-growing legs.

On the tips of my toes, I passed from one corridor to the next, driven by familiarity, a lightheadedness, a peculiar feeling Mama sometimes called *déjà vu.* A thing Miss Wessie called a Remembrance. In the darkest passage, I heard it, the piano. Fast arpeggios. Broken chords. Off the grand marble foyer, it grew louder, sending red-hot quivers through my feet, pulling me into a mahogany paneled room.

Beneath a tumble of chandelier crystals, a woman, her back to the doorway, played a black, baby grand piano. Dust motes waltzed in shafts of light falling across the piano, casting her in a spectral haze. Her hands, a beautiful chaos. Her shoulders, impossibly still.

Barefoot, I crept across the wide-planked floors, my fingers twitching and fidgeting at my sides, following and copying the notes. The weight of my body released the slightest creak. The woman's hands froze above the keys, the hysterical notes scattering the dust motes and tangling in the chandelier.

Then the other feeling returned, that red-hot sensation making its way from my feet to my knees burning all the way up my legs. Something was telling me I should run from the place.

In a breath, she stood—her movement so quick I questioned if she in fact had ever been sitting. Her face—it stupefied. The angles and curves and shadows—all of it assembled into a masterpiece. Her hair was blond, a sort of color I never encountered before, a weaving of different shades creating a rich depth of color tumbling in soft waves above her shoulders.

From across the room, she studied me, tilting her head from side to side. She moved across the floor, the movement so fluid and light, her crocodile pumps hardly made a sound. She took hold, grabbing me by the shoulders. Her touch was hot, urging the burn I felt to move from my waist and spread across my chest. She leaned in, her stunning face so close I thought she might kiss me. When she set her breath against my face, she whispered a single, melancholy word. "Patton . . ."

Not until then was I frightened. *Patton.* I struggled, wriggling my shoulders. That is when she did it. I could smell the blow before it reached my cheek. Perfume and setting lotion. When her hand fell hard against my face, it was the softness of her skin I first noticed, then the sweet bracing sting. There was a shocking joy in her slap, a thrill of tingles—like riding in the back of a truck in a thunderstorm. Rain pelting hard against my face. *A thousand little needles.*

"My name's not Patton. "I'm Analeise. Analeise Newell."

Something swirled in the depths of the woman's green eyes. Her long, slender fingers eased their grip, worrying in her double strand of pearls. "Newell?"

A voice crept softy into the room. "Mother?"

A miniature version of the woman stood at the door, a girl near about my age. Her skirt, the same color of jade as the woman's, was full and cut above her pale knees. In lustrous waves, her blond hair fell below her shoulders. She was a dazzle of girl. A story book princess.

Mama's panicked voice echoed from the foyer. "Analeise?" She rushed into the room, her hands busy pushing loose strands of hair back into her sloppy twist. Her momentum slowed as she entered the room, her eyes bouncing about, surveying the proximity of each inhabitant from the next.

"Mrs. Mayfield. I'm so sorry. I thought you already left out for Tallahassee."

The Mayfields. I was standing in the room with the Mayfields.

Mrs. Mayfield smoothed her pretty skirt, lacing her elegant fingers at her waist. "That appears quite obvious." She set her words and gaze upon me.

Mama and Marlissa moved across the room, joining Mrs. Mayfield and I upon the red Persian carpet, a magnificent affair unfurled across the room like a giant tongue. I always thought Mama a lovely woman until she stood there next to Mrs. Mayfield.

Mama began to speak, but Mrs. Mayfield silenced her with a wave of hand. "Grace Newell, my home is not a place for this child."

Mama was in trouble, and I wanted to help. "Aren't you going to the picture show?" I looked at Marlissa, trying to shift the conversation.

She studied me with curiosity, her eyes moving from my face to my bare legs and naked feet. When she did not speak, I spoke again, "Your dress sure is pretty," I moved forward to touch her skirt as I might a butterfly wing.

"Thank you." She took a step away from my reach. "We are going to Abel Darlington's birthday party." Her eyes were verdant and lovely as her mother's.

Unable to control myself, I spoke again. "I have a jewel for a crown. Etta Mae gave it to me. She's the Cicada Queen." I reached for the pocket of my dress, retrieving a single cicada shell, presenting it to Marlissa in the palm of my hand.

Her scream came quick, her hand swinging violently against mine. The hull caught air landing at the toe of Cordelia Mayfield's shoe. In one movement, the shell was crushed.

I eyed the crumbled remains on the carpet at the toe of Mrs. Mayfield's crocodile shoe. "It's just a shell. It won't hurt you," I said.

A shifting of clouds extinguished the light filtering through the windows. Quickly as the sun left, the room swelled again with light.

"Let's go find your father," Mrs. Mayfield said, walking toward Marlissa. "Before that girl pulls anything else out of her pockets." Cordelia and Marlissa walked hand in hand to the door, a sight so glorious I longed for it to last.

"Grace, do not bring that child here again." Mrs. Mayfield did not turn around when she spoke. She hummed the song she had played, slowing it to slurry tempo.

Mrs. Mayfield and Marlissa stepped across the threshold into the foyer. The room turned sad, a dallop of clouds passing across the sun. The light turned dim, a rapture of heat and prickles still rising from the cheek Cordelia Mayfield slapped.

Chapter 3

At first, the night sky stirred like firefly flicker. Mama mistook it for heat lightning until the faint grumble of thunder intensified, rattling the house, rousing my fascination with the Mayfields.

"Sounds like the Lord has a bee in her bonnet," Mama said, pulling the sheet to my chest.

I ran my feet beneath that old threadbare sheet, searching for cool patches, contemplating Cordelia Mayfield's redolent, floral scent. I tried my best to seem interested in Mama. "That's what Miss Wessie always says."

"I reckon that's where I got it from." Mama touched the tip of my nose with her index finger, the aroma of Ajax still clinging to her hands, shooing away all the good Mayfield smells I was busy remembering.

"Virginia Fenton says it's blasphemous to call the Lord a woman. Blasphemous means it's a sin." Another rumble of thunder sent tremors, vibrating my nightstand and the three nickels I found beneath the Mayfield's sofa cushions. There had been no time to hide them in my keeping spot, the space in the floor beneath my bed. And I hoped Mama had not seen them, that she was distracted by the storm and knowing that Daddy would be coming home soon.

"Guess I wouldn't set much store in what that Virginia Fenton has to say."

"I don't. Not really." In truth, it was hard to ignore her politics, especially in the crush of a Virginia Fenton headlock.

Mama sat down on the bed next to me and smoothed my forehead. "You know why Miss Wessie thinks the Lord's a woman, don't you?" Mama knew I did.

Miss Wessie spoke of it often, a saying so frequent it needed to be cross stitched and hung in a frame. "Because the sweet Lord above has to be a woman to put up with all the mess men folk done made down here on this here earth."

Mama smiled, a rare and beautiful thing. "She's a smart woman, that Miss Wessie."

I stared up into the wood slat ceiling, eyeing the tea-colored water stain shaped like Florida. "Wonder why the Lord doesn't do something about it?"

"About what?"

"Men and the mess they done made."

Mama tried to smile again but gave up. "Women. If we don't have anything else in this world, we have patience." She twirled strands of my hair around her finger. "And hope." She held her hand to my cheek, the place Cordelia Mayfield slapped, Mama's eyes anything but hopeful. I wanted to push her hand away, the rough edges of her fingers and the smell of cleaning solvents—all of it upsetting my recollection of the day.

"Mistletoe must be the biggest house in the whole world." I wanted to switch the conversation to a matter of most pressing interest to me, the Mayfields.

Mama touched the tips of her fingers to her forehead. "I can't speak of the world. But it's the biggest one around these parts." She hesitated, her eyes drifting up to the water stain and back again. "Sweet baby." She cleared her throat. "Before I walked into that room today with you and Mrs. Mayfield, did she say anything? Anything to upset you."

"No, ma'am." Right then I might have told Mama that Cordelia Mayfield slapped me. That it felt good and bad all at once, like telling lies or stealing nickels. That she shared a secret, told me a riddle. I liked the thought of it, a secret with Cordelia Mayfield, a lovely something of my very own. The soles of my feet grew warmer, my toes wriggling beneath the sheet, hankering for cooler places.

Mama tickled at my earlobe. "I hope she didn't hurt your feelings when she said what she said about not bringing you back again."

"Don't feel hurt." I was hesitant to believe Cordelia Mayfield meant what she said. For the briefest, most glorious of moments, she appeared happy to see me there in the music room. The sky threw another hissy fit, rolling thunder and slinging lightning—upsetting the electricity in my lamp. Mama and I both held our breath, staring up at Florida until the threat of darkness passed. "You ever wish we could live in a place like Mistletoe?"

Mama chewed her bottom lip. "I reckon here is just about a good of a place as any." She did her best again to smile, but I knew she didn't mean it. Mama's eyes shifted up and to the right the way they always did when she was too tired to be good at lying. She bent down and kissed my forehead. "Baby, do you wish we lived in a big, fine place like the Mayfields?"

My feet searched the sheets, finding nothing to soothe the heat creeping up my legs. "Might be nice to have a little more room. Could be nice to have one of those black, shiny pianos, don't you think?" Daddy's old upright was a battered thing, the front right leg shimmed up to keep it from tilting. Seemed to me that everything in the place, even Mama and Daddy were delicate things—the whole kit and caboodle propped up with cardboard and held together with rusty nails.

"A new piano might be nice."

"Mrs. Mayfield sure is pretty. And so is Marlissa."

"Pretty is a easier chore for some than others." Loose strands of hair drifted like broken bits of spider web about Mama's face. She tried to tidy herself, pushing and threading the hair behind her ears.

"You ever wish it could be easy? Being pretty." Right away, I knew my words came out wrong—a peach cobbler pulled out of the oven too soon—uncooked and running all over the place. I grabbed hold of Mama's arm. "I didn't mean you're not pretty. You are pretty. I just mean . . ."

Mama squeezed my hand. "I know what you meant, baby." She touched my cheek again, rubbing away a little bit more of Cordelia Mayfield. "Been a long day and we both need to get us some rest." She patted my chest and eased up off the bed.

"Don't go. Not just yet, Mama. Tell me the story." I needed to keep her there with me a bit longer, to know she was okay. To make her believe I thought she was an easy kind of pretty. I grabbed hold of her arm and tugged her back down.

"You've heard that story a hundred times before. You can tell it better than me." Mama's shoulders drooped, an invisible bushel of weariness strapped onto her back.

"Pretty please." Mama was right. Miss Wessie, Etta Mae, and I could all tell it, the story of the night Mama danced with a rattlesnake at the River's Edge Church of Holiness and Light. The night that snake sunk its fangs, leaving Mama with two faded scars on her arm and clairvoyant tendencies.

Mama tried to push herself up from the bed, but I held tight. "Be sweet and turn Mama loose."

The sky threw another fit, abandoning us to darkness. "You have to stay now," I said. "She wants you to."

"Who wants me to?"

"The Lord," I said, whispering back. "Don't go and rile her up. She already sounds plenty angry."

Mama gave up then, pulling back the sheet and tucking herself in next to me. "You're burning up. You feel alright?"

"My legs are hot is all." It was not the complete truth. In fact, I was feeling a little strange, not quite myself, and I was a little bit worried. I never had a fever in my feet and legs before. Was I on the cusp of an exotic illness? "Mama, have you ever heard of anyone tasting music?" I wondered if it might be a symptom, an explanation for my newly acquired condition.

"Can't say I ever have." There was amusement in Mama's voice. "Why you ask?"

I lied, not wanting to worry Mama, deciding to try and sort it out on my own. "Virginia Fenton said she tasted it one time." There was probably no reason to worry. Mama was right, it had been a long day, and it had been a peculiar one. Maybe I was just tired.

"What did I tell you about that Virginia Fenton?"

"Pay her no mind."

The sky took pictures, setting off a frenzy of camera flashes. In between the strobes, I tried to find Cordelia and Marlissa Mayfield's beautiful faces, but it was only Florida I spied blinking back down at me. Only, it looked different in the quick repeat of light. Had it always looked a little like the letter "P"?

The ground grumbled, a long roll of a timpani drum, vibrating the stolen nickels across and off the nightstand. The heat spread over my knees and up my thighs. At last, I found Cordelia Mayfield's stunning face in the storm, her lovely song playing in my ear like a Miss Wessie Remembrance.

Right then, right there, I wanted Mama to go, to leave me there in the storm with that queer thing I needed, to feel again what I felt when Cordelia Mayfield slapped my face. Joy. And prickles. And heat.

* * *

Etta Mae and I did not see one another on Sundays, so I languished until Monday when I could finally regale her with my visit to Mistletoe. After helping Miss Wessie put away the breakfast dishes, and after she released us to the day, I stole into the pantry on the tips of my toes and tucked two white aprons beneath my arms.

On the back porch and free from Miss Wessie's glare, we took off skipping hand in hand behind the house to Mama's garden. Etta Mae led the way, her lovely soprano singing us to the place.

Mama once called the garden her Thinking Spot, a gift from Daddy before I was born. He configured the outdoor space from plantings of azaleas, boxwood, and juniper trees, positioning them all in a large square around the old oak tree. He even repurposed a section of iron fence he salvaged from the junkyard, constructing a fine looking, black garden gate.

Mama said I took my first steps there, she and Daddy coaxing me to them with their arms stretched wide. On rare occasion, Mama spoke fondly of those days in the grass, the time before Daddy took to drinking. I always wondered if it was the Old Crow whiskey that did it—making her abandon that special place.

Once I wrestled up the courage to ask Miss Wessie. "Why doesn't Mama go to the Thinking Spot anymore?"

"I guess she's all thunk out," she said, her eyes remaining steadfast upon her ironing.

"Is it because of Daddy? Did he do something? Was it the whiskey?"

Miss Wessie put the iron to rest, squinting at me as if I stood off in the distance. "I don't know if there is any one thing that did it." She straightened her back, placing both hands on her hips. "Most times it takes two to squeeze out all the goodness."

"What does that mean? I don't understand."

"Then you ain't ready to know." Miss Wessie picked back up the iron and spit on the thing, releasing a sizzle and puff of steam.

Etta Mae and I, with our novice gardening skills, now tended Mama's Thinking Spot, keeping it from going completely to seed. Where Mama and Daddy once watched my first steps, Etta Mae and I now played.

Close to the garden, Etta Mae let loose my hand, pushing through the gate. She leapt onto the rickety, wooden bench. Her muddy, bare feet took hold, and when her balance was secure, she concluded her vocal processional with one sensational trill. "You want me to sing my solo from church?"

These questions were never more than pronouncements that a song would follow. There was so much I wanted to tell her about my visit to Mistletoe, and I was hoping just once, she might refrain from singing. I smiled, looping my hair behind my ears and nodded, hoping she would hurry things along.

Etta Mae straightened herself, pulling her shoulders back. With the slight upward tilt of her chin, she set her gaze beyond the garden as if looking into a crowd, awaiting the moment the congregation would settle into quiet, nothing remaining but the shuffle of poster board fans. She rested her hands by her sides. Her lips parted. And she sang.

It was never the lyrics that stirred emotion, but the lovely timbre of her voice that cast spells, her tiny hands moving with the rise and fall of her voice. At Etta Mae's right foot, a cicada wiggled from its shell, another straightening its crumpled wings just beneath the bench's seat.

With the last lovely note drifting off to melt in the summer heat, Etta Mae jumped down from the bench. "Did you like it?"

"If a bird can fly on wings, a person can surely take to the air on the glory of your singing." I swished the saliva around in my mouth wondering if I might taste her song again.

Etta Mae kissed my cheek. "You're sweet like pie."

I held gently to her kiss, touching the place with the tips of my fingers. "I know a song. Well, it's not a song with words."

"Where'd you learn it?" Etta Mae said, a hungry look in her eyes.

"Just listen." I pulled and scrunched the hem of my dress humming the melody Mrs. Mayfield played on her fancy, black piano.

Despite my poor vocal ability, Etta Mae deciphered the melody and joined in. After a few moments, Etta Mae broke away from our duet. "That's pretty. Kind of like a waltz."

I placed the aprons on the bench away from the clumps of mud Etta Mae's feet left behind. "I heard it at Mistletoe when Mama was cleaning the other day." I sat down on the bench ready to talk. Etta Mae joined me, both of us fidgeting until we faced one another, both of us sitting cross legged with little regard for the unladylike flash of white underpants the other displayed.

"Mistletoe." Etta Mae clapped her hands together. "Where the Mayfields live." Her voice was filled with a Christmas morning kind of excitement.

"Yes. That's the place. Mr. Kingston Mayfield is Mama's boss, you know. He owns the Mayfield Pickle Company."

"And lots of other things, too. Granny says he owns half of Georgia."

Of course, I could not help but feel the slightest annoyance at her interruption. After all, it was my turn to talk. Etta Mae had not actually met or visited the Mayfields, which really made me the true authority on the topic. "Umm hmm," I said, smiling and nodding. I placed my hand on her knee, a reprimand and signal to pay better attention.

Etta Mae's eyes widened and narrowed with every detail I offered of Mistletoe. It was with careful attention I described Cordelia and Marlissa Mayfield, from their exquisite dresses to the gentle wave of their luminous blond hair. She remained silent except for those times she would exclaim, "My sweet baby Jesus," her customary expression of awe.

When I finished recounting my visit, Etta Mae was the first to speak. "Were they nice to you?"

Forthrightness bound the edges of our friendship, but in that moment, I let loose a corner, let it fall right out of my hand. "Yes. Very nice." Why did Etta Mae need to know that Mrs. Mayfield slapped me? Why did anyone? That was a secret between the beautiful Cordelia Mayfield and me. And with inexplicable ease, I told another lie. "Marlissa invited me to the party, but I couldn't go because I had to help Mama."

Without any hint of jealousy, Etta Mae smiled, her amber-tinted eyes filled with sincere happiness I made a friend as lovely and impressive as Marlissa Mayfield. I knew that deep down in the ugliest corner of my soul where I tucked away all the bad parts of me, that I would not have extended the same generosity. The sun, filtering through the leaves of the oak tree, illuminated the flecks of green in her eyes. Swimming in those shimmery pools, I began to feel the press of the lies I told. I leaned backwards to steady myself, my hands resting on the aprons.

"What are those for?" Etta Mae caught sight of the surprise.

"Our party dresses." I grabbed hold of the aprons, spinning around, dangling my feet over the edge of the bench and pushed off. I unfurled the aprons like sails, tightening my grip to keep them from falling into the mud.

Etta Mae squealed, clapping her hands, planting her feet on a damp patch of grass. I held the aprons at arm's length to study them. One apron was for Sundays and special occasions. Mama took great care to fashion a ruffle from a remnant of fabric left over from curtains she sewed for the preacher's wife. The other, bearing the discoloration of kitchen chores, was for regular days.

Etta Mae reached out for an apron, and I met her hand with the shabby one. She hesitated for a moment, then took the apron, wrapping it about her teensy waist, concealing the brown, cotton dress I outgrew.

Once my apron was in place, I greeted her with a curtsey. We both began to spin, our makeshift party dresses floating above our knees. Etta Mae stopped and fanned out her apron. I followed her lead.

Etta Mae studied my feet. "Why are you wearing your shoes?"

I took a look at her mud-caked toes. "Because ladies always wear shoes." In my attempt to capture the elegant cadence of Mrs. Mayfield's speech, I inserted the slightest pause between each word.

Etta Mae turned loose her apron, her smile diminishing as she looked down at herself. She wiggled her toes and flexed her feet. She began to giggle, the sound catching as winter flu.

When our laughter subsided, she hummed the melody again, slowing the tempo, transforming Cordelia Mayfield's song into a melancholy waltz.

We took hold of one another, spinning off around the garden, gliding about to her lovely humming. Shards of light rolled across us like a honky-tonk mirrored ball.

She sang, weaving her own words into the melody. "Beautiful, beautiful boy. Oh where, oh where did you go?"

I could taste it again, Etta Mae's singing. Sweet then sour, like the first suck of a lemon drop.

Faster and faster, we spun, her hands on my shoulders and mine about her waist. We were a single, sinewy knot of girl. A cicada landed on my hand, then another on Etta Mae's neck. We kept spinning, neither of us afraid.

Etta Mae's singing grew louder. In the rise of her voice, my legs turned warm, and I felt an urgency to tell her my secrets—that there was a good kind of hurt. To tell her I lied. That I was a nickel thief. That I could taste her sweet-angel music.

Louder and louder, she sang. "Beautiful, beautiful boy."

That cicada on her neck antagonized me, fluttering against my cheek. My legs burned hot, a meanness boiling my insides. Sweat beaded at my lip, and when I could take it no longer, I put my mouth to Etta Mae's ear. Anger shot through me, exploding like a canning jar. Right then I whispered the only word I could remember. The only word that was, and I shoved Etta Mae. Hard and mean. To spin and tumble off beyond the oak tree and into the weeds.

Patton . . .

Chapter 4

"Looks like you gonna live to see another day," Miss Wessie said, dabbing salve at the scratches on Etta Mae's legs.

"We were dancing in the garden. Our hands slipped loose." Etta Mae dangled her legs over the side of the counter, smiling. If Etta Mae suffered the slightest discomfort from her topple, she did not show it. Did she like the way it felt? Did it tingle like a Cordelia Mayfield slap?

Perhaps Etta Mae really thought it was an accident. If she was lying to protect me, I was grateful. How could I ever intentionally hurt Etta Mae? And what could have made me do such a thing? Was it the heat from my fast-growing legs? But if I was completely honest, anger pushed me to it—the feeling Etta Mae might have been trying to pry loose my secret.

"Your ole' brown dress gonna need some mending. And that poor apron." Miss Wessie rested her hands on her hips. "Looks like that poor apron gonna need to be laid to rest." The very idea of that mud-splattered apron being put to rest must have amused her. Laughter worked itself up deep from her throat and spilled out into the room. She raised her right hand up to the ceiling. "Lord Jesus."

Miss Wessie's laughter tickled like fingers against my feet. Etta Mae and I joined her, interspersing shrill short catches of breath with her soulful bass. Our laughter subsided, smiles still stretched across our faces.

Miss Wessie smoothed and pulled long strands of my hair through her fingers. "Baby, go turn on that radio."

Such a rare request from Miss Wessie so early in the morning, with chores yet to be done, held the promise of fun. In case she might change her mind, I hurried over to the Sears and Roebuck Silverstone Radio. I turned the dial until there was music and spun around searching for Miss Wessie's approval. After several adjustments of the dial, she nodded.

"Now that's a song a body can move to." Miss Wessie kicked off her shoes, lacing her fingers, stretching her hands—knuckles popping.

Miss Wessie began with a few gentle twists of her upper body followed by a series of shoulder rotations. Though Miss Wessie was not a petite woman, there was beauty in her generous proportions. Her full bosom gave way to a waist, a feature not typically bestowed upon a woman her size.

Miss Wessie motioned for me. "Miss Lady, get your fanny on over here."

I tossed my hair over my shoulders hurrying across the floor. She spun me around, a mere warm-up for what was to come next.

"What about me Granny?" Etta Mae said.

"What about you?"

"Can I get down from here?" Etta Mae fluttered her legs over the counter.

"I think that's the safest place for you to be," Miss Wessie said with a half-cocked grin.

Miss Wessie helped Etta Mae from the counter then took each of us by the hand and twirled us like lassos. "Now pay close attention," she said, placing her hands on her hips. She swayed—bending her knees, lowering herself to the floor, and then back up again. Her body, a magnificent pendulum. She raised her hands to the ceiling, executing a series of slow revolutions showcasing her plentiful backside.

Etta Mae and I made sorrowful attempts to match her undulations, both of us star fragments amidst her glorious constellation.

Mama stood at the doorway. "Looks like I walked into the Bait and Tackle on a Saturday night."

Daddy's bait shop, a wooden shanty on the river, was notorious in Providence as a makeshift juke joint in the evenings. Its and Daddy's reputation, an indelible stain on the family name.

"Mama, I thought you were at work."

"Starting late," Mama said, giving Miss Wessie a sideways glance.

"Don't give me that uppity look, Grace Newell. We just having a little fun is all. If the sweet Lord didn't want us to dance, she wouldn't have give us legs." Miss Wessie lifted her dress above her knees.

Etta Mae and I both lifted our dresses, mimicking Miss Wessie.

"Dear Lord," Mama said, regarding the three of us. Etta Mae's legs caught Mama's attention. "Etta Mae, sweetheart, what on Earth happened?"

"Just a little accident is all," Miss Wessie said. "She gonna be just fine."

Etta Mae's face grew somber, her breathing labored from our honky-tonk dance. "Miss Grace."

I took in a deep breath, staring at the greasy dollops of salve on Etta Mae's legs. Was this when she would do it? When she would rat me out. *I should have pushed you harder.*

Mama smiled expectantly at Etta Mae. "Sweetheart?"

"It stings a little, is all."

Mama glanced up at the kitchen clock. "Best be on my way." She walked over kissing the top of Etta Mae's head, then mine. "You put that apron up," she said, squeezing my shoulder. Something seemed to catch her eye. She reached down, taking the apron's ruffle in her hand, glancing across it from left to right, as one reads a sentence.

Mama saw something. "What's it say?" I said.

She bit at her lip, her eyes still clinging to the hem. "Nothing." She looked up hesitantly. "Sometimes, a stitch is just a stitch."

She was lying, I was sure of it—the way concern crinkled around her eyes. I might not have been able to see into the future like Mama, but I could read a face, especially hers. "What is it, Mama?"

"You mind Miss Wessie." She lifted my chin with her index finger, then hurried off, the screen door slapping behind her.

Miss Wessie fiddled with the white kerchief covering her head. "Guess we best get on back to the day." Her eyes drifted down to my feet. "Miss Lady, how come you took it into your head to wear your shoes out to play?"

"Because ladies always wear shoes," Etta Mae said, smiling.

"Is that so?" Miss Wessie directed her gaze at me, her hands resting back on her hips. "Well, ain't you something."

Etta Mae answered once again on my behalf. "Yes ma'am. They always wear shoes out at Mistletoe. Even when they don't have any place to go. Isn't that so, Analeise?"

Miss Wessie moved closer and leaned down. "How you know what them Mayfields do out at Mistletoe?" Her eyes narrowed, her words slow and suspicious.

"Be Bop A Lula" played on the Silverstone, stirring the silence. Wafts of Miss Wessie's homemade salve mingled with the lingering smells of breakfast, unsettling my stomach. Anger was swelling up in Miss Wessie, this I knew. But why?

There was a noise. A knock at the front door.

"Analeise, turn off that radio," Miss Wessie said.

I hurried to the Silverstone and fiddled with the knob.

The three of us stood still, listening.

There was another knock, the sound faint and hollow.

"Someone's at the front door," Etta Mae whispered. A visitor was a rare occurrence.

"Just a minute." Miss Wessie located her shoes, wiggling her feet back inside. She turned to me and spoke in a mocking sing-song. "Ladies always wears their shoes when folks come to call." With a flourish of her hand, she adjusted her kerchief, walking from the kitchen down the hall to the front door. Etta Mae and I grabbed hold of one another, following close behind.

"Flowers for Mrs. Grace Newell," a man said, a gorgeous bouquet covering his face.

Etta Mae and I squealed, hopping all about the place.

"Get on back in that kitchen." Miss Wessie snapped her fingers and pointed down the hall.

We complied, neither of us particular fans of Miss Wessie's wrath. Miss Wessie walked into the kitchen, the lovely flowers reaching out from a cut-glass vase. She placed them on the table. The three of us stared in silence, mesmerized by the vibrant colors of the things, most of which we had never seen before.

It was Etta Mae who broke the spell. "Who they from?" She reached out for the small gold envelope tucked within the blooms.

Miss Wessie swatted Etta Mae's hand. "Says right here on the card they belong to Miss Grace. Is your name Miss Grace?" Etta Mae shook her head, her bottom lip bowing out just a bit.

"I bet Daddy sent them. Maybe he's trying to say he's sorry." I relished the thought. Of Daddy being kind—of the three of us in the garden again. "Wouldn't that be nice?"

Miss Wessie crossed her arms. "Would be real nice."

Etta Mae hummed the song I taught her in the garden, stopping after just a few bars. Miss Wessie and I followed Etta Mae's widening eyes to the collar of her dress beneath which was the slightest movement. Etta Mae froze, holding her breath. Our eyes held onto the emerging thing. Red eyes and then the spread of translucent wings. *A cicada.*

She might have screamed, might have shaken herself all about until she was free of the thing. But she stood stock-still, resuming her beautiful humming, serenading the cicada as it crept up her neck to light on the top of her ear.

Beautiful, beautiful boy . . .

Chapter 5

Everything would change soon as Mama saw the flowers Daddy sent, I was certain of it. Yet, the day lolled along with a relentless lack of urgency waiting for her to return home from work.

Etta Mae and I passed the hours in the garden, exiled there by Miss Wessie to swelter, and leak like faulty spigots.

"You reckon Mama's flowers need watering?"

"Granny told us to keep our little fannies out here and stop bothering her."

I moved my mouth repeating back her words without making a sound, then stuck out my tongue. "I don't care what she said."

"That's mighty big talk." Etta Mae flashed her tongue back at me.

I grabbed Etta Mae by the arm, pulling her to the house. "Come on."

We peered into the kitchen through the screen door and listened.

"This is a bad idea," Etta Mae whispered.

"It's a bad idea to let them flowers wilt before Mama sees them." With the precision of a safecracker, I coaxed the door open, charming the springs to stretch without so much as a mewl. "Hurry up. Before she comes back. And grab that watering can."

Etta Mae scuttled on the tips of her toes over to the edge of the porch and back again. 'It's got something in it." She reached in and pulled out a pint of Old Crow whiskey. Her eyes widened. "Sweet baby Jesus."

"Shush up. She'll hear you." I took the bottle from Etta Mae and held it up, examining the golden-brown liquid. "Daddy must've hid it in there. Here you take it." I handed back the bottle while retrieving the watering can. I hurried over to the sink, filling it while counting silently to ten.

"They're so beautiful." Etta Mae leaned in and gave them a sniff. "Don't you wish you could smell just like this?"

I nodded, lifting and tilting the can above the arrangement. "Is that enough, you think?"

"Mmm hmm." Etta Mae hugged the bottle of Old Crow to her chest.

I blotted at the excess water that spilled onto the table, a result of my anxious hand. We stood back gazing at the bouquet, each of us silent, mired in adoration.

"You gonna drown them flowers." Miss Wessie's voice boomed from behind us. Etta Mae and I screamed, unaware she was watching from the door. Miss Wessie straightened her shoulders, puffed out her chest, then sucked in what seemed to be all the air from the room. And she yelled, "Git."

I dropped the watering can onto the table. Etta Mae and I squealed, scattering from the table to the door.

"Don't make me break off a switch," Miss Wessie yelled, as the screen door slapped behind us.

Within the shifting shade of Mama's Thinking Spot, Etta Mae and I sought refuge beneath the oak tree, both of us sprawled and soaked through with perspiration—the bottle of Old Crow resting on Etta Mae's chest, rising with each short breath.

"That was a close one," Etta Mae said.

I sat up and leaned against the tree. "I reckon it was." I took the bottle from Etta Mae.

"What you gonna do with that?"

"Never you mind." I unscrewed the top. I lifted the bottle to my nose.

"Analeise."

"I'm just smelling it." The scent was not altogether unpleasant. "You wanna a sniff?"

Etta Mae leaned away from me, swatting at the bottle. "You're gonna get us killed. If Granny catches us with that bottle, we won't be sitting down until the good Lord calls us back to glory."

"Daddy sure likes it." I rotated the bottle, watching the contents shimmer and swirl.

"He likes it a gracious plenty." Etta Mae reached out and touched my wrist. "Now you go and put that up."

I did not care for her tone. *A gracious plenty.* "Did your daddy ever drink?" It was a mean thing to ask, a question for which I already possessed the answer. A topic on which she did not care to speak. Etta Mae never knew her father.

She shrugged, pressing her back against the tree. I was immediately sorry for what I did. The last thing I wanted was to send her drifting off into grief, thinking of her dead mama and her run away daddy.

"I wonder what all the fuss is about." I pulled the whiskey so close to sniff it grazed my nose, a drop splashing up on the tip. I dabbed my finger against my nose, then my tongue, tasting the hint of buttery sweetness. It was then I decided to do it. I tilted back the bottle and gulped a mouthful.

"Analeise Newell."

"Hush up." I shut my eyes, taking in the slow burn trailing down my throat, blossoming across my insides. Like the smell, the taste was not as bad as I anticipated.

"Are you crazy?" Etta Mae squeezed my wrist.

"Might be." I opened my eyes to make certain the ground had not split apart to swallow me up.

"You drunk yet?" she whispered, leaning into me, scrutinizing me for any hint of drunkenness.

"Don't be silly. It takes more than a little ole' sip to get drunk." I spoke as if I were an authority on the matter. Truth be told, I did feel woozy, like the end of a good spin on a tire swing.

"You feel any different?"

"A little." I planted my palms into the ground to stop the spinning.

"What's it feel like?"

The lightheadedness intensified, and for no explicable reason, I giggled. "Like I swallowed down a piece of sun." I passed the bottle beneath her nose. "Want some?"

She swatted my hand. "The devil's done grabbed hold of you, Analeise Newell. Don't send him chasing after me."

I screwed the top back on the bottle, propped it against the tree, then laid myself down in the ramble of grass and weeds, my head against Etta Mae's legs. Could this be how it felt to be Daddy? Giddy. Floating and bobbing. Not at all eaten up with meanness. I blinked up into the big oak's branches twisting and reaching toward the house, the sun weaving through, casting shadows of lace all around us.

Etta Mae hummed to Mrs. Mayfield's song, her right hand combing my hair through her fingers. "Beautiful, beautiful boy . . ."

Etta Mae's singing stirred a peculiar longing that sat heavy like a stone in my stomach, her enchanting voice urging the grogginess brought upon me by Old Crow.

Beautiful, beautiful boy.

I thought of Mistletoe. Of Mrs. Mayfield, and Marlissa. How lovely they were. Both, fuzzy-edged remnants of a beautiful dream. Would I ever see them again?

The press of melancholy and whiskey nudged big glossy tears to swell and spill from the corners of my eyes. A heaviness slowed my breathing, coaxing my eyelids shut.

Mrs. Mayfield's peculiar word was the last thought to float across my consciousness before the world fell away, before I drifted into a dreamless sleep.

It came to me like a whisper.

Patton . . .

* * *

The vibrations of the old Ford's engine woke me. Cotton-mouthed and confused, I tried to focus my eyes there in the diminished light, the corners of late afternoon peeling away into evening. "Mama's home," I said, pushing myself up from the ground. Etta Mae had fallen asleep alongside me. I nudged her shoulder. "Wake up. Mama's home."

Etta Mae woke with a start, her eyes swollen from sleep. "The flowers," Etta Mae said, a smile spreading across her pretty face.

Etta Mae and I hurried through the garden to the front of the house where Mama parked the truck. We both jumped up and down, grabbing hold of Mama's arms before she could properly settle her feet to the ground.

"Mama. Guess what?"

"Miss Grace. Miss Grace." Etta Mae squealed, her words tangling in mine, both of us battling for the honor of announcing her surprise.

"My heavens. What a welcome." Mama laughed at our spectacle. "Don't I feel special."

Etta Mae took Mama's left hand, and I grabbed hold of the other, both of us pulling her toward the house.

"Hurry, Mama."

"Okay. Okay," she said, speeding up her pace. "Is the house on fire?"

Etta Mae and I both yelled, "It's a surprise."

We led Mama into the kitchen, turning loose her arms, pushing her to the flowers. Etta Mae and I fidgeted in silence, awaiting Mama's rapture, both of us wound and ready to join her in celebration.

Mama moved slowly, approaching the arrangement with caution, reaching for the envelope affixed to the bouquet.

"Aren't they pretty?" I said. Mama looked at me for a moment, turned and pried the envelope loose with her ragged nail.

"I think Daddy's sorry for being so mean," I said. "Is that what the card says?"

Mama pressed the card into her bosom. The late afternoon light cast a dullness across the room, accentuating the shadows beneath her eyes. The odor of pickle brine saturated her clothing, overpowering the flowers' delicate scent. I studied Mama in her stained work blouse and trousers, corkscrews of lush blooms reaching out to her.

Miss Wessie entered the kitchen, breaking the silence with a hand raised to the ceiling. "Praise be. These here girls been cutting the fool and carrying on all afternoon waiting for you to get home to see them flowers." She wedged her index finger beneath her kerchief, scratching at her head. "Looks like Claxton Newell finally done rolled some dice that turned up the right way." She glanced at Mama from the corner of her eyes.

Etta Mae tugged at one of Mama's belt loops. "Don't you like the flowers, Miss Grace?"

Mama looked down, touching the top of Etta Mae's head, then reached over and stroked my cheek. "Girls, I think they're real pretty. Thank y'all for bringing me in to see them." She folded and tucked the card into her pocket. "I best get cleaned up and get myself a nap before my shift."

"No." I said, elongating the word, melting it in my mouth. "Don't go."

"Analeise, please don't start with me. You know I've got to work."

During the summer months, after pressing pickles into jars, Mama would come home to rest before venturing out to the Panty Factory, stitching together lady undergarments until morning. These were special days because Etta Mae and Miss Wessie stayed the night.

Mama squeezed my shoulder and started for the hall.

"Aren't you gonna call down to the Bait and Tackle and thank Daddy for the flowers?"

"You girls mind Miss Wessie, and don't make too much noise out here."

"Mama, you call Daddy right now. Before you go off to sleep."

"Wessie, can I see you out here a minute?" Mama ignored me, as if I had fallen through the floorboards and clear from sight.

My feet turned hot, anger shot up through me, pounding at my temples. "Mama!"

Miss Wessie turned and snapped her fingers at me, shooing me back. Etta Mae and I hurried to the door, straining to hear the rise and fall of their murmurs. Miss Wessie returned to the kitchen staring ahead, the same veil of distraction Mama wore moments before.

"What did she say? Why won't she call Daddy?"

"I reckon that's your Mama's business." Miss Wessie stared at the flowers.

"She's gonna ruin everything," I said.

Miss Wessie looked at us both. "Time to fix dinner." She rubbed her hands against her apron.

"Did you hear what I said?" I stomped my foot. "Mama's gonna ruin everything." Etta Mae backed away slowly, giving me a wide berth.

Miss Wessie moved in my direction, her index finger pointing down at my face. "I heard what you said, Miss Lady." She sucked in a deep breath. "And now you listen to what I got to tell you."

"Leave me be." I stepped back just outside of swatting distance.

"You mind your tone. You hear me?"

"I ain't gone deaf. Of course, I can hear you. They can hear you all the way over in Tallahassee."

Etta Mae gasped.

It was my hot, fast-growing legs I blamed—watching my plans for Mama and Daddy spinning off in a direction I failed to anticipate. Had my wits not deserted me, I would have run from the place. Begged forgiveness.

Miss Wessie grabbed hold of my left arm just above the elbow. Her words were slow and loud. "Good. I'm glad you ain't gone deaf, so you and them folks over in Tallahassee will be able to hear the thing I'm about to tell you." I tried to wriggle free, but Miss Wessie took hold of my other arm.

Miss Wessie leaned down close. Her breath puffed against my cheek, hot and spearmint sweet. "Your Mama say she want them flowers gone from this house. She wants no part of them. Told me to sling them out back with the food scraps."

"No. You can't throw them away."

Miss Wessie gave me a quick shake. "I can and I will." Her kerchief shifted, exposing a shock of cotton-white hair at her temple.

Her anger twisted and knotted around mine, becoming a breathing, dangerous thing. Something separate and apart from both of us.

"I hate you."

"And I hate you," Miss Wessie said.

It was the shock of her words, hard as red, packed clay that stopped me, that shook my tears and breath loose. Miss Wessie loosened her grip, jostling me just a little, trying to help me swallow down some air. "Now you know Miss Wessie here didn't mean that. Didn't mean that one bit." She lowered herself to her knees.

I wobbled backwards, taking a place next to Etta Mae who already sat balled on the floor hugging her knees.

Silently counting, I steadied myself until I could speak. "I didn't mean it either."

That was our way, Miss Wessie's and mine, forever drawing lines in the dirt. Forever crossing them.

"Sometimes you get the best of me, Analeise Newell." Miss Wessie lowered herself onto one shiny black knee and then the other, until she rested her weight against the balls of her feet, her skirt pulling up her thighs. "You is hard headed just like your mama."

"I'm not anything like Mama. Nothing at all." I smudged the tears across my cheek with the back of my hand. Right there, right then, in the pot-boiling center of it all, I hated Mama. I hated the pickle stink clinging to her sweat soaked clothes. I hated her tired eyes. I hated her throwing away a chance to make nice with Daddy.

Miss Wessie spoke, stopping me from the next awful thing I might say. "You can't take words back, Miss Lady. Just like you can't take back a bruise you put on another." She leaned forward, resting the palms of her hands on her knees. "You can't take back a hurt."

Hurt. I repeated the word over and over to myself. I nodded, shaking loose another round of tears. Etta Mae scooted closer, resting her head against my shoulder.

I pressed my fingernails into the palms of my hands trying to steady the waves of emotion. Perhaps I was more like Daddy than I thought.

Maybe he understood a hurt that feels good, a feeling nice as a Cordelia Mayfield slap. Maybe that is why he drank. To feel good.

I looked over at Mama's flowers, imagining them scattered in the far back of the yard. Flies and rot. Perhaps if Miss Wessie had slapped me, I would have felt some relief. I dug my fingernails harder into my palms, wishing I could take another sip of Daddy's whiskey. A little something to bring back the woozy.

Late afternoon light hung low and heavy in the room, the three of us there on the floor, our shadows pressed and fading into the boards. I imagined the whiskey bottle tipped to Daddy's lips and then to mine, the two of us sharing a secret. That a bad thing can be good. That there is a glorious, hallelujah kind of burn.

Chapter 6

After all the ruckus I caused earlier in the kitchen, Miss Wessie agreed to discard Mama's flowers after Etta Mae and I went off to bed.

"Why don't you girls snip off one of them blooms and pretty up your hair a bit," Miss Wessie said, washing the supper dishes.

Etta Mae and I elbowed our way to the table, each reaching for the same queer, orange and blue bloom holding court amongst the other flowers—a large exotic bird in a bush. "It's mine," I said, slapping away her hand.

Etta Mae laced her tiny fingers below her chin. "Okay. You can have it."

I glanced over at Miss Wessie, her stare burning hot, her chin dipping forward then tipping back, as if wanting to see me from different angles.

"No. You take it." My concession was mostly selfish, a tactic of sheer self-preservation. But there was a thimble full of guilt swishing around my insides right along with remnants of Daddy's Old Crow whiskey. Remorse for having been unkind to Etta Mae in Mama's Thinking Spot, for bringing sadness into her pretty, green flecked eyes. I fiddled with the flower until it snapped loose, leaving just enough stem to tuck into a plat close to her ear. "So pretty," I said, stepping back to regard my work. And I meant it. Etta Mae was a lovely thing, everything about her face—just right—every feature in perfect proportion to the next.

Etta Mae smiled big, the tips of her fingers gently nudging the floral plumage sweeping across her prominent cheekbone. "You think so?"

"You sure is," Miss Wessie said. She folded her arms over her bosom. "But remember. Pretty is, is pretty does." Miss Wessie cast a glance my way.

I never much cared for that saying—this cautionary tale on the true meaning of beauty. Nor did I care for Miss Wessie flicking it my way. In truth, I did not regard myself as beautiful. But I also did not think of myself as homely either. "I don't know," I said. "Pretty looks like pretty to me." I flashed my loveliest smile at Miss Wessie.

"You next," Etta Mae said, taking hold of my shoulders. "Pick one."

Etta Mae had already taken the best, the only one I wanted. The one that was rightfully mine. "You choose." I wondered if she would do me justice, if she would pick the second prettiest flower in the bunch, the perfect white rose opening up big as a camellia blossom.

I shut my eyes, turning the wait into a sort of game. Her petite hands were busy, fussing with my hair, settling the flower behind my ear, caressing my face with puffs of sweet breath.

"There," she said. "All done."

I opened my eyes and glanced over at the arrangement. She had chosen the rose. "Thank you." I was grateful I would not have to pretend to be pleased with a wrong selection.

"Look, Granny. Look at Analeise." Etta Mae held her hand beneath my chin, proud of herself. "Isn't she beautiful?"

What did she see that made her so happy? She, better than anyone else knew I had me a mean streak—coiled up just like a snake. I waited for Miss Wessie to speak, wondering if she might try to toss another life lesson my way.

"Pretty as a picture," Miss Wessie said. "You both is."

Etta Mae and I smiled at one another, happy to have Miss Wessie's approval, happy to possess a bit of lovely, if only for an hour or two. If only Mama could turn loose her anger and love Daddy for being sweet this one time, for trying to make nice.

I imagined Mama in Mrs. Mayfield's green dress, sweet smelling with butter cream hands. Her hair brushed smooth and glossy—Daddy's flowers sprouting through her tresses—a garden tumbling down her shoulders.

"Analeise. Why don't you go play something nice for us while I finish up these here dishes," Miss Wessie said.

Etta Mae bounced up and down, pulling me to the hall. Any opportunity for me to play the piano was an opportunity for her to sing. Before Etta Mae could make her request, I knew what I would play. "Play that song. The one you taught me in the garden," Etta Mae said.

Daddy's upright was wonky, a piece of wood wedged beneath one of the legs to level the thing. What mattered most was the tone, and Daddy took good care when voicing her, tending to the worn hammers and bass strings. Daddy said playing her was like hearing an ugly girl sing pretty. A shock that something so wondrous could come from such a sad state of affairs.

Etta Mae took her seat next to me on the bench covering the heart Daddy scratched into the dull, black paint long before I was born. Mama and Daddy's initials captured on the inside. "C" for Claxton and "G" for Grace.

I could not recall anything as lovely as Mrs. Mayfield's song ever being played on that old upright, mostly Daddy's river rabble music—Hank Williams and Jelly Roll Morton. A gospel hymn here and there.

The clink of dishes from the kitchen comforted me, that and Etta Mae leaning against my shoulder settling herself on the piano bench. "You look like the prettiest hula girl that ever was." Etta Mae pushed at the rose until it rested more securely behind my ear.

I shifted, admiring the bird flower adorning Etta Mae's hair. *My bird flower.*

"And you are the Cicada Queen," I said, smiling. "Only, where have all the cicadas run off to?" Digging around in the pocket of my skirt, my fingers brushed against crumbly bits of cicada parts, until I located three intact shells. *One, two, three . . .* It occurred to me then that the number three might be my favorite of all numbers. That it is special, that if I were a number, I would want to be the number three. "Three," I said. "Three perfect shells for the Cicada Queen." I placed them carefully, each one in Etta Mae's hair like they were snooping around my bird flower.

"How does it look?"

"Like a crown fit for a queen." I tried to tamp down my last bit of envy. I positioned the tips of my cicada dusted fingers below Etta Mae's lips. "Make a wish."

Etta Mae giggled, shut her eyes, and blew. There was no sense in asking her what she wished for. She was a stickler for such rules, convinced speaking it aloud would ruin any chance it might come true. I could only imagine she hoped to have back her poor, dead mama.

"Wishes are kind of like prayers," Etta Mae said.

"I reckon they are." I hovered my fingers across the top of the keys, unsure of where to start—only having heard a section of Mrs. Mayfield's song. I hummed best I could remember. "Help me," I said, wiggling my hands over the keys.

Etta Mae hummed. The music took hold after the first few notes, as it always did, as if little magnets were stitched to my fingertips. And I played.

Yearning. That was the sound. Something far off and out of reach. Was that what Mrs. Mayfield's song was about? But what could people like Cordelia and Marlissa Mayfield not already have? What could they need? My breathing quickened.

"Oh, where did you go?" Etta Mae sang with a grown lady's voice, fully formed and lovely. "Beautiful, beautiful boy. Please come back to me."

I tasted it right away, the feelings in Etta Mae's soprano—the taste of want. It was like cinnamon. Only a smattering. Red hot and honeyed. Then fading. Lingering just long enough to scald my tongue. And my legs—how they ached and burned.

Etta Mae pushed herself up to stand on the bench next to me. "Pretty girl, pretty girl, pretty girls for thee," Etta Mae sang, her voice rising three octaves, her arms lifting with each one.

Etta Mae held the last note—a spectacular crescendo, the highest note I ever heard her sing—an invisible knife slicing open the very air in the room and everything in it, pimply flesh popping up through my wounds.

"Lord above." Miss Wessie spoke from the doorway. "That sure was something else." She held the vase of Mama's flowers at her waist, some of them tickling at her chin. "Folks would come from all around and pay good money to hear what I just heard." She rested the vase on the top of the piano. "You two sure is something else," she said, her breathing as labored as mine.

Clapping her hands, Etta Mae smiled big. "You really think so?"

"Sure do," Miss Wessie said. "But who this beautiful boy you be singing about?" You could hear the playful mischief in her tone.

Etta Mae giggled. "Don't rightly know. Who is he, Analeise?"

"How would I know? You made up the words." I took a few deep breaths, an attempt to settle myself. I rested my head against Etta Mae's hip, looping my arm through and around one of her legs. I blinked into the single bare bulb above, staring just long enough to distort my vision.

"Did I?"

I pressed my cheek against her leg, soft and slick with perspiration. "You did." I became aware of the growing sting at the tip of my tongue—the raw skin at the roof of my mouth. I was certain then. This exotic illness—this bit of hurt. It was left there by Etta Mae's singing.

* * *

Bedtime came too quickly, and my attempts at prolonging the inevitable were not lost upon Miss Wessie. "March your little fanny on down to your room, Miss Lady. I ain't gonna ask you again."

"Can Etta Mae sleep with me? Just this once? The whole night through?" It was our custom, on nights Etta Mae and Miss Wessie slept over, that Etta Mae would fall off to sleep with me. Miss Wessie would retrieve her from my room before Daddy came home to sleep on a pallet of blankets next to her Granny's cot in the pantry.

Miss Wessie situated her hands in that dangerous place just below her hips right where an invisible holster hung. An anchoring spot just before her patience gave way. "You know your daddy, Claxton Newell, ain't gonna have no part in any of that."

Etta Mae lingered quietly, treading in the space between Miss Wessie and me.

Daddy did not much care for Miss Wessie and Etta Mae, passing by them with little regard. Not so much as a nod and rarely ever a word spoken. It was not that Daddy disliked colored folk. No, he liked most of them just fine. "Maybe tonight he won't mind," I said, hoping a change had come with the flowers he sent to Mama.

"He'll mind as much as he always do," Miss Wessie said.

I poked at the white rose, tucking it more securely behind my ear. "What did you do to him, anyway, to make him not like you?"

Anger sometimes came upon Miss Wessie like a trance. Slowed breathing and narrowed eyes. I knew quick as anything, even before she could squeeze and pinch at that place below her hip, that I pushed too far.

Etta Mae began to sway slightly, casting a glance at her granny and then me. She hummed, slowly and lullaby sweet.

Surely, she isn't going to sing. *Not now.* My heart thumped in my ears.

Miss Wessie turned loose of her dangerous place, resting her arms at her side, lifting them up to fold over her bosom. "I reckon I ain't done him a harm." She took in a deep breath. "Nothing but clean his house. Cook his meals." She walked past Etta Mae, squeezing her shoulder. "Watch after you," she said, nipping my chin between her thumb and index finger. "What is you done?"

Her question was not new to me. I asked myself that very thing on many occasions. What had I done to Daddy to make him not love Mama and me anymore? Still, it did not hurt any less. Actually, it hurt more, hearing it spoken aloud, and by another. I guess I deserved it. I refused to let Miss Wessie see me cry. To let her win. *I hate you.*

"You ain't done nothing," Miss Wessie said, tilting my chin up. "Just like I ain't done nothing."

Etta Mae still hummed, standing off by herself. The lovely sound accompanied by the sensation flowing warm through my veins. A sort of sedative.

"Sometimes folks are like memories. That's all we are. That's all we did," Miss Wessie said.

Etta Mae stopped her humming.

"What do you mean? How are we like memories?"

Miss Wessie's shoulders tensed, her hand drifting from my face. She turned to look back at Etta Mae and then to me. She shook her head as if shaking something loose. "I don't mean nothing. It's been a long day is all. I guess I just be talking out of head from tiredness." She turned me away from her and gave my backside a swat. "Off to bed."

"What about me?" Etta Mae said. "Can I go, too?"

"Okay. But just like always. Just until you fall off to sleep."

* * *

My body jerked awake to a clap of thunder. Flashes of lightning illuminated the room. I sat up, looking about, trying to sort things through, my breathing quick. Panic. Rain beat at the roof, the wind pushing through the open windows, sending the curtains reaching for the bed.

Etta Mae's body snapped forward as if hinged by a spring. She grabbed my hand, her breathing hurried as my own. "What's happening?"

"A storm's come." I pushed the sweat dampened hair from my face. Another clap of thunder split the ground, rattling the windows. I threw back the sheet and stood up on the bed, grabbing for the string tied to the light bulb chain. I gave it a quick yank. Nothing.

"Turn on the light." Etta Mae tugged at my nightgown. "Hurry."

I gave the string a few more tugs. "The power's out." I lowered myself back to the bed next to Etta Mae. Between claps of thunder, I heard the voices. "You hear that?"

"Hear what?"

"Shhh."

"You're scaring me."

"I think I hear Daddy. And Miss Wessie." In the pulse of lightning, I could make out the bird blossom clinging at Etta Mae's ear, smashed flat against her head.

Etta Mae squeezed my arm. "I'm not supposed to be in here."

She was right. How long had we been asleep? And why had Miss Wessie forgotten to fetch Etta Mae? I grabbed hold of Etta Mae pulling her across the room with me. I pressed my ear to the door and listened to Daddy's angry voice.

"What are they saying?" Etta Mae whispered.

"Don't know. Can't make it out." A knot tightened and swelled in my stomach. "But something's wrong." I opened the door, just a little crack.

"Is he drunk?"

"Don't know."

"Is it a mean kind of drunk?"

"I don't know. I can't hear." Something fluttered against my cheek. I pulled at it until it came loose. A dangling rose petal. "You stay here."

"Don't leave me by myself. What if your Daddy comes?" she said, grabbing hold of me.

I pried her arms loose. "Go hide under the bed." I gave her a kiss on the cheek and opened the door just wide enough to squeeze through. I reached for the wall, feeling my way the short distance to the kitchen, the voices growing clearer with each step. A bead of sweat let go of my neck traveling down beneath the collar of my gown.

"You shut the hell up old woman." Daddy said, his words slurring. Something shattered, tiny fragments of the broken object skidding across the kitchen floor.

I held onto the doorframe peeking into the room. A long pulse of lightning exposed the kitchen. Daddy stood at the table. Miss Wessie several feet in front of him. The room fell dark, remnants of light still swirling in my eyes. *One, two, three.*

"Where is she, goddammit?"

"I told you where she at, Mister Claxton. She at work."

Thunder muffled Daddy's response. The power flickered. The back porch light burned steady once more, washing the kitchen in sepia tones. Daddy held Mama's flowers. Miss Wessie had not thrown them away. Did she forget? Had Daddy come home early? Why was he so angry?

Daddy lifted the vase up over his head.

He was ruining everything. I dug my fingernails into the doorframe, biting down on my tongue, anything to keep from screaming out, from being found.

The weight of the vase kept it upright until it met the wall. The force of water pushed bits of broken glass across the planks, ruined stems and petals mangled in a watery heap.

"Mister Claxton, you needs to settle down. You hear me? Children be sleeping in this here house."

"Children?" Daddy said, laughing. "That's funny."

"I don't see what's so funny."

"You must think I'm fucking stupid."

"No sir, but I thinks you is stupid, stinking drunk."

"And why do you think that is exactly? Why it is I'm stinking, lousy, drunk?" Daddy took a few steps toward Miss Wessie.

"I have my suspicions," Miss Wessie said, extending her right hand, presenting a black iron skillet.

Daddy raked his hands through his hair then pointed at Miss Wessie. "You think you can come in my house and threaten me? You think you can come in here and taunt me day in and day out? You think you can get away with hitting a white man?"

"What I'm getting ready to hit ain't a man," she said, bringing the skillet up to her lips to kiss. "And this here ole' black skillet sure don't cares if you white."

"You bitch." Daddy stepped forward.

Run, Miss Wessie. I clutched at the front of my nightgown trying to breathe. Daddy had not changed. How could I have ever thought such a thing?

Miss Wessie pulled the skillet up and over her head. "Mister Claxton, don't you make me do it. You keep to that side of the room. You hear?"

Daddy laughed again, bending forward placing his hands on his knees. Thunder struck—a series of heavy concussions. He lunged forward. The power blinked off, throwing the room into darkness. Lightning mimicked the thunder's rhythm. Daddy charged Miss Wessie, tackling her to the floor, twisting the skillet from her hands.

I could barely make it out, their struggle in flashes of storm. Clenched fists. Tangled limbs.

Daddy struck Miss Wessie across the face, her head whacking hard against the floor. She lay still.

Daddy pulled himself up onto his knees, bending forward to assess his violence. "Look what you went and made me do."

I thought of Etta Mae hiding under my bed. First, her burned up Mama and now Miss Wessie. All of them dead. Then and there, with Miss Wessie lying dead on the floor, I knew I loved her, perhaps as I much as I could love a grandmother of my own, if any of them were still living. My knees buckled.

Just as a scream scratched and dug its way up my throat, Miss Wessie's fist connected with Daddy's jaw knocking him backwards against the table legs.

"Now look what you done gone and made me do," she said.

Daddy rolled over, pushing himself onto all fours, grabbing the table, pulling himself up from the floor. He limped over, picked up a broken flower, sniffed it, and threw it at Miss Wessie. "You give that to Analeise. Tell her it's from her daddy. I'm afraid she's gonna grow up to be a bitch just like her mama."

Did he know I was there hiding at the door? Is that why he said that horrible thing? Was it not enough he hurt Miss Wessie? Did he have to hurt me, too?

Daddy turned and walked to the door.

Miss Wessie yelled after him as she pushed herself up from the floor. "Where is you going off to in that pitiful state?"

"Where do you think?" he said without turning back, pausing long enough to shatter the porch light with his fist. Miss Wessie followed behind, yelling after him, his tires spinning into mud and grass.

Anger rose up inside me, a powerful kind of rage. I pulled at the front of my gown. I thought it was Mama that ruined everything, but I was wrong. It was Daddy who done it, who broke everything beyond repair. I backed away from the kitchen door and ran for my room.

"Etta Mae?" I hurried to the bed searching for her with my hands.

"I'm under here," she said. I knelt down on the floor, reaching around for her in the dark until I found her. I grabbed hold, pulling her out.

I jumped onto the bed, hoisting her up with me. I thought more than anything I wanted Daddy to love us again. For things to be as they once were. But that had been foolish. I was foolish. *Stupid bitch.*

"What's wrong? What happened?"

"Shhh." I dug my knees into the mattress and clasped my hands beneath my chin. "Dear Lord, I hate my daddy."

Etta Mae pulled at my arms. "What are you doing?"

"Shut up." I pushed Etta Mae away. I balanced myself and looked to the ceiling. "Dear Lord, please punish my daddy."

Etta Mae gasped. "Analeise."

"Be quiet." I squeezed and flexed my fingers until my knuckles popped. "Lord—make sure he's sorry for all the awful things he's done."

I found Etta Mae's face in a single flash of light, her eyes wide with fear. I pulled the flower from behind her ear and then mine.

One, two, three. And I slung them both off into the darkness.

Chapter 7

Halbert, the gatekeeper's dream whisper woke me. *They got secret's they keep.* His stale breath blew hot, his melted ear scraping against my cheek leaving behind candle wax droplets of skin.

I lay, staring into the wood plank ceiling, my eyes tracing Florida and listening to the morning hum of insects, the rise and fall of their vibrations setting the day to an uncanny song.

The whole room sagged with heat. My cotton nightgown surrendered to the humidity, expanding, and drooping at the neck, giving the appearance I had shrunk.

The clink of dishes and smell of burned toast wafted from the kitchen. Miss Wessie never burned anything. Right then, I remembered Daddy and Miss Wessie wrestling on the kitchen floor.

Etta Mae. I studied the shallow indentation in her pillow, lingering over the spot, taking in the scent of Miss Wessie's homemade hair potion. "Etta Mae?" I whispered, wondering if she might be sleeping under the bed.

I rolled onto my stomach, scooted to the mattress's edge, hanging over to peek beneath. "Are you down there?" No Etta Mae, only dusty tumbleweeds and my keeping place, the small space beneath loose boards. The place where I hid away three nickels, a single sparkly ear clip that had the good sense to drop off Miss Minnie Jean's droopy ear lobe, and the copy of *Jane Eyre* I stole from the library.

I lingered there in the topsy-turvy, my hair spilling about my face tangled and damp, allowing the rush of blood in my head to throb, drowning out the cicada chorus.

"Miss Lady," Miss Wessie said.

I jerked up, slinging back my hair, pushing the rest of it free from my face. "You nearly scared me to death."

"Lucky for you that nearly and being ain't the same," she said, managing a partial smile, her upper lip swollen and split.

Daddy. What on earth must he have looked like after meeting up with the wrong side of Miss Wessie's angry fist? In the spill of daylight, my hate, like everything else in the room melted, leaving behind a puddle of disdain. All I wanted was a better kind of Daddy.

"When did you take to sleeping upside down like a big ole' brown Georgia bat?"

"I was looking for Etta Mae." I could not help but stare at her lip. "What happened?" I said softly, rubbing at my mouth, hoping she might feel some relief and sympathy in my touch.

She followed suit, touching her own lip. "Miss Wessie here tripped in the dark. Gave the door frame a big ole' juicy kiss."

It was a slippery lie, all greased up and coming out quick and smooth. I admired her ease in telling it. "Does it hurt?"

"It'll pass."

Was that another lie? I nodded. "You burned the toast."

"I reckon I did. But you ain't got to eat it." She took a step forward, her bare foot resting on the discarded rose. She stopped, crossing her right foot over and to the side, peeling the flower from her meaty heel.

"You left Etta Mae in here to sleep last night."

Miss Wessie patted the flattened bloom in her hand back and forth like biscuit dough. "I fell off to sleep. Didn't mean to. Just like I didn't mean to burn the toast."

And what of Mama's flowers? Had she fallen asleep before she could toss them out before Daddy came home? Did she also want to keep them? "I reckon you threw out Mama's flowers."

Miss Wessie tapped at her lip, letting a few breaths pass before she spoke. "I did what your Mama wanted. Like I always do." She looked down at the floor to the left of her foot where Etta Mae's bird blossom lay. She bent down pinching it between her fingers just as I once watched her kill a roach. Her lip curled up, nostrils flaring. Like the whole business had a stink to it.

"Where's Etta Mae?"

"Outside." Miss Wessie stepped closer, tossing the tattered blooms onto the bed beside me. "Miss Lady?"

There was a crinkle in the narrow space between her eyebrows. The spot where she squeezed her worry. "What's wrong?"

"Not really sure," Miss Wessie said. "Might be nothing."

Was that another oily lie? "But what?"

Miss Wessie fluttered her fingers over her swollen lip. "Your Mama's arm be tingling."

That place that tingled, the spot where the rattlesnake bit her all those years ago, flared up on occasion. It was these times Mama's sight into the future was clearest, the stitches and embroidery by her own hand, easiest to read. My eyes drifted over to the flowers. I tamped down the urge to touch them, tugging up the collar of my nightgown. "Is it something good?" I already knew the answer. When Mama's arm went to buzzing, I had come to learn that today was almost always better than tomorrow.

Miss Wessie reached out touching the tip of my nose, then gently pulled a handful of my hair through her fingers. "She say it's your daddy."

My heart went to thumping. "What about Daddy?" I pulled away from Miss Wessie, a web of tangled hair catching in her fingers, the shock of it, soothing in an odd sort of way.

"She say something's wrong."

"Where is he?"

"Don't know."

"Did he come home?" I said, leaning back, propping myself up on my elbows.

"No."

My heart caught again, stealing a breath. "At all?"

Again, she fluttered her fingers at her lip, squeezing at her worry. "No."

Another lie. I was less impressed. More angry than anything, wishing I was snarled once again in Miss Wessie's fingers, feeling something other than the raw beginnings of fear. "Where's Mama?"

"She on the porch fretting over the hem of her dress."

"What does it say?" I said, pushing myself up and off the bed, passing Miss Wessie, hurrying to the door. Had the Lord, with my nudging—had she done something to Daddy?

"Don't you go bothering your mama, leave her be."

I ran by the kitchen, stopping long enough to look in, no sign of the shattered vase and flowers. Outside on the porch, the swing swayed empty, Mama nowhere to be seen.

Before I could call out, I saw her walking in the distance, the muddied, red clay path sucking at her feet, the hem of her dress caught in her hands, I stood, holding tight to the porch column listening to the drone of cicadas. And what was it they knew? Had they seen the terrible things I had done. Is that what cicadas did? Gobble up all the secrets in the world until they ripped at the seams, popping clear out of their skin.

I heard Etta Mae before I saw her, her soprano trill sweet tasting as a peach. She sauntered around the corner of the house, her fingers picking daintily at the ruffles of Mama's fancy apron, my play pretend party dress. Her hair was adorned with cicada husks—a crown of secrets. Which ones of mine did she wear?

I might have run down the steps of the porch to shake her hard and mean had I not cared she might spill her beans. Tell all she knew, my whiskey drinking and prayer to hurt Daddy. And there were other things—the list sure to grow longer if only I had time to think. "Mama's arm is a tingling," I said.

Etta Mae stopped to listen, dropping the apron to dangle dangerously close to her mud splattered shins. "Is it something good?"

Stupid girl. "Miss Wessie said something's happened to Daddy." I dug my nails into the post.

I could see it *snap* in her eyes, lifting the apron to hurry up to the porch. "Oh no. You don't think . . ." She stopped to stand one-step below me.

"Hush up. Your granny's inside. Do you think the Lord heard me?" I whispered

"She hears everything."

It would have been easy to push her down those porch steps. It might hurt just a little. "What if something really bad happened?"

Etta Mae took the next step up to stand at my side. "Maybe it's not too late." She grabbed hold of my arm. "Maybe you can take it back."

"Can you? Take back a prayer." I leaned into Etta Mae, feeling the weight of the thing.

"I can't say for sure. Never needed to." She took hold of my hand, lacing her fingers through mine, raising our hands together to kiss the top of mine.

The crunch of gravel caught our attention, the two of us standing fused together, looking to the road.

The screen door whined. "Y'all get on back in this house," Miss Wessie said.

"Who is it, Granny?"

I loosened my fingers taking back hold of the porch column.

"Did you hear me?" Miss Wessie said.

"Is it your Daddy?" Etta Mae said. It was not until then I could make it out, the big blue lights on top of the Sheriff's car. I took two steps down, the beats of my heart too quick to count.

"Miss Lady, you come back up on this here porch," Miss Wessie said. "You hear me?"

The Sheriff's car slowed, turning down the drive stopping where Mama stood. I took off running, red clay oozing through my toes. "Mama?" I yelled as I ran to her. A broken strand of a spider's web drifted across my face catching in my lashes. I kept my pace, pulling at the invisible thing grabbing hold of me.

Miss Wessie hollered from the porch. "Get back here."

I turned back only once, Etta Mae standing wide-eyed beneath her granny's arm, cicadas strewn across the top of her head.

By the time I reached Mama, the Sheriff stood next to his car, his hand resting on Mama's shoulder. "Mama, what's happened to Daddy?"

"Miss Analeise, you best get back on up to the house," the Sheriff said.

Mama held her skirt all the way up to her thighs running her fingers beneath the hem, sliding them across the thread, not turning my way, as though she did not see me there. "He's dead isn't he?"

We stood still, Mama and me, staring at the Sheriff, waiting for him to speak.

Finally, he nodded, glancing at me then turning back to face Mama.

My knees buckled. "I didn't mean it," I said, tears already streaming hot down my face.

The Sheriff shot me a strange look before Mama's hysteria unraveled.

Mama yanked at her dress pulling it up so high her garters showed. "He drowned in the river. I saw it," she said, over and over.

"Take hold of yourself, Grace," The Sheriff caught Mama's frantic hands, her skirt falling back below her knees.

I killed Daddy. I stepped backwards in the muck, then turned to run. Miss Wessie and Etta Mae stood on the porch, bouncing in my vision, the sodden ground working hard to hold me in place.

My right foot stopped me. The shock of stepping onto something sharp toppled me forward onto my knees. The pain, a wincing sort of throb followed by a penetrating burn. I rolled onto by backside, lifting my foot up to look.

The broken neck of an Old Crow bottle dug deep into my arch, the look of it like a syrup tap hammered into a tree. I jiggled it and gave it a tug. Blood poured—a warm, unstoppable gush. It was the sight of the blood that did it, that sent my head spinning.

"Analeise," someone called off in the distance.

The ground reached up to catch me. I lay there blinking into the dazzle of blue. All the storm clouds nearly cleared away, only a single puff of gray pushing through. I kept blinking until the light went dim.

Chapter 8

I killed Daddy. Drowned him in the Chattahoochee. Left him to bob with the catfish during that summer of storms, the summer I learned that a prayer could be a dangerous thing.

Etta Mae comforted me, the only one, aside from the cicadas and God, who knew what I did.

And Daddy? He had at least one terrible secret of his own. Mama learned the Bait and Tackle was in foreclosure, soon to become the property of Mayfield Bank. "Your Daddy never had a head for business," Mama said.

Had Daddy been a different kind of father, a provider—a sober, kinder heart—our lives might have experienced a greater shift, his absence punching a bigger hole in the world for us to tumble through.

In the weeks that followed, before Etta Mae and I returned to school, life commenced almost to how it was before Daddy fell drunk in the river. Mama returned to work—Miss Wessie to her chores, and Etta Mae and I to Mama's Thinking Spot. Me pulling out Daddy's Old Crow beneath the floorboards to sniff.

Miss Wessie and Etta Mae came to live with Mama and me, a decision I found agreeable. I loved them both, understanding the economy and convenience in such an arrangement. Most of all, I appreciated the opportunity to keep an eye on Etta Mae. After all, she had my secrets to keep.

Of all these happenings, it was the change that came over Mama that niggled at me most. At first, it could hardly be noticed. Sweeps of color returned to her face. First her lips, spreading to her cheeks, until one morning she glowed. Her heels played staccato notes upon the floor, the rhythm of confidence.

She quit her second job sewing panties, explaining Miss Wessie would take in laundry and clean a house or two on Saturdays to help sort out the difference. "We're going to be just fine," she said. Oh, how I wanted to believe her.

Miss Wessie's words continued to poke at me hard. *Pretty is, is pretty does.* I studied myself in the mirror, every angle—every curve, wondering if the ugly might set in—what I might look like turned inside out.

With school not far away, Mama began preparing our wardrobe. Etta Mae and I were to each have five outfits, one for each day of the week. For me, she purchased a few basics and sewed the rest. For Etta Mae, Mama refurbished and refitted clothing I outgrew, Mama's clever hand transforming cotton feed sacks into stylish designs, stitching our futures into each piece.

Mama surprised both Etta Mae and me with the promise of a new dress sewn from the same Butterick pattern using fabrics of our own choosing. These were to be the dresses we would wear the first day of school, me at Providence Elementary, and Etta Mae at Booker T. Washington, the colored school.

To stir our excitement, Mama promised us a new pair of shoes and a picnic at Mayfield Park. Etta Mae and I spoke of little else, and I welcomed the distraction from the guilt dragging behind me.

* * *

The night before our trip to Woolworth another storm blew through, chunks of ice clattering against rooftops, shaking all of Providence awake. Even the lightest of sleepers took notice—the wind catching in all the hollow spaces, playing the town like an out of tune oboe.

The morning after, Etta Mae and I awoke a tangled mess of girl, to the sound of Mama's voice. "Girls, we have a busy day ahead."

Etta Mae wrestled herself loose, pulling the tail of her gown out from under me. "Good morning, Miss Grace," she said, running past Mama down the hall to the bathroom.

"Glad to see the storm didn't carry you off," Mama said. "You sleep all right?"

I nodded, rubbing my eyes into focus along with the slow creep of memory Daddy was dead. "Pretty good, I reckon."

Mama bent down kissing the top of my head. "Thought the wind might rip the roof right off."

I imagined us exposed to the sky. Our home, a dollhouse. A big hand reaching to scoop me out and flick me into the tops of the pines. "I hope Woolworth didn't blow away." I tried my best to tamp down my anxiety with thoughts of a new, shiny pair of Mary Jane's.

I hugged Mama around the waist. A lovely new smell drifted off her, a fragrance hypnotic as a gulp of whiskey. "You smell pretty. Is that perfume?" To the best of my recollection, Daddy never let Mama wear it.

"If you don't slow poke about, I'll dab a little on you and Etta Mae."

For the first time I could remember, I wanted to smell like Mama. Something other than sweat and pickle brine. I jumped up, running down the hall to the bathroom. "Etta Mae. Guess what?"

* * *

On our way to town, Etta Mae and I entertained ourselves sniffing and admiring the perfume Mama dotted onto each of our wrists.

"Looks like we were lucky," Mama said, inspecting the debris strewn about.

A good piece down the road, Miss Minnie Jean Carter, the church organist, stood in her front yard, hands upon her hips, gazing up at the tippy top of a magnolia tree, laundry scattered all about.

Mama stomped the brakes. "You okay?" Mama poked her head out of the window.

"Not a scratch, praise the Lord." Miss Minnie Jean curled her big-knuckled fingers over the windowsill. "Came so quick, it blew the linens right off the line before I could bring them in." She leaned into the truck, her coif kept safe by a ring of toilet paper secured in place by an army of bobby pins. She stared across the seat at Etta Mae, her upper lip turning up, breathing out a barely audible, *hmm*.

"So glad to hear you're well," Mama said. "Aside from your laundry, of course. But that can be replaced. You can't."

Even though one time Miss Minnie Jean complimented my piano playing, I could not help but think the world a better place without her. She was always a little mean to Mama, prickly pieces sticking out of her words.

"You might of warned us," Miss Minnie Jean said, tapping the sill with the tips of her light pink painted nails, a shade of girlish she did not wear particularly well.

"Of what?" Mama said.

"The storm. I thought you might've known it was coming is all." She slowed her words at the end, tilting her head to the side. She managed a smile, revealing teeth a little too large for her mouth.

Mama appeared rattled but managed to speak. "I'm afraid not," she said. Though Mama never discussed her clairvoyant tendencies—all of Providence knew, regarding it as an unfortunate predicament. A harelip of sorts.

Right then I wished the storm had carried off Miss Minnie Jean, slung her up in the trees with her pillowcases. I worked hard to tamp down the wicked thought. Had I not learned my lesson?

"Morning, Miss Minnie Jean," I said, struggling to sound pleasant.

"And where are you off to today, Analeise?" Miss Minnie Jean regarded me with suspicion, as if she knew it was I who swiped her ear clip, hiding it away to keep company with a half-drank bottle of hooch.

"Woolworth," Etta Mae and I said in unison.

"School starts Monday. Last minute errands." Mama smiled pretty.

"We're getting new shoes," I said.

Miss Minnie Jean raised one of her drawn-on eyebrows, a shade oddly dark for a woman her age. "Well, isn't that exciting. Sounds like you're up to your knees in cotton."

She lifted her chin, staring at Mama down the barrel of her nose— nostrils flared, eyes narrowing into a crinkly squint.

Mama looked out of the window and up to the place Miss Minnie Jean was eyeing when we drove up. I followed her stare to the piece of laundry caught in the branches of the tree. "We're hardly up to our knees in anything but weeds these days," Mama said.

Miss Minnie Jean bit at her lip, chewing off a little of her orangey-red lipstick. "I guess you're right. Must be hard—Claxton dying in such a tragic way. Lucky for you to have that Wessie Johnston living with you now."

With the mention of her Granny, Etta Mae leaned into me, gazing up at the window, her breath warm against my shoulder.

"It's been a blessing," Mama said.

"Hmm," Miss Minnie Jean said, the sound of it like air escaping a tire. "Well, that's something, ain't it?" She glanced over at me and then Etta Mae—that same look of judgement she cast over the congregation from her organ bench.

"I reckon it is," Mama said.

"Oh, did you hear?" Miss Minnie Jean said. She raked at her lip again with those big teeth. "Perhaps you already know—seen it in one of those feed sacks you sewed up to look nice and pretty."

I imagined Miss Minnie Jean dangling from the top of an oak tree, hollering down for help, her underparts showing. The very thought proffered a slight bit of comfort.

"Perhaps I did see it," Mama said. "Why, just this morning the threads of one of those feed sacks told me to be on the lookout for a donkey in the road."

Oh, how I loved Mama right then. Miss Minnie Jean did look just like a donkey.

Miss Minnie Jean blinked at Mama, oblivious to her insult. "A donkey?" she said.

"Never mind that," Mama said. "What was it you wanted to tell us?"

Miss Minnie Jean nudged at her bobby pins. "Yes—I remember what I was going to say." She ran her tongue over those unsettling teeth of hers. "The school burned down last night." She slowed her words as though they sat heavy on her tongue.

"What?" I yelled, making Mama and Etta Mae jump.

72

Miss Minnie Jean appeared to take pleasure in the commotion she caused, her lopsided smile lingering before she spoke. "Not your school, honey. That private school over in Thomasville. Glenmore Academy." Miss Minnie Jean scratched at her toilet paper tiara. "It appears to have been lightning that did it. Wonder where the Mayfield girl and that Darlington boy will go off to school now?" Her question dangled in the air alongside her laundry.

Marlissa Mayfield. "Maybe at my school," I said, making poor Etta Mae jump again.

"Wouldn't that be something?" Miss Minnie Jean puckered her mouth, accentuating the vertical lines above her lips, the remains of her lipstick bleeding into the crevices.

"We best be getting on into town," Mama said, lifting her arm, examining some phantom watch only she could see. "See you in church on Sunday." Mama patted the tips of Miss Minnie Jean's fingers, a cue to step away.

"You mind yourself," Miss Minnie Jean said. "To God be the glory." Her words tumbled into the rev of the engine.

Except for the *whoosh* of wind in our ears, we sat in silence, me inhaling my wrist. *Marlissa Mayfield.* The very thought of her coming to my school set my mind on fire. The two of us running across the playground together, the other girls trailing behind.

Etta Mae rippled the quiet. "That sure was a big ole' pair of panties caught up in that tree," she said, yelling above the whip of currents flooding the truck. "How do you reckon she's going to get them down?"

Mama leaned into the steering wheel, laughing. Etta Mae and I joined her, surrendering our bodies to the sway of the truck, laughter swirling around us mixing with Mama's intoxicating new smell.

* * *

Broad Street crackled with talk of the storm, people gathering to share tales of calamity and near misses. Etta Mae and I could hardly wait to get to Woolworth, both of us holding hands and hurrying behind Mama along the storefronts.

"We've got all day. The store isn't going anywhere. Enjoy yourselves," Mama said.

The rustle of people and swinging shopping bags made me nervous. Might the last pair of shoes in just my size might be tucked into one of them, the last pair of Mary Janes lost to me forever? I had to look perfect the first day of school. Perfect for Marlissa.

Two stores down from Woolworth, Mama stopped, shaping her hands like binoculars, pressing them against a large plate-glass window.

"What are you looking at?" I said, mirroring Mama, inspecting what was beyond. "There's nothing in there."

"Let me see." Etta Mae pressed her small hands next to mine. After giving the place a good long look, she said, "There's nothing in there."

I pulled back from the glass. "Did you think I was lying?" Etta Mae shrugged.

Mama stepped away from the window, her patent leather purse sliding down her arm until it caught on her wrist, the fog of her breath remaining on the glass.

I wrote the letter "P". "*P" for Patton.* I stepped back watching it recede, dissolving from the outside in.

"You might not see anything, but I do," Mama said.

Had she seen me write the letter? Did she know what it stood for?

"What do you see?" Etta Mae said. "Is your arm tingling?"

Mama reached out touching Etta Mae's cheek, smiling so perfectly—so beautifully that I longed for it to last—for us and her smile to be frozen into an ice cube forever.

"No," Mama said. "Nothing like that," she whispered. "Possibility and seeing the future are two different kinds of things."

"What are you talking about?" I said.

Mama laughed. "I'm just saying that a person can know something with certainty without it coming to her in a vision."

Etta Mae twisted a plait around her index finger. "So your arm's not tingling, Miss Grace?"

"No, sweetheart. It's not."

"Good Lord. Just say what you mean," I said. "What kind of possibility do you see in that dirty old place?" I pulled Etta Mae's hand, yanking her finger free from twisting in her braid.

"Never you mind." Mama tended her reflection in the expanse of glass, touching at her hair, smoothing her dress.

I regarded the three of us, our images hazy in the dusty window. The letter "P" floated between Etta Mae and me—etched in the grime. Nothing more than a shadow. The weight of a whisper.

Chapter 9

The heat bore an oppressive weight the first day of school—a damp,
steamy washcloth draped over the world. A perfect place for moldering
things to grow.

I opened my bedroom door just enough to reveal the tiniest slice of
myself and called to Etta Mae. "You just about ready?"

"Um hmm. What about you?"

"Yep. Now remember, just like we practiced."

Etta Mae and I had not seen the other's new dress, and though the
design was identical, we agreed to keep our fabric choices secret until
that first day of school. To ensure we saw one another at the same time,
we devised an entrance requiring us to walk backwards.

I sang though the opening of my door. "I sees a kitty."

"I sees a cat," Etta Mae sang back.

"I can't finds you."

"Where you at?"

Our giggles erupted even before we started to move.

Etta Mae's path required twelve steps from her room off the kitchen,
and mine, only seven, to the meeting spot in the center of the hall. My
distance was shorter, and when I came to the scar on the floor that
marked the spot, I stood still waiting for the press of her back against
mine.

Though it was only 7:00 a.m., a slick of perspiration crept from the
small of my back—the slight pressure of Etta Mae against me, tacking
my dress to my skin.

"Okay," I said. "On three." I paused for a moment, heightening the
anticipation. "One."

"Two."

We both finished the count together, both of us spinning around to face the other. We grabbed hold of one another, swinging our arms like jump ropes.

"You're beautiful," I said. The royal blue fabric she selected played upon the amber flecks in her eyes giving them the appearance of topaz, her smile made even brighter by the white Peter Pan collar fitting perfectly to her delicate neck.

Etta Mae's eyes swept over me. "So are you."

I selected a shade of green for my dress, a color close to the one Marlissa and Mrs. Mayfield wore the day I met them.

We compared our dresses, pulling our skirts together to examine Mama's work. Though they were exactly alike in design, our fabric selections transformed them into magnificent one-of-a-kinds.

The prior evening, Miss Wessie took loose Etta Mae's plaits. "I'd rather be shelling peas," she said, pretending to be put-upon.

After Etta Mae's hair had been washed and dressed with her granny's special hair potion, Miss Wessie fashioned two simple ponytail braids, one on each side of her head, accentuating her cheekbones and exotic tilt of her eyes.

"Your hair's so pretty," Etta Mae said, reaching gently to touch the curls at the end of my ponytail, an effect achieved by Mama rolling and twisting discarded strips of fabric into wide sections of my hair, a process not nearly as tedious as the one inflicted upon Etta Mae.

Miss Wessie called from the kitchen doorway, "You two peacocks quit your preening and get on in this kitchen and let me take a look at you." Her tone was playful, an occurrence as special as a hard candy treat.

Miss Wessie sang along with Peggy Lee on the radio, the two of them in duet to "Love Me or Leave Me".

Etta Mae and I twirled into the kitchen in time to the music, walking in a circle around Miss Wessie, showcasing our first-day ensembles.

Miss Wessie's eyes went wide with her smile, her head nodding while she sang. She spread her arms out in front of her like a fancy lady singer on *The Ed Sullivan Show*. Etta Mae and I took our places at her side, the two of us, her backup singers.

Mama walked into the kitchen, clapping her hands after we let go of the last note. "Look at you two," she said from across the room. Mama wore a floral print, summer dress with short, French cuffed sleeves, her small waist accentuated by the fullness of her skirt.

Etta Mae was the first to fuss over Mama and the new dress she had sewn for herself. "Miss Analeise, you sure are a picture."

"I must say, I do feel particularly good today." Mama rotated once, slowly and elegantly to give us the full effect.

"Looks like I got me three peacocks in the kitchen," Miss Wessie said, placing the emphasis on "three". She shook her head, returning to wipe out her well-seasoned skillet, the one she aimed at Daddy the night I drowned him in the river.

Would I ever be able to carve away the memory of what I did? I looked down at my prettied-up self. My new dress was buttercream frosting spread over a lopsided cake—a disguise to an ugly truth.

"You okay, baby?" Mama said.

I nodded, trying desperately to tamp down that horrible, brick-heavy feeling that was sure to come. Was it selfish to want to feel good? "Are you wearing that to the Pickle Factory," I said.

Mama laughed. "Nope." She kissed the top of my head. "Mama's got an important meeting today."

"What meeting?" I was taken off guard by her announcement. Meetings and pretty dresses were rare as snow.

Mama cast a glance at Miss Wessie. A charge of electricity passed between them, a collision of static energy so shrill only a passing dog might have heard. Miss Wessie's smile melted in the exchange, our hard candy treat dissolving in the moment.

A speck of old Mama crept through her powder and blush, her eyes heavy with worry. She spackled over it, spreading a smile back into place. Was Mama a lopsided cake like me?

"Never you mind," Mama said, stirring mischief and mystery into her words. "You'll just have to wait until later. Until I know for sure."

I wondered if the answer to her mystery meeting might be in the undersides of our new dresses, hidden in back tack and blanket stitches. Had she even looked at what would come?

A horn blew from outside the house, three goose-like honks. Sister McLeod, Miss Wessie's friend from church had arrived. For as long as I could remember, she drove her own grandchildren and Etta Mae to school each day.

Miss Wessie dried her hands on her apron, "My baby's a big ole fifth grader now—all grow'd up and pretty."

Etta Mae beamed as we gathered around to see her to the porch, Miss Wessie carrying her packed lunch and homemade school bag.

Sister McLeod rolled down the window and waved to us. "Looks like I got the honor of driving me a princess to school."

I could not see her face, but I knew Etta Mae was smiling. I yelled out after her. "I sees a kitty."

She sang back without turning around, "I sees a cat." I could taste the bittersweet in her voice. The flavor, like sugarcane with stalk peeling at the edges.

I felt a swell of affection for Etta Mae, of the sadness and uncertainty that comes with a goodbye. I blinked away mutinous tears.

Mama, Miss Wessie, and I watched the old Cadillac drive her away, Mama's squeezing hands warm on my shoulders.

I looked up at Miss Wessie, her face dim and troubled. Was it the shadow of a farewell—of the passing of another summer? Or was it Mama's important meeting that troubled Miss Wessie most? She reached down and kissed my cheek, tugging playfully at my ponytail before she turned to walk inside.

Mama fiddled with my collar, inspecting her work, running her finger along the dainty edge. She looked so beautiful on the porch in the gentle wash of morning light.

I pretended to be happy, smiling up at New Mama. The drone of cicadas agitated the nervous churn in my stomach, that down-yonder place thankfully no one could see.

* * *

A pack of boys ran crazy through the playground, savoring the final moments before the school bell rang. Machine gun noises and wounded cries of pretend soldiers fell across the battlefield.

Had Marlissa already arrived? Would she remember me?

I gave Mama one final wave before walking into the lobby where the other girls sought refuge from the heat. How I wished I could take her with me, to show everyone how beautiful she looked. *Pretty Mama. New Mama.*

I stepped over the boy that fell at my feet, turning to give the nuisance a dainty kick with my new pair of Mary Jane's. "Rest in peace, soldier."

Virginia Fenton cornered a group of girls from my class, regaling them with the events of her summer. By the time I walked from the door to the group, I learned she and her family traveled to Disneyland. Though she found it enjoyable, the whole affair failed to live up to her expectations. Little ever did.

Virginia stood a good head taller than the others, and took it upon herself, as if with height came privilege, to direct and dominate our days. We tolerated her like a fly at a picnic.

Jane, my friend—Virginia's twin sister, stood slightly away from the group. Had their mother not insisted they dress identically, one would have been pressed to discern they were twins. Jane, the smaller of the two, possessed a prettiness that eluded her sister. Even the sprinkle of freckles across Jane's tiny nose possessed a pleasing symmetry that was in direct contrast with Virginia's, a thoughtless, haphazard ramble.

Jane and I hugged, assessing the changes that summer brought upon the other. "I love your new glasses," I said. They were cat-like in shape, offsetting the puppy dog slope of her eyes. Virginia, also near-sighted, refused to wear her glasses, resulting in a perpetual squint which contributed to an unwavering countenance of intimidation—an effect I suspected she embraced.

"Thank you. I love your new dress," Jane whispered, careful not to disturb Virginia's recitation of summer happenings.

"Mama made it. Gosh, what happened to Virginia's hair?" Until now, she and her sister wore the same style. Jane's bangs were precise, as if cut with the aid of a ruler, the rest cascading in large, reddish-brown finger waves to her shoulders.

"She fell asleep with chewing gum in her mouth, a big ole wad of it." She began to laugh. "Mama had to cut it. Now, she looks just like Buster Brown."

"What's so funny?" Virginia folded her arms across her jumper.

"Not a thing in this world." Jane chewed at her lip, eating away her smile.

Virginia turned her attention to me, her big boy-hands planted on her hips. "Analeise, what did you do this summer?"

I killed my Daddy, I thought to myself, wondering what the others might do if I spoke it aloud, if I sent my confession to drift in the halls.

Jane spoke softly. "You know Analeise had a difficult summer."

"Did you hear Jane and I got air conditioning in our rooms?" Virginia steered the conversation back to a topic she thought more interesting, herself. The group nodded, temporarily silencing her. "It would get so hot up there, I'd have to sleep buck naked."

"Virginia Fenton." Jane scolded, her voice becoming part of a collective of girlish gasps and nervous giggles. Virginia managed her thin lips into a snarl, the closest thing to a smile she could muster. She was pleased with herself, never refusing an opportunity to shock and titillate. The prior year she took up dipping snuff, a habit not known to exist amongst any other fifth grader at Providence Elementary.

I imagined a crater-sized hole sprawled across Virginia's insides. A never-ending need for attention.

"Analeise, you weren't here earlier when I explained the plan for welcoming Marlissa Mayfield and Abel Darlington." She flared her nostrils. "My Daddy's a lawyer," she said. This was a fact of which we were all aware, but one which Virginia felt required constant reminding. "He's in charge of all the lawerying for the Mayfields and Darlingtons. Also, I'm good friends with both Marlissa and Abel." She jerked her shoulders back and lifted her inadequate chin. "They are very important people, and it's our job to make them welcome."

Jane leaned into my ear, "We hardly know them. Just been to a few of the same gatherings. And we go to the same church."

"Are you listening to me, Jane?" Virginia said.

Jane rolled her eyes. "With great anticipation." Jane sometimes sounded like an adult when she spoke.

"When they arrive, I'll meet them at the door and lead the introductions." She looked around the group for confirmation. Everyone nodded. "They'll probably be coming in their Rolls Royce—the only one in all of Georgia."

"I don't know how she knows that," Jane whispered. "I think she made it up." A smile passed between us.

"They're here. Stand back." Virginia spread her arms wide as if keeping us from danger.

A flush of excitement spread across me and the others. We were all tippy-toes and straining necks. The black car was sleek, with a luster that gave the appearance it was wet. Morning sun caught pieces of chrome creating small camera-like flashes of light.

A boy wandered in from somewhere behind us. "Somebody die?"

"Put a egg in your sock and beat it." Virginia poked her finger into the middle of his forehead and gave him a push.

"Dang, Virginia," he said, walking off rubbing his head.

A colored man wearing a suit and hat exited the driver side. "That's the shop-fur." Virginia said.

Jane nudged my ribs with her elbow. "That's the chauffeur."

"Are you deaf, Jane?" Virginia said. "Can't you hear nothing? That's what just came out of my mouth." She pointed her finger at her sister. "Pay attention."

"I beg your pardon," Jane said, tamping down her smile.

A boy was the first to exit the car. "That's Abel Darlington." Virginia looked back at us to ensure we were paying attention.

Jane leaned in once again to whisper. "He's so handsome, isn't he?"

"The shop-fur? He looks right nice in his suit," I said, smiling.

Jane giggled. "Behave yourself, Virginia will put you in the corner."

Abel Darling was a handsome boy, or at least appeared to be from a distance. Dark hair and olive skin. Then he smiled, a sort of happiness electrifying anyone lucky enough to look.

"You know, his mama died two years ago." Jane cupped my ear with her hand. "Lady cancer," she whispered. "The Mayfields and Darlingtons are real good friends. Mrs. Mayfield's been like a second mama to him."

What must it be like to have Mrs. Mayfield as your mama? For her to love you—to look upon you with those stunning green eyes.

"Look," one of the girls yelled. "It's her."

A small, delicate hand reached out from the car to Abel. In one smooth movement, Marlissa Mayfield stood at his side. Her dress, the color of periwinkle, was a shock against the summer haze. Sun caught and gleamed in her hair.

"That's Marlissa Mayfield," Virginia announced.

Another tumble of whispers rolled across the girls. My finger twisted in my ponytail.

Wonderment choked the chatter. A gloved hand in a shade of lilac reached from the car, posing elegantly in the air.

Abel once again reached toward the door. A high-heeled shoe, the color of the glove, appeared beneath the door. With the same fluidity as her daughter, Cordelia Mayfield floated from the car.

"And that's Mrs. Mayfield," Virginia said, her voice a sleepy, dreamy-time croak.

Mrs. Mayfield wore a two-piece, linen suit matching her shoes and gloves. The skirt was narrow. A slope-brimmed hat topped the look, her Grace Kelly hair tucked from sight. The combination of hat and sunglasses concealed much of her face, a slash of cheekbones and peek of red lips were the only features in view, as if one might be unable to look upon her all at once—that it was safer to gaze upon her in small sections at a time.

Would the Mayfields remember me? Would the others be jealous we were acquainted?

The party of three entered the lobby walking toward the group. Virginia spread her arms, her signal for us to await her direction. "Good morning, Mrs. Mayfield." Virginia bowed her head. "On behalf of Providence Elementary, I, Virginia Fenton, would like to welcome you, Marlissa and Abel, to our school."

"Oh, brother," Jane whispered.

Mrs. Mayfield spoke, her eyes hidden behind her sunglasses. "Thank you, Virginia."

The name, Virginia, for me would always be scabbed knees and peculiar smells. Mrs. Mayfield elongated it—disregarding the "r", a sort of rechristening, bestowing a kind of beauty upon Virginia, if only for a moment. Virginia, her jaw gone slack, seemed taken by its lyrical quality, that such a name could be her own.

Abel and Marlissa stood on each side of Mrs. Mayfield. Abel smiled to the group, his dark features a stark contrast, but stunning compliment to the Mayfields. Marlissa, slowly blinking her pale, spider lashes, stood with a Mona Lisa countenance, an expression lingering somewhere on the cusp of an emotion.

"I would now like to introduce you to some of my classmates," Virginia said.

Marlissa walked toward Virginia through the parting girl-herd until she stood in front of me, my fingers spreading and clenching. Did she remember me?

Virginia's nostrils flared.

A swell of hope caught like a lump in my throat. Would she speak my name as lovely as her mother spoke Virginia's?

Her lips, the shape of a bow, pulled apart. "You're that bug girl."

Bug Girl. My knees melted away.

The school bell rang—a horrible clanging that startled us all. The wild boys spilled into the lobby in a frenzy of *whoops* and *hollers*.

Jane stood by me, chaos swirling around us. Each girl of the group regarded me with strange curiosity, pity smeared across their faces.

Mrs. Mayfield's beautiful scent settled over me as she and Marlissa walked by. Her fragrance was familiar—hints of jasmine and lily of the valley? It was the new smell of Mama, and I had stolen a drop for each of my wrists—sneaking it down from the dresser, carefully returning it to the rest in the exact spot at just the precise angle.

Virginia lingered, her face, a mangle of disgust and satisfaction. "Bug girl." She pointed a chubby finger at my face, bits of her spittle landing on my cheek. She turned to walk away, letting loose a goblin's laugh.

I raised my right wrist to my nose and inhaled, relinquishing myself to the current of the crowd, my body directed by the push and knock of shoulders and hips.

Jane grabbed hold, guiding me down the hall.

Mrs. Mayfield's lilac hat hovered in the distance, that troubling heat creeping up my legs.

How easy it would be to pray Virginia Fenton dead, to send her to the river's bottom, her stubby feet snagging in the weeds.

The vibrations of the bell pounded in my ear, driven deeper by the blow of Virginia's receding cackle.

Chapter 10

Virginia Fenton was furious. Mrs. Lawrence's alphabetical seating arrangement placed me directly behind Marlissa with Virginia sitting two rows away. Amidst Virginia's protestations and assertion she be allowed to sit behind Marlissa, Mrs. Lawrence did not concede.

"Miss Mayfield will be just fine where she's sitting," said Mrs. Lawrence. Thirty years of teaching sixth grade had dulled Eudora Lawrence, layering her in a patina of ambivalence even Virginia Fenton could not rub away.

Bug Girl. How is it the day went so wrong so quickly? I could think of little else sitting behind Marlissa—her cascade of blond hair, a sheen so brilliant, I might have seen my reflection had the light been just right.

The stirrings of my classmates signaled it was time to go out and play, that the recess bell had rang.

The boys scurried, bumping into one another, shoulder-to-shoulder, clogging the doorway. "No running in the halls," Mrs. Lawrence said.

Virginia jumped up from her desk. "Marlissa, wait for me." Her jumper caught the side of her desk sending it to topple, the contents of her desk spilling onto the floor. Dozens of marbles rolled across the room.

Marlissa paid no mind to Virginia. She rose, placing the double handles of her school bag across her up-turned wrist. The bag matched her dress, periwinkle with a gentle tumble of embroidered, white flowers down the front.

"Miss Fenton, you aren't leaving this room until you clean up your mess," Mrs. Lawrence said.

"Dang-nabbit to heck," Virginia said.

"Miss Fenton, mind yourself. Don't let me hear that kind of talk again, or I'm sending you down the hall."

Jane took advantage of her sister's detainment, coming to my desk to greet Marlissa. "Have you been properly introduced to Analeise Newell?" she said. "I'm sure it was just an oversight, but I think you got her name wrong earlier." Oh, how I loved Jane Fenton.

"Did I?" Marlissa said, her eyebrow arching above her green eye.

Virginia's heavy breathing was audible from across the room. "Almost done," she said, scooping up her marbles, dropping them into her pockets, her hips growing lumpy.

"Would you like to swing with Jane and me?" I said, taking a chance she might spend time with the one and only Bug Girl. "We'll have to hurry—they're the first to go."

Marlissa looked to Jane as if she asked the question. "I couldn't possibly swing wearing a dress."

Jane and I had been swinging in dresses since first grade. Though it was a bit awkward, if you tucked your skirt between your knees and kept them together, a girl could get along just fine. On occasion, when no one was looking, we jumped from the swings, our dresses parachuting for a brilliant moment, until they fell back into place.

"What would you like to do?" Jane asked Marlissa, stealing a look in my direction. "It's your first day. You pick." The other girls in the class gathered around awaiting Marlissa's decision, all of them content to just be close.

"Be right there," Virginia hollered, picking up the last marble only to drop it again.

Mrs. Lawrence spoke from the door tapping her leg with a ruler. "Miss Fenton, when you are done removing those marbles from your pockets, I will require your assistance cleaning the erasers."

"Good Lord a-mighty," Virginia said, stomping her foot, planting her hands on her lumpy hips.

"That's it, Virginia Fenton." Mrs. Lawrence pointed into the hall with her ruler. "Down to see the Principal."

Jane smiled big, relishing her sister's predicament.

Virginia Fenton stomped passed us, her face the color of an overripe tomato.

Marlissa appeared unaffected by the whole affair. "I brought along some things. Gifts," Marlissa said to the group, looking down at her bag. With a smooth turn of heel, she glided to the door and down the hall. If you listened closely, you could have heard it. The quiet tap of her expensive shoe—a sort of Morse Code only girls can hear. *Follow me. I am in charge now.* We hurried behind her, our heels tapping back, agreeing to this new order.

Marlissa sat herself upon a concrete bench beneath a magnolia tree. The rest of us assembled closely, awaiting to view the contents of her lilac bag.

She pulled out a tidy, glittery stack of sparkle held together by a gold ribbon. With a gentle pull, she unfurled the ribbon, the contents fanning in her hands like an oversized deck of playing cards.

There was a buzz in the momentary silence, only the yowls of wild boys stirring the quiet circle. Somewhere off to the side, someone spoke. "What's that?"

"Mes belles poupées," Marlissa said, not looking up from her task, her ankles daintily crossed, legs swinging ever so slightly.

"Pardon?" Jane said.

Marlissa looked up from her chore, the sun dissecting her face, illuminating the right half. "It's French," she said, "It means my beautiful dolls."

I repeated her words to myself. *Beautiful dolls. Beautiful dolls. Beautiful dolls.*

"Where did you get them?" Jane said.

"I made them. From Mother's *Vogue* magazines."

Etta Mae crept into my thoughts, the sound of her angel-voice. Was she having a good day?

Marlissa looked down again, her dolls shimmering in dappled light. "I think I have enough for each of you to have one, if you'd like."

Giddiness spun the girls into near hysteria. I could feel it myself. The paper dolls were unlike any I ever saw, and from the commotion breaking out about me, unlike any the group had seen.

The cutouts were reinforced with card stock giving structure to the flimsy magazine paper. Bugle beads, rhinestones, and glitter embellished the dolls' dresses. On occasion, bits of ribbon and cording enhanced an ensemble. The most striking feature assigned each doll was a set of expansive wings affixed and coordinated in similar detail.

Though the winged creatures were breathtaking, there was something unsettling in their design, an otherworldliness that seemed incongruous with a girl's paper doll. I, like the others, could not resist their allure.

Marlissa took the first doll and looked to the girls around me searching for the proper pairings. Her decisions were careful and subject to a methodology known only to her. The introductions to her new classmates that morning had been brief, but somehow, Marlissa remembered each girl's name, personalizing each presentation. Even Jane seemed held in the grip of her thrall.

I, the only girl without a doll, stood facing Marlissa. The other girls clustered in conversation comparing one doll to the next.

Marlissa put her hand into the bag, and for the first time that day looked directly into my eyes. Her gaze lingered, the sun now fully covering her face, the whole of her revealed. The direct light gave her green eyes a fluorescent quality—two glorious, wonderland rabbit holes to fall away into.

I tugged at the side of my dress, self-conscious, unsure of what to do with my hands.

"This one's for you," Marlissa said. She continued to look upon me without blinking.

Finally, I looked away and down at her gift. I knew immediately something was wrong, unbalanced. It was missing a wing. I turned it over checking to see if it might have folded back, requiring a mere adjustment to set it right. But the wing had been torn away, only the scalloped edge remaining.

The paper doll's eyes unsettled me most. They were pushed through—only holes remaining. I held the doll in front of me looking through the perforations, Marlissa looking back from the other side. A sick feeling came over me. Wobbly legs and sour stomach.

Jane examined my doll. "What happened to it?" she whispered.

I shrugged my shoulders.

"Marlissa," Jane said. "Analeise's doll is . . ." She hesitated, staring down at the thing. "Broken."

Marlissa pulled a green book from her bag. "That's the last one." Marlissa rubbed her hand over the cover, not looking up.

"You can have mine," Jane whispered. Her glasses slid down the sweaty slope of her nose.

"That's sweet, but you keep it." I squeezed her arm.

"Jane, let me see yours," someone said. Jane's eyes met mine, and I nodded her away.

Several girls fussed over the black dress that Jane's doll wore. Marlissa turned her attention to their conversation. "That's Christian Dior," she said, Mother says he's a genius."

I studied my doll, imagining what she might look like whole. I turned it over, running my hand over the plain, white backing. Then I noticed it—something written on the bottom. I pulled it close, positioning it at an angle until it became clear in the mottled light. *Analeise.* My name was written on the back. Girlish cursive—all swirly and slanted.

Marlissa pushed her hair behind her shoulders and ran her hands over the emerald green book resting in her lap, her tapered fingers tracing the gold lettering of the title. *Fairies of the Flowers and Trees.* She opened the book.

I stepped forward taking a closer look, my legs heavy in the thick, summer heat. I stood so close I cast a shadow over the page, blocking the light. For the briefest of moments, I thought she might look up at me with her lovely eyes. But she only stared down at her book, turning one page and then another.

Chapter 11

Marlissa's paper doll left me undone.

I needed time to think, and Mr. Lucas Bloom's music class was a welcome reprieve. An opportunity to melt into the seat with my thoughts, free from the tap of Mrs. Lawrence's ruler.

Mr. Bloom, the High School Choral Director, visited Providence Elementary three times a week teaching a variety of musically themed topics from theory to great composers. On occasion, he would arm the class with cymbals and tambourines—the maracas being reserved for only a few possessing what Mr. Bloom referred to as *exotic flair.*

Unlike Mrs. Lawrence, Mr. Bloom did not subscribe to the convention of assigned seating, allowing us the discretion to sit where we pleased. The boys sat in distant rows, constructing a mote between them and Mr. Bloom's creative whim. Virginia and the other girls flanked Marlissa, each cradling her very own paper doll.

Virginia, who had been detained by Mrs. Lawrence through recess, held a paper doll as lovely as the others. Just how did she manage to have one? Had Marlissa hidden one away just for her? My deformed paper doll remained pressed between the pages of my math book, left behind in my desk cubby.

"Good afternoon, and welcome." With a sweep of hand, Mr. Bloom wrote his name across the board, the slide and *swoosh* of the chalk creating a comforting rhythm, a sound—if repeated, might lull one to sleep. He blew the chalk from his fingers then brushed his hands together.

"Good afternoon, Mr. Bloom," the class repeated back—only the girls expressing anything resembling enthusiasm.

"It's my understanding we have two new students with us this year," Mr. Bloom said. As if shielding his eyes from a debilitating brightness, he placed his hand above his eyebrows and scanned the room. "Mr. Abel Darlington, where are you?"

The other boys patted Abel, playfully punching at his arms until he stood. A huge smile spread across his tanned face, revealing the slightest gap between otherwise perfect teeth. Strands of black hair fell across his forehead, his hands tucked into his back pockets.

There was a joy about him—an ease that drew the eye—that stirred one's breathing. Within the span of a day, Abel Darlington already found his place amongst the other boys, a magnet every bit as strong as the one Marlissa wielded over the girls.

Mr. Bloom approached the front riser slowly, as if to capture a butterfly perched on a branch. "And you must be Miss Marlissa Mayfield."

Virginia's body swayed with smugness, looking back over her shoulder at Jane and me. Jane crossed her eyes at her sister. Virginia returned the gesture, embellishing the look by sticking out her tongue, the effect all together unsettling.

"Miss Mayfield is a classically trained pianist," Mr. Bloom announced to the group.

Marlissa Mayfield plays the piano? I sat up straight in my seat.

Mr. Bloom bent over placing his hands on his knees. "I had the pleasure of hearing you play at one of your mother's charity events." Marlissa affirmed with a nod, but there seemed to be little recollection. "Would you do us the honor of kicking off our year with a selection of your choosing?" Gripped by the prospect, the girls applauded, Virginia's hands the loudest of all. Marlissa took the bench with perfect posture, her face expressionless. Mr. Bloom clasped his hands beneath his chin. "What will you be performing today?"

"A piece by Chopin. The Waltz in D flat major, Opus 64," she said, her eyes looking out at the class, but at no one in particular.

"The Minute Waltz." Mr. Bloom touched his hand to his face, leaving behind a chalk smudge. "Wonderful."

"Vals du petit chien," Marlissa said.

"I beg your pardon."

"It is another name for the work." Marlissa said. "It means, The Little Dog Waltz." She ran her hand through her glossy hair. "Mother said he was inspired to write the piece while watching a little dog chase its tail."

The girls all leaned forward, elbows into knees, enraptured by her words.

"Splendid," Mr. Bloom said, clasping his hands together as he turned to write "Chopin" on the board. Some of the boys chuckled at his flourish of movement.

"Chawp-in," Dink Hammond yelled from the back. "That's a stupid name." For effect, he used it in a sentence. "I saw your mama chawp-in wood wearing your grand pappy's overalls."

Laughter erupted amongst the boys, the girl tribe holding them in frigid glares, arms crossed against their chests.

"Stink Hammond, shut your stupid yapper," Virginia said.

"That's enough." Mr. Bloom snapped his fingers. "Let's give Miss Mayfield our undivided attention.

The room settled into quiet. Marlissa shifted upon the bench, then looked down at the keys. And she began to play.

As it often happened, it seemed I knew the piece—could play it myself, anticipating each note before it came. I played along with her, my fingers moving in my lap.

Marlissa was exciting to watch, her pretty hands running the keys. The girls looked upon this happening with adoration, the boys bobbing their heads and tapping their feet.

She was good. But somewhere deep inside—where the good and bad parts of me battled and swirled—I could not help but think . . . *I'm better.*

When she finished, she sat, her Mona Lisa smile unmoved by the applause.

Mr. Bloom could hardly contain his elation. "We are so fortunate to have such talent in our presence," he said, bowing toward Marlissa. He grinned big, placing his hands on his hips.

"Mr. Bloom," Jane said, waving her hand in the air, the one holding her paper doll.

"Yes, Miss Fenton?"

"Analeise can play the piano."

"Shh." Had Jane Fenton lost her mind? What was she doing? I tugged at her sleeve. Aside from Mama, Daddy, Etta Mae, and Miss Wessie, Jane was the only person I ever played for.

"You're good," she whispered back. "Just as good as Marlissa."

Virginia whipped around, contorting her face, as if suffering the indignity of an unpleasant odor. "What kind of music can you play, Bug Girl?" she said. "Something from your Daddy's trashy ole' juke joint."

"Be quiet, Virginia," Jane said.

"Another prodigy amongst us?" Mr. Bloom said. "Would you do us the honor of playing for us, Analeise?"

I wanted to kill Jane Fenton, snatch that paper doll from her hand and slap it against her face. What was she trying to do to me? She squeezed my arm, smiling, radiating what seemed to be a genuine confidence in my abilities.

"Yeah, whatcha gonna play, Bug Girl?" Dink Hammond placed his hand under his shirt and into his armpit producing a flatulent sound. "Why don't you play a song I wrote special for you. I call it 'Bug Girl Blues'." Virginia let loose a cackle, rattling the boys loose from their unnatural reserve—stirring a temporary chaos.

"If you don't settle down, Mr. Hammond, I'm going to send you off to Mr. O'Connell's." The threat of Principal O'Connell quieted the room. Mr. Bloom breathed in and leaned forward. "What are you going to play for us, Miss Newell?"

What am I going to play? I could hardly think in the rush of panic.

"Miss Newell?"

Virginia snickered. "Big dummy."

"You don't have to play if you don't want to," Mr. Bloom said.

I found Marlissa on the front row, her gaze steady upon the chalkboard. I hesitated. "I just don't know the name of the song, and I haven't exactly played it before."

"She don't know the name of the dang song," Dink said. "Then how's she gonna play it?"

Virginia turned loose her goblin laugh.

Mr. Bloom clapped his hands together. "Settle yourselves, class. Well, that's okay. I suppose you don't have to know the title of a song to play it. But if you haven't practiced—that's okay. You can play another time."

I nodded. "I'm ready, sir." I sat down on the bench and looked down at the keys, calling forth a song from memory, the one Cordelia Mayfield played the day I visited Mistletoe.

I sat with my eyes shut. In that temporal stretch of quiet, the beginnings of a storm grumbled inside me. My toes tingled. Next came the heat—akin to a match lit and passed beneath my feet. I opened my eyes. Bent my fingers. And I played. The notes came to me like a Remembrance, as if tattooed behind my eyelids.

In the vibrations of the final note, I sat, the static sound of the world creeping back into consciousness. I looked out at the class—all of them sitting silent, a bit wild-eyed, all of them but Marlissa who sat unblinking. She chewed at her lip like I sometimes did.

What had I done?

Mr. Bloom broke the spell, the others following quickly behind with applause. Virginia sat on her hands, studying me closely, looking for some explanation of my ability, the answer to the magic trick.

Marlissa gently put her hands together, only the strain and set of her jaw giving clue to any discomfort. Dink played his armpit again, this time, a compliment.

"Analeise. Dear sweet child. That was brilliant. Just brilliant." He wiped at his watery eyes. "And you don't know the name of the piece?"

"No, sir."

"A lovely mystery then," he said.

Mr. Bloom discussed Chopin the remainder of the class, a tribute to Marlissa, though I heard little of his lecture. I spent the time contemplating my performance and the reaction of the class. The sound of applause was a rapturous thing. I wondered if this is what it felt like to be Marlissa Mayfield. To be beautiful. To be adored.

* * *

The school bell rang, shaking me from daydreams. Mr. Bloom's class was over and so was the day. Jane and I gathered our things from beneath our seats.

Abel Darlington called my name from across the room, startling me, my head hitting the seat of the chair as I retrieved my books. *He knows my name.*

"You were great today," he said. Sweet puffs of boy breath wafted across my face when he moved close, the smell of it like Wrigley's Spearmint Gum, the kind Miss Wessie kept inside her Sunday purse.

"Thank you, Abel." My voice came out thick and unfamiliar.

"Marlissa, I'll meet you outside at the car. I forgot my math book," he said, waving his hand in her direction.

Jane pinched my elbow as he hurried to the door.

Marlissa's voice rippled the air. "May I have a word?"

I turned to find Marlissa and Virginia Fenton behind me. "With me?"

"Only a moment of your time," Marlissa said, her eyes blinking slowly, allowing her lashes to rest before sweeping them upwards. The effect, altogether stunning.

"Okay."

Marlissa turned to Jane and Virginia. "If you two would be so kind."

The two sisters stuttered and stammered, both taken aback by Marlissa's dismissal. "Of course," Jane said. Virginia remained oddly silent, her puffy face unattractive with disappointment.

Marlissa waited, watching the sisters leave the room.

What does she want? My stomach turned somersaults.

Finally, the two of us were alone, standing beneath the eerie serenade of fluorescent lights, my heartbeat thumping in my ears.

She walked toward me, herding me backwards, her embroidered bag dangling from her arm.

My back pressed against the wall, she grabbed hold of my wrist. She squeezed hard and mean, her eyes glittery and beautiful. She made her business quick. "Why did you play that song?"

Her nails dug into my skin. Just like her mother's slap, it was a good kind of hurt. How lovely to be in the grip of a Mayfield. My mouth opened, but nothing coming out.

She asked again. When I did not answer, she leaned in close. I could smell the scent of her Mother's perfume, the same as my mama's. "That song is not for you."

"I'm sorry," I said. "I didn't know.

She leaned in closer, her cheek against mine, her lips pressing to my ear. *"Avez-vous peur des fantôme?"* she whispered.

I shook my head, her words unknown to me.

She turned loose my wrist and stepped back. "Thank you for your time." She turned and glided away, her movement, the slow drift of a dandelion bloom.

My wrist burned from her squeeze. When she was gone, I lifted it and watched the red marks recede slowly, until only the crescent indentations of her fingernails remained.

Fantôme . . . Fantôme . . .

Chapter 12

The school bus pulled away, red dust kicking up from the tires, leaving me standing in a thin veil of grime. It was a tender mercy to be home.

The first day of school was hardly what I expected, having left home as Analeise Newell—returning as Providence's very own, newly christened, Bug Girl.

How would I explain the day to Etta Mae? To Mama and Miss Wessie? No doubt, I would have to lie. But how big?

I pulled my ponytail over my shoulder running my fingers through the length of it, examining the ends. Mama's curls had turned to fishhooks. I inspected the walls on both sides of the front door. Ribbons of paint curled away from the house, clinging tenuously to the clapboards.

The urge to poke and pull at the paint, to peel back the layers, came over me, and I obliged it, fanning my hand across the siding, releasing scales of paint to the floor. Perhaps I was only meant for broken things.

A note was tucked in the screen door. *Gone to the Piggly Wiggly. Be back soon. Love Mama.*

The front door and windows were open—Miss Wessie's relentless struggle to shoo away the heat.

I walked inside. "Etta Mae? Miss Wessie?" I was alone with the whir and hum of box fans. The churn of gravel and dirt from the driveway followed. *The Sheriff.* Had something bad happened to Mama? Or was he coming for me?

I dropped my school bag on the floor, crouching down beneath the window beside the sofa. I was ready to run if I had to. Down the hall and through the kitchen.

A car door opened and shut, and then the sound of another automobile crunching in the yard. I lifted myself just enough to peek out the window. Mama was home. And alive. The Sheriff must have come for me.

The tin roof popped, vibrating under the late afternoon heat. I resisted the urge to yell to Mama for help. I knelt just below the window and listened.

"Is everything okay?" Mama said.

"No emergencies, Grace. Just stopping by." I imagined his lack of urgency a trick, to relax Mama and then carry me away, his blue lights flashing and sirens sounding. *Analeise Newell murdered her daddy.* He cleared his throat. "I just need to have a word in private."

I lifted up for another look out the window. Miss Wessie stood to the left of Mama and Etta Mae in the rear. Grocery bags crinkled under Miss Wessie's arms with the shift of her hips.

"Okay," Mama said.

"Go on to the house." Miss Wessie urged Etta Mae along with the bob of her head.

Etta Mae walked by the Sheriff, looking up the length of him, taking in his uniform. He took off his hat and bowed his head as she passed.

A hint of smile passed across Etta Mae's face. *Judas.*

"Is the porch good?" Mama said.

"The porch is just fine." His voice was deep and rich, the receding notes of a tuba.

"Best get these groceries on in the house before they get to spoiling," Miss Wessie said.

"Let me help you with those," the Sheriff said.

"Thank you, but I got 'em."

I lowered myself back down below the window. I imagined Miss Wessie's *boom boom* hips as I listened to the *crinkle* of the grocery bags. I hummed the sound of her walk to myself. It calmed me—helped me think through the fear.

Boom. Boom. Crinkle.

Etta Mae and Miss Wessie were close to the porch. I grabbed my school bag and hurried to my room. I tossed the bag out the window and jumped out behind it.

Our house was raised on brick piers, and on countless occasions Etta Mae and I crawled beneath. Refuge from heat and boredom. We would lay on our backs gazing up at the underbelly, listening to Miss Wessie shuffling and singing.

I crawled under the house, the cool, damp earthy smells rising up to meet me.

Etta Mae called out my name. "You home?" She sounded far away, her voice tinny and distant.

I reached up to touch the floor, feeling the vibrations of her steps above me. I crawled closer to the backside of the steps, the Sheriff and Mama's muffled conversation becoming clearer. I settled myself on my knees.

"I sure hate to come out here and bother you." Silence stretched between them, the shifting of someone's weight causing the floor to whine.

"Briar, if there's something needing saying, then say it." It was the first time I heard Mama call Sheriff Dobbs by his first name. She said it soft and gentle, and I imagined her reaching out to touch his arm. Mama once shared with me that she and the Sheriff were sweet on each other long before she married Daddy.

He softened his baritone to match the tone of Mama's voice. "It's about the night Claxton drowned."

A loud and unsettling glissando, fingers scaling down piano keys played in my head. The Sheriff had come to take me away. I leaned forward and grabbed for something to hold onto, to keep myself from toppling. There was no anchor to be found, only clumps of dirt that pulled away through my fingers.

"Someone mentioned you called in sick out at your second job the night of the accident."

"Yes." Mama drew out the word, stretching it into syllables. Her voice, a question.

"Don't give me that look, Grace. I know it's nothing, but I have to ask."

The timbre of Mama's voice changed. "I don't believe you've asked me anything, Briar. What exactly is the question?" I could hear the slow boil in her voice.

"Now, settle yourself down."

"What do you need to ask me?" She paused between each word.

"Okay, okay." He cleared his throat again. I imagined him reaching his hands out to settle Mama. He spoke slowly, with caution. "Where were you the night Claxton drowned?"

Moments passed before I realized the shift. Implication hung low and heavy like the floor beams above. I raised up onto my knees, opening my hands slowly, the clumps of dirt spilling back onto the ground. Stillness. Even the cicadas held tight and silent in the moment waiting for Mama to speak. I couldn't breathe.

Boom. Boom. Crinkle.

Her words came quickly. One word fired after the next. "I was home and in bed. I came home from the Pickle Factory and went right to sleep. You can ask Wessie if you don't believe me. Wessie, come here."

"That's not necessary."

"I think it is."

The floorboards vibrated under Miss Wessie's quickened stride. I could tell from the cushion of her step she still wore her shoes. A sign I took to mean she was ready for trouble. She pushed the screen door with force, the spring squalling like a cat.

I raised my hands above my head, pressing my fingers into the beams to steady me—to keep the whole place from falling in.

"Ask her, Briar. Ask her the question."

"Wessie, I've just come out here to see about something." There was calm and kindness in his voice that soothed me a bit.

"Yes, sir," said Miss Wessie. I knew from her tone she was kneading her hands into her apron.

"I've come to ask about the night Claxton died. Miss Grace says she was sick the night he drowned. That she was here at home with you. Is that true?"

Miss Wessie answered without hesitation, "Yes, sir. She was just about sick as a dog, and I looked after her."

My shoulders relaxed on their own, and I breathed out slowly. There was certainty in Miss Wessie's words.

"That's all I needed to see about," he said. "I don't see any need in bothering you ladies about this any further. I thank you kindly for your time."

I could see clear up to the Sheriff's waist when he descended the stairs. He turned around to face the house. "Good evening, ladies." He lingered, and when no one spoke, he turned to leave.

"He didn't need any help from me. Claxton died like he lived. Drunk and foolish." Mama's words stopped the Sheriff and sent him back around to face the porch.

"Like I said, my business here is done. Don't expect to be having to bother you again." I watched as dust rose to cover his polished shoes, until he was in his car driving away.

Mama and Miss Wessie stood above me, their heavy silence pressing down. *Boom. Boom. Crinkle.*

Miss Wessie exhaled long and hard. "You think he coming back?" Mama must have answered with her head, because Miss Wessie said, "I hope you right."

I felt I would shatter in the spanning stillness until Miss Wessie spoke. "My heart just about give out."

"I would have never known it. You're a smooth lie, Wessie."

Smooth lie. What lie? Did Miss Wessie lie to the Sheriff? I struggled to collect my thoughts. Where had Mama been? Had she done something? Something to Daddy.

The cicadas stirred, reminding me they were still there, that they heard the lie.

I stared at the redbrick piers before me, attached to the house like giant teeth. I realized then I was crouching within the mouth of something horrible. I had to get out of there. I had to free myself. Before I was gobbled up.

Chapter 13

Etta Mae recounted her first day of school at the supper table, her voice possessing the trill of a nightingale's song. Mama and Miss Wessie clung to her every word. Her chatter was the perfect cloak to hide behind, and I welcomed the diversion.

Between halfhearted bites, I pretended to listen. Most of her words were lost to me—only the occasional note of her aria finding my ears. Mama's words whirled in my head. *You're a smooth lie, Wessie.*

How was it they both appeared so relaxed, unaffected by the Sheriff's visit? The two of them, cucumber cool. What did it all mean? What tumble of events had my prayer set into motion? What part did Mama and Miss Wessie play?

"Analeise?" Mama smiled as she looked across the table. "Did you hear me?"

"Pardon?"

"Mama's surprise?"

Etta Mae grinned, squirming in her chair, repositioning herself up onto her knees.

I spied a crack in Miss Wessie's visage, some of her coolness spilling out, tiny beads of condensation scattering across her brow.

Mama leaned into the table, her fingers gripping the edges. "I'm opening up a fabric store."

"A fabric store?" I said.

"I met with the bank and finalized it all today. Rented the old Marcus Insurance space down from Woolworth." Mama's eyes widened with the quickening pace of her voice.

Etta Mae squealed, clapping her hands together. She reached across the table and grabbed hold of my wrist.

"There's no place in this town to buy decent fabric. Only Woolworth, and there isn't much to choose from." Mama laughed rubbing at her arm, back and forth over the old rattlesnake bite.

"Ain't that something, girls?" Miss Wessie said, nodding at Etta Mae and me. She looked at Mama. "Sure is something." Miss Wessie's smile receded.

Mama gave Miss Wessie a sideways look, one resembling a reprimand. "Along with selling fabric, I'm going to setup a sewing shop inside the store. Going to take orders for curtains, and dresses, and anything else that needs sewing. I found a real nice place in Atlanta that can supply my fabrics." Mama took a deep breath. "And Lona Ezell, a girl I went to school with has a decorating business over in Tallahassee. Says she can keep me busy with special orders." One excited word tumbled into the next.

"What are you going to call the store, Miss Grace?" Etta Mae hollered out.

Mama pulled her shoulders back and took in a big gulp of air. "Graceful Stitches." She stretched her words like taffy. She tightened her jaw, holding her breath, awaiting our reaction.

Etta Mae let loose another squeal. "It's got your name in it."

"Well now, ain't that another something." Miss Wessie looked at Mama and then at me. "Look at what your Mama done gone and done." There was something prickly poking into her words. Something not quite right in her smile.

"What do you think, baby?" Mama said.

"I think it sounds real pretty." I was unsure of what to say. Unsure of what to think.

"Are we going to be rich?" Etta Mae said, clapping her hands together.

Rich? I did like the sound of that. A rich Bug Girl was certainly better than a poor one. "Rich like a Mayfield?"

"Rich like a Mayfield." Etta Mae repeated. "You know, they own the whole bank."

It was as if I poked a hole in the room, all the air spilling out of a punctured balloon. Etta Mae felt it, too, settling back into her chair—resting once again on her fanny.

"A Mayfield?" Mama said.

"Ain't nobody in this room gonna be like a Mayfield." Miss Wessie crossed her arms.

"Of course not," Mama said. "We won't ever be rich like that." She touched her hand to her chin. "But if we're lucky, things will get better."

"If we're lucky." Miss Wessie stared at Mama.

If things were looking up, I should have felt better—what with the new store and the Sheriff believing Mama and Miss Wessie's lie and all.

"Graceful Stitches," Etta Mae said. She sang it over and over in a round of arpeggios.

I stared down at my plate to find I almost had eaten my entire pork chop. Only a few small bites clung to the bone.

* * *

Etta Mae and I sat on the back porch in the swing while Mama and Miss Wessie cleaned the kitchen.

The sun was all but gone, brilliant orange and red rips in the clouds smoldering like campfire embers. I divided my attention between the conversation in the house and Etta Mae. I listened for clues, for admissions.

"Can we swing now?" Etta Mae asked, an edge of frustration in her voice.

"Shh," I said, restricting her movement, anchoring my bare feet against the porch floor to settle the swing. Still, I could hear nothing—only the *clink* and *rattle* of supper dishes.

Etta Mae leaned into my ear and whispered. "Wanna know a secret?"

Could I manage another? I moved in close, our foreheads touching. Warm bursts of lemonade scented breath blew into my face.

"Not here," she said, looking out into the gloaming.

"Where then?"

Etta Mae pointed to the yard. I did not want to leave the porch, did not want to miss even a whisper. But who could hear anything over Etta Mae's prattle?

We stepped from the porch, all but a crimson ring remaining in the horizon. We held hands and walked to the garden. Etta Mae was the first to see the quick pulse of a lightning bug. "Look," she said, pointing with her free hand.

Impatience got the better of me. "What's the secret?" I hoped she heard Mama and Miss Wessie talking on the porch after the Sheriff left—heard something I missed while I hid beneath the house. A puzzle piece, perhaps?

A cluster of lightning bugs flashed in quick succession. The quick firing of their lights sounded like the *ping* of quarter notes.

"Miss Hamilton says I can be an opera singer when I grow up." She squeezed my hand turning to me, her delicate features diminishing with the light.

"Who?"

Etta Mae dropped her shoulders and pushed out a sigh. "Miss Hamilton, the wife of the doctor that just moved to town. From Atlanta."

"Who?"

"Didn't you hear me tell y'all about her at supper?" Etta Mae seemed incredulous.

I had more important things to pay mind to—like her granny, Mama and me all being carted off to jail for killing Daddy. Then there was Marlissa Mayfield's awful paper doll hidden next to the bottle of Old Crow in the keeping space in the floor beneath my bed. I shrugged.

"Sweet—baby—Jesus!" Etta Mae ennunciated each word.

"I'm sorry." I squeezed her hand, touched my forehead to hers. A thin slick of perspiration settled across our brows. "Tell me all about it." I blew into her face hoping my breath smelled as sweet.

"Okay. But you better listen this time." We walked through the gate of Mama's old Thinking Spot, our fingers curled into the other's, our arms a slow swing. "She's not a teacher, more like a volunteer, but she studied music at Spelman College in Atlanta. She's going to come teach us music a few days a week. The school can't afford a real teacher. I reckon she's probably as good as the real thing. Better even."

"That sounds nice," I said, sitting on the garden bench.

Etta Mae laid back and rested her head in my lap. "She's real pretty. And smart. She can sing in different languages. You should've seen her dress." I could hear the broad smile in her voice. "She asked me to sing for her, and I did."

Ping. Ping. Ping. More lightning bugs burned around us. I pressed my hand into the soft spring of her hair, running my index finger down her perfect part. I crossed my ankles and set my legs to a slow sway, trying my best to push everything out of my head, focusing on all she had to say.

"Is she colored?" I knew she must be, but for some reason, I asked anyway.

"Umm hmm."

Though I only had a general idea that an opera was some kind of musical, I pretended to understand all its intricacies. "Wow. She must be talented." Still unsure of the reason for our clandestine trip to the garden, I asked, "So, what's the secret?"

Etta Mae let out another exasperated sigh. "Didn't you hear anything when you were gobbling up that pork chop?"

Etta Mae was the first to start giggling. The lilt of our laughter was the perfect complement to the lightning bug song. When we fell quiet, our faces warm and flushed, she answered. "I'm gonna be an opera singer one day, but I don't want to tell Granny or your mama just yet."

"An opera singer sounds like a fine thing to be." I stopped swinging my legs, making them still as the air. "Why aren't you telling Miss Wessie and Mama?"

"I didn't want to make them feel bad."

"Why would they feel bad?" I stopped smoothing her hair.

"Cause you can't be a opera singer and live in a small town like this. I don't want them to worry or feel sad just yet . . . that I'll have to move away one day. My poor, sweet Mama is gone, and now your Daddy. They might feel lonely."

"Move away." The rise of some kind of powerful emotion was traveling my legs.

Etta Mae pulled herself up from my lap and stood on the bench. "Maybe New York or Europe," she said. "You wanna hear what Miss Hamilton taught me today?"

I did not. I stood up and backed away from the bench.

"She taught me to sing . . ." She stopped for a moment trying to remember. "A chromatic scale." She sang a staircase of notes. Her voice soared higher and higher until she came to the top, sustaining it beat after endless beat, slowing it until the vibration of her voice dissipated.

Hundreds of lightning bugs winked around us. I took in Etta Mae's tiny silhouette against the sky's ambient light. I did not like the thought of being left behind. My insides sank, hard and fast.

"You can come with me. I told Miss Hamilton you play the piano better than anyone I ever heard. She said that's good 'cause all opera singers need accompaniment." Etta Mae held out her right foot and pointed her toes.

Accompaniment.

"Miss Victoria says I'm a soprano." Etta Mae dropped her head looking down in my direction.

"Who in the sweet heck is Miss Victoria?"

"That's Miss Hamilton's first name. Isn't it pretty?" Etta Mae spread her arms out to her side executing a careful rotation.

"Do they even let colored folk sing opera?"

If she noticed the bite in my voice, she did not let on. "Sure, if they're good. Miss Victoria says if I practice hard, I can travel the world one day . . . and sing for important people."

I did not know this Miss Victoria Hamilton, and I already hated her. "Sounds nice."

Over and over, Etta Mae sang, "Lightning bug," her voice lush and beckoning.

I felt woozy headed again. Like I just took a swig of whiskey. Charmed by Etta Mae's siren song, droves of lightning bugs sparked about us, more than I ever had seen, thousands of quarter notes hovering about. *Ping.*

I could better make out the movement and extension of her arms in the incandescent light. Her voice latched onto my anger and jealousy. I could feel the soothing nature of it—an invisible embrace. I did not want to feel better. I wanted to hate. I wanted to be mean.

Her singing was irresistible, witchcraft tamping down the swell of my emotions. I fought it, tears welling in my eyes.

In beautiful cascades, her voice rose and fell. More lightning bugs came, millions of twinkling lights all about us, stars sung down from the firmament. Bright like the rising sun. I loved and hated her all at once.

She would not control me. She would not leave me. I would not be her accompaniment. I clenched my fists, fingernails digging into my palms. "I'm going inside." I turned and hurried to the gate.

"What's wrong?"

"I'm sick." I plugged my ears with my fingers, not taking any chances she might try to enchant me back to her. I ran, looking back only once, lightning bugs receding in the hush—the sad silence when her signing was done.

The garden grew dim, Etta Mae reduced to a tiny silhouette.

Chapter 14

Etta Mae did not come to my room after I stormed from the garden, disrupting her lovely lightning bug song. So, I slept alone, one crazy dream after another. Dreams of Etta Mae running off to tour the world, the Sheriff pulling me out from beneath the house, Marlissa's paper doll flapping crooked, chasing me about the place.

I lay there, unsure of the time, staring at the ceiling. I kicked at the sheet, fanning away the mugginess, trying to dry the sweat settling where my back pressed the mattress. How much longer before I would have to begin getting ready for school?

Into the kitchen, I crept to peek at the clock. The room was dark. I moved close to make out the position of the hands. *5:32 a.m.* I did not have to get up until 7:00 a.m., but Miss Wessie would soon be up.

I opened the refrigerator and tipped back the water jug to my lips. The cold liquid cut a bracing path down my throat, startling my insides. The cooling effect was only temporary, the awful heat rushing back in around me. I would never be able to find my way back to sleep in that oven.

Perhaps it was cooler on the front porch. Not wanting to risk the screen door waking the place, I climbed through the open window.

The sky cracked open in the horizon, allowing the beginnings of morning to push through. A distant hum broke the early morning quiet. Someone was driving down the road toward the house.

Curiosity took over. I made my way from the house to the mailbox. Headlights bounced and flickered as the truck dipped along the uneven road.

I stood to the left of the mailbox, a safe distance from the path of the vehicle, preparing myself for a round of Genie in the Bottle. Sometimes, Etta Mae and I would play this game, offering ourselves to the gust of wind and stir of dust an automobile would bring. After it passed, we would twirl about, emerging from the dusty commotion and grant the other wishes.

More than anything—more than the want of a momentary thrill, I wanted to cool myself. I rested my arms at my sides, shut my eyes and held my breath, preparing for the *whoosh* of air. Nothing. Only the squeal of brakes and drag of dirt and rock.

I opened my eyes to the pickup truck idling at the mailbox, and the colored man who drove it. "Analeise?" His voice was boyish, only slightly lower than a girl's. "Analeise Newell?" I blinked incredulously. He spoke without moving his mouth. Perhaps, I was still dreaming.

"Yes, sir?"

"Back here, Analeise. It's me. Abel Darlington."

Abel Darlington. I walked to the back of the truck, my heart thumping with each step. He remembered my name. I pulled my mouth apart, my tongue sticking to its flypaper lining. "What are you doing here?"

He laughed. "Good morning to you, too." He smiled, his dark eyebrows arching above his chocolate drop eyes.

Could he see the flush of color I felt spreading across my face? "I'm sorry. I didn't mean to be rude. Just surprised to see you is all."

"I've come to deliver your paper."

"The paper? We don't take the paper." I followed his eyes down my nightgown to my bare feet. I was outside half-dressed in front of a boy. I pulled up at my collar.

"Eli?" Abel yelled to the cab of the truck. "What's that delivery schedule say again?"

"It say Miss Grace Newell's first paper come today. New subscription."

"She didn't tell me." We never had a subscription to anything before. I remembered what Mama said at the supper table. *But if we're lucky, things will get better.* Sounded like things were already looking up. I pulled my fingers through the gnarls in my hair. "I didn't know you delivered papers." Immediately, I felt ridiculous. Of course, I didn't know. I hardly knew Abel Darlington at all.

Abel laughed. There was kindness in his laughter. "How else am I going to earn my allowance?"

"Allowance?"

"My dad owns *The Providence Weekly.*" His voice was soft, without conceit. Just stating the facts. He pushed back at the hair falling across his eyes.

The Darlingtons own the newspaper. They must be rich. *Rich like a Mayfield.*

"I'm going to be a writer one day," he said. "Dad says the newspaper business is good a start as any." He smiled that crooked smile.

"Sounds like a wonderful thing to be. Like Charlotte Bronte. *Jane Eyre* is my favorite." The words just tumbled out, and I felt silly. "I mean, you won't be like Charlotte Bronte because she's a girl."

Abel laughed. Not in a mocking way, but sweetly. "I know what you mean. I also consider *Jane Eyre* a favorite." He bowed his head.

Was he just saying that to be kind? "What's your favorite?"

"Golly, that's tough. I just finished *The Red Badge of Courage,* and I can't stop thinking about it." He poked at his temple with his index finger. "So, for now, I'll pick that one."

Eli called from the window. "Mr. Abel, you about done back there?"

"Just about," Abel hollered back. He took a deep breath and smiled down at me. "On behalf of *The Providence Weekly*, it is my honor to bestow upon you, Miss Analeise Newell, the first issue of your new subscription." He held the paper before him.

I moved closer, raising up on the tips of my toes, reaching for the paper. Abel moved forward to meet me. His breath was fresh from Colgate. I became even more self-consciousness of my unkempt state.

"Thank you." I was careful not exhale too hard, not having the benefit of a recent, good teeth brushing.

"There's a picture of Marlissa in it this week. She played the piano for the Garden Club." He lost his balance and leaned back on his heels, the newspaper moving just out of reach.

"That sounds . . . nice." I tried to match his tone. The thought of Marlissa featured in the paper pinched and excited me all at once. I wanted to snatch the paper, run to the porch and lay it out to look. "She's so good," I said, struggling to remain sane looking, to temper my teeter-totter emotions. Jealousy and adoration.

"So are you."

Abel Darlington thinks I'm good. But was I Marlissa Mayfield good?

"She wants to be a concert pianist when she grows up."

I did not know what being a concert pianist entailed, but I knew one thing to be certain; if Marlissa wanted to be one, it must be a glorious thing. How was it, that at the age of eleven, both Abel Darlington and Marlissa Mayfield had assembled plans for their futures? Even Etta Mae knew her destiny, opera singer. God, how I hated Mrs. Hamilton for putting such foolish ideas into her head.

"I'd like to be that too." I looked down at the ground, pinching the dirt with my toes. "A concert pianist." It was not entirely a lie. Had the topic of future vocation ever presented itself, perhaps I might have chosen concert pianist, if I knew such a thing existed. Maybe I would be a concert pianist. I was every bit as good as Marlissa Mayfield. Could she even taste music?

"Patton might have been a concert pianist, too." Abel said.

Patton. The name was a wallop in the stomach. Not since Mrs. Mayfield whispered softly into my ear had I heard the name spoken aloud. My legs nearly gave out.

Abel hurled the rolled-up newspaper up into the air right above his head. I watched it rotate end over end, until gravity took hold, sending it back down again. He grinned in my direction, the paper hurling toward him, catching it in the hand he held behind his back.

His trick was impressive. Had I not existed for only one thing in that moment, to know the meaning behind this Patton, I might have clapped and carried on.

He leaned back into his laugh, his brown eyes lined with thick, black lashes, closed for a moment. "You should consider yourself lucky, Miss Newell. Not all my customers get such special treatment." He handed the paper to me.

"Who's this Patton?" I said, desperate to know.

Abel blinked those ridiculous baby doll lashes. "I'm sorry. I just thought everyone knew that Patton was Marlissa's brother."

"Her brother. Where is he? Where does he go to school?" There was a feverish hysteria in my voice.

"He doesn't. I mean . . . not anymore." Able bit at his lip. "Well, he died is all."

"Died."

Abel nodded his head. "I'm afraid so."

Eli called out. "Mr. Abel, if you done delivering that paper then we best be getting along."

"Yes, sir." Abel looked to the cab of the truck and then back at me. "Miss Analeise, it's been a pleasure."

"How?"

"Pardon?"

"How did Patton Mayfield die?"

The engine revved. The truck rocked back just a little.

"It's an awful thing," Abel said, grabbing hold to the side of the truck, securing his balance.

More than anything, I wanted to know that awful thing. What it was that killed Patton Mayfield. "What happened?" The truck moved forward. I resisted the urge to pull myself up into the back and grab hold of Abel by the shoulders, demanding he tell me, his baby doll eyes widening from shock.

"Another time."

The truck gained speed. I trotted behind yelling into the dust. "When?"

He hollered something back, but his words were lost in the space widening between us.

Chapter 15

Patton. Patton Mayfield. How would I be able to think of anything else? I made my way into the kitchen, *The Providence Weekly* tucked beneath my arm. Marlissa's picture was inside, a treat wrapped up like a Starlight mint to untwist and savor when no one was looking.

"Is that you, Miss Lady?" Miss Wessie called from the back porch, her voice quiet as a booming thing can be. "I know it's you. That sneaky tippy-toe you got."

"Yes, ma'am. It's me." I hesitated, contemplating whether to leave the paper behind or keep it in my charge. I kept it tucked under my arm. I pushed the screen open with my index finger, just wide enough to squeeze through, me and my wild-woman hair. My heart raced. *Marlissa Mayfield has a brother.*

Miss Wessie sat in the swing, a scorched pot at her side, a hamper at her bare feet. A heap of unshelled, white acre peas rested in her lap within the scoop of her blue, cotton housedress.

"Your mama got her a sneaky tippy-toe, too. I reckon you got it honest." There was a lightness in her voice—a signal that all was well if only I minded myself.

"What you doing out here?"

"Now, Miss Lady, I know you got some sense about you. What it look like I'm doing?"

Churning butter. I chewed my lip, resisting the urge to sass. "Shelling peas."

"Smart girl. What no-good is you up to so early this morning?"

"Too hot to sleep."

"That it is."

"Why aren't you fixing breakfast?"

"Same reason you ain't sleeping."

If I was not careful, I was sure to shake the hornet's nest. It was much too early for a Miss Wessie kind of sting. Besides, I needed to know everything she knew about Patton Mayfield.

"Biscuits already in the oven and ham in the icebox leftover from yesterday," Miss Wessie said.

"Sounds nice."

"Do it now? Glad you approve." She hummed a jazzed up, honky-tonk version of "Wade in the Water".

I lowered myself to the porch floor, gathering and arranging my nightgown to sit cross-legged a couple of feet from Miss Wessie. I placed the newspaper behind me, unsure if she saw it there in the gauzy, early morning light. I sat, studying her rhythm, her method of pea shelling, gauging the right time to ask, to gather any information she might have about the Mayfields.

She snapped a bean in two, slicing and dissecting the length of shell with her thumbnail. She pried the peas loose, emptying them into the pot on her right, tossing the empty shells onto a small pile on the floor. I watched her repeat this activity, listening to the *plink* of peas in the bowl, enjoying the release of that raw, green, earthy smell. There was serenity, a hypnotic quality to the process emphasized by Miss Wessie's humming.

If there ever was a time to find out what I needed knowing, it was then, right there as the veil began to lift from night. Before the day spilled in and ruined the moment.

Fantôme. The peculiar word Marlissa spoke at school wiggled its way into my brain. It must have been French. It sounded like some of those fancy, foreign, French words she spoke in music class.

"Miss Wessie, can you speak French?" I knew as soon as she looked at me that it was a ridiculous question to ask.

"Can I speak French?" she said. I only had to wait a moment before she laughed. "Did you fall down and bump your head, Miss Lady?" She tossed a bean at me, almost ringing the empty space between my legs. "You sure do get some crazy ideas in your head. Why you ask?"

I reached for the bean, placing it between my index and middle finger, bringing it to my lips like a cigarette. I inhaled, pretending to smoke the thing, then breathed out slowly, giving me time to think what to say. "Marlissa Mayfield speaks French."

"Do she now?" Miss Wessie paused, her big toe steadying the swing. Her fingernail sliced down the middle of another bean.

"Yes, ma'am." I took another puff of my white acre bean.

"I reckon them Mayfields can do a lot of things you don't need to be doing."

"What's wrong with speaking French?" I blew an imaginary smoke ring to float in the space between us.

"I guess there ain't a thing wrong with it if you French."

"Are they?"

"Is who what?"

"Are the Mayfields French?"

Miss Wessie tossed another empty hull on floor. "Mayfields been here as long as anyone can remember. Now, Miss Cordelia, her people are from Charleston. I don't know if she got any French in her, but her kin came over a long time ago on that boat."

"Boat? What boat?"

"Guess you gonna wear me out with questions."

"I reckon," I said. "Now tell me. What boat you talking about?"

"The one them pilgrims came over in."

"The Mayflower?"

"That sounds about right."

"Goodness," I said, flicking the ashes off my white acre bean. "Well, Miss Cordelia sure is pretty."

Miss Wessie raked her fingers through the pot, stirring the peas. "You shouldn't bother with them Mayfields."

"How come?"

"Them Mayfields ain't for you is all." Miss Wessie reached down to grab another handful of beans. "You're just like your mama."

"How so?"

Miss Wessie snapped a bean in two. "In a lot of ways. Both of you with them sneaky, tippy-toes."

I giggled, but was unable to coax a smile from Miss Wessie, to grease up the next part of my plan. "I heard something just awful."

Miss Wessie's big toe reached for the floor. She shifted herself around on the swing, the extra chain rattling at the top. "Is that so?"

She would never let on, but I had unnerved her. I threaded together a lie. "Jane Fenton told me Marlissa's brother, Patton, died. Isn't that sad?"

Miss Wessie cleared her throat. "It's almost always sad when a body up and dies."

Something in her words caught hold and snagged. I thought of Etta Mae's poor, sweet mama all burned up. Then I thought of Daddy, drowned down in that river—the part I played in it, and what Mama and Miss Wessie might have done to help it along. A heaviness pulled at me, like I was metal, and the porch floor, a big ole magnet. *Yes. It's sad when a body up and dies.* "What happened?"

"He fell out a window," she said, as though it were a sort of ordinary thing. She ran her fingers through the shelled peas then pulled them out to sniff. "And he died. Just like that Jane Fenton say."

"How old was he . . . when he died?" I put the end of the play-pretend cigarette in my mouth, bit off the tip, and spit it in my lap.

The light grew brighter, dissolving the dark walls that shut out the world, the onslaught of day threatening to spoil our intimacy. "Come here," Miss Wessie said. "Away from that door."

Miss Wessie's toes reached for the floor to stop the sway. The swing vibrated, the effect of gravity playing a spooky chord through the tension in the chains. The early morning chatter of insects, all the hidden things that rub and chirp, shushed to hear.

When Miss Wessie spoke, her voice was low and distant as though tossed down a well. "I'm gonna say a few things, and when I'm done, I'm done. You hear me?"

I nodded.

"Miss Lady, I asked if you heard me."

"Yes, ma'am."

"I need to know you aint' gonna tell your Mama what I'm gonna say, you hear?"

Again, I shook my head.

"Miss Lady?"

I could hear the frustration swell in her voice. "Yes, ma'am," I said, nodding with the conviction of a woodpecker.

"You put them Mayfields out of your mind."

"How come?"

"Cause nothing good will come of it." Her dress rose above her glossy knees. She tugged at it, trying to pull it back down. "You asked about that that Patton Mayfield. Well, I'll tell you what bit of it I know. He was a good-looking boy, an almost kind of pretty. Blond as the rest of them, his eyes greener, a kind of shine that makes you feel a strange kind of way. That makes you want to be close. All of them—Mr. Kingston, Miss Cordelia, and Marlissa. They all got it. An unnatural kind of charm."

I understood what she meant. I knew what it was like to stand in the shine of a Mayfield. So blinding you have to squint.

"Remember that time you twisted your ankle when you went to chasing after that butterfly?"

"Couldn't walk for a week."

"This world is full-up of pretty things to chase after. Some ain't what they seem."

I opened my mouth to speak, to tell her I did not understand.

She pointed at me, then put her finger to her mouth. "Shh . . ." Her lips grew fuller, puffing up and reaching to kiss her finger. "Patton was about fourteen when it happened. When he fell from that window out at Mistletoe. It was a terrible, awful thing just like you said. The kind of awful that makes people . . ."

A wonderful surge of excitement shot through me—the way a good girl should never feel when hearing an awful, horrible, terrible thing. "That makes people what?" I said.

"Mercy McLeod, the Mayfield maid. She go to my church. She was there when it happened."

"I know Mercy. Met her when I went with Mama to help clean."

Miss Wessie scrunched her nose. "She ain't got no business taking you out there."

I felt the beginning tumble of something, a momentum of words that might come spilling out. Before I could urge her on, she put her finger to her lips again. She leaned back a little in the swing, the chains giving a *jangle*. "A nightmare come to life when she heard that little girl screaming."

"Marlissa?" The thrill returned. The thought of hysterical, perfect Marlissa crying big, beautiful tears. Diamonds sliding down her cheeks.

"Miss Cordelia went out of her head with grief. After the funeral, she woke up every morning and put on one of her fancy evening dresses, her hair all done up on the top of her head. Sparkling with jewels and walking down that big staircase like she going to a party." The railroad track lines between Miss Wessie's eyebrows grew deeper. "Sitting at that piano playing that song she always play. The one Mr. Kingston give her when they first got engaged."

Song. What song? Was it the song she was playing that day at Mistletoe? The one I played at music class. I could hardly stand it. My bladder was full-up, a mild distraction there in the thrum.

"What about Marlissa? Did she go crazy like her Mama?"

"Mr. Kingston sent her off to Charleston to her Mama's people for a spell. Until Miss Cordelia came back around to herself."

"Is Miss Cordelia better now?" I remembered the sting of her slap—that good, burning, sweet smelling hurt. She still must be a little bit crazy.

"She always been a strange one. One to be careful of. A mean streak cutting right through the middle." Miss Wessie leaned forward, the swing creaking, the chains taut and playing that unsettling chord. "But I reckon she good as a woman can be after losing her baby."

120

If anyone knew the grief in losing a child, I supposed it was Miss Wessie, her own daughter, Etta Mae's mama—dead and gone. Had Miss Wessie gone out of her head? I needed something to do with my hands, something to fidget with. *Where is my white acre bean?*

"Miss Lady, come here to me?"

I scooted the short distance on my knees, a splinter pricking the top of my foot. I grabbed hold of Miss Wessie's buttered knees, pulling myself up. The thrill of knowing more of the Mayfields swelled with my bladder. For a moment, I thought I might wet myself.

Miss Wessie grabbed hold of my shoulders, the two of us close as cat's breath. "You stay away from them Mayfields." She squeezed my shoulders. "You hear?"

"I'll stay away." It was a lie.

"Butterflies and twisted up ankles. That's all there is."

The day crept in allowing Miss Wessie and me a clearer look of the other. A breeze pushed through the yard across the porch, the air filling with the pungent scent of peas, the smell of things lay bare.

Chapter 16

Mrs. Lawrence stood at the front of the class carrying on about long division, a topic of which, under the best of circumstances, failed to hold my attention. There was simply too much to think about sitting there staring at the back of Marlissa Mayfield's pretty head. *Poor, dead Patton.*

Before heading off to school, Mama did little to help settle my anxiety, inspecting the seams and collar of the pretty pink dress I wore, the one she sewed special for me. As if reading braille, she ran her fingers across the plain of her work the way she did when she found some hint of message, a glimpse into the future. When she was done, she stood back rubbing at her arm.

"What is it, Mama?"

"Not a thing, baby." She tried to smooth her face, relaxing the vein that sometimes wiggled up in her forehead thick as an earthworm.

"You see something. What is it?"

She smiled. "All I see is a pretty girl in a pretty pink dress." I knew she was lying. She kissed me on the cheek, swatting my backside before sending me down to the mailbox to catch the bus.

I turned back to wave. "Bye, Mama."

She stopped rubbing her arm long enough to lift her palm in my direction. "Analeise?"

"Yes, ma'am."

She put her hand to her mouth like she might be trying to push something back inside. "If you have to run . . . run fast."

Run fast. What in hellfire did that mean? I almost ran back to her, to demand she explain. But I was in a between space, smack in the middle of something. Too many places to be. Too many things to think, so I hurried to the bus.

I shut my eyes listening to Mrs. Lawrence scrawl numbers in chalk across the board, looking for some calm in the rhythm of her frenetic *peck* and *stab*.

"Miss Newell?"

My eyes popped open. Mrs. Lawrence and the whole class stared at me. "Yes, Mrs. Lawrence?"

"It's a bit early in the day for a cat nap, don't you think?" Mrs. Lawrence rolled the chalk nub between her fingers.

"Do bugs take naps?" Dink chuckled, loosening up the others to laugh along, prying loose a Virginia Fenton cackle.

"Settle down," Mrs. Lawrence said, scowling at Dink, holding up her dusty hand to settle the class.

The recess bell jostled the room, disturbing the order Mrs. Lawrence had nearly managed.

"Walking feet," Mrs. Lawrence said. "No running."

* * *

Outside, at the concrete bench beneath the old magnolia, Virginia Fenton pulled the newspaper clipping from her pocket and passed it around the group. I already saw it, pouring over every inch before Miss Wessie called me to breakfast. I tore it gently from the paper, folding and tucking it beneath the floorboard alongside that horrible paper doll.

When Jane handed the clipping to me, I lingered with it long enough to appear polite, before passing it along to the girl to my right.

Marlissa sat on the concrete bench chatting with some of the girls surrounding her, meeting all their attention with a poised modesty. I wondered if she missed her dead brother, if they shone so bright together people had to squint when they looked upon them standing side by side. What might she do if I went over and told her how sorry I was to hear? That her brother fell out that window and died. That her mama went a little bit crazy. *Is that why you never smile?*

Virginia broke into the circle, pushing two girls aside, raising her voice above the others. "I think you are the only one of us to ever make the paper." She put her hands on her thick waist and pushed out a hip.

This was not a true statement. In fact, Virginia once appeared in the paper when she was in the first grade, a celebration of her victory at the Providence Fair's Watermelon Seed Spitting Contest. Not only was she awarded a blue ribbon, an accessory she wore to school for two weeks straight—her picture was also featured in the newspaper.

Jane cleared her throat, obviously stricken with the same recollection. We both looked to the other, wondering if we should set the record straight. Obviously, Virginia had moved beyond her seed-spitting glory days, a hobby that would no doubt leave an unfavorable impression upon the likes of Miss Marlissa Mayfield.

"I'm just so excited." Jane beamed at her sister. "I could just spit."

"Just spit," I said.

Virginia cut her eyes in our direction, red blotches spreading across her neck. "Put a sock in it," she said. "Can't you see I'm talking?" Virginia scanned the group. "Where's that paper?"

A girl in the back raised it above her head waving it like a surrender. "Right here," she said.

"Don't just stand there like a big dummy. Bring it here." When the girl was within arm's length, Virginia snatched it from her hands. "You wrinkled it." Virginia cleared her throat. "If I may," her words more of a command than a request for permission. "Miss Marlissa Mayfield, a confection in pink organza, mesmerized the membership of the Providence Garden Club with her masterful playing of Debussy." Virginia paused, looking around the group, and then to Marlissa before continuing. Marlissa never bothered to look up from her book of fairies and flowers.

Pink organza. I could have recited the entire thing without so much as a glance at the clipping, having read it over and over before leaving out for school. My fingers were still slightly stained from the ink, minuscule particles of Marlissa lingering at the tips and just beneath my nails.

Jane leaned in and whispered. "Good gravy."

"Miss Mayfield is the daughter of Mr. and Mrs. Kingston Mayfield," Virginia continued.

"Look out!" Abel Darlington yelled, pulling our attention from Virginia and to the stampede of boys running in our direction.

Girls squealed and scattered. Jane and I grabbed hold of each other, taken off guard by the fuss.

An enormous pinecone bounced off Virginia Fenton's head.

Dink ran backwards, arms flailing. "I got it," he yelled, crashing into Virginia. Virginia was hardly disturbed, but the force of the impact sent Dink to fall hard against the ground.

"Stupid idiot," Virginia yelled, rubbing her head. "What are you doing?"

Abel pulled Dink up by the arm. "Playing ball. What does it look like?" Dink said, putting his hands on his hips, mirroring Virginia. He contorted his face into an uncanny Virginia-like scrunch. Then he yelled, "Idiot,"

"Who plays ball with a dang pinecone?" Virginia said. She raised up her foot and stomped down hard into the makeshift ball. *Crunch.*

The boy herd booed and moaned.

"Maybe if you weren't such a midget and could run faster, you could catch it." Virginia pushed her freckled nose into Dink's face.

"I can run faster than you any day, Virginia Fenton," Dink said. "Everybody knows boys are faster than girls." He spit on the ground dangerously close to her shoe. "My daddy says God made it that way on purpose."

Virginia squeezed her hips, her face pulsing purplish red. "Is that so?"

"Yeah, so we can get away from the ugly ones. Cause they're faster than the pretty ones." He slapped his leg and turned around, winking at the boys. "They have to be." The other boys, all but Abel, joined him in a fit of laughter.

Abel stepped close, touching Virginia's shoulder, holding his hand there for a moment. "It was an accident, Virginia. It's not Dink's fault. I misjudged the distance."

Virginia's face relaxed, her color almost restored to its everyday ruddiness. When she spoke, her voice was softer. "You can't help it if Dink is . . ." She looked away from Abel and then to Dink. "Retarded."

Dink moved toward Virginia. Abel motioned for him to stay put. "Let's handle this with a friendly competition," Abel said. "How about a race? Dink and Virginia." He looked around the assembly. "Better yet, how about one big race? Boys against girls."

The boys came to life first, their chatter escalating to a war chant.

Abel scanned the faces of the girls, his smile stopping and resting upon me. "Well?" he said, "Miss Analeise?"

My heart made a loopty-loop inside my chest. Abel Darlington was smiling at me. I smiled back, wondering if he thought I looked better by the light of day—all dressed, and my hair smoothed back from my face. For some ridiculous reason I felt the need to raise my hand. "I'll do it." Girl whispers tickled the air, mixing with the boys' gladiator *whoops.*

"That's the spirit," Abel said.

"Bug Girl." Virginia cleared her throat and gave me a nod as I approached.

"Count me in," another girl spoke from behind.

Annette Everston. She was a shy one, her participation surprising the others.

"Annette Everston. That ain't no fair," Dink said. "Everybody knows farm girls can run fast. They get all that practice chasing chickens and hogs." He turned and laughed with the other boys. "And she's ugly, just like Virginia.

"You shut up, retard." Virginia said.

"Now that's enough of the name calling," Abel said, looking at Virginia and Dink. He clapped his hands together. "Now, who else? Who's in?"

Two more girls came forward, a few boys following behind.

Virginia looked around. "This is stupid."

In the distance, the Pickle Factory's steam whistle wailed—calling morning break, a happening always lasting exactly ten seconds. I began

126

my silent count. *One . . . Two . . .* I blinked up into the sky, the clouds pulling apart like puzzle pieces. I half expected to see the clouds ripple from the squawk. I thought of Mama and the last words she spoke. *If you have to run . . . run fast.* Lord, was this what she meant? That there would be a race. *Eight . . . Nine . . . Ten . . .*

The whistle stopped, trailing off into an echo. A hush traveled through the playground, blowing like a breeze through ponytails and the leaves of the old magnolia. There was a sudden stir in the back, everyone turning to look. The wall of girls parted like picture show curtains, pulling back to reveal Marlissa standing in front of the bench, her book tucked beneath her arm. A glorious sight in her royal blue dress.

Marlissa stepped forward. "I will join the race." Her voice was legato, pausing a half beat between each word.

Abel ran over to her. "That a girl," he said, squeezing her shoulders. Her face shifted into an almost-smile. There must have been magic in Abel Darlington's touch.

A wind stirred, bringing in a waft of pickle brine from the factory. Marlissa's hair fluttered back over her shoulders. The sun caught hold of her, conjuring an altogether brilliant effect, accentuating that Mayfield Shine.

Virginia, like the rest of us, was taken off guard by this recent turn of events. Marlissa Mayfield refused to swing in a dress. How was it she was agreeing to run a race?

"Me, too," Virginia stuttered. "I'll join the race."

Able lined us up along the fence facing the school. Jane volunteered to signal the beginning of the race and drew a finish line in the dirt.

Run fast. Had Mama seen this coming? I looked down the line to my right. Annette Everston stood between Marlissa and me, and then Virginia beyond her. My heart thumped in my ears. An uneasy feeling came over me.

A safe distance from Virginia, Dink yelled, "If I were betting on girls, I'd put my money on Virginia. She's the ugliest." Laughter rolled down the line, Virginia's face glowing red.

Jane counted to three, then dropped her arms.

War cries spilled from the boys' mouths. I pushed forward and ran, chaos and wind filling my ears. I could see no one else in front of me, only the flash of Marlissa's blue dress in direct line of my peripheral vision.

She was keeping up with me, running in long strides—gliding across the ground. Her white ankle socks—a blur.

Run fast. I turned my head to look at her, our eyes meeting for a moment. Long waves of blond hair swept across her face. She tossed it back and looked ahead.

Marlissa moved ahead of me. I pumped my arms and legs harder. Faster. I joined the boys in their warrior howls, opening my mouth letting loose a feral scream. Anything to push me forward and ahead of Marlissa.

Her hair floated over her shoulders—taunting curls unfurling just beyond my reach. I stomped at her shadow.

Marlissa's upper body remained erect, her chin lifted to the sky. She moved ahead, pulling her shadow from beneath my feet.

I ran harder, closing the distance. Marlissa approached the finish line. I let out a final scream as her patent leather shoes crossed into victory.

Momentum kept me moving forward several feet beyond the finish. For a moment, I thought I might keep running all the way home. But reason, and lack of breath conspired, and I slowed my pace.

The girls rushed to Marlissa, closing in around her.

I watched Abel cross the finish line behind me, followed by a rush of other racers. Virginia near the back. Dink just a few steps ahead.

Abel jogged over to me. "Congratulations."

"I didn't win," I said, bending forward to ease the slow burn in my lungs.

"You almost did."

The recess bell rang. "Almost . . ."

He touched my elbow. "Next time," he said, turning to jog over to the swarm of girls fussing over Marlissa. He turned and hollered, "I guess Dink and his daddy were wrong. The pretty ones are faster."

Marlissa emerged from the girl swarm making her way over to me. Virginia followed a few steps, but Marlissa turned and pointed to the school, sending her the other way.

I felt a swirl of fear and excitement. *Run fast.* Was this what Mama had seen? Did I need to get away from Marlissa Mayfield? And what was it Miss Wessie said? *You stay away from them Mayfields.* Marlissa got closer, and I knew that was something I could never do. Would never do. "Congratulations," I said.

Had it not been for the dust on her shoes, there would have been no clue she ran a race. Her breathing, smooth. Her dress, tidy. God, how I hated her and wanted to be her all at once.

Her lips pulled apart. *"Au vainqueur va le butin."*

I shook my head. "I don't understand." Was she leaving me with another mystery, another thing to decode?

"It's one of Mother's favorite sayings." Marlissa pulled a gold, heart-shaped locket from the collar of her dress. With her delicate, tapered fingers, she opened it. Her shoulder brushed against mine, to offer a better view, a closer look at the engraving.

I pressed myself closer, enjoying the intimacy, the feel of a Mayfield. "What does it mean?" I whispered. Something clawed at me sharply beneath my bodice. I shifted, trying to make myself more comfortable, but not too quickly to break the spell, to send Marlissa away.

She placed her lips to my ear just as her mother had done, her warm, sweet breath feathering against my face. "To the victor goes the spoils," she said, loudly enough to ensure I heard. Words meant for me to remember.

The prickly thing beneath my bodice fluttered, but I refused to make a fuss, to disrupt what might come next.

The factory whistle blew again. Marlissa pulled away, walking slowly back to the building. I watched her recede in the squall, the thing crawling and scraping, making its way up my chest, wriggling out of my collar and down my front.

Five . . . Six . . . Seven . . . The cicada unfurled its crumpled wings, its tymbals vibrating frantically. *Eight . . . Nine . . . Ten . . .*

Chapter 17

The aroma of fresh brewed coffee and buttery smell of praline cookies met me at the door. Miss Wessie's cookies won prizes, and as with all sumptuous things, a happening rare as the hothouse flowers Daddy sent Mama that summer.

News traveled fast in Providence, and I could not help but wonder if she already knew I lost the race to Marlissa. Was all this for me? Some sort of consolation prize? I rested my school bag at my feet.

Mama called from the kitchen. "Analeise, is that you, baby?"

What was she doing home?

"I'll go see about her," Miss Wessie said, her voice lighter than usual.

I held my breath listening to Miss Wessie travel across the floor, her *boom boom* gait punctuated by the squeak of leather. *She's wearing shoes.*

Miss Wessie rounded the corner. "Miss Lady, what you doing just standing there?"

She was wearing Lucinda and her daisy-yellow linen dress. Lucinda, her favorite wig, was treasured like her praline cookies, coming out only for church and other special occasions. Birthdays, holidays, and funerals. When Lucinda was centered and styled properly, Miss Wessie bore a striking resemblance to Miss Pearl Bailey.

"We got company," she whispered, fingering the edges of Lucinda.

"Company?" So, all the fuss was not for me. "What's Mama doing home? Isn't she supposed to be downtown working on the store?"

Etta Mae poked her head around her granny's hip, her face glowing, pink satin bows adorning her pigtails. "She's here," Etta Mae said. "Just wait 'til you see her."

I was hardly in the mood for surprises. "Who's here?"

Etta Mae took my hand pulling us past Miss Wessie and into the kitchen.

"There you are?" Mama said, putting her coffee cup down onto the table. "We have a special guest."

Next to Mama sat a beautiful colored lady.

Etta Mae pulled me closer. "I'd like you to meet Mrs. Victoria Hamilton," Etta Mae said, her tongue rolling lushly over her guest's name.

Mrs. Hamilton rose from her chair. "You are every bit as lovely as Etta Mae said you were."

God, I hated Victoria Hamilton. Putting fool-crazy ideas in Etta Mae's head. "That's sweet." I squeezed Etta Mae's hand harder than necessary.

Mrs. Hamilton was a young woman, her complexion smooth and lighter than Miss Wessie's. Her dark hair, which appeared to be her own, was similar in style to Miss Grace Kelly's, similar to Cordelia Mayfield's.

She wore a pale gray dress with fitted bodice, her tiny waist accentuated by a wide matching belt. A red chiffon bow was tied at the small wing collar. The red was a near perfect match to the color of her lips. In her pointy-toed stilettos, she rose a few inches above Mama. All in all, upon closer observation, I could hardly imagine why Etta Mae made such a fuss.

"It is a pleasure to finally meet you," Mrs. Hamilton said, her voice possessing a melodic quality similar to Etta Mae's.

"Uh-huh." Was this some sort of ambush? A plot to traipse Etta Mae through Europe. I turned to Mama. "Why aren't you at work?"

Mama looked at me from the corner of her eyes, a signal to remember my manners. "Mrs. Hamilton has come to speak with Miss Wessie and me about Etta Mae."

"Why? What did she do?" This was a perfectly ridiculous thing to ask. Etta Mae never misbehaved.

Mrs. Hamilton laughed. "Good heavens, Etta Mae is a dream—a well-mannered young lady." She smoothed her dress, lowering herself back to the chair. "I'm not here to talk about something she's done wrong. I'm here to talk about her singing."

I knew it. I took a cookie from the plate on the table, pressed it hard against my teeth. Etta Mae just sat there beaming at Mrs. Hamilton. I felt myself starting to unravel.

Miss Wessie rejoined Mama and Mrs. Hamilton at the table. I studied our visitor and all her pretty wrapping. I did not trust her, not one little bit. That heart-shaped face and delicate cheekbones. And those perfect manners. Who did she think she was fooling?

Mama pulled my hand away from my mouth and took the cookie. "You can have that later," she said, her words sharpened at the edges. "Victoria, please continue."

"Etta Mae has a talent I have never experienced. And to have had no formal voice training . . . well, it's just astonishing."

Miss Wessie touched Etta Mae's chin. "My baby was born with a song in her heart. You can't teach that."

"So true, Wessie. There are some things that can't be taught," Mrs. Hamilton said, holding Etta Mae's complete adoration.

"What is it you say her voice be again?" Miss Wessie pressed her hands onto the tabletop.

"A coloratura soprano."

Miss Wessie repeated it silently to herself, her full lips painted red as an apple.

"I can sing a high F," Etta Mae said.

Etta Mae was not typically one to brag. This unfortunate turn was no doubt the product of Mrs. Hamilton's meddling.

"And with a little work, we can train you to extend it higher," Mrs. Hamilton said, winking one long-lashed, caramel-colored eye at Etta Mae.

"What in the sweet heavens above is a color—a—tura soprano?" I executed a Jane Fenton inspired eye-roll, at the end of which, I caught glimpse of Miss Wessie.

Miss Wessie leaned back in her seat—her eyes narrow—reptilian. When she was certain Mrs. Hamilton was not looking, she pointed at me, mouthing wide and slow. *You better mind your biscuits.*

I was standing at the crumbling edge of a cliff, my stomach filled with only a single helping of defeat and a half-eaten praline cookie. I looked to Mama—her eyes reaffirming Miss Wessie's warning.

"That, my lovely child, is a very good question," Mrs. Hamilton said, her voice remaining pretty and patient. She put the tips of her thumb and index finger together and pecked at the air, her nails, glossy red mirrors. "It is a light, but very agile voice, someone who can sing in a range of middle C to a high F." She took a sip of her coffee. "Miss Etta Mae here can sing a bit lower, and with training, a bit higher."

Mama smiled at Etta Mae. "What do you know about that."

Oh, my God. Did no one care about me? That I lost a race to Marlissa Mayfield. That she whispers crazy things in my ear. That my name is Bug Girl.

"I'm going to learn to sing in different languages. Miss Victoria is going to teach me." Etta Mae's pink hair bows fluttered with the movement of her head.

"What good is that, if no one can understand a dang fool thing you're singing?" More pieces of that cliff I was balancing upon fell away. I could feel Mama's and Miss Wessie's glares. I held onto the table and fixed a stare onto Mrs. Hamilton.

Mrs. Hamilton held her smile, blinking only once before answering. "Opera is transcendent." She paused a moment to look up at the ceiling. "Emotion is universal. Love, hate, and jealousy. They are all the same in any language. If you can listen, if you are capable of feeling, you'll understand without knowing the words. Singing is like painting a picture."

There was a shift in her voice, something akin to a reprimand. I felt a little sick to my stomach. I was pushing things too far, but I could not help myself.

"Analeise, guess what?" Etta Mae spoke quickly.

I looked up from the table, reaching down deep for something resembling interest. "What?"

"Miss Victoria is going to give me private lessons two days a week." She held her hands to her face as if she might turn loose a scream.

"Now, baby, we still be talking about that. There's a matter of money," Miss Wessie said.

Mrs. Hamilton held up her hand, "I certainly do not expect compensation, nor would I consent to take it. Working with someone special as Etta Mae is a once in a lifetime opportunity. And payment enough."

La-tee-dah. I wondered if the others could see the poison apple Victoria Hamilton clutched in those soft, slender fingers.

"I couldn't go and let you do it for free. You a busy doctor's wife. You got responsibilities."

"Victoria," Mama said.

I looked at Mama expectantly, awaiting her to confirm what Miss Wessie already said, that there was no money for Etta Mae's lessons. Really, it was better this way, no sense in putting foolish notions into her head. *Colored girls can't be opera singers.*

"How about this? Anytime you need any fabric or need something sewed, you come see me down at the store," Mama said. "I'll be opening up in the next week or so."

My bottom lip caught in my teeth. I thought for a moment I could hate Mama.

"That would be lovely. I just might take you up on that." Mrs. Hamilton set our one good coffee cup down onto its matching saucer.

"I have a surprise for y'all," Etta Mae said.

What now?

"What's that, baby?" Miss Wessie said.

Etta Mae looked to Mrs. Hamilton. "You wanna tell them?"

"We have been working on Etta Mae's very first opera piece." Mrs. Hamilton turned loose another one of her long-lashed winks.

"Is that so?" Mama said.

Oh, shut up, Mama.

Mrs. Hamilton nodded at Etta Mae to continue. "The title of the aria is 'O Mio Babbino Caro' from the opera *Gianni Schicchi*," Etta Mae said, with an uncustomary hint of prissiness. "I'm going to sing it in Italian."

I thought of Marlissa. I had my fill of foreign languages, of things I could not understand.

"Italian," Miss Wessie said slowly. "Mmm . . . Mmm . . . Mmm."

"Etta Mae also has a gift for language. She can hear a recording and sing it back almost perfectly. I've never experienced anything quite like it," Mrs. Hamilton said.

Miss Wessie narrowed her eyes. "Lord have mercy."

"Grace, would you allow me the use of your piano to accompany Etta Mae?" Mrs. Hamilton asked.

"It's my piano," I said.

Mama cleared her throat. Miss Wessie mouthed, *biscuits.*

"I mean, it was my Daddy's piano." I spoke with as much gentility I could muster. "Now it's mine, and you are certainly most welcome to play it." I bent slightly at the knees, an awkward attempt at a curtsy. I led the way from the kitchen to the piano, wanting to end this misery soon as possible.

We gathered in the front parlor. Mrs. Hamilton took her seat at the upright. Etta Mae moved away from us and stood at the screen door. The windows were open, the August afternoon still and humid.

"This aria was written by Giacomo Puccini, and Etta Mae will be singing the part of . . ." Mrs. Hamilton motioned to Etta Mae with a gentle turn of her wrist.

"Lauretta," Etta Mae said, standing with perfect posture—her chin lifted like she did before she sang one of her funeral songs.

"And?"

"And she is in love with . . . a boy," Etta Mae looked down at her shoes and giggled. "His name is Rinuccio."

Etta Mae's eyes met mine. She looked tiny standing within the frame of the door—delicate and vulnerable. The sight of her nervous and happy pushed away at my anger, making me remember I loved her.

"Who is Lauretta singing to?" I asked. I imagined myself singing to Abel Darlington.

"Oh, yeah, that's important to know," Etta Mae said. "She's singing to her daddy. She's telling him that she loves Rinuccio and that she wants to be with him." She sucked in her lips to settle another round of the giggles. "She's pleading with him to have mercy."

"Very good," Mrs. Hamilton said.

Miss Wessie tugged at the back of Lucinda. "Sounds like a right interesting story."

Unfortunately, I had to agree. It did.

"Remember, Etta Mae, dig deep down into that well of emotion we talked about. Find that special place," Mrs. Hamilton said. "Just nod when you're ready."

"Yes, ma'am," Etta Mae shut her eyes for three long breaths. She nodded her head and opened her eyes.

I imagined Etta Mae dropping a bucket down into her insides and filling it with thoughts of her poor, sweet mama.

Etta Mae's first note drifted, pulling across the room like a veil, the color, a shade of pale blue. She extended her hands, singing to her imaginary daddy. A breeze awoke, pushing through the screen, causing her hair bows to tremble. Sun spilled from the windows outlining her in a golden shimmer, a sparkle melting and turning blue at the edges.

My eyes darted about the room, my heart running a race. The veil billowed, waltzing, and curling around us. It seemed I was the only one who saw it. The only one to see Etta Mae's voice turn into a real, seeable thing—puffs of breath blown in the winter's cold. What was happening to me? And I could taste it. Love and want. More of a texture than a flavor, cotton candy melting on my tongue, dissolving to a sugary grit.

I felt lighter, my burdens seeping out through the toes of my shoes, my heart reduced to a thump. The weight of my dead daddy, of needing to be close to a Mayfield—all of it caressed away by Etta Mae's heavenly voice.

Setting the last note adrift, Etta Mae opened her little hands, her voice ebbing, the blue, translucent shawl she sang into the room— fading.

* * *

We returned to the kitchen, all of us working to compose ourselves after the performance. Mama, Miss Wessie, and Mrs. Hamilton all prattled on, making a big fuss over Etta Mae.

I took a few sips of Mama's coffee and ate the other half of my praline cookie. My taste buds were askew, everything bitter after Etta Mae's aria. That familiar heaviness returned, my thoughts tumbling back in on top of me. Should I mention I might be seeing things?

"Victoria, what are your favorite languages to sing in?" Mama said.

Mrs. Hamilton placed the tip of her shiny nail to her lips. "Italian and French." She then spoke in a hush. "German is my least favorite."

Italian and French. I sat up straight in my chair. "Did you say French?" I startled the others.

"Yes," Mrs. Hamilton said. "Why do you ask?"

Everyone stared at me. "No reason."

Miss Wessie raised her eyebrows and mouthed, *biscuits.*

Mrs. Hamilton glanced at her watch. "Time has completely gotten away from me. You probably think I came to stay the night."

Etta Mae appeared to like that idea, joy blossoming across her face.

The last thing I wanted was a slumber party with Mrs. Hamilton as guest of honor. I needed her help. I needed to get Mrs. Hamilton alone and away from the others for just a few minutes. My eyes followed the scrapes and nicks of the pine table to Mrs. Hamilton's black, leather purse and the white linen handkerchief poking out of the top. And there it was—my plan. When no one was looking, I pulled the handkerchief from the purse, scrunched it up and hid it behind my back.

Mrs. Hamilton walked to her car. Mama, Etta Mae, and Miss Wessie waved from the porch. I stood inside the house watching at the screen door.

When her gloved hand touched the door handle, I counted to three. "Mrs. Hamilton." I kicked the screen door open, leapt across the porch and onto the ground. "You forgot your handkerchief," I said, waving it wildly in the air.

"How on earth did I manage to do that?"

"Found it on the floor under your chair."

"Thank you." She placed her hand against my cheek. "That is so sweet of you."

I glanced back at the porch. They all looked on, most likely suspicious of my new interest in Mrs. Hamilton. "Can I ask you something?"

"Certainly."

"If you can sing in French, does that mean you speak it?"

"I am fairly fluent. Why do you ask?"

I looked back at the porch again. Etta Mae's face was a filled with curiosity. She took the first step down. I knew she wanted to join us, to be close to her Miss Victoria. I had to hurry. "I was wondering if you could tell me what something means."

Mrs. Hamilton seemed amused. "I certainly will try. What is it?"

"I'm not certain if I'm saying it correctly, but it's something close to this." I shut my eyes trying to recall Marlissa's exact words. *"Avez-vous . . ."* I chewed at my lip. *"Peur des fantôme?"*

"Where on earth did you hear that?"

"I don't remember," I lied, bouncing on my toes. Etta Mae took another step down from the porch. I bounced harder.

"Are you afraid of ghosts?"

"What?"

"In French. That's what it means," Mrs. Hamilton said. "Are you afraid of ghosts?"

Ghosts?

"Sweetheart, are you okay?"

Why would Marlissa ask me if I'm afraid of ghosts? "Yes, ma'am. I'm fine." Another lie.

Mrs. Hamilton glanced over at Etta Mae and then back at me. "I saw it in your face earlier. It's hard to shake. You can feel it. Even now, can't you?"

"The ghosts?"

Mrs. Hamilton laughed again. "No, the magic. In Etta Mae's voice." She took my chin in her hand. "It has a way of holding on."

Etta Mae made her way to us in the afternoon sun, her shadow stretched like pull candy. Mrs. Hamilton was right. There was enchantment inside that girl, that special something that might take her from me one day. I could hear it, taste it, and for the first time—see it. I felt sick, my stomach sour from coffee and that one praline cookie.

I studied Etta Mae's shadow. Of everything, what frightened me the most? Ghosts? The Sheriff? The Mayfields? Or being caught there in that cool dark space trailing behind Etta Mae?

Chapter 18

The sky hung low and gray over the playground the morning after Mrs. Hamilton's visit, a strange energy sparking about the place. My classmates swooped in and out of clusters, huddling, and then breaking apart again.

I drifted, pulled along in the tide, knocking, and brushing shoulders until Virginia Fenton grabbed hold and pulled me from the stream.

"Hey, Bug Girl." Virginia said, breathless and wild in the eye. "You get yours?"

"Get what?"

Virginia snorted. "Your invitation, dummy. To Marlissa's birthday party." She angled her chin offering an unfortunate and unobstructed view up her nose. "It's going to be at Mistletoe." A little bit of Virginia spittle landed in my right eye. "There's going to be hot air balloons and fireworks at dark."

"Morning, Analeise," Jane said, walking up behind us.

I was happy to see Jane, but for the first time I could remember, I wanted to hear what her sister had to say.

Virginia swept her eyes over me. "Everybody's going. Even the Governor is coming all the way from Atlanta. He's friends with the Mayfields." She leaned down and scratched her ankle. "And there are other things I know."

I was desperate to know everything Virginia knew, but not wanting to seem too eager. "Like what?"

"I'm sworn to secrecy, and I'm certainly not gonna tell the likes of you." Virginia stuck out her chalky tongue. "I can say I received a special invitation which makes me a special guest. Only ten girls get special invitations, and I'm one of them. Everybody else gets regular ones."

Jane circled her finger in the air. "Whoop-tee-doo."

Virginia grabbed at her sister's finger. Jane pulled it back in the nick of time. "You're just jealous because you're not a special guest like me. You just got a plain one. Plain Jane and her plain ole' stupid invitation." Virginia bent forward and cackled, then quickly straightened herself. "Oh, my God. Marlissa's here." She waved her hand in the air. "Marlissa. I'm coming. I'll be right there." Virginia left, skipping over to Marlissa. "Plain Jane . . . Plain Jane," she sang over and over, out of time to her clumsy gallop.

Jane shook her head. "She hasn't shut up since yesterday when she got that special invitation."

"What's special about it?"

"I have absolutely no idea. She won't let me anywhere near it, but it does look different from the one we got, the one addressed to our family."

Across the playground, girls swarmed Marlissa. I could only catch glimpses of her and the pale blue ribbon banding her hair. Why did she like Virginia better than me? What had I ever done, aside from frightening her that day at Mistletoe with the cicada shell?

"Hardly anyone ever gets invited out there. It's quite a big deal. Mama read all about it in the Tallahassee paper. They're calling it the Mayfield Gala. It's not only a party to celebrate Marlissa's birthday, but it's also the unveiling of Mrs. Mayfield's conservatory."

"What in the world is a conservatory?"

"A big fancy greenhouse made of glass. Mama read it was brought over in pieces all the way from England from some old estate and put back together right there at Mistletoe. It dates all the way back to 1870 something and has over 16,000 panes of glass."

16,000 panes of glass. I could hardly grasp the number. "That's a bunch of glass."

"It sure is. They say it's the biggest, private conservatory in the South—maybe even the whole United States." Despite Jane's whoop-tee-doo finger circling in the air, I could tell she was impressed, her eyes twinkling a bit.

I imagined acres and acres of flowers overflowing an enormous building made of glass.

"What are you going to wear?" Jane asked, her words tumbling. "Mama's going to take me down to Tallahassee to shop. Virginia doesn't need a new dress—something to do with her special invitation." Jane gave extra attention to the word "special" crossing her eyes when she spoke it. She took a big breath. "So, what about you? What are you wearing?"

An awful sinking feeling took hold, anchored deeper by embarrassment. "I didn't get one."

Jane's smile receded. She hesitated, looking unsure of what to say. She reached out touching my elbow. "Surely it will be in the mail today."

"Maybe." More than anything, I wanted to go to that party, to go back to Mistletoe. I looked across the playground trying to find Marlissa. She was hidden in the throng, but I could sense her, could feel a kind of energy. I thought of what Miss Wessie said, about Marlissa and her brother shining so bright together. *That Mayfield Shine.* "Jane? Did you know Patton Mayfield?"

"Why do you ask?"

"Just wondering is all."

Jane pushed her glasses up her nose. "I remember seeing him. They go to our church, but they never went to Sunday School or anything, so I didn't even know Marlissa until she came here to school. They have a pew reserved up front just for them, a plaque with their name on it and everything. They come in and they leave when it's over."

"Do you know what happened to him?"

Jane leaned in and whispered. "Well, I don't know much, other than it was a horrible accident. Nobody really talks about it."

"I heard Mrs. Mayfield went a little crazy after it happened?"

Jane's eyes widened. "Who told you that?"

"I can't remember," I said, not feeling right about telling her it was Miss Wessie.

Jane took hold of my arm, guiding us away from anyone within earshot. "I haven't heard anything about her being crazy, but Mama says she's a bit stand-offish. Not too friendly with people around here. Mama says all her friends live in other places. Rich folks. Some of them even famous."

"What did he look like?"

Jane's face reddened. "Every bit as handsome as Marlissa is pretty." She poked at her glasses again. "Sometimes I'd just sit there staring at them."

I knew what she meant. There were times I could hardly look away from Marlissa, me sitting so close behind her at school, that urge to reach out and touch her, to nudge my nose up in her hair and sniff. I was glad I was not the only one with these inclinations.

"What do you think it's like?"

"What?"

"To be a Mayfield. To be that pretty."

"Analeise Newell. You hush your mouth. You're every bit as pretty as Marlissa Mayfield, and you certainly are kinder . . . sweeter."

"Jane, that's such a nice thing to say." I squeezed her arm and then hugged her. Aside from Etta Mae and Mama, no one ever called me pretty. Was it possible I was lovely as Marlissa Mayfield?

But what did pretty matter if my inside parts did not match? I imagined my innards, discolored and mushy, a half-eaten watermelon left too long in the sun. I was layers of mean thoughts and murderous prayers. Just how awful could I be, what else might I be capable of if a thing needed doing? To what lengths would I go to get my hands on an invitation to Mistletoe? Was sweet Jane Fenton even safe? I pulled her closer and squeezed tight.

Is anyone?

* * *

News of the party spread quickly through Providence. Etta Mae spoke of little else after school, as excited as if she had been invited. That night, we lay there in bed. Me—blinking up at the ceiling. Etta Maes on her side burning a hole in the side of my face with those topaz eyes.

"I wonder when it's coming," she said. "I don't think anybody ever mailed us an invitation before. I wonder what it looks like. Do you think she just might give it to you at school? What did she say?"

How would I ever be able to explain it to Etta Mae? That it was all a lie. That Bug Girl was never and will never be friends with Marlissa Mayfield. That I will never be invited to that party. She was there the night I prayed Daddy dead, heard every word, and still she liked me—loved me. Perhaps she could forgive a lie. Should I tell her the truth?

"I'm getting one of her special invitations. They take longer."

"Special invitation," she said slowly, rolling onto her back, staring up at the ceiling. "Gosh, you're lucky." She reached over and laced her fingers through mine. "What are you going to wear?"

A full-length taffeta gown, the color of Marlissa's pale blue headband. "Don't know. Haven't thought about it."

"Maybe Miss Grace will sew you something special."

"She's probably too busy, getting the store ready to open and all. It would be awful if I couldn't go because I don't have anything to wear." I was already planning excuses, little white lies to cover up the fact I was not invited.

"What do you think Marlissa is going to wear? Bet it's gonna be beautiful. Did she say?"

"She didn't."

"What about Jane and Virginia?"

"Don't know." Would she ever stop her infernal blabbering? "I'm getting sleepy."

"I'm too excited to sleep," Etta Mae said.

"Try . . . please."

"Okay." Etta Mae rolled onto her side and kissed me on the cheek. "Time to pray."

Before Daddy died, Etta Mae and I regarded prayers with the delicacy of wishes, never saying them aloud, fearful they might go unanswered. But it did not matter, did it? God listened. She listened to every prayer. Those sent silently, and those cast aloud in a storm. I had not meant for Her to hurt Daddy. That was an angry, horrible mistake. Was I to be punished forever and always? Would anything good ever happen to me again? I was truly sorry for what I did, and sorry to have Mama and Miss Wessie tangled up in the mess. If I asked forgiveness, might I be allowed an invitation to the party? Perhaps I was pushing my luck. What did I have to lose?

Dear God. Please make Marlissa Mayfield invite me to her party. I promise I won't ask for anything else. Not ever. I lay there listening to Etta Mae's puppy dog breathing, her fingers loosening their grip as she drifted off to sleep. *And dear God, can you make it one of those special invitations? Like the one Virginia Fenton got.*

* * *

Mama screamed, the awful sound slicing open the night, ripping us from sleep.

"What's wrong," Etta Mae panted, pushing herself against me.

Mama's voice pealed in the darkness. "Fire!"

My heart beat in my chest like a fist. I reached for Etta Mae pulling her across the bed and onto the floor.

I prepared myself for smoke and flame, pushing Etta Mae a safe distance behind me. The white of Mama's nightgown helped me find her in the darkness. She tripped, bumping into the walls, her arms flailing about.

"Mama. We're here." I screamed, grabbing hold of her gown, her pace so quick and fierce, she pulled me into the doorframe, forcing me to turn loose.

Miss Wessie ran behind Mama, bare feet slapping the floor. "Grace," she yelled, "Ain't no fire in here."

I took hold of Etta Mae's hand pulling her behind me into the parlor. Mama spun about the room, her eyes open and wide with terror. She coughed and gasped for air. "Help me!"

"What's wrong with Mama?"

146

Miss Wessie stood close to Mama as she could get, her palms reaching out, careful not to touch. Miss Wessie glanced back at me.

"She stuck in a dream."

Etta Mae backed away into a corner. Sliding down onto the floor, she hugged her knees.

Mama gulped for air, stomping at the floor. She beat at the hem of her nightgown. In one sudden jerk, she ran across the room to the windows, her hands beating at the glass.

"Lord Jesus!" Miss Wessie yelled, running to Mama, catching her around the waist. Miss Wessie picked her up and pulled her back from the windows. Mama kicked and twisted, curtains catching in her hands.

"Settle yourself," Miss Wessie yelled, struggling to keep her balance. "You gonna get us hurt." The curtains pulled at the rod until it all broke away from the window, clattering onto the floor trailing behind Mama and Miss Wessie, a train of ruffled sheers snaking behind them.

Mama arched her back, violently thrusting her legs sending both she and Miss Wessie toppling over the coffee table. Mama's head knocked hard against the floor.

There was quiet then. Our ragged breathing and Etta Mae's whimpering cracked open the hush.

Mama lay motionless, her eyes shut. I squatted down, crawling over to her and Miss Wessie. "Is she breathing?" Panic blew up inside me like a balloon, my mind leaping into dark places. What if Mama died? Who would take care of me? I would be left all alone in the world. No daddy. No mama.

Etta Mae cried. "What's wrong with her?"

"She done gone and knocked herself out." Miss Wessie said.

I lay my head on her chest and listened, to find out for myself. She was still breathing.

"Miss Lady, you get back on over there with Etta Mae," Miss Wessie said.

I touched my hand to Mama's cheek. "She's burning up."

Miss Wessie squeezed my shoulder. "You get on away from here like I told you."

Just then, I heard it, a peculiar sound coming from Mama. "Shh," I said. "She's saying something?"

"What's she saying?" Etta Mae said.

Mama's eyeballs rolled beneath her lids. Her lips were twitching—a mumbled sound coming out. I leaned down to listen. The sound grew louder, the murmur more pronounced. "She's humming something."

Miss Wessie massaged Mama's hand. "Grace? You come on back to us."

Mama's humming grew louder. It was familiar, something I heard before, but could not quite make out. Her eyes fluttered, then popped open, startling me. "Mama? You okay, Mama?"

"There she is," Miss Wessie said. "There's my Grace."

Staring up at the ceiling, Mama rubbed her hand over her old snakebite, her hair fanning across the floor—the puddle of window shears framing her sweat-slicked face. She possessed a queer sort of beauty laying there in the wreckage. Her humming trailed off, winding down like a broken music box, the spooky sound prickling my skin.

"You gonna be just fine." Miss Wessie smoothed Mama's damp hair.

A chill caught hold, causing my teeth to chatter. I recognized it. I remembered. I knew where I had heard Mama's dream-fire song.

Chapter 19

Several weeks passed, another Saturday rolling around, and still no invitation to the Mayfield Gala. Etta Mae and Miss Wessie were visiting family over in Thomasville, and I spent the day at Graceful Stitches. After Mama's night terror, I was glad to have the opportunity to keep an eye on her. Mama claimed to remember little of the affair, the goose egg knot on her head now reduced to a teensy bump.

Though she seemed herself again, I remained a bit undone. Mama's dream-fire song was the one Mrs. Mayfield played that day at Mistletoe, the same piece of concerto I played in Mr. Bloom's music class. How had it made its way into Mama's head—into her dream? She lay there rubbing at her arm, over the old snakebite, the way she always did after catching glimpses of the future.

"Baby, why don't you come over here and tidy these notions."

"Yes, ma'am." I was happy to have a chore, a distraction. On my way, I ran my hands across the fabrics lining the wall. I stopped at my favorite bolt. Days before, when Mama was not looking, I cut a tiny swatch of the taffeta, an elegant robin's egg blue. I kept it with me, a talisman of sorts, to help summon an invitation to the Mayfields. Right then, the swatch rested in my sock, smooth against my ankle.

I imagined this fabric sewn into a party dress, a matching velvet ribbon tied neatly at the waist. Poofs of fabric gathered into sleeves, and a full skirt reaching all the way to the floor.

"You still eyeballing that fabric?"

I pulled my hand away. "So much my eyes ache."

Mama slid her stocking feet into her high heels and walked over. "You have good taste. One of the most expensive fabrics in the store." Mama unfurled a couple of yards and wrapped it around my neck. "So nice against your coloring." She touched her finger to the tip of my nose. "This taffeta also comes in emerald green. It would set your eyes off right nice."

"I guess that would be pretty, too." My heart was set on the pale blue, the color of one of Marlissa's hair ribbons, the ribbon she wore the day I first learned of the gala.

"Baby, I know you're hoping to get one of those invitations to the Mayfields, and I hate to see you disappointed."

I was uncertain how Mama felt about me going to the party, but I knew Miss Wessie was hoping an invitation would never come. Just the day before, I overheard them whispering in the kitchen. "She ain't got no business traipsing out there to that Mayfield party," Miss Wessie said. "If an invitation do come, what you gonna do?"

"I don't know, Wessie."

"What you mean you don't know? Is you crazy?"

"Keep your voice down."

"You is prideful, and you is playing with fire."

What did Miss Wessie have against the Mayfields? *Them Mayfields ain't for you.*

Mama plucked at the taffeta, arranging it into an exaggerated collar framing my face.

"Etta Mae has taken it into her head that you have some kind of special invitation on the way from Marlissa Mayfield." Mama lifted my chin. "Any idea how that came to be?"

Etta Mae ran her mouth entirely too much. I shrugged. "Don't know. She gets that way sometimes."

"I have a surprise for you. I was going to wait until tonight, but I reckon now is as good a time as any."

My heart thumped in my ears. "I could use a surprise right about now."

"Mr. Bloom." Mama paused. "He knows Miss Victoria."

Was this the surprise? Who cared who knew that Miss Victoria. "Mr. Bloom, my music teacher?"

"Yes," Mama said. "Mr. Bloom's been talking about you to Miss Victoria."

Given that Miss Victoria was involved, I was immediately suspicious. "About what?"

Mama laughed. "Nothing bad, little girl." She knelt in front of me. "Mr. Bloom thinks you have real talent . . . a gift."

I felt a little tipsy all wrapped up in taffeta and a compliment. "Me?"

Mama leaned back, her shoe leather squeaking. "Yes, you." She poked her finger into my stomach right above my belly button.

I never regarded myself as possessing anything special. Playing the piano was something I always had known, something passed onto me from Daddy. I supposed I had him to thank for my gift. *Poor Daddy.* Mama and I spoke very little of him since he died. Being there so close to Mama, shrouded in taffeta, I wondered if she missed him. I did. I missed the man from before, the one that did not drink and swear, the gentle man that loved Mama and me. Would Mama forgive me if I confessed, if I told her about the prayer? About the awful thing I did. I felt heavy, like bricks had been sewn into the hem of my skirt.

"Mr. Bloom asked Miss Victoria to have a word with me to see if I'd be open to lessons."

I was confused. "What's he going to teach you?"

Mama laughed. "Not for me. Piano lessons for you."

Piano lessons.

"If you want them."

Marlissa—I heard she took piano lessons. I was already better than Marlissa. How much better might I get? As good as a concert pianist?

I pulled Mama into a hug, immediately feeling lighter. "When can I start?"

"You have an hour lesson every Tuesday after school."

"Can we afford it?"

"You let me worry about that." Mama kissed my forehead and rose from the floor, unwrapping the fabric from around me, smoothing it back onto the bolt.

The bells above the store door *jangled,* noise from Broad Street spilling right behind.

A woman's voice called from the front. "Anybody here?"

Miss Minnie Jean. I recognized her nasal drawl.

"Be right there," Mama said.

"It's as cold as Alaska in here," Miss Minnie Jean said.

"What an unexpected surprise." Mama said. "So good to see you."

I followed close behind. "Morning, Miss Minnie Jean."

Until that day, Miss Minnie Jean had not once visited Graceful Stitches. All the other ladies of the congregation made regular stops, but not Miss Minnie Jean, her lack of patronage, most likely an intentional slight.

"A body could up and freeze to death in here," Miss Minnie Jean said. "I'd been told you done went and bought one of them air conditioners." She pulled her black, patent leather purse into her chest. "Business must be booming to already be able to afford such luxuries." There was inflection at the end of her words, a question.

Mama ignored her. "And what do I owe the pleasure of your visit?"

"Just wanted to see what all the fuss is about."

"Have I gone and caused a fuss?"

"Haven't you?" Miss Minnie Jean held out her vowels until she wore out their welcome.

"Looking for anything in particular?" I asked.

Miss Minnie Jean lifted her purse a little higher, squeezing it tighter to her bosom. "I buy my fabrics at Woolworth."

"Well, please feel free to look around, Miss Minnie Jean," I said. "We have much nicer fabrics than down at Woolworth."

She looked at me down the crooked barrel of her nose. "My, aren't you getting all grown up helping your mama down at this here store."

"Did you do something different with your hair?" Mama asked, no doubt, an attempt to divert Miss Minnie Jean's attention from me.

"I just came from the beauty parlor." She fingered the nape of her neck.

Mama stomped on the truth. "It's quite becoming."

Miss Minnie Jean's hair, a severe shade of black, was curled tighter than usual at the temples, a look accentuating her horsey features. "It's real pretty," I said, getting in on the fun with Mama.

"Just getting myself ready for tomorrow's service."

"It suits you," Mama said.

Like lipstick on a mule. "I'm gonna take piano lessons," I said. "Starting Tuesday."

"Isn't that something?" Miss Minnie Jean flared her nostrils and glanced around the store again. "I must say, things sure are looking up for Grace Newell. A new fabric store, air conditioning, and now piano lessons for you. I reckon the Lord does work in mysterious ways. After losing a husband, most women are near about broken." She lowered her purse, pinching the handles, letting it dangle at her knees. "I know I was after I lost my Edgar."

That squiggly-worm vein in Mama's forehead poked out. "It's been a difficult time, but there's nothing to be done but move forward."

"And to think you were on the brink of financial ruination," Miss Minnie Jean said. "Hardly a nickel to your name and the bank coming to take back Claxton's Bait and Tackle."

Mama glanced over at me and then back to Miss Minnie Jean. "I'm not certain this is the time or place to discuss such things."

"Grace, I only say all of this as a compliment. To celebrate all that you've . . . accomplished. And in such a short time."

I always suspected it, and now I knew it with certainty. Miss Minnie Jean was an awful woman. "I'm proud of Mama."

"Is that so?" Miss Minnie Jean moved closer. I could smell her then. Musty hymnals and old lady smells—the odor camouflaged with Chantilly dusting powder. "I will say this about your mama. If she's never had anything else, she's had pockets full of . . . in-gen-u-ity."

"Minnie Jean," Mama said. "How about a nice cold Co-Cola from the back?"

Miss Minnie Jean ignored Mama and kept on talking. "When she was a girl, probably no older than you, she used to sell fortunes to the other children just like a traveling gypsy. And all it cost was a dime."

Mama selling fortunes. This was news, another thing I did not know. Most of the town knew of Mama's ability, but as far as I was aware, it was a thing only ever mentioned in whispers.

"Analeise, why don't you get on back to your chores," Mama said, trying to keep her face smooth and pretty.

Still, Miss Minnie Jean just kept on talking. "In-gen-u-ity. Some children might take it into their heads to sell lemonade or cookies, but not your mama." Miss Minnie Jean smiled, pulling back those thin lips over her big teeth, lipstick bleeding into the wrinkles around her mouth. "She'd cut up these pieces of burlap or feed sack and stretch it over an embroidery hoop." Miss Minnie Jean hugged her purse to her chest again. "Then she'd do something kind of like cross stitching, making these little pictures she'd rub her fingers over."

"That was a long time ago. I was just a girl with silly notions." Mama's purple, wormy-vein bulged to the point I feared it might burst.

"Hardly silly," Miss Minnie Jean said. "Quite a serious thing, seeing the future if you ask me. It's a dark kind of business. But that was then, just like you said, wasn't it? When you were a girl. Before you knew such a thing was wrong . . . not of God? Before you and your Mama left that holiness church and saw the right side of things."

I felt heavy again, like it would be easy to just flop over. Mama, a traveling gypsy.

"You're right, Minnie," Mama said. "Seeing the future can be a dark and terrible thing. A heavy burden to bear." Mama took a step toward Miss Minnie Jean. "I don't know who's more foolish—me agreeing to look or the person asking." Mama touched Miss Minnie Jean's shoulder. "Sometimes I wonder if it's me seeing the future in what I stitch, or me stitching fate into the future."

Miss Minnie Jean stepped backwards. "What are you saying?"

Mama laughed. "Just me being silly again, Minnie." Mama took a step back from Miss Minnie Jean. "You and I go way, way back. Your daughter, Odette, and me . . . we played together when we were little bitty things. I've listened to you finger at that old church organ for just about long as I can remember. So, should you ever need anything. Anything sewed or anything you need knowing, is all you have to do is ask." Mama touched her fingers to her throat. "And I won't charge you. Not even a dime."

The three of us stood there staring at each other, an uncomfortable quiet lingering thick as Miss Minnie Jean's body talc. "That is most kind of you, Grace. But there is nothing I need knowing other that what I already know." Miss Minnie Jean's words were dense, something clinging heavy to the undersides.

The bells over the front door *jingled*. "Hey, Analeise."

Abel Darlington.

He walked over, buoyant strides and crooked grin. "I thought I saw you in here," he said. "Looks like we're both working today." He pushed his hands into his front pockets. "So, this is your mother's new store." He looked around smiling. "Sure feels nice and cool in here."

Miss Minnie Jean cleared her throat.

"This is my mama," I said, pointing in her direction. "Mama, this is Abel Darlington."

"Well, if you aren't just the very image of your Daddy," Mama said. "I haven't seen you since you were an itty-bitty little bit of nothing."

How strange to think Mama knew the Darlingtons when I never knew they existed. Then again, Mama had been around longer than me. And the Darlington's, like the Mayfields lived strangely in a world so close, yet fully apart from our own.

"It's nice to meet you, ma'am," he said, pulling his right hand from his pocket extending it to Mama.

"And this here is Miss Minnie Jean," I said.

Abel and Miss Minnie Jean exchanged pleasantries, Miss Minnie Jean managing something close to a genuine smile.

"What brings you in the store today?" Mama said.

"Just taking a break. I'm working at the paper today." He motioned across the street. "I was on my way down to Woolworth for a Coke when I saw Analeise here. Just thought I'd come in and say hello."

Mama clasped her hands together and held them at her waist. "How sweet."

"Analeise, would you like to join me? My treat."

I looked at Mama. "I think you could use a break," she said, giving Miss Minnie Jean a glance.

Alone with Abel Darlington. I felt like I swallowed down a handful of butterflies, their powdery wings flapping around, dusting up my insides. "That sounds nice."

I hugged Mama. "Are you sure you don't mind me leaving you here?" I didn't want to leave her alone with that old werewolf.

"I'll be fine. Just don't stay too long."

"Bye, Miss Minnie Jean. See you at church tomorrow," I said, happy to be away from her.

"Nice to meet y'all," Abel said, touching my back, leading me to the door, a million pin prickles setting my skin on fire.

Miss Minnie Jean spoke as Abel and I walked through the store, my ears wide as I could make them. "She sure is gonna be pretty just like her Mama. That will come in handy, don't you think? Wonder if she's got some of her Mama's in-gen-u-ity."

Abel pushed at the door, the bells sounding hollower than before. The suck of cool air pulled Miss Minnie Jean's stale, old lady smell onto the street with us, mixing with the brine from the pickle factory.

In-gen-u-ity . . .

Chapter 20

There in the Saturday clamor of Woolworth, I sat with Abel Darlington, the swarm of butterflies still dusting my insides.

Abel bent his head to the straw, his glass resting on the table. "I'm glad you like cherry Coke. It's my favorite," he said. He took a few hands-free sips and grinned. "I know I'm not suppose to do that, but for some reason it tastes better."

"I won't tell." I zipped my lips with my fingers. I was happy to follow suit, as my palms were unusually sweaty, a potential hazard when lifting the tall, slick Coca-Cola glass.

"You know what else I'm not supposed to do?"

"What?"

He leaned back to his straw, blowing bubbles into his glass. "That."

"Rude." I giggled, bending forward to join him. The two of us sat there tucked into the red vinyl booth, hunched over the table making a racket.

"My lands. What's all this carrying on?" At the half-wall separating the dining area from the store, Miss Minnie Jean stood, head cocked back, chin melting into her neck. I turned loose my straw and pressed my back into the booth. Abel followed.

Awful woman. Had it not been for the aroma of patty melts and French fries, I might have smelled her standing there so closely. "Hi, Miss Minnie Jean. You find something at Mama's?"

She rattled a small, brown, paper bag. "Buttons." She pinched her purchase between her fingers. *Butt—onzzz.* She stretched the word until it vibrated on her tongue.

"That's nice."

"Can't afford anything else over yonder," she said. "I reckon your mama thinks a lot of what she's selling." She opened her purse, dropped the small bag inside, and snapped it shut.

Butt—onzzz . . .

Miss Minnie Jean turned to leave, pointing her crooked finger to the ceiling. "You mind yourself, Analeise Newell." She paused and pointed again before walking away. "All is seen. All is known."

It was if she stole all the air while she stood there, sucking it up through those horse-sized nostrils and wrinkled lips, all of it rushing back in and crashing like a wave when she was gone. My shoulders drooped from the sweet relief of her departure.

Right then was the moment I could have been unkind, when any child might have been disrespectful to a mean old woman like Minnie Jean Carter. Eye-rolls and sniggers. But I refrained, awaiting Abel's reaction, staring at those chocolate drop eyes—lacquered and gleaming. He smiled sweetly, his kindness giving off heat. He was not like other boys.

"Hey, do you like words," he said, excitement building in his voice.

"I guess."

He reached around and pulled a small notepad from his back pocket. "I get a word a day. It's been a pretty good week so far." He flipped open his pad. "A writer has to have an expansive vocabulary."

"Where do you get them?" I never heard of such a thing. I knew boys who made hobbies of arrowheads and old coins, but not words.

"Mostly my dad. But sometimes other people—people who know I collect them."

I had a collection. Cicada shells, whiskey, secrets, and lies. *Does that count?*

"Monday was a good one. You want to hear?"

"Sure."

He ran his finger along the page. "Obfuscate. It means to hide or conceal."

To hide or conceal. I would have to remember that one. *Obfuscate. Analeise Newell is good at obfuscating.* "Hmm." I fluttered my fingers over the table. "What was Wednesday?"

He lowered his eyes to the table, one lazy sweep of charcoal lashes. "Beguile." He dipped his head back to his straw.

"That sounds like another good one. Who gave it to you?"

He blew another blast of motorboat bubbles through his straw. "Dad."

Moments passed while we sat amidst the din of shoppers. Crinkling bags and heeltaps.

"Are you going to tell me what it means?"

He nodded. "If you want to know."

"Tell me."

"To charm or attract." Abel moved away from his straw. "Dad said he was thinking of my mom when he chose it. He said the first time he laid eyes on her, she beguiled him and stole away his heart."

There was sweetness, and love, and loss in his voice. I recognized the sound of loss—of sorrow. I heard it sung in Etta Mae's voice. I had tasted it, knew it for myself.

"My mom died when I was three," he said, his dark eyes floating in watery pools.

I lay my hand on the table, wanting desperately to swat at the air, to shoo away the shadows. Was it possible something bad could ever happen to a golden-skinned boy? A boy wrapped up in sun shards and glittery moon dust. A boy like Abel Darlington would never kill his daddy.

"What y'all doing here?"

Jane. She startled me, like I was smack in the middle of no-good. I could feel my face flush.

"Hi, Jane," Abel said, his brightness returning. "We're taking a break."

Virginia Fenton moved out from behind a crisscross of ladies, an enormous, pink bubble swelling from her mouth.

Jane obstructed her sister's view. Not having yet seen me, Virginia collapsed and sucked the wad of gum back into her mouth—*clicking* and *popping.* When she reached the half-wall, she stiffened, turning slowly to find me in the booth. She set those guinea hen eyes on me. It was always chilly at the end of a Virginia Fenton stare.

I looked to Jane—her eyebrows arching, lips set in a smirk. She was positively giddy finding me with Abel Darlington.

Virginia's chapped lips pulled apart, the gum residue peeling away bits of dry skin.

"I think that was the biggest bubble I've ever seen," Abel said.

Virginia pried her lips apart. Before she could speak, Abel held up his index finger, pressing it into the air, shuffling through the pages of his notebook with his free hand. There must have been magic in that finger, because it possessed the power to silence Virginia Fenton.

Abel's other index finger rested at a place on the page, then set to tapping. "Virginia, that bubble was . . ." He drummed his hands on the table. "Colossal."

The muscles of Virginia's face twitched and pulled into something resembling joy.

"The trick is three pieces of Bazooka," Virginia said. "The best bubbles come when the sweetness is gone."

"No wonder you're so good at it," Jane said.

Virginia turned loose her face muscles, her expression shooting back like a rubber band into its most familiar and natural countenance. Menace.

I giggled. I tried to recover, quickly masking my misstep with a cough.

Virginia leaned into the half-wall, her eyes nothing more than slits. "I hope you're not coming down with something." She shifted the gob of Bazooka from her right cheek to her left. "It would be a shame if you had to miss the Mayfield Gala."

Jane nudged her shoulder into her sister's. Virginia jerked away.

"Betcha got something real pretty to wear. Maybe something your mama made?" Virginia sneered. She knew I had not been invited. Virginia Fenton was a Miss Minnie Jean kind of awful.

Abel seemed oblivious to the female induced shift of barometric pressure. Oblivious to the secret language of girls. The carbonation from my cherry Coke bubbled up and burned my throat.

I stared at Abel's notebook laying there open on the table. *Beguile.* I met Virginia's close-set eyes. "I bet nothing could be as pretty as what you're wearing." I leaned down to my straw and took a swallow of Coke.

For the second time in less than five minutes Virginia Fenton was silent, confounded by my compliment. Jane shot me a sideways glance.

"What are you going to wear, Virginia?" I asked.

"You know that's a secret. You know I'm a special guest and can't say."

Jane circled her finger in the air. *Whoop-tee-do.*

"Girls?" Mrs. Fenton called from across the store. "I'm all checked out. Off to the next stop." Mrs. Fenton waved over to Abel and me.

Jane nodded at me and flashed her eyes. There would be questions later.

Virginia did not say good-bye; instead, she stepped backwards, kneading, and chewing her gum. She pushed it from her mouth. The baby bubble stalled. For a moment, I thought it might wither. But it swelled into a sheer membrane, bulging, and pulsing until it nearly concealed her face.

"Colossal. Virginia Fenton's bubble is colossal." Abel played table drums again.

Virginia held up three fingers. *The trick is three pieces of Bazooka.* Jane rolled her eyes.

Virginia turned away from us and walked right into a lady, the bubble flattening and popping between her face and the woman's white, cotton blouse.

The best bubbles come when the sweetness is gone. I clapped and called out from the booth. "That was a good one, Virginia."

* * *

Abel walked me back to Mama's store from Woolworth. The time passed too quickly, and I did not want to go back inside. The sky shared my disappointment, clouds clumping together, hiding away the sun.

"Thank you for the Coke," I said.

"My pleasure." He grinned and bent at the waist. "I guess I best be getting on back to work."

A horn honked. Dink poked his head from the passenger window of his daddy's rusted Studebaker. "Abel McDable," he hollered, his thumb sticking in the air.

"Dink McStink," Abel yelled. Abel turned back to me, his face lit with a grin. "Sorry," he said, shrugging his shoulders, as though the customs of boys might be too difficult to explain to a girl.

He underestimated me. I stuck out my thumb and hooted, "Stinky Dinky." The rusted heap clattered across the railroad tracks, Dink's head jerking and swaying from side to side.

Abel raised an eyebrow. "Not bad." He scratched his head. "Hey, you working next Saturday?"

I had no idea. "Yes."

"Great, we'll take our breaks together again. If you want."

"Sure," I said, hoping I did not sound too anxious. He bowed again, turned, and walked away, his notebook sticking out from his back pocket. Wanting to keep him there a moment more, I called out. "Abel. You never said. What's today's word?"

He turned back around smiling. "It's a beauty." He stretched his arms out wide. "Conflagration."

I could hardly make it out. "What?" I said, cupping my ear with my hand.

"Con-fla-gra-tion."

"That's a good one. What's it mean?"

He framed his face with his hands, making a makeshift megaphone. "A terrible, awful fire," he hollered back. "Miss Cordelia gave it to me."

A gift from Cordelia Mayfield? "Use it in a sentence," I said. A short distance behind Abel, the railroad-crossing signal chimed, the lights flashing red. I heard only bits and pieces of words. "I can't hear you."

162

He yelled louder above the din, breaking it up in sections. "They all . . . burned up . . . in . . . the . . . con-fla-gra-tion." The railroad crossing gates lowered, the ramble of traffic halting on both sides.

Sheriff Dobb's car drove by slowly. He dipped his head, nodding in my direction.

Abel crossed the street. He bounced on his toes, winsome and carefree carrying a pocket of words. Would I ever be that light? Could I ever be that good?

I locked my eyes on the Sheriff's car. Watched it roll to a stop. The brake lights, a slow blink, then shining steady.

Chapter 21

We took in the Saturday evening air—Etta Mae, Mama, and me on the front porch swing, Miss Wessie in a ladder back chair brought outside from the kitchen.

"Looks like summer might be leaving out early this year." Miss Wessie said, wriggling off one shoe and then the other. Tucked between her legs, Lucinda rested on a wig stand, strands of dark brown hair wound around pink sponge curlers. "Turned off right cool. Sun done gone and got lazy." She picked up Lucinda, rotating her in the air, inspecting all her angles. "Turkey time be here before you know it." She set Lucinda back down in her lap and removed another curler.

"Good Lord, Wessie, don't go scooting the year away," Mama said, pushing her stocking feet against the porch floor setting the swing in motion.

Etta Mae laughed as we swung close to her granny, then back again to the edge of the porch. Mama reached out her feet to touch Miss Wessie. Etta Mae laughed harder, joining Mama's game, stretching out her tiny toes.

"Get on away from here," Miss Wessie said, smirking and swatting away the team of wiggling toes with her hand. "Don't you go and make me mess up Miss Lucinda here."

Sitting between Mama and Etta Mae, I felt heavy drifting across the porch cradled in the swing. I let my body go limp, allowing my legs to dangle, enjoying the momentary release of control. It felt good to let go. I shut my eyes, concentrating on the loose strands of my hair tickling and drifting across my face like broken bits of cobweb.

"Did you tell Etta Mae about your trip to Woolworth?" Mama said. I opened my eyes. She grinned and pushed off again, causing the swing to buck backwards. Her voice was playful, her eyes filled with mischief.

"No, ma'am. I forgot." There had been little opportunity to edge in a word. I planned to tell her, but Etta Mae chirped on and on through dinner about her trip to Thomasville and the choir solo she would sing the next day at church.

"What did you do at Woolworth?" Etta Mae said.

"I'll tell you later." Talking was the last thing I desired. I only wanted to shut my eyes and float above the porch floor, the September air feathering over me.

Mama laughed. "Why so shy all of a sudden?" She put her arm around me. I leaned into her, my cheek against her chest.

A curler bounced out of Miss Wessie's lap and rolled across the porch. "Son of a bucket. Lucinda didn't wanna let loose of that one." She picked at the perfect curl with a snaggle-toothed comb.

Moments passed with no one speaking. Somewhere between the swing's squeak and *jingle* of chain, I realized something was different. The ambient sounds of night had grown dimmer.

"Mama, I don't hear them."

"Hear who, baby?"

"The cicadas. I don't hear them anymore."

The swing creaked forward and back again. "I reckon it's time for them to move on along."

They got secrets they keep. I was happy they were gone, a handful of pebbles pulled from my pockets, one less thing to fret about. I pulled Mama's hand into mine. Her skin was softer now, free from the gnaw of pickle brine. I loved the feel of New Mama. Smooth, confident, and pretty. But I was still acquainting myself with these fresh, green pieces. How else might she change? Would I still love her when the mold was set?

Etta Mae hummed, sweet and gentle.

Another curler fell onto the floor. "Have mercy," Miss Wessie said. Etta Mae giggled, covering her mouth with her hand.

Mama's breathing began to change, the long, lazy measure of her chest giving way to a quickened beat. She anchored her feet to the floor, stilling the swing. She touched her left hand to her right, then ran it up the length of her arm.

"Mama?"

Etta Mae's humming wound down like a tired music box.

Mama pulled her dress up above her knees, her fingers running over the hem. She looked up, staring into the horizon, into the smattering of clouds, purplish black bruises beaten into the sky.

"Miss Grace? Are you okay," Etta Mae said.

"I'm fine." Mama stood up and walked to the railing. "Somebody's coming."

All went quiet, the late evening noise peeling away from Mama's words. Mama stood. Etta Mae and I followed, abandoning the swing.

"Mama, who's coming?"

Etta Mae and I stood with Mama at the rail, shoes and errant curlers strewn behind us. Miss Wessie followed, Lucinda tucked beneath her arm. We looked off in the distance, Etta Mae humming again.

Miss Wessie was the first to see. "Grace?" She pointed with her free hand. "Is that them there you saw coming."

Mama nodded.

I could not see anything. "Is it the Sheriff?" I said.

Miss Wessie shot me a look out of the corner of her eye. "Why'd he be coming here? You hush up with that foolishness."

Mama squeezed the rail harder, her red lacquered nails bending from the pressure. "It's not the Sheriff."

I could see now. I could see the car that drove toward the house, black and long as a mile.

"Looks like a Mayfield done come to call," Miss Wessie said.

The blood rushed out of my head and down to my toes. An odd look passed between Mama and Miss Wessie—something close to panic.

Etta Mae's humming dwindled to a kitten's purr.

The front passenger door opened slowly. A dark, stocking-clad leg, and then another.

"Mercy?" Miss Wessie placed Lucinda on the rail, her shoulders relaxing "What you doing here?"

Before Mercy could answer, Mama spoke. "You come alone?"

"Yes'm." Mercy stopped a few steps from the house.

Mama loosened her grip on the rail.

"Sorry I'm calling on you so late. Won't keep you long. Just a quick errand for Mrs. Mayfield."

Etta Mae called out into the yard. "Hi, Miss Mercy."

Mercy waved back, a flash of something in her hand. "Hey, sweet girl," she said, walking to the bottom porch step.

"Sure is late for errands. Don't them Mayfields ever turn you loose from work?" Miss Wessie said.

Mercy smiled. "You be sweet, Wessie."

"What's the errand?" I said, so anxious, I thought I might pop.

"Miss Analeise, it seems there was an oversight. Looks like your invitation didn't get put in the mail with the others, so I was asked to bring it out to you . . . to hand deliver it special."

I was a kettle, burning hot and ready to howl. *Invitation.* "To the Mayfield gala?" My throat tightened, pinching off the end of the question.

Mercy looked down at the ground as if her next words were scrawled in the dirt. "Mrs. Mayfield would like to apologize for any inconvenience suffered from the delay."

Etta Mae hopped up and down, clapping her hands. "Your special invitation to Mayfield Gala. Your special invitation."

I wanted to join her, but I tempered the tornado of wild-girl whoops and hollers that might spin out and level the place. I smoothed the wrinkles in my dress and tossed my hair over my shoulders.

Mercy took the first step, and I followed—to meet her halfway. Mama's hand came down firm and tight on my shoulder. I wiggled around gazing up at her face. She looked to Miss Wessie, an invisible current coursing between them, scorching the air.

I pried my shoulder loose from Mama reaching for the creamy beige envelope extended in Mercy's hand. "Thank you," I said, stepping back to study the black, scrolly letters. I pressed the envelope to my chest. "Mama, may we be excused?"

Before Mama could speak, I grabbed hold of Etta Mae's hand and ran to the door. Once inside, I ran my fingers across the envelope's elegant, linen weave.

Etta Mae laughed, bouncing up and down. "Open it."

"Shush." I lifted the envelope to my nose breathing in the smell of it—the lush, florid scent of Cordelia and Marlissa Mayfield. I turned it over working my fingernail beneath the gold-foil seal until the flap was free. The stiff card pulled easy from the sleeve.

Etta Mae latched onto my arm, tipping me sideways. "Read it."

My eyes scanned the invitation, my index finger tracing the cursive script. I angled the invitation to leverage the last bit of sun until it could be read in the dim light of the parlor.

Time: When day begins to trickle. When truth is no longer illuminated by the harsh glare of light. When the world is bent and folded into fantasy and cast in the flickering glow of flame. Half past enchantment: 7:00 p.m.

Etta Mae pulled at my arm. "What are you going to wear," she asked, each word a note on an ascending scale.

I handed her the invitation and knelt to the floor, plunging my fingers into my sock, searching for the tiny swatch of fabric. "Something made from this." I held out the piece of pale blue taffeta in my hand, pulling it back again from Etta Mae's reaching fingers.

Etta Mae twirled around with the invitation. I let go my restraint and joined her in a spin. I walked to the open window, rubbing the fabric against my cheek. The Mayfield car pulled away from the house. Mama and Miss Wessie stood a few breaths apart, the seeping light erasing their faces.

"Grace, you ain't gonna let that child go off to that party is you?"

I crouched beneath the sill. What reason could she and Miss Wessie have to keep me from the party? How could they be so selfish?

I heard only a mumble, then the groan of boards as they walked down the steps into the yard.

Etta Mae waltzed over to me, pulling me up from the floor. We took off, reeling about the room, Etta Mae trilling a familiar tune. A moment passed, and I placed it.

It was Cordelia Mayfield's concerto—it was Mama's dream-fire song.

Chapter 22

The Fenton's Cadillac smelled of lilac and Brylecreem, an amalgam of scent agitating my jitters. Thankfully, Jane's family invited me to accompany them to Mistletoe, rescuing me from the embarrassment of arriving at the Gala in Daddy's old jalopy. Since Virginia's special invitation required she sleep over at Marlissa's the night before, there was oodles of room.

The weeks leading up to the event were contentious—fantastic and covert battles fought between Mama and Miss Wessie, all of them centered on my attendance at the party. Though I did my best to eavesdrop, I was unable to discern the source of Miss Wessie's concern, only managing to steal away scraps of these fierce exchanges. *You done lost your mind, Grace. Don't turn that child loose to them Mayfields. You is prideful. Playing with fire.*

"Analeise, your Mama sure did outdo herself with your dress?" Mrs. Fenton said, turning her head to the backseat giving me another look over. "I've never seen anything quite so lovely."

"Thank you, Miss Fenton." I folded my hands neatly upon my lap. Though Mama was forced to hurry, she indeed had outdone herself. Even Miss Wessie, with her contrary ideas about the party, could not help but be impressed. My dress was a dream—yards of exquisite, pale blue taffeta, each pass of Mama's needle stitching together perfection.

Miss Minnie Jean called Mama a gypsy fortuneteller—her intentions obviously cruel. But I rather liked the thought of it, Mama having a gift, possessing ingenuity. If Mama could sew the future into a thing, I hoped she hemmed a bright one into my dress. If ever I needed a night to unfurl in my favor, it was right then—the night of the Mayfield Gala. *Goodbye and so long, Bug Girl.*

"You look beautiful, Analeise. Just wait until everyone sees," Jane said, reaching over to touch my shoulder.

"So do you." In truth, I did feel pretty, not quite like my regular self, as if all my better parts sprouted up and overtook the bad. Mama executed great care in her preparations, washing and curling my hair, smoothing it into shiny, chestnut waves cascading down my back. What would Marlissa think? Would she like the new, prettier me?

"You're all stunning," Dr. Fenton said. "I'm the luckiest man in all of Providence."

"Sweet talker." Mrs. Fenton smiled at her husband.

I thought of Mama and Daddy, of the kind things they once said to each other, imagining the three of us in a nice car riding off to the Mayfields. If not careful, the dark edges of guilt and memory would corkscrew around me, ruining my mood. I hummed along with the radio, to Roger Williams singing "Autumn Leaves".

We followed slowly behind the procession of cars to the gatehouse. Halbert stood to the right, holding up a lantern with his left hand, motioning for cars to roll down their windows with his other.

"Welcome to Mistletoe," he said. "Please be so kind as to turn off your lights before you and your'n enter Mayfield Wood." One car after the next, all headlights went dim.

"Why on earth do you imagine we have to turn out the lights?" Mrs. Fenton said.

I watched Halbert as we passed, wondering if he remembered me. The flicker of his lantern cast a spookiness upon his face, shadows lingering in the crevices of his burns, his melted ear more gruesome than I recalled. His eyes caught hold of mine and held on. He nodded and smiled, the scars pulling down his eye. "When the day begins to trickle," he said. "Half past. Half past enchantment."

"Who's that man?" Jane said. "He's creepy."

"Jane Louise Fenton, you mind your manners," Mrs. Fenton whispered. "He's obviously experienced some sort of misfortune."

"I'll say."

Conflagration. I thought of Abel's word, the one Mrs. Mayfield gave him. A chill blossomed up my back.

"Take a look at that," Dr. Fenton said, angling his head looking out into the space before us.

Mrs. Fenton clasped her hands just below her chin. "My goodness-graciousness. Have you ever seen anything so glorious?"

Jane grabbed hold of my hand and squeezed. "Analeise, get a look at this."

A constellation of lanterns hung from the tree canopy, all of them arranged at varying heights, everywhere above us and all the way around. The candlelight shimmied giving the impression the very air we breathed glimmered and pulsed.

Gasps tumbled from the lowered windows from the cars ahead. Jane threaded her fingers through mine, both of us looking in all directions, each of us not wanting to miss a single, glorious detail.

The song on the radio dissolved to static, leaving us to ride along in the lightning bug tunnel to the monotony of *sizzle* and *hiss*. Minutes passed, and finally, Dr. Fenton reached over, turned the knob, extinguishing the sound.

We wilted in eternity, and still, I could not see the Mayfield mansion. I fingered the choker Mama strung together from a strand of imitation Woolworth pearls and rhinestone beads.

"Look at that," Mrs. Fenton said. "Isn't it divine?"

Before us was the end of Mayfield Wood, an opening offering the dreamy vista to Mistletoe. Hurricane lamps defied gravity sitting atop round topiary shrubs, hundreds of luminaries interspersed and lining the way.

Cars entered the expansive circular drive that wound about the fountain, a series of basins cascading water into an enormous concrete pool below. Colored men in black tails assisted guests from their cars then drove the emptied automobiles away.

Jane's knees bounced up and down. "I wish they'd hurry on up."

172

"Jane, the party isn't going anywhere," Mrs. Fenton said. "We'll be to the front of the line soon enough."

Jane's anxiousness mixed with mine, infecting my own knees with her fidgeting.

"They sure are taking their sweet time about it," Jane said.

"Sweetheart, if you are in such a hurry, why don't you and Analeise go on ahead and get out of the car here while we've stopped. Your mother and I will meet up with you along the way."

"Thank you, Daddy." Jane pulled at the door handle. "Come on, Analeise. Let's go."

"Jane Louise Fenton, you mind your manners," Mrs. Fenton said. "Remember yourself. And if you see Virginia before I do, tell her the same."

Jane poked her head through the car window and kissed her daddy on the cheek. She hurried over to my side, grabbed hold of my hand, pulling me toward the house, our party slippers sinking and crunching in the gravel.

Amber light spilled from the windows falling in columns across the lawn. A string quartet played just inside the marble foyer. Jane and I stopped before entering, both of us smoothing our dresses.

"Analeise, you are a living, breathing angel."

"And you look just like a dream."

We laced our fingers together, passing across the threshold, wedging ourselves into a cluster of guests, folding ourselves into the *swish* and *swoop* of party dresses—into the elegant swell of music.

We followed the guests to a place called the loggia, an expansive hall long and wide as Broad Street with floor to ceiling windows to the right, a gallery wall of oil paintings and sculptures perched on plinths to the left. Silver trays hovered above us, hands from everywhere reaching for crystal champagne flutes. *Clink* and *clank*. Jane and I, both of us confections, bobbed along in the stream.

The light from the cut glass chandeliers fell against the windows, transforming them to mirrors. I stopped to find my reflection, my necklace catching the light. I loved the effect—the sight of me twinkling.

Someone called from up ahead. "Jane! Analeise!"

"My goodness, that can't be Annette Everston," Jane said. "Look at that."

I hardly recognized her, that fast running farm girl in a handsome, peach colored dress, her hair swept up in a tidy bun.

"You look so pretty," Jane and I both said in unison, our girlish chirp mixing with the hum of the crowd, becoming part of the collective fervor reverberating through that grand hall of magic mirrors.

Annette reached out to touch the sleeve of my dress. "I could just eat you up, Analeise Newell," she said. "You sure do clean up right pretty." She glanced at Jane. "You look nice, too."

Flattery was a scrumptious thing. Had there been time to waste, I might have taken slow, savory bites. "Have you seen anyone else from school?" I looked over Annette's head and down the way, hoping to catch glimpse of Marlissa.

"A few of the girls from class." Annette puffed her cheeks. "And the flower-fairy court."

"The what?" Jane said.

"The flower fairies," Annette said. "You know, they're in that old book Marlissa totes around with her—the green one?"

"I know it," I said.

"Turns out that it's part of that special invitation Virginia's been going on and on about for weeks now. One of only ten?"

I nodded briskly to keep Annette talking, desperate for every detail.

"Three girls from our school, and seven from Marlissa's old school."

"Whoop-tee-doo," Jane said.

I would have pushed Miss Jane Louise Fenton to the side if I could. Slung her off into the corner. "Pay no mind to her, Annette," I put myself in the middle of the two girls, looping my arms through theirs. I gently tugged us forward and back into the elegant drift of people. "What else?"

"Mrs. Mayfield had fairy costumes made for all of them to wear tonight."

"Fairies are dumb," Jane said.

"Hush up. Annette's talking."

"They even have wings. Just like those paper dolls Marlissa gave us. Can you even stand it? Wings."

My pace quickened, matching the giddy, staccato beat thumping in my chest like a second heart. *Wings.*

We walked faster—the string ensemble paling to an echo, feather-light and tingling in the small of my back.

"And guess what else?" Annette said, abruptly stopping, jerking me back.

We unlatched ourselves from the other and gathered close. Jane spoke first, her feigned ambivalence unhinging, ripping loose like a shutter in a ferocious wind. "What else?"

"Mrs. Mayfield sent away all the way up to New York City for charm bracelets from a placed called Tiffany's. They all get one. All the fairies."

Jane gasped and grabbed hold of her throat. "Tiffany's?"

I never heard of it, but I knew it must have been a place fine as Woolworth to rile Jane into such a state of apoplexy.

Annette breathed in and exhaled slowly, the color in her cheeks deepening. "And every bracelet comes with a fairy charm."

Then and there I hated Virginia Fenton, begrudged her those fairy wings and that fancy charm bracelet brought down all the way from New York City.

"And that's not all," Annette said. "We all get a bracelet. All the girls at the party. Every last one."

The three of us leaned into the middle, fingers lacing and squeezing—all of us on the verge of hysteria. I grabbed hold of Jane's hand, and Jane took hold of Annette. We made our way down the loggia, the three of us a pastel, patchwork centipede.

We stood at the end of the hall in a bottleneck, guests moving slowly through the doors leading to the grounds. Fronds of light from the last chandelier fell over our arms and faces. Jane, Annette, and I held our hands out in front of us admiring the speckled effect.

"She's that Grace Newell's daughter," a woman spoke from somewhere behind. Something in the tone was familiar, but there were only strangers behind me—chandelier sparkles distorting faces.

I walked to the doors, turning back to look. "Where's her Mama?" another woman asked, her voice a swirl of singsong and taunt.

"I can't imagine she wouldn't have been invited. Anybody who is somebody is here tonight," the other woman said. A devilish peal of laughter followed.

I realized I did not know the women who spoke. It was not the voices, but the Miss Minnie Jean tone that rang familiar. Innuendo. *Ingen-uity.*

Jane reached back and pulled me forward. She seemed to have not heard the women—preoccupied and deafened by anticipation, a crazy smile smeared across her face.

Outside the air was cooler. The chatter dissolved, the only sound, a waltz unfurling in the distance. We passed through the doors, the view obstructed by the adults in front of us.

The reverent hush untangled, a rise of awe rumbling up through the crowd. "What is it, Jane? What do they see?"

Jane grabbed hold of my wrist, yanking us through the crowd, hurrying across the veranda to the balustrade.

Colossal. A dozen or more brilliant white, hot air balloons hovered, tethered to the ground below. Moored at different heights, the balloons created a chandelier effect. Bursts of flame released—puffs of dragon breath illuminating the sky—the sound, a loud and exhilarating *whoosh.*

In the distance, a white tent, at least the length of a football field, emitted a soft, golden glow. An orchestra played within. Like a spinning zoetrope, dancers twirled and dipped, casting shadowy silhouettes visible from outside the tent.

"Where's Annette?" I said.

"We must have lost her."

We zigzagged through the crowd over to the first of the double staircases curving to the ground below. Momentum and the late evening breeze fanned my dress, my curls bouncing soft against my shoulders—the affect, a wondrous sensation. I turned loose a laugh. Jane joined me, her bird-like tweet making me laugh even harder.

At the bottom, my feet sank into the cushion of grass, perfectly shorn and crayon green. I held out my arms, balancing myself, securing my footing on the otherworldly terrain.

A tribe of boys in suits hurried past, skipping and whooping to the cadence of an Indian chant. Dink led the pack.

"Hey, Dink McStink," I said.

"Who on earth let him in?" Jane said.

"Didn't you hear?" a voiced asked sheepishly.

Abel Darlington. I was winded from the sight of him, the feeling exacerbated by the spectacular commotion all about. His white, dress shirt glowed, setting off his smile and year-round tan. "A tribe of Indian warriors are on the loose and hunting scalps." He smiled wider, those black, lash-rimmed eyes slowly blinking.

Jane tweeted again, only more demure this time as she fingered the ends of her hair.

Oh, brother. Jane was flirting with Abel Darlington. *My Abel Darlington.* For the second time that evening, I wanted to fling her away, push her down to sprawl across the ground in that tacky, mint green dress.

A ball of flame escaped from the balloon right above, framing us in a brilliant bolt of light and spectacular *whoosh* of heat.

"Miss Cordelia sure knows how to throw a party," Abel said, smiling up at the hot air balloon. His hair was tamed, the work of a good-smelling, glossy pomade—a meticulous part somehow managed in that dark thatch of hair. The sleekness of the style accentuated his cheekbones and almond-shaped eyes. It was the square of his jaw that balanced all the pretty. How could Jane help herself? How could anyone?

I straightened my back, letting my arms drift by my side into the folds of my gown. "And why aren't you running about collecting scalps?" I asked.

"I got plenty already," he said. He pushed his hands into his pockets. "Besides, you both look like you might need protecting. That's some mighty fine-looking hair you ladies have there. Probably fetch a real nice price."

Jane touched Abel's arm. "Mama took me to the beauty parlor today for a wash and set."

"Is that what happened," I said, cutting my eyes at Rapunzel.

"Actually, I was wondering if you two would do me the honor of allowing me to escort you both down to the conservatory." Abel nodded off in the distance.

Jane and I followed his gaze down the slope of the grounds. A fountain splashed below, spilling and streaming down a series of cascades for hundreds of feet, the end of it concealed by a drop of terrain.

"To the Chrystal Palace of the South," Abel said, pointing his long, slender fingers.

The orchestra fell silent, the last of the waltz playing out.

Jane spoke first, squeezing an exclamation into a whisper. "Wowie. Take a look at that."

The building burned bright, light refracting from all the beveled edges as though the sun had been stolen and tucked inside. A trumpet pierced the silence. The orchestra followed, flourishing quick like a whirlwind.

Four fairies skipped our direction, all shimmer and twinkle, and girlish giggles. They flitted, then darted in front, moving quickly down the path. Marlissa and Virginia were nowhere to be seen.

"Ever pull the wings off a butterfly?" Jane asked.

"Nope. But I've caught one in a jar," Abel said.

I thought of the one-winged paper doll hidden beneath the boards of my floor, crumpled and broken. Before I could think more of it, Jane grabbed my hand, and Abel took the other, pulling me along.

Everything buzzed, the air faint with honeysuckle—all that remained of summer. We trailed down the path behind the soft rustle of fairy wings, the babble of water cascading to our right.

I felt it then, the surge of emotion that comes with happiness. For an instant it did not matter that I killed Daddy, that I was a girl capable of terrible things. All I cared about was then. That single moment of bliss. I blinked away at the tears that rose and threatened to spill, squeezing the hands I held. I knew it would pass too swiftly as all happiness does.

We ran faster, gaining speed, so close I could hear the huff of fairy breath. All of us running together, wild and happy, to the gleaming light of the Chrystal Palace.

Chapter 23

The inside of the conservatory was a profusion of elaborate detail, the overwhelming immensity of the place causing the pressure in my ears to shift, setting off a woozy spell—the sudden feeling I might keel over.

How might a body even venture to describe such a place—the arched panels, the hand-carved corbels, the putting of a jungle inside a room of glass?

Jane, equally undone by the sight of the Chrystal Palace, leaned into me, lingering for a moment, regaining her balance.

Abel was the first to speak, those chocolate drop eyes sweeping across the space. "Mon-u-mental."

"I'll say." Jane blinked up into the trail of chandeliers lighting the intricately laid brickwork paths below.

The four fairies remained a good distance ahead, darting down the walk, paying no mind to the magnificence about them. The babbling fountains, statues tucked into the foliage—ancient marble faces keeping watch.

We followed behind, taking in the *monumental* place, walking to the assembly of people ahead. Drawing closer to the gathering, I could feel it, the shift, the slowing of time, that moment before something might happen. The moment before a wingless girl might be swept into a jar, lid screwed tight.

Shh . . . If you are quiet, you can hear it, even now, the moment I first heard Cordelia Mayfield laugh. *Feathers.* The sound of it was light as a fistful of feathers tossed into the air, drifting, and falling slowly to tickle.

I could see her only from behind, soft blond hair pulled and twisted into a chignon at the nape of her slender neck. Her back, bare to the waist—red gown smoldering against her cool nakedness. Cordelia

Mayfield was magnificent, and I desperately wanted to be close to the bright and hot of her. Everyone did.

I slipped my fingers from Abel's and Jane's, shifting on my feet to test the queer terrain, toeing at the courage to move closer to the knot of people surrounding her.

"Who are all these folks?" I said. "I've never seen any of them before."

Violins began to play, the source—a group of musicians positioned at the top of the floating stairs leading to the catwalk that surrounded the place.

"Most of them are visiting from other places. New York, Atlanta, Savannah," Abel said. "The Mayfields know a lot of people."

"New York? That's a long ways away." Jane said. It seemed to me that Mistletoe was a long ways away, a world separate from everything else.

"You see that man with the cigar?" Abel said. "He's from Random House, a big publishing company up in New York City."

"Wowie," Jane said, smiling too big and wide at Abel.

"And you see that lady next to Miss Cordelia? The one with the black and white dress?"

I nodded. "Uh-huh."

"That's Miss JoAnne Woodward. She's an actress."

"How does she know the Mayfields?" Jane said.

"She's originally from around these parts. She and Miss Cordelia have known each other for as long I've known the Mayfields. Probably longer."

"She's pretty," Jane said, and she was, but her light, only an ember aside that Mayfield Shine.

Mrs. Mayfield laughed again. I glanced up into the ether imagining a shower of downy-white feathers. Her back, still turned to us, shifted, curving into the shape of the letter "S" before straightening again. She clapped her hands, commanding the room's attention. The knot of people loosened around her, all of them standing back to take her in.

The last pass of the violin bows released an eerie hum settling the conservatory into quiet.

Cordelia Mayfield turned, her patrician profile in full view. "I want to thank you for joining us tonight here at Mistletoe for this very special occasion."

She moved as if she stood upon a lazy Susan, rotating for the convenience of her guests—easing the labor of their gobbling eyes. The train of her dress wrapped slowly around her feet, then unfurling perfectly behind her. She stood with her arms at her sides, her chin—a regal tilt. "Tonight, we celebrate the birthday of our only living child. Our dearest Marlissa." The room applauded. Mrs. Mayfield pressed her palm to the bodice of her strapless gown. "We also pay tribute to the memory of our son, Patton." The applause ebbed—the room falling somber. "The world will never know what he was meant to be. What he would have become had he lived." She stepped forward, the train of her dress trailing over the brick floor—the slightest of scrapes amplified in the hush. "He will never grow to be like his father."

Mischievous little girl laughs rustled and stirred within the thick elephant-eared foliage surrounding us.

A smile tugged at Cordelia Mayfield's face, pushing away the cloud. She put her finger to her lips, looking about the room as if poised to tell a secret. "Did you know that there are sprites about the place?" She touched her fingertips to the hollow of her throat. "Fairies that dwell amongst the flowers. Fantastical creatures that fly about on gossamer wings." She turned her head from side to side, her diamond and ruby earrings dangling and shimmering above her shoulders, dusting away particulates of melancholy floating in the air.

The room smiled, a look of intrigue spreading across all faces. More whispery giggles shook at the leaves.

Mrs. Mayfield spread her pale arms wide, fluttering her fingertips, her stunning smile dissolving. The room looked on raptly, suspended in the theater of the moment. She quickly blinked three times and spoke again. "Wings. . ." She said it slowly holding it out until there was nothing left of it but the soft pout of her lips. Her eyes widened—her face betraying a glint of happiness. The room breathed again. "I've always thought that beautiful things were meant for wings."

Cordelia Mayfield's eyes flashed across the conservatory, landing upon me for a moment, then just beyond, her head turning back slowly to find me once again in the room. She looked up at the landing of the conservatory steps. Marlissa shimmered at the top, an icy-blue princess with butterfly wings.

"The world is a dangerous place for a beautiful thing," Mrs. Mayfield said, holding her gaze upon her daughter.

More titter rustled beyond the potted trees.

"I think you might be mistaken, sweetheart," said a man hidden away, barely visible in shadow.

Cordelia Mayfield returned her fingertips to her throat, not turning to look at the man.

"I believe it is the world that is in far greater peril from the charms of a beautiful thing," the man said, moving into the light, walking between two lit candelabras perched on plinths, his sculpted features carved deeper by the candlelight. He raised his crystal tumbler into the crowd's laughter and then to Mrs. Mayfield. She smiled a coy, narrow-eyed smile—her cheekbones sharper, more dangerous. He coiled his arm about her waist.

"Who's that?" I said.

"Mr. Kingston." Abel said. "Kingston Mayfield."

Marlissa's daddy. He was a nearly indescribable kind of handsome, the dangerous sort that flusters and taunts. He was a warm, summertime glow against the Mayfield women's snow-blanket complexions. His hair was deep shades of wheat. Cordelia and Marlissa—both fairer shades of blond.

"So, tell me, Cordelia, where does one hide her wings in a dress as exquisite . . ." Kingston Mayfield unwrapped his arm from her waist. "And as spare as this?" He rubbed his left hand along the perfect plain of her back.

Something was strange about that hand. From a distance, it appeared dark and wrinkled. A withered old man's hand—not at all a match to his right one.

Cordelia laughed again, only this time heavier. "A woman can be just as good as a man at concealing things." She raised her hand as if holding a glass. She looked to the assembly and then at her husband.

Laughter rippled across the room, and I joined them, unsure of why, only aware that I was happy to be there, happy to be a part of it all—to dwell within that dream world. To be close to that Mayfield Shine.

Mrs. Mayfield moved away from her husband and over to the staircase running her hand up the iron railing forged in the likeness of braided branches and leaves. She looked up the stairs and nodded. The violins played again—a sort of introduction.

Mrs. Mayfield glided across the room. The pace of her stride, brisk enough to fan her gown. She made a wide sweep, her train catching the air, lifting for the briefest moment from the bricks until she stopped at the grand piano tucked into the crook of a vestibule.

A blanket of velvety flowers draped the Steinway, cascading and spilling across the floor. Only once had I ever seen such stunning flowers as these, the flowers Daddy sent to Mama, the bouquet he smashed to the floor. There in the lush warmth of the Chrystal Palace, acres of flowers grew magnificently and abundantly as the weeds tangling and choking the grass in our yard.

"Mr. J.M. Barrie once wrote." Mrs. Mayfield paused, settling the room into quiet. She dropped her voice into a stage whisper. "When the first baby laughed for the first time . . ." She stopped again, the room leaning to listen. She fluttered her fingers like raindrops. "His laugh broke into a million pieces." The pianist wiggled his fingers into the keys playing a mischievous tinkle.

Mrs. Mayfield touched her hand to her throat. "And they all went skipping about," she said, undulating her other hand in the air like a wave. She breathed in heavy and smiled, unsheathing those cheekbones. "And that was the beginning of fairies."

Stillness settled within the glass, jungle box—heads looking beyond, expecting perhaps for a curtain to rise. I joined the room searching, anticipating what might come next.

The piano ebbed. Violins woke, bows sliding into strings.

And then, singing. Soprano voices. A duet.

"That's opera," I said, turning to Jane.

"Really? I would have never figured that out on my own." She smiled, and I pinched her elbow.

I followed the gaze of the room to the top of the stairs where Marlissa had been. Two women dressed in identical, white chiffon gowns now stood at the rail. Their voices, a silvery blue, drifted and spread across the room like dandelion seeds. Not since the night of Mama's dream-fire song had I seen music. I looked up, watching their notes bob about. I thought of Etta Mae, knowing she would love to have been there to hear them.

A fairy peeked through the trees. Then another. And another. Their wings springing free from the hold of branches and leaves. Each of the girls wore a different costume, each representing a flower. A collective of breathy *aww's* and *mmm's* spilled across the room.

Finally, out popped Virginia. I pressed my elbow into Jane's side. "Oh, brother." Jane rolled her eyes. Virginia was draped in yellow—not the best choice for her sallow coloring. Standing there, swaying in the palm of illusion, Virginia Fenton might have been mistaken for almost attractive.

I leaned in and whispered, "What kind of flower is she?"

"A stink weed," Jane said, her deadpan expression making it all the funnier. Abel heard, turning loose a snigger. Jane and I joined him, covering our mouths—our shoulders heaving as Virginia and the others spun and twirled ribbons, their new charm bracelets rattling in time with the music.

The fairy court huddled into a circle, then unfolded like petals into a semi-circle. Posed in the middle was Marlissa *en pointe*, satin ribbons crisscrossing up her legs, her arms rounded above her head in fifth position.

Applause blossomed as she stood effortlessly on the tips of her toes, the faceted jewels of her tiara tossing off sparks.

"I didn't know she could dance," I whispered to Jane.

"Me neither."

Abel brushed his hand against mine. He spoke in a hush. "Resplendent."

Resplendent. Abel used my word, the word I gave him just that Tuesday morning when he delivered the paper, a word to add to his notebook, the word I found for him special in a dictionary in the school library.

He dared to say it again. "Resplendent." Only this time he gestured with those long-lank fingers at the butterfly-fairy. He used my word on her, passing my gift to Marlissa, the girl who had everything.

Kingston Mayfield stood to the back of it all watching his daughter spin, her spiral curls bouncing against her shoulders with each pause. He regarded her with great intensity, a studying eye.

A gentle wave of yearning pushed against me—the sort akin to jealousy. Had Daddy ever looked upon me in such a way? I lifted my eyes up from Marlissa to Kingston Mayfield. He looked away from his daughter, settling his eyes on me.

Startled, I looked away quickly, an awkward jerk of the head. *Resplendent.* I flashed my eyes at Abel. Again, I looked at Mr. Mayfield, this time willing my eyes still—surrendering to his aqua eyed-stare—keeping him from Marlissa, taking a little something back for myself. Was it stealing? Did I care?

My skin thrilled, millions of pushpins sticking into me. Someone else was watching. I pried my eyes loose, scanning the room. *Mrs. Mayfield.* I fought the urge to look away, holding onto her for as long as she would have me. At last, she looked away, settling her gaze back upon Marlissa.

The room was adrift in an imaginary woodland, caught in the spell of Marlissa's flawless arabesque and *jeté grand.* She spun in a whirl of perfect notes collecting like snow upon the guests—notes clinging to her lashes when her body slowed, an effect I was certain only I could see.

Maybe I was not resplendent, nor could I dance on my toes. But I possessed other things, wondrous things lost to all the others. I could taste music, could see it—right into its soul. This was my gift and my gift alone. And that made me special, did it not?

I smiled back across the room at Mr. Mayfield, lifting my chin a little higher. There could be no harm in taking just a little more from a girl with so much.

The last of the notes fell over the room lightly dusting Marlissa as she held her final pose, the fairy court bowing in a circle all around her. I glanced over at Mrs. Mayfield, her eyes passing across her husband and me.

Then came the scream, a hot, shrill shock, and then another.

"Fire!"

Chapter 24

Flames licked at the hem of the woman's gown. She turned in circles, her movement giving breath to the fire. The room came fully alive then, shaken from the dream of Marlissa's fairy dance.

The room swelled with panic, women shrieking. Fairies squealed, scampering back into the trees.

Kingston Mayfield grabbed hold of the woman, stilling her. He stomped at the flame until there was nothing left of it but a soft billow of smoke at the woman's feet, giving the appearance she hovered upon a cloud.

"Are you alright?" Mrs. Mayfield hurried to the woman.

"She's going to be just fine. No harm done," Kingston Mayfield said, placing his arm around the breathless woman. "Looks like she stood a little too close to the fire."

I inspected the scene finding no candle burning low to the ground.

"You've always been one for attention," Mrs. Mayfield smiled, lightening the mood and the woman's face. The room breathed out nervous laughter.

Mrs. Mayfield called up at the quartet. "Play something splendid. Something adagio. Something to smother a flame." Music spilled again over the rails.

Mrs. Mayfield took hold of the woman's arms, leaning in to kiss each of her cheeks. She pulled away, snapping her fingers. "Mercy?" In just a moment, Mercy emerged from beneath the stairs. "Please take Mrs. Parker up to my room and find something lovely for her to wear."

"Yes, ma'am," Mercy dipped her head.

As quick as that, order was restored.

Jane looked pale, her coloring all leaked out. "You all right?" I asked.

"I think," she said, her voice warbling.

From behind us, a woman whispered. "That's how he died, you know."

I would have turned around if my attention had not been demanded by the mere existence of Kingston and Cordelia Mayfield standing together, light fluorescing and igniting around them.

Mr. Mayfield took hold of his wife's elbow. She pulled away, but he grabbed hold tighter, wrapping his arm around her waist. His body swayed to the music, coercing Mrs. Mayfield to move with him. He pushed his mouth against her ear, his lips moving slowly. Mrs. Mayfield jerked her head away, pulling herself apart from Mr. Mayfield.

I turned back to Jane. Her color slowly returned to her face. "Where's Abel?"

Jane pointed. "Over there with Princess Butterfly and her merry band of mosquitoes."

Abel stood close to Marlissa, smiling and laughing his golden-boy laugh. What other words of mine was he giving away? The fairies crept back in from the trees to surround them both.

"Miss Jane Fenton, you are a picture this evening," Mr. Kingston Mayfield said, walking over, his baritone voice, elegant—the ends of his words melting lazily off his tongue. His sudden approach flustered me, and I was overwhelmed with the sense I should run.

Jane's cheeks splotched when she smiled. Before she could speak, he moved in closer, turning to look down at me. "I have not had the honor, but I do not believe introductions are necessary." Mr. Mayfield was even more handsome up close, his eyes more crystalline-blue than appearing at a distance. "I knew just the moment I saw you that you had to be Grace Newell's child. I would know her face anywhere. You know, she worked for me until your daddy passed on." He touched his hand to my cheek, my stomach lurching like a dream-fall. It occurred to me then that Mama had not been back to Mistletoe to clean since we were there together. Did she quit? Did Mrs. Mayfield fire her?

He lifted my face with his ruined hand, the dark and wrinkled one that did not belong. He pulled at my chin until my eyes met his. He studied my face, the moment passing long and awkwardly. Finally, he spoke. "Tell me, do you possess your mother's gift?"

It was impossible to move my head with my chin clasped in his hand. "I don't think so." I stood motionless, unsure if he meant her gypsy ways.

"Perhaps another extraordinary something?" he said, releasing my face. I locked my eyes onto his disfigured hand.

With a half-cocked smile, he regarded and rubbed at his bad hand with his good. "You want to know what happened, don't you?"

I did not speak or gesture. He bent down so close I could smell the exotic tang of liquor and lemon peel on his breath. His smile began to evaporate, and when it was completely gone, his lips parted to speak.

Mrs. Mayfield floated our direction, her earrings hardly moving. She reached out touching Jane's shoulder, acknowledging her presence. "Hello, dear," she said. "I hope my husband is not boring you with the details of his personal tragedy." She took her husband's strange hand to hold against her cheek. "Did he tell you of the time he tried to hold fire in his hand?" Mrs. Mayfield laughed. This time there was weight to her laughter. She turned from Jane to me, all mirth gone from her face. She released Mr. Mayfield's hand. Mr. Mayfield held it out in front of himself, blowing upon it as one might extinguish a match.

Cordelia Mayfield leaned down, her dress making the slightest rustle. A rush of *déjà vu* took hold. I held tight in my focus to keep my legs from buckling. Was she going to slap me? A violin clucked, the out-of-tune note causing my shoulders to flinch. Her face grew close, those green eyes shifting across the color spectrum in the changing light. Her warm cheek pressed into mine, her ruby and diamond earring scraping my face. She whispered so only I could hear.

"Some things in this world are meant to burn." *Burrrrnnn.* She stretched this word sending a stream of warm air into my ear.

Across the room, Abel's laughter caught in the chime of fairy chirp. Recklessness took hold, hurried and untempered a thing as it is. And then I did it. I pushed her word back at her—Abel's secondhand gift to me. "Conflagration." I spoke it barely above a murmur, but she heard. Her eyes held mine, binding us there together until finally she blinked. She pulled her stunning face away, leaving behind her deep, floral musk, a tiny scratch on my cheek, and the want for more of her—the good kind of hurt I knew she could give. The sort I craved.

Kingston Mayfield and Jane looked on as Mrs. Mayfield regained her impeccable posture. "Kingston, we have guests to attend to up at the pavilion. Shall we?" she said, her voice, lullaby-sweet.

"If you two ladies are done sharing secrets?" Kingston Mayfield said.

"For now," she said.

Kingston Mayfield extended his arm for Mrs. Mayfield to slip her hand through. "Evening ladies," he said, nodding to Jane and me. He turned back to look at me as they walked away—his face, queer, a look I can hardly describe. Hungry. Deprived. Beguiled.

"What did she say?" Jane asked, grabbing hold of my arm.

"Who?" I watched the Mayfields draw closer to their daughter.

Jane shook my arm. "Mrs. Mayfield."

I lied, a thing I grew better at with each passing day. "She likes my dress."

"Is that all?" Jane's voice sank.

"Uh-huh," I said, watching Cordelia Mayfield glide across the room, guests leaning in to speak and admire. Perhaps Miss Wessie was right. Maybe Mrs. Mayfield did go mad when Patton fell out that window.

Abel yelled from across the room. "Analeise. Jane. I'll meet you up at the party tent. Mr. Kingston wants to introduce me to someone."

Jane and I waved back as he walked away with Kingston and Cordelia Mayfield. Marlissa and her entourage stayed behind, staring in our direction.

"What are they looking at?" Jane said.

"I think they're looking at us."

They stood quiet at first, a gnarl of wings and spangled tulle. Somewhere within the clod, the vibrations began—girl jabber.

The green fairy blew into a wooden flute, a few quick notes ascending a scale. The shake of a tambourine followed, and then the hollow clank of rhythm sticks. Those without instruments twirled ribbons as the fairy band riled. A moment passed, the noise gaining some semblance of unison; and when it did, it transformed into something close to music.

Marlissa pirouetted and pointed to Jane and me. I prepared for what was coming. I braced myself, holding my breath. Waiting for them to swoop.

Chapter 25

Jane and I stood captive in the quiet eye of the fairy circle, the two of us waiting for them to dive and sting.

Marlissa stepped forward, a bewitching simper electrifying her already magnificent face.

I knew there must be truth in Kingston Mayfield's words. *The world is in far greater peril from the charms of a beautiful thing.*

"Happy birthday," Jane finally said. Jane's offering seemed to please Marlissa, so I repeated the sentiment.

"Thank you for coming," Marlissa said, speaking with the ease and flow of a party waltz.

Marlissa came closer—so near I could feel the pull of static crackling in the tulle of her ballet costume.

"Your dress is pretty," Marlissa said, looking at me. There was no hint of jest in her voice. Surely, she was speaking to another.

Jane cut her eyes sharply at me. "She's talking to you."

The fairies laughed.

"Mama made it." Immediately I regretted sharing too much, that my dress was homemade. I waited. There was no laughter—no looks of pity or revulsion.

"It's splendid," Marlissa said. "Isn't it?" Marlissa looked around the circle.

Splendid. I liked the sound of it—a fairy word.

The sprites nodded and tweeted amongst themselves. The green fairy blew a few short toots into her flute. Virginia was the only one amongst them who stood silent, fiddling with her charm bracelet.

Marlissa reached out and touched her tapered fingers to my skirt. "Taffeta," she said.

"From Mama's store."

"It's beautiful." It was the first time she ever smiled directly at me, the sensation hot like a sunburn.

"I liked your dance." I was unable to think of anything else to say.

Marissa smiled again. Jane, visibly unnerved, wrapped her arms about herself.

"Fairies!" Marlissa commanded, scooping the air with her hands, her arms moving up and over her head. The edges of the circle melted. The girls moved closer. The smell of rose water and lavender lay heavy upon the group. Their warm, cloying, sugary breath overpowered as they pulled in tight.

Marlissa pried herself loose from the huddle, leaping atop an enormous, copper mushroom. "Tonight, we fairies are in search of a mortal girl," Marlissa pulled her shoulders back, her crown sparking with the slightest movement. "A very special, mortal girl worthy of wings."

The fairies clapped and trilled.

"She must be fair, and graceful, and mischievous," Marlissa said. "Might you be that girl, Analeise Newell?"

Jane's face flushed, red splotches making their way up her neck.

Yes, I was desperate to be that girl. A special girl with wings. I looked away from Jane, my voice louder, more frenzied than I intended when I spoke. "Yes."

Fairy-hoots echoed about.

Marlissa held up her hand. "It won't be easy. Fairies must not only be beautiful, they must also be cunning." She sucked in her cheeks and tilted back her head, her costume tossing mottled light up her neck.

The air in the room turned viscous, bottlenecking in my throat.

"You must earn your fairy wings." She rounded her shoulders touching her fingers to her throat just like her mother. "Solve this riddle and you may join us."

The fairies were quiet, their eyes lustrous and hungry with anticipation.

Marlissa placed her feet into first position. "Be careful. You have but three chances. Are you ready?"

I nodded, looking away from Jane.

Marlissa pressed her Cupid's bow lips together and spoke.

Underneath a cupola—swathed in Claire de lune
I stood within a garden where
Stone flowers are known to bloom.

When she finished, she held her hands before her as though holding a bouquet of flowers. A rhythm stick struck the floor. I followed it with my eyes until it rolled to a stop at the base of an urn. A breeze stirred through the open windows, pushing the faint drift of music into the conservatory.

"I ask you Analeise Newell, where do I stand?" Marlissa's voice had grown deeper—womanly.

Garden. Stone flowers. I could not think. *I don't know.*

Marlissa recited her poem once more. "I ask you Analeise Newell, where do I stand?"

I glanced over to Jane, standing alone, shoved away from the group.

What grows from the ground? Stone doesn't grow from the ground. Then, a thought. No—more like a memory. *Daddy's funeral.*

"Where do I stand?"

I shut my eyes, feeling safer in the dark.

"You must answer me now," Marlissa said.

"You stand in . . ."

"I stand where?"

"A cemetery?"

The pause grew and spread, wrapping tight around me until finally it splintered—fairy chirp leaking through the cracks.

"You are a cunning girl, Analeise Newell." Marlissa said.

I opened my eyes to the room's golden hue.

"Congratulations," Marlissa said, her pretty face brightening, her hands planted upon on her hips. "You have earned your fairy wings."

Rejoice broke out amongst the fairies. Marlissa clapped her hands and hollered over the squawk. "Be quiet, and bring her to me."

The girls swept around, pushing me to stand at the base of the mushroom.

Marlissa pointed her finger down at me. The others backed away leaving me to stand alone with her, the proximity unsettling.

"Are you prepared?" Marlissa said.

I nodded. But I was hardly ready, the sudden shock of it all leaving me discombobulated.

"William Butler Yeats. Do you know him?"

"Does he go to our school?"

The group turned loose its raucous laugh, Virginia's goblin cackle the loudest. Even across the distance from where they stood, I smelled their fairy breath.

Marlissa's face remained stoic. I stared up at her, my neck aching from standing so close.

"Mr. Yeats was a poet and has long since passed." Her voice once again was queer, possessing the quality of someone older.

My face grew hot. "I didn't know."

"Shall we?" Marlissa asked, looking out at the fairies.

They clapped and trilled.

Marlissa placed her finger to her lips to settle the commotion. "Come away, O human child!" she commanded.

The fairies repeated her words, together, their voices booming and echoing through the vast Chrystal Palace, now emptied of everyone but us.

"To the waters and the wild. With a fairy hand in hand." Marlissa's tone went soft and wistful, the little girl quality returning to her voice. "For the world's more full of weeping, than you can understand." Marlissa crossed her hands and held them to her chest until the others finished repeating her words, and then she lowered her arms to her sides. "Analeise. For you to receive your wings, another fairy must sacrifice her own." Her proclamation anchored the room. "Virginia." Marlissa looked to the back of the huddle.

Fairy heads turned, eyes glinting in Virginia's direction. Virginia's face drained to pale, all the sallow and pink gone away. She fiddled with her bracelet, rubbing at the fairy charm as if conjuring luck.

Marlissa jumped from the mushroom and grabbed hold of my hand. Lacing her fingers through mine, she pulled us quickly through the flap of wings. Virginia's eyes shifted from side to side, a quiet plea for help from the others.

"Your wings, Virginia." Marlissa said, still holding onto my hand, the perfect fit of our fingers undoing me.

Virginia, who stood taller than the rest of us, bent forward. "Marlissa?" Her voice cracked. Would Virginia Fenton cry? Could she?

"They were never meant to be yours to keep," Marlissa said, her voice legato once more. "It's my birthday. I decide." Marlissa's grip on my hand tensed. "Virginia."

Virginia stroked her bracelet.

"You can keep the bracelet, but your wings belong to Analeise now."

My heart sank for Virginia. She flashed her eyes up and down me—an unmistakable and familiar look of disgust rushing onto her face. This was the Virginia I liked best—the Virginia from whom I could steal wings. The one I could hate.

"Help her," Marlissa said.

A tizzy of fairies whorled around Virginia, pulling and tugging until her wings came free. At first, she stood stiff and defiant, making the task difficult, the inevitability of the moment passing across her eyes. Finally, she relented, her arms flopping loose at her sides.

Marlissa let go my hand. The girls closed in around me, tying the wings over my shoulders, belting the gold cording around my waist—the excess dangling with tasseled ends.

"Splendid," Marlissa said, using her fairy word again. "How do they feel?"

I looked over at Virginia, her face and shoulders gone slack. They felt heavier than I imagined. "Perfect." I averted my eyes from Virginia.

The fairies all swarmed and fussed pushing Virginia over to stand with Jane. *Jane.* She was colorless as her sister.

Marlissa took my hand again pulling me closer. "You've never seen my room before, have you?"

I shook my head.

"Would you like to?"

"Yes." More than anything, I wanted to go.

"Fairies! Go on up to the party. I'm taking Analeise to my room."

The girls struck up their instruments and marched away, leaving us in the wake of their racket.

"Shall we?" Marlissa said, extending her hand.

I turned to find Jane. Her face had changed—a countenance I did not recognize. "Jane?" I said, tilting my head to beckon her forward.

"Jane can't come," Marlissa pulled me a few steps forward. "No mortal girls allowed." In that moment, I could tell they were sisters, both Jane and Virginia's faces similar with hurt and confusion. "Analeise, are you coming?"

No mortal girls allowed. Who wanted to be a mortal girl? Not me. I had my wings, and I wanted to wear them. Surely, Jane would understand. "We won't be long," I said. "We'll meet you up at the party."

Jane's face hardened, looking more like Virginia than ever before. I smiled back, nodding as if all were well—that nothing had or would ever change.

Marlissa held out her hand to me, and I took hold, curling my fingers through hers, to savor our perfect fit.

Outside, Marlissa led me along the path running aside the water cascade. At first, my wings resisted the night air, pulling heavily against my shoulders, unsettling my balance, my body no longer feeling like my own.

I imagined myself a cicada, squeezing myself free from my shell. Each step forward, shedding and leaving the old Analeise Newell behind, the new version of myself wriggling loose.

Half-way up the slope, I began to learn the trick of it, the trick of wings. I hastened my pace, working to be gone from myself all the quicker.

Hot air balloons hovered above, the flames dappling the ground. The night crackled. My skin hummed. Marlissa glided at my side.

Soon. Very soon. I would become someone new.

I am a beautiful thing.

Chapter 26

Marlissa and I wound our way up the floating staircase, the enormous place almost completely quiet—only distant party sounds seeping through the walls.

Slowing my pace, I admired the portraits and landscapes hanging in massive gold frames curving along the wall. Marlissa did not look about as I did. Her ordinary, my extraordinary.

She alighted the landing before I did, turning to find me steps below her. "You're slow."

She was a girl born to win races, I thought, remembering her playground victory. "And you're fast," I said, my eyes drifting up to the last picture hanging above Marlissa's head, a portrait of the Mayfields.

The painting was magnificent, possessing a three-dimensional quality—a moment so real it seemed to jut from the frame. I took the next three steps, desperate to be closer, wondering if I might feel the warmth of their brilliant, Mayfield skin. I took hold of the railing, to root myself there upon the Persian stair runner.

Immediately, I knew whom it was standing in front of Kingston and Cordelia. *Patton Mayfield.* I fought the urge to gasp, to reach out and touch him. He appeared to be the brightest of the four, his skin, a warmer gold than his father's. His eyes, fluorescent green, and lips—full like Marlissa's parted ever so slightly—perhaps a single, beguiling word sliding out.

Marlissa stood in front of her mother and next to Patton, her snowy-blond hair falling to her waist. Kingston Mayfield's ruined hand rested on Patton's shoulder, except that in the painting, his hand was as perfect as the other.

"Mother doesn't much care for that piece."

"Why? It's so pretty," I turned back to the portrait. It was nearly impossible to look away from the thing, as if the Mayfields themselves stood there beckoning within the frame.

"Mother says it might as well be a photograph. It's flat and soulless." Marlissa lifted herself onto the tips of her toes then lowered herself slowly back to the floor. "Mother hates soulless things."

"It's much better than an old photograph." I reached out to touch the frame, as if the very act would bring me closer to them, change me in some way.

"Mother would disagree. Perhaps you don't understand such things." Marlissa sucked in her cheeks. "Father says it's no easy task to capture the essence of a Mayfield."

"I see." Still, I thought the painting perfect. The artist had captured what Miss Wessie called the Mayfield Shine. To me, that seemed plenty.

"The artist took liberties," Marlissa said. "Those aren't even the clothes we wore." She lifted herself up again onto her toes. "Do you ever wonder what you look like to other people?"

"Sometimes," I said, staring up at the portrait. I studied their clothing, Kingston and Patton's white, loose cuffed and collared shirts. Cordelia and Marlissa wore pale yellow dresses, Marlissa's falling just above the knee. Mrs. Mayfield's was more formal, flowing to the edges, nearly tumbling from the frame. Mrs. Mayfield's shoulders were bare, her hair gathered up loosely, soft tendrils tickling her neck.

The weight of my wings began to lighten, fanning my confidence, but still I needed to hold tight to the rail. "Your mama looks resplendent," I said, reclaiming my word—using it to my liking.

"Doesn't she?" Marlissa looked to the painting for the first time. "My room is this way," she said, turning to walk across the landing.

I hurried up the stairs behind her, trying to keep time with her ballet walk. I turned my feet out just as she did, my duck-like gait in stark contrast to her lovely march.

Her hair was a slightly warmer shade of blond than depicted in the painting, but a coolness still mingled within the strands of gold. The curl loosened since her performance, now hanging in lustrous waves, a look I thought even more becoming. I resisted the urge to reach out and touch her. Was this what it felt like to be Etta Mae? Always chasing close behind.

I followed Marlissa through towering double doors. "Is this your room?"

Marlissa continued across the carpets that covered the wide-planked floor, her slippers making the faintest thud. *"Oui."*

The room was incandescent, the light, golden and bronzed at the edges. A chandelier hung from a wind-swept sky, its crystals tumbling from a cluster of gilded, leafy vines.

A silk wallpaper of a woodland covered the walls, an effect meant to deceive the eye. An elaborately carved tester bed anchored the space— miles of mossy green silk draping across the canopy and puddling onto the floor.

"Do you like my birthday gift?" Marlissa asked. She stood at the side of a black, grand piano occupying a large, recessed space framed in floor to ceiling windows.

"It's beautiful."

"You can play it if you like."

"Really?"

Marlissa stepped to the side, motioning to the bench. "You play well," she said.

"That is so sweet. Thank you, Marlissa." I wanted to roll myself up in her flattery, to be alone for a moment to enjoy it. I tucked my chin and lowered myself onto the seat, positioning myself so the bottom of my wings cleared the edge.

"With whom have you studied?" she said, her voice formal but soft.

I repeated her elegant string of words silently to myself. "Mostly just me, but Mama hired Mr. Bloom to give me lessons."

"Mr. Bloom." She spoke more softly than before. "Is anyone else in your family musical?"

"Not really," I said, not wanting to make mention of Daddy, of his honky-tonk influence, of his backwater blues. I ran my fingers across the covered keys. "Your mama sure plays pretty."

"Mother plays well," she said. "But Father is the true talent."

"Your daddy?" I regretted my lie, the lost opportunity to connect us through our fathers. I thought of Mr. Mayfield's large hands, what must have been a great effort to manage the keys.

"It's a gift he mostly keeps to himself. Unless he needs it." Her delicate cheekbones lifted with the spread of her smile, a startling and beautiful effect. "Mother says that's how he wooed her. Mayfield men are dubious that way." She reached up, touching at the highest point of her tiara with her index finger. Marlissa brought her hand back down, examining her finger, then extended it to me to inspect the tiny droplet of blood that formed on the tip.

"You cut yourself."

She put her finger to her mouth, shutting her eyes. "It's just a prick," she said, showing me the tidied finger. "All better now." She smiled, tilting her head to the side, the light from the chandelier catching and shimmering in her eyes.

Did Marlissa know hurt the way I did, that it can be good, that it can comfort and soothe? "Did Patton play the piano?" His name was thick on my tongue. I immediately regretted the question, afraid I might unhinge the moment with talk of her poor, dead, beautiful brother.

Marlissa straightened herself. "Of all of us, Mother said he was the most talented." She leaned into the piano with both hands. "Nature is such a wicked thing, don't you think? How is it that a boy can play so beautifully, with so much feeling, when he has none?" She paused, studying my face before speaking again. "Nature's camouflage," she finally said, pushing herself from the piano.

Camouflage? "I'm sorry. I don't understand."

"That's what Mother calls it. A way to hide . . . to trick . . . to appear to be something different than you are."

I shook my head. I still did not understand.

"Like a lizard that can change colors and blend. Or . . ." She rested her hand at her throat. "Or a beautiful flowering plant that eats flies."

"You mean Patton was like a lizard?"

Marlissa's soft edges began to harden. "I'm saying that some people are not always what they seem."

I stared out through the window into the darkness, her gaze following mine. Moments of silence passed, only the *creak* and *pop* of the floor marking the void. Finally, she turned and walked away from me to her dressing table. "Play something for me," she said, tossing her hair over her shoulders.

The cover lifted easily, the smell of newness rising to meet me. I knew immediately what I would play, Mama's dream-fire song. The song Cordelia Mayfield played that first day I came to Mistletoe, the song Marlissa said did not belong to me. I wanted to give it back to her, play it one last time, leave it there forever—a thank you for letting me back inside, for giving me wings. I played, presto agitato.

Instantly, I could see the colors of my own playing, the pink throb of light around my fingers, the color flicking off as my hands ran the length of impossible arpeggios.

Marlissa stood to the side of her dressing table. The shards of light glowed cotton candy pink, deepening to vermilion. The chunks of light came together outlining Marlissa, caressing, and then crowding her contours, as if to devour her. She cast a stare upon me, a look I hoped was awe or something akin to jealousy. I knew jealousy, all its prickly tines. Her jaw tensed—fingers curling into fists. No, it was not jealousy. It was anger.

She made her way to me, her steps slow at first, then quickening with the beat. I looked up from the keys, knowing where my fingers should go. I should have been frightened, but I could not look away from that face. The evening breeze pushed through the open windows, meeting her stride, lifting her hair from her face—her cheekbones shadowed from the color of my music, her wings striking hard at the crimson air.

Still, I played, hungry for what might come next. For the first time, I tasted my own music, swallowing down the sweet peony-flavored notes, the rapid accumulation of saliva clotting and forming a knot in my throat.

Marlissa's lips moved, forming a string of words I could not hear, deaf to all but my playing. She reached out her slender hand slamming the cover over the keys, my fingers barely escaping the piano's bite.

The hammer of the lid echoed with the hum of aborted bass strings. I jerked and blinked from the clatter. Marlissa appeared as shocked as I that it happened, as if someone else did it. We stood there, the two of us silent in the ebb of vibration and fading tint of magenta.

"Patton hated playing that," she said, her breathing rapid and jagged. "But Mother made him anyway."

"Why?"

"Why did he hate it? Or why did Mother make him play it?"

"Both, I guess." I looked upon Marlissa, her angry edges tucking back inside, her face softening, her breathing calm again.

"It was an engagement gift to Mother from Father, a sonata written just for her. Three perfect movements."

I never knew such a thing existed, that a person could own a song, could give it as a gift. "Why did he hate it? Was it too hard for him to play?"

Marlissa laughed, wrapping her arms about herself, her wings giving a slight flutter. "Hardly. He could play anything with little effort. He was technically perfect."

"Then why did he hate it?"

Marlissa took in a whisp of air, her back straightening from the effort, her wings more regal. "The third movement, the piece you played. It requires playing with what Mother calls 'abandon'. You have to let part of yourself go. You have to—you have to balance it with emotion."

"Did he play with abandon?"

Marlissa looked quickly over her shoulder and leaned in close. "He could never let go." She spoke in a hush. "He was always in control. That's why Mother made him play it over and over again."

"To help him play with abandon?"

Marlissa reached up for her tiara. For a moment, I thought she might prick her finger again, but she lowered her arm, resting it at her side. "No," she said. "To help him feel something." Marlissa stepped back from the piano. "I have to ask that you don't play that song again. It belongs to Mother. No one else." She looked about the room and then back at me. "It upsets her."

It occurred to me that the song distressed Marlissa as well. "I won't. Cross my heart," I said, drawing over my chest. "But why does she play it, if it makes her feel sad?"

Marlissa held my gaze, the gentle blow and suck of curtains reminding me to breathe, far off party sounds stirring the quiet. "To keep away the ghosts . . ."

Her words shook me, that topsy-turvy feeling of stepping into a hole—of quickly trying to right myself. *Ghosts?*

Solemnity unraveled from her face, a smile slowly forming, and then that Mayfield, feathery peal of laughter. She reached out, laying a comforting hand upon my wrist as though it had all been a joke.

"Silly girl," she said.

The light from the chandelier spilled into her eyes, setting them to glisten, and I took hold of the edges of the bench, steadying my shaking hands, eager to put aside our peculiar conversation. I was unnerved. *Ghosts.* The word lingered.

Marlissa spoke of ghosts before—that day at school in the music room. She had asked me the question, and now it seemed I should ask her. No—that I must ask her.

"Marlissa, are you afraid of ghosts?"

She clamped her hand more fiercely around my wrist. "Only the bad ones," she said, her breath warm and sweet, a strange bit of laughter tumbling out. She turned loose, looking down at herself, smoothing her fairy gown. "We should freshen ourselves before we return to the party." In one fluid movement, she was gone, walking back to her dressing table. "Join me."

I followed slowly, hoping to purchase more time with her, to stretch the moment there in that strange place.

Marlissa swept her hand across the tufted vanity seat. "Sit."

Beautiful things lay atop the polished mahogany surface. A suite of monogrammed silver. A brush, comb, and hand mirror rested at an angle on the right. On the left sat an exquisite, cut crystal perfume bottle just like Mama's. I slid my hand across the vanity's cool, smooth finish touching the bottle with the tips of my fingers. "You have the same perfume as my Mama," I said, excited to have this, another thing in common. I faced the looking glass studying Marlissa's reflection.

"Mother always gives me the last little bit when a new bottle arrives." She stood behind me fingering and arranging my curls. "A par fumier in Paris makes it for her. It's her custom scent." She glanced up at me then. "Meant only for her."

It was evident from the tone of her voice she thought I was lying, that Mama's perfume could not possibly be a twin to Mrs. Mayfield's. I picked up the bottle and brought it to my nose, taking in the richly layered, floral fragrance. I smelled my own wrist—the single squirt I stole from Mama's room, still aromatic and alive on my skin. There was no mistaking, Mrs. Mayfield's perfume was the smell of New Mama.

Marlissa put her hand on my shoulder, a consoling gesture with the slightest pinch of condescension. I found the glow of her green eyes once again in the mirror, and then my own. Perhaps she was correct.

Marlissa moved her hand to my homemade necklace. "Pretty. Would you like to see my birthday gift from Father?"

I could hardly imagine anything more spectacular than a grand piano. "Of course."

Marlissa moved from behind me and pulled at one of the vanity's drawers revealing yards of rolled up hair ribbons. She opened another.

"Mercy must have moved it." She moved past me across the room to an armoire.

I watched her from the mirror, the tilted angle erasing the floor beneath her slippers. Her fluid movement gave lazy sway to her wings, creating the appearance she rode a gentle breeze.

I looked down into the drawer of hair ribbons. So many of them. Would she ever miss one? I watched my hand, a separate living thing grab at a lovely, sky-blue ribbon.

"I found it," Marlissa said.

I stuffed the ribbon into the bodice of my dress watching her float back across the room holding a pale blue velvet box in the palm of her hand. *It is just one little ribbon. Just a little something to remember I was here, that I was with Marlissa in her room.*

At my side, she stood, opening the box, its hinges protesting ever so slightly. Inside was a golden heart-shaped locket, the edges of the heart encrusted with small diamonds.

"Are they real diamonds?" I reached out to touch the edge of the box.

"Aren't all diamonds real? Shall I try it on you?"

She unfastened the clasp, reaching around, pressing gently into my wings, threading the chain beneath my hair and around my neck.

"It's spectacular," she said, pressing into me again, careful not to bend my wings. She studied me in the mirror. "It becomes you."

I stared back, confused by the reflection, of the two girls' faces hovering within the frame—high cheekbones and bright burning eyes, unsure of where I began and Marlissa ended. I pressed the cool locket against my skin. Was it possible that I was pretty? Every bit as lovely as Marlissa?

"Do you want to know a secret?" Marlissa pressed her cheek to mine, her hands squeezing my shoulders.

Of course, I did. Anything to be closer to her, any excuse to stay. "Yes, please."

She leaned down, her lips fluttering against my ear. "I hate Virginia Fenton," she whispered, pausing between each word.

A chill shot up through me, not because of the sentiment, but because of the weight—the uncanny nature of her words. "But I thought she was your friend."

Marlissa smiled. "That's the point." She looked into the mirror, pinching at her cheeks. "Now it's your turn."

"My turn?"

"Yes. It's your turn to tell me a secret."

I killed Daddy, and Mama and Miss Wessie helped. It was the greatest of all my secrets, and even the promise of friendship with Marlissa Mayfield could not pry the ugly truth from me. My mouth opened a bit, quickly thinking of what I could share that would not send me off to jail.

"I'm waiting." A few moments passed, and she spoke again. "Secrets between fairies are the most sacred of all." Her voice soothed like the cool side of a cotton pillowcase. She placed her hand on my shoulder. "I'm quite good at keeping secrets."

I stood there silent, thinking. What could I give her? Why would she need anything more than she already had? Why would she want my secrets?

"Do you not believe me?"

Beguile. Who could ever resist her smile? That shine. "I believe you."

Her smile diminished. Her features sharpened. "Good, because I have already kept a secret for you, my dearest fairy friend." She wound one of my curls around her finger.

"Silly girl," I said. I waited for her to laugh, to show me that once again she was playing another of her games. There was nothing that betrayed her—just somber resolve.

"I don't know what I would do." Marlissa coiled more of my hair around her finger. "If I were in your place."

I attempted to turn my head, to face her, but she held firm to my hair, keeping me face to face with my reflection in the looking glass.

"What place?"

"I don't know how you carry the burden . . . the shame of it." She studied her reflection as if just discovering some new striking angle to her face.

Again, I tried to get free, but she was unrelenting, wrapping my hair tighter around her finger. The pain was glorious. I enjoyed the feeling of being bound to her—being held firmly in place. It was the feeling that something was about to shift that frightened me.

"The shame of what?"

"Of having a colored sister," she whispered.

Colored sister. She released my hair—the curl unwinding, my senses spiraling with it. My head went heavy, bobbing forward, as though Marlissa had been holding it up with marionette strings. *Colored sister.* I stood up and turned to face her. "I don't have a colored sister." As I finished, I felt the realization, the weight of it like a punch in the gut.

"Mother says these things happen. It's your father who is to blame," Marlissa touched my elbow with her cool hand. "Mother says that all trouble of the world is laid upon it by men." I thought of Miss Wessie, of what she said about God being a woman. "No one can hold it against you. Can they?" She released her question slowly from her lips, letting it drift between us. "Certainly, I would never."

Bile rose in my throat—a cold beady layer of sweat creeping across my brow.

"You look unwell. Sit down."

I dropped back down onto the seat. How could I not have known? How could I have been so stupid? I gripped the seat. My head ached, questions spinning and whipping. *Does Mama know? Is that why she hates her old Thinking Spot? Is that why they live with us?* "Etta Mae." Her name slipped softly from my lips. *Does she know?*

"Is that the colored girl's name?" Marlissa ran her index finger across one of her eyebrows and then the other. "Are you sure you're well? You act as if you didn't know."

"I didn't." Somewhere within, I guess I always knew, the way one knows things deep, deep down. Cool musty, cellar spaces.

"Forgive me," Marlissa said, turning away from the mirror kneeling beside me. She placed her hands on my knees. "But it's much better to hear such a thing from a friend. Don't you think?"

Friend. How I loved the sound of that. If only she might have spoken it sooner, not tangled it into the ugliness spun into the room. I folded at the waist. "Who told you?"

"It is not common knowledge, if that's your concern."

"Then how do you know it's true?"

"We're Mayfields. It's our place to know these things," Marlissa said, reaching up to hold my face within her hands. "Your secret is safe with me. No matter what." She threaded her fingers through my hair pulling my face to hers, pressing her lips against mine. She lingered until my breath was spent, pulling back slowly leaving my lips moist and honeyed. "Fairy kisses are the sweetest."

"Marlissa?" A voice spoke from across the room. Mercy stood at the door. "Your daddy done called for you." Her eyes shifted between Marlissa and me. "Best get on down to your guests."

"We just finished freshening up." Marlissa pushing herself up from her knees. "You can run on along now." She flicked her wrist at the door.

I wobbled up from the bench and stood beside her. She took several steps forward and turned back to me. She smiled, extending her arm. "It's almost time for the fireworks." I hooked my arm inside hers, allowing myself to be pulled across the room. "I just adore fireworks," she said. With her free arm, she swept her hand above her head, wiggling her fingers down through the air like a rain of confetti.

Somewhere along our way outside, I stopped breathing. My body, suddenly aware and desperate, I turned my face to the breeze, parted my lips and gobbled up the air. My chest heaved inward, causing the stolen hair ribbon to slip and tickle my stomach.

"It's mine."

I turned back to look. Marlissa's mouth moved again, but I could not hear her amidst the tumbling laughter and *whoosh* of flame.

I moved closer. "I can't hear you."

"Please . . . just give it back. I won't tell. I promise."

Was she talking about the hair ribbon? I stopped, my feet sinking into the cushion of grass. I shut my eyes, then opened them to a flash of light from the hot air balloon above, my sight trailing beyond the basket to the star-strewn sky.

"I only wanted a small remembrance," I said, raising my voice above the applause that followed the conclusion of the orchestra's song. "I'm sorry." There was truth in my words, a swell of hope that it would be enough. I fingered at the bodice of my gown prepared to retrieve the ribbon.

A question rose in her eyes, her head tilting to the side. The orchestra fluttered to life again, fingers sliding up piano keys—twinkling at the end. A man's voice sang from somewhere beneath the tented pavilion, his voice amplified by a microphone, the bravado of his tenor unable to overtake the creeping shadow of disaster.

"Did you hear me? Give it back." She extended her hand to me. "I have another necklace you can have. But that is a gift from my father."

The diamond locket. I forgot to take it off. I touched the pendant. "Help me," I said, fumbling with the clasp.

Marlissa stepped forward yanking my hands to my side holding them there. "Let me go," she said. "You're hurting me."

"I'm not touching you," I struggled to push her away. Her fingers gripped and pinched, her violence, glorious and terrifying. "What are you doing? I don't want your necklace. Help me take it off."

Marlissa screamed, "Stop hitting me." She lunged forward, pushing me back.

"I didn't hit you." My feet crisscrossed catching in the hem of my gown, the quick ripping sound causing my breath to catch. I steadied myself with a stumble and flap of my arms. I surveyed the distance between us. What was happening? People walking toward the pavilion turned to look. I took notice of the ruined edge of my dress, of the lonesome tenor voice still singing.

"Please stop." Marlissa looked from side to side, throwing her arms in front of her face, shielding herself from imaginary blows.

I knew then with certainty she meant to deceive, to give the appearance I was attacking her. I moved quickly, my finger to my lips. "Shh. Be quiet. Please."

She grabbed onto my arms, pushing them into my chest. I pulled free, grabbing her wrists.

"Let me go."

We pulled and pushed into the other, the two of us stumbling across the grounds. I released her arms just as she yanked them away from me, the momentum driving her own fist hard into her nose. *Pop.*

I froze. Marlissa's eyes went wide from the shock of the blow. Blood pooled in her right nostril, trickling to her lips. She lifted her fingers to her nose and pulled them away, regarding her own blood as she had when she pricked her finger. I expected her to scream, to lose herself in hysterics.

"I didn't mean to. I'm so sorry." My words deteriorated into small chokes. I stepped closer with caution as if happening upon a bird—careful not to startle, my arms spread and ready to grab.

She looked from side to side, for anyone who might be watching. Her eyes met mine. I thought then she might scream. I clenched my toes, mooring myself to the soft ground. The night sky blazed above us. *Poof* and *swish.* Still no screams, only the tenor crooning from the tent. He held a note. The blood dripped and spread across Marlissa's lower lip.

Where there should have been fear, there was sparkle; an eerie glee passed across her face. Viscous crimson seeped into the soft contours of her mouth. She smiled, showing her blood-washed teeth.

I took a step backwards. She followed, her palms flat in supplication. Had she come to her senses? A drop of blood clung to her chin, pulsing and growing. She took hold of my wrists, her sudden movement jarring the blood-tear loose.

The droplet fell onto my shoe. *Plunk.* "Fairy blood," Marlissa said, staring down at the dark splatter absorbing into the toe of my slipper. "Does it burn?"

I tried to yank away from her, pry myself from those elegant fingers. "Turn me loose."

She released my left hand, swinging her right hand, landing a blow against my cheek, my body jerking from the shock and brute force of it.

She grabbed hold of my shoulders and pulled me close. Our eyes caught in a stare, neither of us blinking until the second drop of fairy blood fell onto her skirt.

The tenor's voice drifted across the grounds. She said it then, rolling her words in spittle and gore, spewing them against my face. "Dirty cunt."

I wrenched myself free, stumbling backwards, no distance feeling safe.

"You are a thief. Give me my necklace back. Please." A gurgle sounded from her throat, then the eruption of a pitch-perfect scream. She did it then, running at me, wings folded, arms held before her like battering rams, her war cry aria piercing the night.

The strike was quick, my body thrust to the ground. Breathless I lay, air knocked from my lungs, the threads of consciousness snapping around me. Sound and light dimming. *Hiss* and *fade.* I lifted my throbbing head only to sink it back again into the grass. *Pretty,* I thought, looking up at the fire-lit sky, the piano playing, the tenor singing. How easy it would be to drift away into all that was beautiful there.

Marlissa pulled me back from the lovely. "Get up."

Colored sister.

"I said get up. Now."

The bent wires from my crumpled wings poked my back. I heaved and wretched into the sweet, crayon green grass, my fingers digging into the soil. I might have broken in two then, one tiny fissure joining the next until I cracked completely through.

Marlissa howled when I rose. "Somebody help me."

"Shut up," I said, lurching forward, grabbing hold of her shoulders. Anger swelled up inside me, nowhere for it to go, no one close enough to pummel but Marlissa. She released her body fully to the pull and jerk of my fury, her head flopping forward and then back again.

"You there. Stop that," a man's voice called from just outside the tent.

Marlissa laughed and I shook harder. "Dirty cunt," I yelled, giving her word back to her.

A woman gasped. "Leave her be." She pointed her champagne glass in my direction.

More people emerged from the tent, all of them hurrying our way. I kept shaking her.

A gong sounded, dozens and dozens of Japanese lanterns released to the sky. I turned to look, my hands slipping from Marlissa's shoulders, droplets of her blood trickling down my hand.

She staggered backwards, wailing.

The crowd moved closer.

I did then the only thing a girl with fairy blood on her hands could do.

I ran.

Chapter 27

Shivering, I stood outside our front door, Sheriff Dobbs and I washed in the paltry light of a single bulb, moths fluttering and clicking against the glass.

The Sheriff, a guest at the Mayfield Gala, had been the one to catch me, scooping me up, tucking me into his car on the seat next to him. What a commotion it had been, him grabbing hold—me kicking and screaming, all the lovely party guests spilling out to watch. Abel, Jane, and that Miss Joanne Woodward, the three of them looking on, their faces aghast.

The Sheriff spoke very little in the car, his voice soft and reassuring. "Settle down now. I'm not taking you off to jail. I'm taking you home to your mama."

I hardly remember the ride, nearly prostrate from shock, the poke of crumpled fairy wing wire keeping me conscious, aware I was still breathing, still a living thing.

The Sheriff rapped his knuckles against the screen doorframe, a sound so jarring I was certain it could be heard all the way to town.

"Sweet Lord Jesus!" Miss Wessie said, swinging open the door, grabbing hold of my shoulders, turning loose, stepping back to take in the carnage. Her eyes flashed wildly over my face, Marlissa's blood smeared across it, and then down to the shredded hem of my gown. "What is happened to you, child?" She glanced up at the Sheriff. "Grace!"

Mama and Etta Mae came running, both wide-eyed, panic prying apart their lips, the two of them resembling catfish with hooks caught in their mouths.

"She's fine, Grace. She's not hurt," the Sheriff said. "A little worse for wear is all."

"Worse for wear?" Mama said, pushing past Miss Wessie, taking to her knees, patting her hands up and down me, lifting my chin, searching for broken bits. "She looks like she's been half beat to death."

"I didn't do it," I said, the last words I spoke before the cork popped off, sending all the awful to spew. Hysterical sobs and a gully wash of tears.

Mama grabbed hold, pulling me into her, squeezing hard. "It's gonna be all right," she said, rocking me back and forth. "Briar, what in the world has happened?"

"Just a ruckus out at Mistletoe is all. An unpleasant bit of business between Miss Analeise here and Miss Marlissa."

Rocking back and forth, wrapped tight about Mama, I was eye to eye with Etta Mae. *Colored sister.* Why had no one told me? I felt a swell of anger, a feeling I enjoyed better than fear. *It's your fault,* I thought to myself. For Mama and Daddy. For everything gone wrong. For what will happen if Marlissa tells? And why would she not tell everyone? Marlissa must have hated me as much as she hated Virginia Fenton to do all she did.

Etta Mae reached out to comfort me, to pet and tidy my tangled mess of hair. "Leave me be," I said, leaning back out of reach.

"What kind of unpleasant business?" Mama asked.

I burrowed my nose into her neck taking in the lingering smell of New Mama, of Cordelia Mayfield's perfume. It was certain to me then, as clear and true a thing as Marlissa's hair ribbon stuffed within the bodice of my dress that Mama stole that bottle of perfume from Mrs. Mayfield.

Before the Sheriff could answer, Miss Wessie yelled at Mama. "I done told you. I told you not to set that child loose to them Mayfields."

"Wessie," Mama snapped, untangling herself from me, leaning back on the heels of her bare feet, pushing herself up to stand. "Enough of that. This isn't the time or place."

"Enough? Don't you go and try to hush me, Miss Grace high and mighty Newell."

"Ladies." The Sheriff stepped forward, tamping the air with his hands. "This can all be sorted through tomorrow. Why don't we send the girls off to bed, and then we'll talk."

There was almost quiet then, only the *clack* of those desperate moths, the sounds of night pushing in around us. The hurried cadence of our breathing.

"Etta Mae, sweetheart. Why don't you help Analeise back to her room," Mama said.

I unsheathed my words quickly, slicing the air with them. "I don't need any help." *Colored sister.* I refused to look at her, to acknowledge she was just inside the door.

"Get on back to your room like your Mama told you," Miss Wessie said. "We'll be back to check in on you in a bit."

Mama kissed my cheek, patted me on the backside, and nudged me through the door.

The Sheriff spoke, stopping me mid-step. "Miss Analeise?"

Mama took hold of my shoulders, gently guiding me around to stand in front of her to face Sheriff Dobbs.

"If you don't mind, why don't I go ahead and take that necklace on back to Miss Marlissa." His baritone was low and gentle, vibrating in his throat.

The necklace. My hand, spring-loaded, jerked up clutching my neck. *Lord help.* I forgot I was still wearing the awful thing.

"Analeise." Mama said. "What's this about?"

"Nothing worth going into now," the Sheriff said. "But if you'd help her with it, I'd appreciate it. I'm a bit clumsy with this sort of thing."

Mama pulled snarled hair up from my sweat-slicked neck, untangling Marlissa's necklace from the fake one she strung with imitation Woolworth pearls and rhinestone beads. I could feel Miss Wessie and Etta Mae's eyes on me, both watching the whole shameful affair. "Here you go," Mama said, her hand shaking as she dropped the necklace in his palm.

I turned to get away, to stop them all from gawking at me. I hurried past Etta Mae and down the hall, her tiny, naked feet padding behind me.

"Go away. I don't need you. I don't want you."

"What happened?" Etta Mae whispered.

I stopped outside my bedroom door, not wanting to turn to look at her, to gaze into those searching, hazel-colored eyes. "I want to be alone. Please, go away."

"Are you mad at me?" Etta Mae took hold of my elbow, trying to pull me around to face her.

"Leave me be," I said, turning to swat her away. It was then I saw it, the paper doll she held in her hand. My paper doll, the one Marlissa gave me. I grabbed her wrist.

"What are you doing with that?"

Etta Mae's eyes went wide. "I . . ." She tried to pull away. "I didn't mean to . . ."

She had been plundering beneath my bed. "Give it," I said, snatching it out of her hand. I pushed her away and ran into my room, slamming the door, to keep me from walloping her, to keep me safe from more trouble and out of the backseat of that Sheriff's car.

"I'm sorry," she whispered from outside the door.

I tossed the paper doll onto my bed. Pulling, yanking, and ripping, I freed myself from those broke-down fairy wings. "Get on away from here," I said. This was my house, my room. My dead Daddy. I would never tell them I knew Etta Mae was my sister. I would not speak it into being. I would not give power to the thing.

"I shouldn't have done it."

I knew what she was doing. I was on to her. She was trying to take over, to take what was mine. I pulled Marlissa's ribbon out of my dress and laid it on the bed beside the paper doll. I could hardly breathe. I tugged at my necklace until it snapped. Cheap pearls and beads bounced and rolled across the floor. What else had Etta Mae taken that was mine?

I crawled beneath the bed, prying open the square of wood flooring, feeling around in my keeping place, pulling out *Jane Eyre*, then Daddy's bottle of Old Crow.

"Please let me in."

Sliding out backwards, a few strands of my hair caught in the mattress springs, my momentum pulling them clean out from the root—the sensation, a feeling as soothing as fingers feathering across my back.

"What happened out there at Mistletoe?" Etta Mae said.

"Never you mind." I lowered myself to the floor leaning against the bed, setting the bottle of whiskey on top of my book.

"Why did you have Marlissa's necklace?"

"Mind your own business." I unscrewed the cap of the whiskey bottle, placed my nose to the lip, and took a great big sniff.

"I mean, if you did something bad, I know it wasn't on purpose is all."

Stupid girl. I had done plenty bad and on purpose and had a mind to do more if she did not leave me be. I tipped the bottle back, taking a swig of Old Crow, just enough to singe my throat, and I began to sob.

"Don't cry, Analeise. Please don't cry." Etta Mae's movements cast shadows in the light spilling and fanning across the floor of my room, her little fingers poking under the door. "Let me in."

"Go away."

"You wanna hear a song Miss Victoria taught me?"

"Leave me be."

"It's from an all-colored opera, *Porgy and Bess*. Did you know there was such a thing? A colored opera."

"Sounds stupid."

"I loves you Porgy," she sang.

Melancholy. That was the sound. From the first note, there was no mistaking the enchantment, the star-dusted wonder that was her voice. Right away, I felt different, a merciful relief. A lightness. I took another swig of whiskey. *Beguile.* I was on to her, to her colored girl voodoo.

Did she think I was some stupid lightning bug she could fool, to hover about and adore her?

I watched her fingers searching beneath the door—wanting and reaching. I tipped back the Old Crow and took another swill. On the floor, I lay covering my ears, baffling the sound, to feel the truth, to sort out a plan. I shut my eyes, enjoying the scorch pulsing in my throat that comes from liquor.

If I knew nothing else, I knew this. *Some things in this world are meant to burn.*

Chapter 28

Mama and I sat in the pickup, the heap idling and bucking in the half-circle drive of Providence Elementary. We stared straight ahead, not a word passing between us, the two of us fresh from the trenches of a spectacular war. Mama insisted I go on off to school. I insisted I could never show my face again.

Sunday, the day before, Mama allowed me the luxury of moping, to hide away in my room and wallow in the aftermath of catastrophe. Absolutely, under no circumstance would she concede. "You gotta go on to school sometime," she said. "Might as well be today. Get it over with. Show them what you're made of."

Exactly what was I made of? If you sliced me open, just what might you see? The bad parts of Mama and Daddy? Thievery and drunkenness twisted up like a pretzel holding my insides in.

Mama reached across the seat and rested her hand on my knee. "Baby, I wish I hadn't let you go off to that party."

I wondered if Mama had seen something, if the whole wretched affair revealed itself to her in the baste and stitching of my party dress— if she knew what was to happen, and still let me go. "Miss Wessie didn't want me there." I said, laying my hand atop Mama's. "How come?"

Mama continued to stare forward, shifting in the seat just a bit. "I reckon she thinks a girl like you, people like us, can't mix with a family as fine as the Mayfields."

"And what do you think, Mama?"

A magnolia leaf fell onto the windshield, sliding and scraping down to the wipers. "You are finer than all them Mayfields put together." She wiggled her hand out from beneath my hand, lacing her fingers through mine. "Every bit as good and better."

"It's all a lie."

Mama squeezed my hand. "What's a lie, baby?"

"What Marlissa said I did. What they all think I done." Until then, I shared very little of the whole affair with Mama, only asserting my innocence.

"Why don't you tell me? Tell Mama what happened out there."

"She tricked me is all. Let me think she was my friend. Made out like I took her necklace. That I hit her on purpose."

Mama turned to look at me. "Briar said you called Marlissa a horrible name. Is that true?"

Once again, Mama referred to Sheriff Dobbs by his first name, the sound as strange as before. "Sort of. I mean, she said it first. Only nobody heard."

Mama nodded. "Go on."

"She made me so mad, so I gave it right back to her. Called her the same thing."

"You ever hear that word before?"

"No, ma'am. Not ever. Not once."

"Baby, promise me, no matter how riled up you get—never, ever use that word. You hear me?"

"Yes, ma'am."

She let loose of my hand, taking my face in both her hands. "Anything else you need to tell me? Anything you want to talk about?"

I might have told her then, the two of us there, close and hitched like love bugs. I might have told her I knew Etta Mae was my sister, told her so we might share the same secret, bear together what Daddy had done. I was frightened what I might set into motion. "No, ma'am." I placed my hands over hers, pressing her cool, soft palms harder against my cheeks. "Mama, why you reckon she did it?"

"Sometimes people do bad things. For no reason at all. For no reason other than to do it." Another magnolia leaf scraped the windshield, and then another.

* * *

The playground seemed as it always had been—a gnarl of girls congregating at the meet-up spot—the boys running wild. I prayed

223

Marlissa would not be there, that she might have stayed home from school. I scanned the girl hive. Thankfully, no Marlissa.

I stopped a good piece away, resting my burlap book tote at my feet to smooth my blouse, tucking it into my skirt. I was intentional when selecting my outfit, settling upon a simple, white cotton blouse, and blue, pleated skirt—my hair unadorned and pulled neatly into a ponytail. An ensemble within which a girl might appear innocent, go unnoticed. I picked up my bag, took in a deep breath, and walked toward the swarm.

Jane and Virginia came across the playground from the other side. I watched the two of them traversing the zigzag of boys, waiting until they were closer. I cleared my throat. "Jane. Over here." I waved my hand at shoulder height, not wanting to draw too much attentnon.

Jane's face hardened—teeth clamping down over her bottom lip. I waved again, hoping she did not hear me the first time—hoping she forgot I chose Marlissa over her. Forgot I took her sister's wings.

"Hey," I said, more softly than before.

Virginia narrowed her eyes, shaking her charm bracelet at me. She tucked her arm through Jane's, pulling her over to the others.

My eyes smarted. *Don't cry, Analeise Newell. Don't you dare cry.*

Dink hollered from the top of a pile of tackled boys. "Hey, look everybody. It's Analeise Newell. Better keep watch over your valuables and keepsakes—ole' Miss Sticky Fingers is here."

I glimpsed the writhing boy-pile hoping Abel was nowhere in the mix to witness the shameful affair. The girls greeted me with a collective of mouth-covered, eye-cutting whispers. A hush fell. The girls unfolded, opening up around the bench. Marlissa sat alone in the middle, girls fanning out around her.

Marlissa stood, burying her hand within her lilac bag, the same rich color as her pearl-buttoned dress. She closed her hand around the object she retrieved from the tote, tightening her hand into a fist.

The bruises, purplish green—a stunning floral swirl matching the color of her dress, were undetectable until she was but a few feet away.

The violence was lovely, a queer and perfect complement to her features.

Playground noise fell away, the last of it vibrating within the metal swings. Everyone watched.

Sand scraped at the bottom of Marlissa's shoes, one delicate foot placed gingerly in front of the other—an angel treading lightly upon a thundercloud. I listened to the scrape—watched her fist clench tighter. She was close, a hint of her mama's perfume in the air. As much as I hated her, I was, in equal measure, desperate to be close to her, to be swallowed up in her shine.

The playground stood still, waiting for her to speak. "Mother says it's my Christian duty to forgive you for what you did." She spoke louder than necessary—an actress playing to the balcony, no doubt the influence of that Miss Joanne Woodward.

Forgive me? I glanced around the playground, everyone hungry for what would come next.

"I can't fault you for admiring my necklace." She touched her hand to the collar of her dress where the locket lay. "It is truly lovely. But it was a gift from my father." She straightened her shoulders. "Mother said you must have wanted it very badly to have done what you did."

My knees buckled, my upper body swaying back a little. Her eyes swept down to her fist, mine following close behind. Was she going to hit me? *Oh Lord, yes please. Hit me. Go ahead and do it. Show them who you really are.*

She presented her fist to me. "I can't give you the necklace because it's so precious to me. But I can give you this." Her pale fingers opened up like petals. A heart-shaped locket similar to the one she wore rested in her palm. "A necklace of your very own."

You sneak. You liar. I wanted to shake her, knock her to the ground and stomp her silly.

The girls cooed at her gesture. A precarious tremble started in my ankles—the kind of shiver that shook tears loose.

She had me cornered, right where she wanted me, standing there looking like a thief. What could I do? She held a secret of mine—ripe for the telling. One wrong move—just one wrong word, and everyone would know. *Colored sister.*

The trembling moved its way up my shoulders. Marlissa grabbed hold of my arms. I braced myself. "I forgive you." She pulled me into a hug, her cheek pressing against mine, my arms hanging limp at my sides.

Her chest rose and fell against mine, her mouth close to my ear. I waited for a word, a warning, a curse. Nothing. Just the tickle of her breath. She pulled away, pressing the locket into my hand—the metal holding the warmth of her body, the dampness of her lies.

The Sheriff's car passed slowly down the street.

"Hey, Analeise. Look, your ride's here," Dink yelled, setting off a grenade of laugher in the crowd.

The school bell rang, laughter dissolving into the shrillness. Pinafore-clad courtiers folded themselves around Marlissa, sweeping her up the stairs.

Jane did not look back, but Virginia did—just a glance and shake of her bracelet. *Marlissa hates you,* I thought, the very idea giving me comfort.

I looked down to study the locket. It bore a surprising weight. Could it be real gold? I lifted it closer for inspection. Similar in size to Marlissa's, it was simpler in design, lacking the diamonds that glittered around the edges. With a few gentle flicks of my nail, I opened the locket, splitting the heart in two. A dusting of black, powdery ash spilled out, just enough to leave a sprinkle of soot across my knuckle.

The squall of the school bell ceased, leaving the vibrations whiffling in my ears. I snapped the locket shut and tossed it in my bag. I spit on my hand, rubbing at the soot, the dark blotches smudging and feathering across my skin.

Chapter 29

Standing at the end of the drive, wrapped in Miss Wessie's old shawl, I waited for Abel to deliver the paper. He was absent from school on Monday which meant we had not seen each other since the Mayfield Gala. My insides gurgled a little from hunger, but mostly nerves. Would he regard me differently? Would he hate me—an assailant and thief—a trashy-mouthed girl?

Of all the words he scribbled in his notebook, I was certain there was one word not included, Marlissa's dirty word, the one-word Mama told me I was never to speak again. Had he been there to hear me say it? I pulled the shawl tighter, watched the truck's headlights move closer, the beams bouncing and growing larger.

"Good morning, Miss Newell," he said, his sleepy time rasp buoyant as always.

I hurried to the back of the truck, my heart hammering my chest. I needed to see his face—his eyes. Only then would I know if things had changed. "And a very good morning to you."

Right away, I knew. I saw it in those sable-colored eyes he thought of me as he always had—fondly. Innocently. He smiled that charming smile. How I wanted to cry, to thank him for not hating me. For being kind.

As was his custom, he tossed the paper into the air, catching it behind his back, presenting it with a gentleman's bow. "Miss Newell, your paper, if you please."

"I'm ever so happy to see you alive and kicking," I said. "I thought you might have taken sick."

"Nope, just rode over to Tallahassee yesterday to see the orthodontist."

"For what?"

"Dad thinks I might need braces. To close up this gap." He pointed at that slightest, most adorable space ever to exist between two front teeth.

"Don't you dare," I said, letting the words spill, leaving me awkward and embarrassed.

Abel laughed. "I'll be sure to tell Dad you find the state of my teeth agreeable."

My cheeks caught fire. I imagined the heat mixing with the cold morning air, a puff of steam born from the collision. "Anything new in Providence?" I looked down at the paper. Something I failed to consider knocked hard against me like a wrecking ball. What if I made the papers? What if someone took pictures of me in the backseat of the Sheriff's car? Surely, he would warn me if such a thing happened.

"Not much, except for the Founder's Day Celebration next month."

"Anything about the Mayfields? About the party?"

"Nope." He scratched his temple. "Well, actually, there is one thing. Mr. Kingston and Miss Cordelia are sponsoring the first ever, Founder's Day Talent Show. Sounds like it's going to be quite the shindig."

"Talent show?"

"Yes, ma'am. And the winner gets his or her picture in the paper, and a grand prize of fifty dollars." He chewed at his lip. "Oh, and you get to ride a float in the Founder's Day Parade."

Fifty dollars. "Can anybody be in it?"

"Anyone in the first grade all the way up to the twelfth."

Possibility crackled the air. "Is Marlissa going to enter?"

"I can't imagine why she wouldn't. Nobody can play the piano around these parts like she can." My heart dipped, and then that awful slap of jealousy falling close behind. He smiled big again. "Nobody, of course, but you."

"You think I could beat her?" I managed to keep my face from ripping into a smile, desiring to remain humble as possible.

"Miss Newell, if anybody could give her a run for her money, it would be you."

Right then, I could not love anyone or anything more than Abel Darlington. Clear as clear could be, I knew what was to be done, that this talent show was the perfect opportunity to beat Marlissa. To show everyone I was not Bug Girl or ole' Miss Sticky Fingers, but that I was Analeise Newell, the girl who could outshine a Mayfield.

"I think I might just enter that talent show."

"What are you going to do with that fifty dollars when you win it?" He cast a sideways glance, his smile charmingly crooked and coy.

"Wouldn't you like to know?" I said, truly not giving a care in the world about fifty dollars. There was only one grand prize I wanted—Marlissa Mayfield's fairy wings stuffed in a jar.

"Mr. Abel, we need to get going," Eli said, hanging his arm out the window, slapping it against the side of the truck.

"Yes sir, just one minute." Abel jumped down, stuffing his hand into his pocket. "Analeise, I've got something for you." He looked down at his shoes, then fixed those sweet chocolate drop eyes on me. He fished something out of his pocket. "You ran off the other night before getting your gift."

"What is it?"

A fairy charm bracelet snaked in his palm. "All the girls were supposed to get one. Didn't seem fair you didn't."

I had been desperate for one of those bracelets. I fought the urge to grab hold of Abel Darlington and squeeze the daylights out of him.

"Does Marlissa know?"

"I reckon I forgot to tell her." He dropped the bracelet into my palm. "But I will."

I wanted to explain, to tell him what really happened that night, that things were not as they seemed, but that dang-nabbit Eli slapped the side of the truck again. "Best be going," Eli said.

Abel winked and climbed back up into the truck bed. He bowed his head, pretending to tip a hat. "See you at school, Miss Newell."

I nodded, afraid to speak, afraid I might crack open a cloud burst of tears. I stood, waving and watching my Abel Darlington shrink and fade in the distance, my fairy charm bracelet still warm from his pocket.

* * *

I passed the half hour between school letting out and my piano lesson with Mr. Bloom by sitting in the music room trudging through homework. The day had been an endurance of isolation—all the girls avoiding me, even my Jane. If not for Abel's kindness that morning and the promise of outshining Marlissa at the talent show, I might have come apart at the seams.

I dared not wear my fairy charm bracelet for fear of questions and accusations, so I stowed it away in my keeping place. Though I vowed to never wear it, I kept Marlissa's locket close in my bag concealed in one of Daddy's old tobacco tins, a real and true thing to paw, a reminder of what she did, a talisman to ward off her black magic shimmer.

Mr. Bloom hummed and dusted away his pretty, curlicue writing from the chalkboard in tiny, rhythmic swipes.

"Mr. Bloom."

He jumped, clutching his chest, and spun around. "For the love of Doris Day," he said. "I forgot you were in the room."

"Didn't mean to spook you, Mr. Bloom." I tried to hide my amusement at the spectacle, his glasses askew, a bouquet of chalk flowers blossoming across his vest.

He chuckled, fingering his glasses back to order, then glanced at his watch. "Is it that time already?"

"No, sir. Just wondering if you heard about the talent show." It was a silly thing to ask. Not since news of the Mayfield Gala had there been such talk.

"You mean the talent show you're going to enter?" he said, crossing his arms, smiling. "And win with a little help from me?"

For the second time that day, I wanted to cry from sheer happiness and gratitude. "You really think I can win?"

"Absolutely."

"What about Marlissa Mayfield?"

"Stiff competition, most certainly, but nothing you can't handle." He pulled sheet music from his satchel, wielding it in the air with a flourish. "I have the perfect selection." He pressed the pages to his chest and hurried to the piano. "Join me, sweet girl."

Sweet girl? Surely, he heard the gossip, the whole sordid account of my shenanigans at Mistletoe. I followed him, resting my bag on the bench next to me.

"This is a Chopin *étude*. Do you know what an *étude* is?" Mr. Bloom opened the music propping it against the stand.

Étude, a fancy Marlissa word. I would have to remember it for Abel. "No, sir, I sure don't."

Mr. Bloom spoke swiftly. "It's a term that describes pieces that are technically difficult, sometimes virtuosic. Chopin was a pioneer—a master of the *étude*. Do you follow?"

"I think."

"If you are going to out play Marlissa Mayfield, you must not only be technically sound, you must also play it with great passion. Convey the emotion—the feeling." His breathing quickened, "That's where you excel. Do you understand?"

"Yes, sir."

"This is Chopin's Opus 10, number 12. It's called 'Revolutionary'."

The door clicked, giving us both a start. The sheet music fluttered.

"*Excusez-moi, síl vous plaît. J´ai perdu mon crayon boîte,*" Marlissa said, standing perfectly still, the only movement, the gentle flit of her lashes.

Mr. Bloom stepped away from the bench, folding one hand into the other. "Miss Marlissa Mayfield, to what do we owe this pleasure?" He bowed at the waist, his face brightening, that hungry look following—the early stages of her enchantment spreading quick as snake venom.

"I seem to have misplaced my pencil box," she said, gliding her way up the risers to the chair where she previously sat. I knew that pencil box, a lovely sterling silver affair with roses engraved on the lid.

"Might I be of assistance?" he asked, his eyes following her, his body straining to stay put and safe from her undertow.

"Thank you, no," she said, glancing around the area of the chair. "I'll only be a moment."

"Any luck?" he said.

"It doesn't seem to be here." She worked her way back down the risers, the momentum lifting her skirt, each step revealing a flash of alabaster knee. "I just don't know where it could be." She turned her attention to me, giving me her loveliest smile. I reached into my bag giving the tobacco tin a shake. "I hope I haven't interrupted anything. A lesson perhaps?"

"Oh no. Just getting started," Mr. Bloom said.

Marlissa glided over to the piano. I marveled at how quickly she healed, the faint green bruising above each eyelid giving the notion she wore eyeshadow. Resisting the urge to touch her, I tucked my hands under my behind.

"Sorry about your pencil box," I said. "It was pretty."

"I didn't realize you admired it." She touched her locket, insinuation popping like firecrackers. She leaned over me, her shoulder grazing mine to look at the sheet music. "What a coincidence." She pulled away, stoking the want in me for her to stay close, to remain there pressed against me. Desperate to ward off her spell, I reached into my bag searching for the tin to shake.

"A coincidence?" Mr. Bloom said.

I grabbed hold of something, only it was not the tin. I peeked into the bag. *Marlissa's pencil box.* I dropped the thing quickly and closed the bag. She meant to ruin me. How had she managed it? When had she sneaked her box into my things?

"I'm playing this very piece at the talent show. I adore Chopin."

Mr. Bloom cleared his throat. "That certainly is the coincidence," he said, looking a bit shaken from the news. "Analeise is playing the same selection at the talent show."

She managed a look of utter delight, her dainty fingers touching her cheeks. "It's absolutely providential. What an honor to compete with you, both of us playing the same . . ." She glanced back over at the music. "*Étude.*"

The tobacco tin was out of reach, but I no longer needed it to shake away her spell. Torrential anger would keep me safe from her devilish charms. What might keep her safe from me?

"Marlissa." I looked up from the piano bench. "I almost forgot to thank you."

"Forever what?"

"For the fairy charm bracelet. It was so sweet of you to send it by Abel." There was only the teensiest pleasure in the look of shock passing across her striking face, replaced immediately with the horror I betrayed my sweet Abel Darlington.

"He's too kind for his own good, don't you think?"

I had angered her, taken her off guard. I used her friend, Abel Darlington, to do it. Had all my senses left me? I was playing a dangerous game. I was playing with fire.

"Looks like its past time for my lesson," I said. "If I'm to beat you, I best get busy." I mustered a laugh.

Mr. Bloom had been too enraptured by Marlissa to notice the time, to sense the danger swelling in the room. "My goodness graciousness," he said. "Quite right, Analeise."

"Please forgive the intrusion." Marlissa glided back across the room, the simple act, astonishing and beautiful. I imagined her standing on an ice-covered pond, her movement so slight, giving the appearance she slid—invisible wires pulling her across from the other side.

"If I should come across your pencil box, I'll let know," Mr. Bloom said, his words no doubt a meager attempt to keep her there with us.

"Thank you, sir. And Analeise?" She smiled her most frightening smile, the one showing none of her lovely teeth. "My best to Etta Mae."

* * *

After dinner, I wanted to run off to my room, to sip a little whiskey and have time to myself to think. But Mama had other ideas, forcing me to join her, Etta Mae, and Miss Wessie on the back porch to take in the evening air. Etta Mae insisted on sitting next to me in the swing, leaving Mama and Miss Wessie to wobble in our only two rocking chairs, both weathered and warped.

From time to time, I glanced over at my colored sister, speculating if there might be a resemblance, something that might give us away. It was the eyes I decided were most alike—the almond shape and color. Etta Mae's eyes were an unusual hue for a colored girl, hazel with tiny flecks of gold. They transformed in the light, sometimes looking nearly as green as mine. Of course, Mama and Miss Wessie both knew the truth, they had to. What about Etta Mae? Did she know?

Oh, I felt sorry for Etta Mae all the years I knew her, singing and pining for her dead, burned up, mama, but not anymore. It was justice, a payback for her mama's sins, for doing what she did with my daddy.

" And a prize of fifty dollars," Etta Mae said, her words snagging hold of my attention. "Can you imagine?"

"That sure is something," Miss Wessie said.

"What do you think, Analeise?" Etta Mae said. "If you enter, you'd win for sure."

I planned to not make mention of the talent show in the presence of Miss Wessie. She was always trying to keep me from fun, or in this case revenge. My scheme was to discuss it later with Mama when I could get her alone. Of course, Etta Mae would spoil it just like she spoiled everything.

Mama eased her rocking, the sound of the chair's counter rhythm, unsettling. "Is that something you'd want to do?"

"Mr. Bloom and I talked about it today. He thinks I'd do just fine," I glanced between Miss Wessie and Mama. "We've already picked out a song."

"Is that so?" Mama leaned back in the rocker.

Miss Wessie stopped her chair. "Is my ears playing tricks on me, Grace Newell?" She rubbed her glossy knees. "Is you saying you'd consider allowing that child up on a stage in front of all of Providence, in front of God and everybody? After all the goings-ons out there at Mistletoe." Miss Wessie slung out her hand, pointing off into the darkness.

"Don't you raise your voice at me, Wessie Johnston." She stopped herself from saying more. I lowered my feet, slowing the swing, readying myself should the need arise to move quickly from the place. She let out a deep breath and spoke softly. "We'll take this up later, you and me."

Miss Wessie shifted in the chair, the woods slats creaking and popping, leaving me to wonder if the whole kit and caboodle might come apart from the strain of her abundance and rage.

"I sure would love to win fifty dollars if I had the chance," Etta Mae said. "Mostly, I'd just like to sing for folks."

I was taken aback, the little mouse speaking up after such an uproar, her timidity replaced with a gleam of confidence.

"Now baby, you know that show ain't for you," Miss Wessie said, a leftover slice of anger rattling in her voice.

With great intention, I turned the screw. "She means it's not for colored folks."

"Analeise," Mama said. "She knows perfectly well what it means, and doesn't need you telling her anything about it."

Miss Wessie shot me a look out of the corner of her eyes. She tugged back her kerchief a bit, revealing a shock of white hair, as if the gesture were a reprimand—a dare.

"I know it's not for me." Etta Mae reached out to touch my leg. "But what if it was?"

"What a wonderful thing that would be," Mama said. "All of Providence hearing an angel sing."

Etta Mae beamed at Mama.

"Imagine, the two of you up there competing for that prize," Miss Wessie said, her head cocked back, a smile spreading across her face. "Miss Lady up there playing the piano, and Etta Mae making all kinds of a joyful noise." She leaned forward in her chair. *Creak* and *pop*.

Not until then did I consider who was most talented. Yes, I knew Etta Mae possessed a gift, but so did I. Who was better? Who would win? Miss Wessie was being hateful. She was stirring the pot. I imagined her shifting about in that chair, nails turning loose, wood giving way at the joints, Miss Wessie sprawled out on the porch.

"What would you sing?" Mama said.

"Mozart." Etta Mae jumped down from the swing, jostling me in the seat. "'Queen of the Night' from *The Magic Flute.*" Etta Mae stood out in front of us, leaning side to side, taking turns balancing on each foot.

Queen of the Night? How had this unraveled? How had it become all about Etta Mae?

"Sounds like some sort of fairy tale," Mama said.

"Is it another one of them opera songs Miss Victoria taught you?"

"Yes, ma'am. But it's not really called 'Queen of the Night'. Miss Victoria says its proper title is *'Der Holle Rache'."* Etta Mae's pronunciation was throaty and unsettling. "It means hell's vengeance boils in my heart."

Hell's vengeance. I liked the sound of that.

Etta Mae spun about once, her movement puffing the hem of her gown. In the *swish* of the turn, she transformed, the Queen of the Night left standing there before us. She opened her mouth, slashing the stillness with her soprano. That first fantastical note seared my tongue. The notes came alive, transforming to cockleburs, thousands of them spinning, pulsing pink—their tines glowing brighter than their core.

A rising breeze rustled the near-naked branches of the oak in Mama's Thinking Spot. Remnant leaves blew and scraped across the porch floor, crunching beneath the Queen's stocking feet.

Across the porch, she marched, her gown gathered up in her tiny hands, a magnificent train of cockleburs rustling behind. She sang in German.

Death and despair blaze around me.

Every bit of it I could understand, could interpret in the vibrations, could read in the throbbing pink. Mama and Miss Wessie sat still.

Mesmerized. Unblinking. Hundreds of cockleburs collected on their skin. The breeze gained speed, acorns pummeling the roof.

Hear, gods of vengeance, hear the mother's oath!

The Queen lifted her arms, stretching across the space, her hands closing to fists. The darkness screamed out. Insects, Birds, and Critters. *Hoots* and *howls.*

She lowered her arms, the last note, hot and perfect as the first. The Queen gave one last spin. When the wind fell still, Etta Mae was herself, her girlish face and sweet smile with us once more.

Mama and Miss Wessie blinked away at the spell, the fragments of enchantment collecting like sleep cracklings in the corners of their eyes. My hand stung, one last cocklebur holding fast. I flicked at the little porcupine until the barbs pulled loose from my skin. I watched as it floated off, bouncing against a porch post and drift into the dark.

Chapter 30

Bits of skin dangled like stalactites from the roof of my mouth, the same sorry affliction one suffers from impatience, from gobbling up something much too hot to eat. Only it was Etta Mae, not my own gluttony, who had done this thing to me. A week later, and still I had not fully regained my ability to savor food—the whole of my mouth scorched raw by The Queen of the Night.

Miss Wessie cooked my favorite supper of fried pork chops, collard greens and dumplings, and I could hardly taste any of it. Etta Mae and her peacock ways ruined everything.

After eating, Mama and I assisted Miss Wessie in the kitchen, the three of us attending the wreckage, black iron skillets and grease splatter swirls.

"Such a shame Etta Mae missed dinner," Mama said.

Miss Wessie dried the last of the chipped Blue Willow plates. "I expect she just as happy to be eating over there with Miss Victoria." Miss Wessie snapped the drying-towel in the air and folded it into a square.

Talk of that Miss Victoria usually scraped me like sandpaper. Miss Victoria this. And Miss Victoria that. I was only partially annoyed, thankful to have time away from Etta Mae, from the confusion I felt when we were together. With the talent show a few weeks away, I needed to free myself from distraction, from the intense desire to hurt and love Etta Mae all at once.

The phone rang. The three of us jumped. Mama, just the week before, replaced the old phone, the new ring—ear splitting and fraught. Like New Mama, it was another something to which to grow accustom.

"I'll get it." I ran outside the kitchen to the phone niche. "Hello, this is Analeise Newell," I said. "Mr. Bloom." His voice was monotone. "Sure, Mama's here." I hesitated before calling Mama to the phone, unsettled by the feeling that something was about to tilt in a bad direction. "Mr. Bloom, is everything okay? I understand. Yes, sir, I'll get her for you." I placed the phone to my shoulder. "Mama. It's Mr. Bloom,"

Mama rounded the corner drying her hands on her Sunday apron which had become her everyday one. "This is Grace." Mama nodded her head, placing the phone to her chest. "Analeise, could you please give me a minute?" She motioned for me to go back into the kitchen. "Wessie, please take Analeise out on the back porch while I speak with Mr. Bloom."

Miss Wessie took me by the shoulders, steering me through the kitchen and onto the porch. "Come sit with me here on the swing."

Before she could lift a hip to sit, Mama called for her. "Wessie, come here please." I knew from the pinched, high-pitched quality of her voice trouble was afoot.

Miss Wessie walked to the screen door, turning to point at me there on the swing, ordering me to stay put.

No doubt it would be another Mama and Miss Wessie conversation—whispers and secrets. My curiosity was too much to bear. Doing my best to console that grumpy swing, I imagined myself a haint, light as meringue, and lifted myself off from the thing. I slipped out of my Mary Jane's and tippy-toed over to the door, kneeling at the perfect angle to listen and peep.

"What kind of trouble we got coming now?" Miss Wessie said.

"Please don't give me any of your hot sauce tonight," Mama said. "My nerves can't take it."

"My ears is open and ready."

"That was Mr. Bloom.".

"That much I already know."

"He can't teach Analeise piano anymore," Mama said, her words hurried and ragged at the edges.

He can't teach me anymore. I leaned into the side of the house, the weight of my shoulder breaking off a ribbon of curling paint. I held my breath, steadying myself, hoping they had not heard.

"And why is that?"

I peeked through the screen. Mama stood a few feet away, her back to the door. Miss Wessie stood facing me, her eyes shifting and slicing into mine. She had seen me. I jerked my head back, my heart shooting off like a bottle rocket. I waited for her reprimand, for the walls to rattle from the weight of her footfall. Nothing.

"The Mayfields," Mama said.

I tried to lasso my heart back into place, to catch my breath. I leaned forward again looking back through the screen. The sliver of paint crunched under my knee. Miss Wessie's eyes flashed over at me and quickly back to Mama. She knew I was there. Was she not going to rat me out to Mama? Did she want me to hear?

Mama untied her apron, yanked at the strings only to tie it back up again. "Seems they made him a very pretty offer."

"And what that be?" Miss Wessie talked louder than she normally might, inviting Mama to follow. Perhaps, so I could hear it all for myself.

"A king's ransom to teach Marlissa," Mama said. "To focus all his attention on only her."

I held my breath to keep from screaming. Marlissa already had a piano teacher, a fancy fella from all the way over in Tallahassee.

Miss Wessie cut her eyes again over at me. "Sweet Lord Jesus. I told you nothing good would come from tangling up with that lot."

"Can't you just listen? Can't you just hear me out?"

"I could, but what of it? Me just sitting here grinning at you and nodding my head. Somebody needs to knock some sense into you."

"I'm in my right head, Wessie. After everything that's happened, I see more clearly now than I ever have."

"You don't see nothing. If you did, you'd see they ain't paying that Mr. Bloom to teach Marlissa. They is paying him not to teach Analeise."

Marlissa Mayfield would do anything to win, and everything to hurt me.

"You've upset my nerves," Mama said, taking off across the kitchen to fiddle with the breadbox.

Miss Wessie looked over at me and put her finger to her lips. What was she up to? "Grace, what else did that Mr. Bloom say?"

Mama pulled out the half loaf of Sunbeam and then a bottle of Old Crow. How long had Mama been drinking whiskey; how long had she been hiding it? She poured a healthy amount into the knuckle of sweet tea remaining in her glass, took a sip and handed it over to Miss Wessie.

"Oh, what the Sam Hill." Miss Wessie tipped back the glass and took a few gulps. She wiped her mouth with the back of her hand and licked her lips. "What else did that Mr. Bloom say?"

Mama took another swallow. "Marlissa is playing the same piece as Analeise at the talent show."

Miss Wessie chuckled. "So little Miss Marlissa be playing games with our Analeise's head. But that ain't what's got you so jittery."

Mama whispered. "It wasn't so much what he said as how he seemed. He wanted to say more; I could tell. But he was . . ."

"He was what?"

Mama tossed back the rest of the whiskey. "He was frightened."

Out of the corner of my eye, something pulsed in the dark, a lazy flash of light just short of the porch. A single cocklebur, translucent and shriveled, came for me, hovering and dipping like a half-spent helium balloon. The look of it spooked me, that desiccated note desperate to find its way back to Etta Mae.

"We ought to be frightened," Miss Wessie said.

I listened the best I could, keeping my eyes on the awful thing creeping toward me. I wanted to swat it away; I wanted to run. It bumped against my cheek, its tines turned brittle and impotent—no longer able to pierce my skin.

"Miss Analeise?"

I jumped, turning loose an awful howl, too startled to properly scream. I teetered on my knees and fell on my backside. "Mercy, what are you doing here? You scared the Dickens out of me!" Had I been in

241

reach of something to throw, I would have slung it at her. I would have knocked her upside the head.

"Lord child, please forgive me." Mercy took the first porch step, holding out her right hand in front of her, tamping the air between us.

"What on earth is going on out here," Mama said, pushing the screen door open, Miss Wessie following close behind.

"Seems I near about scared Miss Analeise here to death," Mercy said.

"Mercy, what is you doing out here?" Miss Wessie said.

I pushed myself up from the floor to stand next to Mama, bits of shattered paint sticking to my knees. The three of us stood there side by side staring down at Mercy, the bouquet of Old Crow teasing the air.

"Miss Grace, I come for a favor," Mercy said, glancing down at the long, black glossy box tucked beneath her arm. "I got me a bit of trouble."

Miss Wessie crossed her arms, an awkward and nearly impossible feat given the ampleness of her bosom. "I reckon there's lots of trouble going around this evening."

Mama cut Miss Wessie a look. "How can I help?"

Mercy cradled the box like a baby, looking behind her out into the dark. "You mind if I come in?"

"My land, where are my manners," Mama said. "Please." Mama opened the screen door motioning Mercy up onto the porch.

Mercy placed the long, rectangular box on the table. "It's a bit of sewing for Miss Cordelia." She stared awkwardly down at the thing.

"Cordelia Mayfield?" Mama said. Her eyes went wide from the shock of it, her right hand pressing her lips.

"Lord help," Miss Wessie said, backing away from the table. "What you done dragged into this house?"

"Cordelia Mayfield asked you to bring this here to me? A sewing job."

Mercy chewed at her lips. She turned loose her gaze from the box, letting it drift to Mama. "No, ma'am. Not exactly."

"Sweet Jesus!" Miss Wessie turned away from the table and back again. "What do that mean?"

"Leave Mercy be, and let her speak," Mama said.

"It mean she don't know I come," Mercy said, glancing at me then back at Mama. "Cause of you know why," she whispered.

What did that mean? *Cause of you know why.*

"Cordelia Mayfield has the best seamstresses between here and Atlanta attending her every whim. Why on earth would you come to me, Mercy?"

"Cause I need to keep it quiet is what. If I go to any of those folks, she might know what happened. And because I know you're magic with a needle. I really need your help." Mercy opened her palms to Mama. "Please."

Mama gestured at the box. "What do we have here? What needs doing?"

"It's Miss Marlissa's talent show dress."

Marlissa's talent show dress. Right here in my kitchen. I hurried to the edge of the table. It occurred to me that Mama and I had yet to settle on a pattern for my talent show dress.

Miss Wessie pulled off her kerchief, the very act brightening the room, her white hair charging the space as if wired to the circuit box. "You done brung Miss Marlissa's talent show dress up in this house." Is you out of your mind?"

"Wessie," Mama said. "Mercy's our friend. Let's hear her through. Figure out a way we can help her."

"Ain't you the angel, Grace Newell," Miss Wessie darted her eyes at Mama. "Helping a friend in need."

Mama turned away from Miss Wessie. "Let's take a look."

"It come all the way from Paris France," Mercy said, removing the lid, revealing endless, puffy layers of tissue paper. "Mr. Christian Dior made it for her. He makes near about all Miss Cordelia's clothes." She pulled back the first layer of tissue. "He done it as a personal favor on account of her being one of his best customers and cause they friends."

"Christian Dior? For a little girl?" Mama said, moving closer to the table with a cautious reverence.

Mercy peeled back layer after layer of tissue, a luxurious and maddening sound. Finally, there was quiet, the last of the paper pulled back.

"Get away from there." Miss Wessie pulled me back away from the table, pushing me behind her.

"Just look at that," Mama whispered. "It's lovely."

"Let me see," I said, doing my best to wiggle out of Miss Wessie's grip.

"Ain't it something?" Mercy said.

I broke loose, running around to the other side of the table. Mama and Mercy both looked down upon the box as if regarding a sleeping baby in a crib.

Mama reached for the dress.

Miss Wessie knocked her fist against the table. "You is a fool, Grace Newell, if you get anywheres near that dress."

Mama held the jewel out before her. "Have you ever in your life seen anything like it?"

We all went quiet, even Miss Wessie, the wattage of her hair brighter than before. We stood stupefied, until Miss Wessie spoke at last, rattling us from the wonderment sparkling in the room. "What color would you say that is?"

"Miss Cordelia, she say . . . let me try to remember it just like she said it." Mercy paused, staring at the ceiling. "She say it be the color of moonlight falling across a snow drift. You know how she talks, Wessie. All fancied up and pretty as a poem. But crazy-like."

How would Miss Wessie know how Cordelia Mayfield talked?

Mama draped the dress back across the box so we could admire the full length of it. "Exquisite," Mama said. And it was—every inch, heaven spun. Star dust collected thick at the hem, swirling up and around the full skirt until there was nothing more than a smattering upon the sweetheart bodice. The color was otherworldly—the palest of blues with smoky grays seeping through. An altogether daring and unconventional look for an eleven-year-old, even for a golden-haired fairy child.

"She's gonna wear that in the talent show?" I said.

"Sure is," Mercy said. "Miss Cordelia says it be a gown for winning."

"Baby, never you mind this dress," Mama said. "It's just window dressing. That's all."

"Don't look like anything on it need sewing," Miss Wessie said.

Mercy placed her hand on her neck. "The netting's all ripped."

"You mean the tulle?" Mama lifted the hem, pulling back the layers, revealing a mangle of shreds and tears.

"Look like a cat caught hold of it," Miss Wessie said.

Mercy chewed her knuckles. "Wasn't no cat, Wessie. It was Miss Marlissa."

"On purpose?" I said. "She did this on purpose?"

"Not on purpose, I reckon." Mercy said. "But she done it just the same."

"Don't seem to be the end of the world, Mercy. You can't even tell what's been done with the dress pulled down." Miss Wessie retrieved her discarded kerchief from her apron pocket and dabbed away the glisten on her forehead.

"Cordelia Mayfield always know what be underneath a thing," Mercy looked at Miss Wessie, then rested her gaze upon Mama, the last of her words dissolving to a whisper.

"So, Cordelia doesn't know about this?" Mama said.

"And she won't. Not if I can help it. Not if you'll help me."

"How did she do it?" I said, desperate to know how such a thing happened.

Mercy cleared her throat. "Miss Cordelia, she put me in charge of seeing after Miss Marlissa's talent show dress." She paused, seeming to contemplate if she should go on.

"The cat already out of the bag, and from the look of things, up that dress," Miss Wessie said. Pleased with her own cleverness, a smile spread across her face. "Keep going child. Too late to turn back now."

"I took it to my room to see about any wrinkles and what not. Miss Marlissa, she knew the dress was coming, and she been doing her best to get at it. But Miss Cordelia didn't want her to see it until later, until after she come back from her Garden Club meeting over in Thomasville." Mercy took a deep breath clasping her hands together beneath her chin. "Miss Marlissa, she was down in the music room with Miss Bouchard taking her ballet lesson, so I thought I had a little time to myself to get a few things done without having to worry about that child. Lord knows, she a handful on a good day. Not that she's a rowdy thing. She's just hard to please like her mama. Never know what she gonna get up to next."

"I reckon tending rich folks is a worry," Miss Wessie said, dabbing at her forehead again, her smile gone away.

Mercy shook her head. "Truer words, Wessie. Truer words."

"What happened then?" I said, looking down at the Christian Dior, anxious for an inside look at Marlissa Mayfield in her natural habitat.

"I was in the linen pantry when I felt a shiver. Like someone just walked across my grave. More like Miss Marlissa walked across it. It's a feeling come over me sometimes when that child is up to no good." Mercy hugged herself. "I feel it a fair amount."

Miss Wessie chuckled. "I know what you mean," she said, cutting me a look. What did Miss Wessie mean by that? I was nothing like Marlissa Mayfield.

"Then what?" Mama said.

"I hurried on over to the music room, and you know what I found?" Mercy took in a deep breath and held it. Mama, Miss Wessie, and I, all of us held our breath waiting for her to speak.

"Good Lord, Mercy, spit it out." Miss Wessie said. "What did you find?"

Mercy exhaled and shook her head. "Nothing and nobody. Just the sweet, pretty smell that child leaves behind," She tapped the tip of her nose with her index finger. "Miss Bouchard done went and finished up the lesson early. That's when I knew I was in for it. I would've kicked my shoes off if it would've gotten me to her any faster."

My stomach ached, nervous for Mercy, and for some reason, anxious for myself. *You know the one. Nothing. And nobody.*

"I was scared to open the door. Pressed my ear against it. The only thing I could hear was my heart thumping. I prayed for the courage to let myself see what was on the other side. Something told me it wasn't going to be good, and I was right. There she was, Miss Marlissa standing there in her ballet costume with her fairy wings tied on her back, hair piled up high with a little crown sitting on top." Mercy took in another big breath and licked her lips. "And that charm bracelet of hers tangled up into the petticoat."

Miss Wessie lifted her hand in the air, her gesture for summoning up the Lord.

"I hung the dress from the door of the chifforobe to let it settle, and there she was with her hand all up in the thing, like she'd been reaching and stretching for it."

"From the looks of things, she must have tried to fight her way out of it," Mama said.

"One thing Miss Marlissa don't like is being caught," Mercy said. "By the time I got to her, she was cool as a cucumber patch, looking like some kind of beautiful bug snagged up in a cobweb."

I loved the idea of that, Marlissa twisted up in a web—spider food. "What did she do?" I said.

"Now, give me a minute. I was getting to that." Mercy kneaded her neck. "She blinked at me with those big, green baby doll eyes of hers, and she said, 'How could you've been so careless, Mercy?'"

Mercy's tale seeped into the floor and walls, all of us gone quiet.

"Devilishness," Miss Wessie said. "Pure devilishness."

Mama tried to stifle a giggle, but it escaped like a sneeze, tickling at Miss Wessie until she joined in—the two of them doubling over with laughter.

Mercy stared at the two of them, her face awash with astonishment. She plopped her hands on her little waist. "I don't see a thing in this world funny about a woman on her way to losing her job or worse."

Mama and Miss Wessie straightened themselves. Their laughter petered, seriousness drifting back into place.

"Now, Mercy, we ain't laughing at you," Miss Wessie said, bending over halfway, lifting her apron to blot the shine spreading across her nose.

"You pay us no mind." Mama said. "You finish telling us what happened."

Mercy looked down at the floor. I followed her gaze, my eyes stopping, catching on the cocklebur clinging to the hem of her dress. *When will that thing every leave? Git.*

"I told Marlissa I was going to tell Miss Cordelia what she done. And she said, 'I'm sure Mother will be beside herself that you let this happen. That you've been so careless.'" Mercy shifted her feet, the movement shaking loose the cocklebur to drift across the table and mope just above the Christian Dior. "She said it could be our little secret—a fairy secret. Just so long as I cleaned up the mess."

Mama walked over to Mercy and touched her elbow. "I'm pretty sure I can help you with this, but we have to figure out how you're going to explain where the dress is."

Mercy grabbed hold of Mama, hugging her around the neck. "Miss Cordelia has me seeing about getting Marlissa's slippers dyed to match her dress. I'm gonna tell her they needed to keep it for a perfect match."

"Sounds like you done thought of everything, Mercy, except where we all gonna run off and hide when Cordelia Mayfield finds out what we all been up to." Miss Wessie breathed out hard, stirring the cocklebur across the table in my direction.

Mama ignored Miss Wessie, her eyes locking onto Marlissa's talent show dress. She lifted it from the table, holding it out in front of her, looking down at it, then over to me.

"Grace." Miss Wessie said, warning wedged in her voice.

A dangerous looked passed between Mama and Miss Wessie— gasoline soaked and matchstick ready. That awful cocklebur wobbled in the crosshairs of their glare, gaining momentum, moving faster in my direction. I swatted at it, pushing it back across the room.

Mama hugged the Christian Dior to her chest. "I think I know how I'll fix things."

Miss Wessie breathed in, preparing to speak, sucking the cocklebur between her teeth. She hesitated and shut her mouth again. The prickly thing popped like a bubble—the sound, a broken guitar string—a tiny explosion of ashen powder splattering across her lips and chin. "Where'd you put that whiskey, Grace?" She dabbed her kerchief across her forehead, and then her lips, spreading the dust across her cheek and up to her ear.

Chapter 31

The talent show stage, an enormous affair, covered the Court House steps, protruding into Mayfield Square like the bow of a great ship. The viewing stands, positioned for maximum advantage were filled to capacity. All of Providence was packed in and bending the boards.

Founder's Day had come around too quickly, hardly giving me time to sort through my preparations. Ready or not, I stood inside the contestant tent adjacent to the festivities—Marlissa Mayfield, yet to arrive.

My nerves were getting the better of me, my stomach, the slow grind of an ice cream churn. There was time, time to change my plans, time to stop what I was setting into motion. If things flowered the way I hoped, I would humiliate Marlissa just as she had me. Only, I would be betraying Mama's plans, and using Etta Mae to do it.

Excitement propelled me the weeks leading up to that day, the way a wicked thought might. A naughty feeling warm and pleasurable as a good kind of hurt.

I looked down at my gray satin, full length cape, checking the closures just like Mama instructed. "Don't let anybody see underneath," she said, before sending me off into the tent. "Wait to take it off at the very last minute."

"Out damn spot! Out, I say!" Across the tent, Virginia Fenton rehearsed her monologue folding one puffy hand into the other, her fairy charm bracelet making a racket. Since meeting Miss Joanne Woodward at Mistletoe, Virginia declared her devotion to the stage, setting out to conquer her place upon it, dwelling within the delusion she would, no doubt, one day become a great actress.

I, along with all the other contestants watched Virginia, all of us unsettled by the look of her. A long brown wig cascaded over her broad shoulders and down the back of her white, floor length tunic. Her feet were bare—ten fat piggies poking and wiggling out beneath the hem.

To my right, the tent flap stirred. Etta Mae's face poked through. What was she doing there? She knew the plan. I hurried over pushing through the flap, into the late afternoon light, taking hold of her arm, hurrying behind the tent next to the shrubs where no one could see. "What's wrong?" I was frightened she might have changed her mind.

"I'm nervous is all," she said. In the gold, autumnal light, her eyes glowed rich like topaz. "Are you sure Granny won't get mad? I've never lied to her before."

Never lied. Was such a thing even possible? "Not telling a thing isn't the same as lying," I said, trying to find the words to steady her. "Think of it as a surprise." Etta Mae nodded her head, wanting to believe me. From the very beginning of my scheming, she had been easy to convince. "You remember what Mama said, don't you? What a wonderful thing it would be for all of Providence to hear an angel sing."

"You said this show isn't for me."

I rolled my eyes. "You hush up now and remember what I told you." I took hold of her by the pink shoulders of the pretty new dress Mama made for her, the exact color of the rose embellishments sewn onto my cape. "Once they hear you sing, everything will change."

"You don't think we'll get in trouble?"

"Trouble?" Oh, I knew there would be trouble—that was what I was planning on, what I was praying for. I was prepared for it. Once the domino was flicked, there would be no stopping the others. I knew I was at risk—in danger of Marlissa telling my secret, of her letting all of Providence know Etta Mae was my sister. That was the bill I was prepared to pay—for the pleasure of humiliating Marlissa in front of the entire town. After all, I was already Bug Girl—Miss Sticky Fingers. What would having a colored sister matter? "Once they hear you sing, all the trouble in the world will melt away."

When that trouble came, whose fault would it be, really? Miss Wessie had been the one to put the notion into my head, setting the wheels to turn. *Imagine, the two of you up there competing for that prize. Miss Lady up there playing the piano, and Etta Mae making all kinds of a joyful noise.* She was right. Yes, I possessed a gift, a gift greater than Marlissa's. Etta Mae, she was the virtuoso; she was the genius. What was the point of any of it anyway? I would never be allowed to beat a Mayfield, even if I did it fair and square.

"Thank you, Analeise." Etta grabbed hold of me, wrapping and folding her tiny self into me.

"For what?" There was no use in trying to break free, her grip as tight as a canning jar lid. I relented, letting her have me.

"For giving me your chance." She began to hum, her body swaying, pulling me along with her.

Right away, I felt it, the soothing vibrations of her voice possessing me. Tricking me. Making me want to love her. "Turn me loose," I said, doing my best to wriggle free. "I best get on back to the tent." Still out of my head from her witchcraft, I kissed her on the cheek and turned to escape.

"Analeise? You know how much I love you?" she said.

I spun around, still not myself, still tethered to her thrall. The words spilled out. "A bushel?" I said. Applause broke loose, a contestant exiting the stage.

"And a peck," she hollered above the noise. She spread her arms wide, her smile a glorious thing. Before she could lure me back to her, before I might change my mind, I gathered up my cape and hurried to the tent

Inside, the place was mayhem, a clamor of tap shoes and twirling batons, everyone preparing for their turn on stage. Where was Marlissa?

"Here's the smell of the blood still: all the perfumes of Arabia will not sweeten this little hand," Virginia said, walking in a circle, her eyes wide as a lunatic's.

Dink put down his harmonica. "Little hand." He bent over laughing. "Virginia Fenton, you got hands as big as a catcher's mitt."

"You shut your face," she said, hurrying over to him, giving him a push, toppling him into Annette Everston and her prize chicken, Doodle Bug.

"Dang, Virginia. I almost squashed Annette's ugly chicken."

Annette scooped up her chicken, cradling the clucking thing like a baby. "Sweet Doodle. My sweet, sweet Doodle," she said, scurrying to the other side of the tent.

Dink brushed the dust off his Sunday breeches. "Who are you supposed to be anyway, Virginia? The bride of Frankenstein."

"I'm Lady Macbeth, you moron." Virginia snatched Dink's harmonica, holding it above her head. "Hell is murky," she hollered, hurling it across the place, grazing poor Doodle Bug, setting her off again into another squawking frenzy.

I hurried past her ladyship, beyond Annette and her hysterical chicken, desiring to steer clear from any brawl which might unsettle my cape, ruining the surprise hidden beneath.

Then there was quiet, all the noise sucked from the tent—as if a lid fell down over the world, extinguishing the sound. I twirled around, holding the cape's clasp close to my neck.

Marlissa Mayfield. She stood still, her magnificent dress casting starlight across the place. The ambient light grew brighter, that Mayfield Shine blooming and brightening all the dim corners. The noise tumbled back in, the girls gushing first. They scrambled to her—all of them colorless, powdery, desperate moths. The boys, they stood dazed, moved in ways then beyond their comprehension. Even Dink held a wonder in his face, a look of tenderness.

Mrs. Lawrence poked her head into the tent, snapping her fingers. "Marlissa Mayfield and Analeise Newell, please come with me," she said. "Time to line up."

We had known the order of performance the past two weeks, contestants organized alphabetically and by category. Marlissa would be first, a detail which could not have been more perfect if I planned it myself.

The girls unfurled, revealing Marlissa. The Christian Dior stunned, the slightest movement shooting off sparks. Her brilliance was spellbinding. Mama managed the impossible, mending the underside of her gown to perfection. Cordelia Mayfield was none the wiser.

My own dress? I could hardly wait to remove my cape. I walked to Marlissa, everyone's eyes slashing the air between us.

Virginia stood aside Marlissa, her chest puffed out. "Mind yourself, Bug Girl."

Unlike Marlissa, I did not hate Virginia Fenton; I pitied her. "My goodness, I hardly recognized you, Virginia. Don't you look fetching?"

"Fetchin," Dink yelled. "The only thing Virginia is fetchin' is a dog bone."

Laughter covered up the place, smothering the tension. "You shut, up," Virginia yelled, charging Dink, laying him flat and winded.

Mrs. Lawrence clapped her hands together. "Enough of that carrying on. Don't make me send for your parents," She snapped her fingers. "Marlissa and Analeise, I need you girls to hurry on up."

"Oui," Marlissa said, turning away, her gown careening into mine, setting off my own dress to tingle and hum. Had Mama sewn her hoodoo into the thing? I followed close behind, our hems swaying and touching, a thrill of tiny electric shocks riding my spine.

We stood below the stage at the foot of the wooden steps—the distance above, a good ten feet. An assault of tap shoes scraped and slapped the stage above—sporadic eruptions of applause in between. "Line up right here," Mrs. Lawrence said, casting glances between Marlissa and me, her eyes measuring the distance between the two of us, assessing the risk of leaving us there unattended. "Don't you two look just lovely. Remember. When you're done, exit off the other side."

"Mrs. Lawrence. Come quick," someone yelled. "Virginia's killing Dink."

"My stars." Mrs. Lawrence scampered off.

Virginia's voice reverberated from the tent. "Hell is murky."

I stood there alone with Marlissa, the sun teasing her dress, feral pinpricks of light having their way upon me—blinding me. I imagined a hole poked clean through her and all that Mayfield Shine spilling out.

A lullaby voice spoke from behind. "You look just like a sparkler."

Etta Mae. Why did she refuse to listen? She knew she was to hide behind the camellia bushes.

"Hello there?" Marlissa said, her voice curious and sweet, her delicate neck angling for a look at my colored sister.

Etta Mae lifted up her hands, shielding herself from the glare. "My name is Etta Mae. Etta Mae Johnston." Tap shoes struck the stage. Another rush of applause.

"Enchanté," Marlissa said.

Etta Mae giggled, her face speckled with light. "You're Marlissa Mayfield."

I backed up into the shade of the stage, angling myself from the sun and reach of Marlissa's brilliance.

Marlissa smiled, her eyes narrowing. "You must be Analeise's . . ." She paused, looking at Etta and then me.

I had to stop Marlissa, stop her from telling Etta Mae, at least until after the talent show. "She's . . .um . . ."

"Your beautiful friend?" Marlissa said, smiling at Etta Mae, walking to her, standing so close she engulfed her in shimmer. "What a pretty pink dress."

"Thank you. Miss Grace sewed it special."

For once, Marlissa spoke the truth. Etta Mae did look lovely—completely transformed. Her little girl plaits removed and replaced with an elegant ballerina bun sitting atop her pretty head.

"Your voice. It sounds like music," Marlissa said. "Like you're singing when you speak. A fairy's voice."

Beguile. That was what Marlissa was doing. I knew her scheme, the net of enchantment she was casting over my Etta Mae, the net she cast over everyone.

"I'm gonna be an opera singer."

"How wonderful," Marlissa said. "You'll have to sing for me sometime."

Etta Mae crossed her hands at her heart. "I'd love to."

"Splendid." Marlissa smiled, folding one hand into the other, resting them at her waist.

"Etta Mae?" Danger was afoot. I stepped out from the stage's shadow, back into Marlissa's dazzle. I squinted into the brightness.

"Maybe you could play the piano for me sometime," Etta Mae said.

"That would be utterly delightful."

I touched Etta Mae's shoulder to try and shake her from Marlissa's grip. "Etta Mae?"

"You know what your ensemble is missing, don't you?" Marlissa said, her left-hand fiddling with her right. Before I could stop her, Marlissa held Etta Mae's wrist.

"Leave her be," I said.

Marlissa fastened her jewelry to Etta Mae's wrist. "A fairy charm bracelet for the girl with the fairy voice."

A fairy charm bracelet. "You can't take that, Etta Mae. Give that back. It's a trick."

Etta Mae ignored me, holding out her tiny hand, admiring all the dangling, glittery pieces. It was as if I vanished, evaporated by that hot Mayfield Shine. I broke apart, covered up and blinded by light, my ears full of bacon grease sizzle. I bent over, unfastening the bottom clasp of my cape, and then the next—a bit of my own sparkle spilling out onto the ground. I stood up straight and spun around again, my cape fanning out and opening just below the waist.

"Analeise, what are you doing?" Etta Mae said.

Another spin, and I opened the next clasp. My dress knocked into Marlissa's. Mama's handy work *buzzed* and *popped.* Around and around I went. I was a twinkling tornado. I spun and spun until my cape came loose, cast off and slung to the ground.

Marlissa gasped.

"You're wearing the same dress," Etta Mae said, squeezing her eyes shut and popping them back open again.

"Are we?" I smiled, struggling to focus, disoriented from spinning and the lustrous effect Marlissa and I made with our Christian Dior gowns. Marlissa wore the original, and I, the one Mama copied to perfection.

A look of utter shock seized Marlissa's gorgeous face, a look as satisfying as the vibrations coming from the stitching in my bodice. Marlissa stammered. "Where did you . . .?"

"Where did I get my dress?" I said, plucking the skirt of my gown with my fingers. "Just some ole' Butterick pattern Mama picked up from Woolworth sometime back."

"Miss Grace made that?" Etta Mae said, every bit as astonished as Marlissa.

"Don't worry, Marlissa," I said. "I doubt anyone will even notice." I touched her elbow and leaned to kiss her cheek. "Fairy kisses are the sweetest, don't you think?"

Applause came again, only this time there were hoots and hollers. The emcee's voice boomed from the speakers. "The Pride of Dixie Tap Troupe," he said. "And now, ladies and gentlemen, it gives me great pleasure to introduce our next contestant, Miss Marlissa Mayfield."

Marlissa shut her eyes, hands balling into fists. "Good luck, Marlissa," Etta Mae gently touched her shoulder. A moment passed and Marlissa stood still, her breathing deep, her body swaying.

"Marlissa. It's your turn. Didn't you hear?" I said.

The applause peeled apart, the awkward ebb followed by the murmur of audience whispers. "Ladies and gentlemen, Miss Marlissa Mayfield."

"Are you all right, Marlissa?" Etta Mae said.

My dress stung like an army of fire ants. What had I done? Why had I not listened to Mama? Why did I take off my cape too soon?

"They're calling you." I tugged at Marlissa's arm.

Another commotion erupted from the tent, Virginia's voice hollering above the noise. "Moron."

I shook Marlissa. Etta Mae joined in, her fairy charm bracelet shaking franticly. "You're ruining everything," I said.

Marlissa's body froze, a deep breath pushing out. Her chin lifted; her eyes clicked open. I was done for.

"Ladies and gentlemen, Miss Marlissa Mayfield."

Chapter 32

"Marlissa, they're calling you," I said. If I did not need Marlissa to get up on that stage, I might have killed her, might have prayed her dead like poor drunk Daddy.

Marlissa grinned and blinked, staring off into the camellias.

Etta Mae pulled at Marlissa's elbow. "She won't budge."

I took to the stage steps, creeping up to take a peek. "Here she is," the emcee said, grabbing hold of my arm, hauling me up the last few steps. "No need to be shy."

A flourish of *oohs* and *awws* arose from the audience. Applause followed. "It's not my turn," I said.

"Miss Marlissa Mayfield," the emcee announced, tugging me over to the black, baby grand piano on loan from the Mayfields.

I did everything I could to anchor my slick-bottomed slippers, to keep from being handled across the stage. "I'm not . . ."

"She's not Marlissa Mayfield, I am."

The audience awoke again, gasps and bacon sizzle. I jerked away from the emcee, preparing myself for whatever treachery Marlissa planned.

The emcee's head ping ponged between the two of us, his hair slicked and glistening with pomade. "What do we have here? Some sort of surprise?" He laughed into the microphone, his nervousness catching and pinching between his eyebrows. Skittish audience laughter followed. "And who might you be," he said, squeezing my shoulder, lowering the microphone to my mouth.

My voice cracked. "Analeise Newell." The audience sizzled again. I dared to look directly into the crowd, searching the place for Mama. That very moment I knew Miss Wessie was coming undone, a fury of tangled bobbin thread.

"We've fallen out of order," Marlissa bowed her head, the sun, an electric current running through her tumble of blond waves.

"I think I might understand the confusion, Miss Mayfield. It would seem you have a twin." The emcee extended his hand to Marlissa. She glided over to us, that peculiar way she had of moving, the illusion of the floor sliding beneath her feet.

My eyes snagged the gilded, framed edge of Patton Mayfield's portrait perched upon an easel, angled at the far corner of the stage. His handsome face, vibrant and amused.

The emcee stepped behind me, pulling Marlissa to my side. Our gowns collided. My skin, a glory of prickles and ant bite stings. The audience rumbled at the site of the two of us standing there together.

"And how might this have happened? Two lovely young ladies wearing the same pretty dress?"

The Mayfields sat side by side in a festooned viewing stand reserved just for them. Miss Joanne Woodward was to the right of Miss Cordelia and Abel to the left of Mr. Kingston. I glanced Patton's portrait, then Marlissa to my left.

"My gown is by Mr. Christian Dior," Marlissa said, pulling the microphone to her Cupid's bow lips.

"Mama made mine," I said, grabbing hold of the microphone. The audience fussed again, heads turning side to side. I imagined Miss Wessie out there in the colored section, laid out on the ground in the throes of a spectacular convulsion. Her favorite wig, Lucinda, come loose and sunning like a bobcat.

Marlissa tugged at the emcee's arm, pulling him down, her hand covering her mouth. She whispered into his ear. He nodded, straightening his posture, his eyes fully taking her in. I knew the meaning of that glassy eyed look, the moment her bewitching took hold.

"Miss Mayfield would like to bestow Miss Newell the opportunity of going first," he said, speaking to the audience, but all the while looking down and adoring her. "What a good sport you are. How about a round of applause for Miss Marlissa Mayfield?"

Providence cast a rapt eye upon Marlissa, following her descent from the stage, taking in her sunset, until the last bit of her was gone, and the light grew pale.

"Miss Analeise Newell, ladies and gentlemen," the emcee said, glancing down at his note card. "Playing . . . Chopin." The applause was feeble at first, stirring to a respectable clatter—to the sound of a lazy rainfall.

What was I to do? Was Etta Mae still down below? Had she deserted me?

Fourth row center, in the section of chairs arranged on risers, I spotted Miss Minnie Jean, her withered lips set in a snarl, bony hands idle in her lap. *Buttooonzzz . . .*

I sat upon the piano bench. Sheriff Dobb's badge glinted in the corner of my eye. There was still time to turn back, to abide Mama's plan. *If Marlissa is going to play your Chopin, you're gonna wear her dress. We'll fix her little wagon.* What a delight it was to be in cahoots with Mama.

The Mayfield Pickle Factory whistle screeched, an empty call to the workers looking on from the stands. All of them set free for the whole of the day.

I counted, waiting for it to pass, until only vibrations and vapor remained, and I played the first of Etta Mae's introduction. The beginning notes, angry and hot.

The top of Etta Mae's head crested at the stairs, raven's wing black. *Good girl. Just like we planned.* She hesitated longer than rehearsed. *Come on Etta Mae. Come on.* I stopped playing and started again. She ascended the last of the steps, standing at the edge of the stage, my cape fastened at her neck and tumbling behind her.

I pulled my hands from the keys, the notes falling away to silence. Etta Mae stood still in the rising murmur. She lifted her chin and stared across the stage.

"Colored gal," a man hollered. "What you doing up there?" Other voices followed, disdain pealing through the horde.

Dink's fat mama hurled the last bites of her candied apple at the stage, landing at Etta Mae's feet. The thud gave Etta Mae a start, her green-flecked eyes blinking down at her slippers.

I snapped by fingers. "Etta Mae. Look at me. Look here." Her eyes locked mine. I raised my hand, counting off with my fingers. *One, two, three . . .* I played again, angrier than before.

Etta Mae took her cue, lifting her chin, spreading her arms. She moved across the stage, her fairy bracelet *jingling*. The cape, fastened only at the neck unfurled behind her, blossoming like a magnificent rose covered parachute. She walked quick in a circle and stopped center stage.

"Get off from there," Dink's mama yelled.

I called to Etta Mae from the piano. "Remember what I said. Sing mad. Sing for your poor, burned up mama."

She turned to me, her eyes, watery and lustrous with fear. She jerked back around—tongue firm on the trigger. She fired her first note, a flawless blast of wrath. The audience jerked from the shock, heads knocking back from the force.

My mouth went hot, scalded from the sound. Her voice, a flash of light, left sunspots swirling in my eyes. She took another turn of the stage, her eyes blazing wild. The Queen of the Night devoured my Etta Mae from the inside out, until nothing remained but the green flecks in her eyes.

I knew every word she sang. Tasted and saw every note. *The vengeance of Hell boils in my heart. Death and despair flame around me.*

The audience sat transfixed, mouths agape. All of them hypnotized— enraptured by every flourish. A grumble sounded way off in the distance, followed by a gust of wind. The courthouse flags *snapped* and *popped.* I jabbed harder at the notes.

The Queen of the Night unraveled in her song. Hands reaching, arms spreading. Her body spinning with the music.

Dark clouds pushed together from every corner, choking out the sun, sealing the sky until the blue was gone. From all directions, the wind blew, birthing whirly winds of dirt and leaves. Still, the town sat. Unblinking. Slack-jawed. Paralyzed with wonder.

The rising storm caught the wide brim of Miss Joanne Woodward's hat, nudging her head to the right and left. Cordelia Mayfield's own lavender hat blew free, caught on a current lifting it higher and higher. Mrs. Mayfield sat unflinching, her eyes hidden behind sunglasses. She reached, pulling a pin from her chignon and then another, until her hair whipped free.

Abel stared ahead, leaning against Kingston Mayfield, his dark hair wild about his face. Mr. Mayfield's tie came alive—berserk in the crosswind. The Mayfield's, my Abel, and Miss Joanne Woodward—all of them, a beautiful chaos.

Etta held out the final, violent note, fists raised to the heavens, her cape in flight. A succession of three lightning bolts slashed the air, each one ripping and drilling into the base of Providence's largest, oldest oak.

Thunder detonated like a bomb beneath us, shaking the wooden stage, rattling my teeth, toppling the portrait of Patton Mayfield. Providence looked on, bewitched and motionless. The rain came, a dense, pounding wall of water moving north across the lawn. The frigid deluge broke the spell, dousing and reviving the town.

Pandemonium struck. The crowd screamed and scurried in all directions. The stage was last to be hit by rain, the drops so profuse and heavy they lay against the piano keys like restless fingers.

Etta Mae turned to me, fully herself once more, blinking giant drops of water from her lashes. That lovely, glistening terror returned to her eyes. I hurried to her, slipping, and sliding across the stage. "What happened?" she yelled.

I grabbed hold of her shoulders and hollered. "You done sang up a storm."

"No, I didn't," she said, shaking her head, rain droplets slinging off her nose.

"Make it stop."

"Where's my granny? I want my granny," she said, snatching away.

Miss Wessie was the last person I wanted to see. "Get a hold of yourself," I said, shaking her.

Squinting into the maelstrom, I searched for Mama, finding only the Mayfields seated in the stands, both of them more shimmery and golden—a steamy vapor hovering about Miss Cordelia. Mr. Kingston looked down upon the mayhem regarding Etta Mae and me. He turned loose a timpani roll of laughter, as if delighted by catastrophe. Marlissa made her way up to the top of the viewing stand, folding into my Abel Darlington, her ruined Christian Dior twinkling in lightning strobe.

Barely above the thunder, I heard the faint sound of my name. Hand in hand, Mama and Miss Wessie hurried across the square, shirking beneath cracking branches, shielding their eyes from the sharp slant of rain. I grabbed hold of Etta Mae and took off for the stairs, Etta Mae's cape dragging soaked and heavy behind her.

"What you both gone and done?" Miss Wessie said, dropping to her knees, grabbing Etta Mae and me, inspecting us for injury. She yanked our arms hard, pulling us in tight for a hug.

Etta Mae sobbed and babbled. "Didn't mean to lie."

Mama was soaked through, her mascara, trailing dark rivers. "We gotta get out of here."

Knotted together, we hurried to the truck, storm clouds swirling and funneling above. Folks ran wild, bumping and knocking.

From behind, a howling gale pushed against us, snatching Miss Wessie's sopping wig. "Lucinda," Etta Mae yelled, her tiny hands reaching. We watched Lucinda, watched her lift and tumble higher until she snagged in the branches of that large oak tree. Miss Wessie pressed her palm against her head. Her white, shorn hair fluoresced, a startling flash of bright in the murk.

Up ahead, the Fenton's hurried to their car. Jane held tight to her father. Virginia looked about, rebuking her mother's reach, her guinea hen eyes wild and darting with excitement.

Right then, I wanted my friend; I wanted my Jane. I screamed her name. She turned, straining to see me through the bluster. I called her name again, hoping she might forgive me, allow me another chance. At last, she raised her hand to wave.

Mr. Fenton pulled the car doors open, pushing in Jane and then Mrs. Fenton. Virginia held out her arms, her Lady Macbeth tunic plastered against her pink skin. She delighted in the storm, a smile spreading across her face in the wash of rain. She let loose her dreadful, goblin laugh, made even more terrible in the squall.

Mr. Fenton yelled from the other side. "Dammit, Virginia. Get in the car."

The wind ripped again, upsetting the branches, playing a monstrous symphony. Virginia yelled her lady Macbeth soliloquy into the commotion. "I tell you yet again, Banquo's buried," she said. "He cannot come out on's grave."

The old oak creaked, the storm tangling in the massive branches. It was not as quick as it might have been, the falling of that tree. Graceful and violent. *Whoosh.* The crush of metal. The shatter of glass. The Fenton's and their car consumed and flattened beneath the glorious old tree.

Mama set off to help them, but Miss Wessie yanked her back. Etta Mae toppled forward, landing on her knees.

Jane. I just stood there blinking, wondering if it might be a dream. My eyes passed over the tree following the trunk to the crater left there in the earth. There in the gape, I detected the beginning of movement. First a trickle, and then a spew. A writhing mound of something grew from the hole, then flattened and spread across the grass.

"What is that?" I said, shielding my eyes from the rain.

"Somebody help." Mama cried, paying me no mind. Sheriff Dobbs came running, stopping short of the wreckage. "Briar, it's the Fenton's."

"Stay there, Grace," the Sheriff called back.

265

The spew from the ground branched off, part of it wriggling across the fallen tree and the other moving toward us.

Etta Mae pushed herself up from the mud and pointed. "Granny, look."

It was quick upon us, the ground squirming beneath our feet. Thousands and thousands of cicada nymphs, fresh from the deep down, covered up our shoes, clawing up our ankles, latching onto the hems our dresses.

Etta Mae was the first to scream, her wail, shrill and terrible. The dreadful sound revived my dress, constricting the bodice—stealing my breath. I tugged at my gown. Ripped and pulled. My knees gave out, tipping me backwards. I screamed, spending the last of my breath. Darkness slithered, curling in around me.

Banquo is buried . . . he cannot come out.

Chapter 33

I awoke in the truck, shoved tight against Mama, soaked and shivering, stripped down to my underthings. My imitation Christian Dior was wadded up and tossed to the floorboard.

My first blurry thought was of my Jane, my dear, sweet friend beneath that fallen oak tree. It was the storm that sobered me, the terrible thing releasing its burden, rattling and booming over the top of us. The force of the rain was so fierce the wipers failed to keep pace. Mama hunched forward, gripping the steering wheel.

Scissored between Miss Wessie's rain-slicked legs, Etta Mae sobbed. "Are they all dead?" I said.

"There she is. There's Miss Lady," Miss Wessie said, a splinter of relief pricking at the fear laying thick in her voice. Etta Mae followed, speaking my name through broken whimpers.

"You gave us quite the scare," Mama said, squeezing the steering wheel.

"All dead," Etta Mae said. "All dead." Stunning globs of tears glistened and spilled from my sister's eyes.

"Hush now, sweet baby," Miss Wessie said, wrapping her arms about Etta Mae.

There was despair in Miss Wessie's voice, a wretchedness I had not heard since that night Etta Mae and her granny first stepped upon our porch, the night Etta Mae's mama died.

Etta Mae's sorrow eased long enough for her to speak. "I didn't mean to."

Didn't mean to . What exactly did she regret? Was she sorry she lied to her granny? Or was she sorry she sang up that storm? The storm that toppled that tree, the storm that killed my Jane Fenton.

"Then why'd you do it?" I said. A gust of wind slammed the truck, rocking us against one another like dice in a Yahtzee cup.

"Why'd she do it? Is that what you be asking, Miss Lady?" Miss Wessie words spun like a twister.

"Not now, Wessie," Mama said, clutching the wheel, her knuckles angry and pale.

"If not now, then when, Grace? From the looks of things there might not be another time. What the two of you pulled tonight, you and Miss Lady here, I just can't get my head around it. How you could've done such a damn fool thing."

"I told you I didn't know about Etta Mae. I told you it was Analeise's and Etta Mae's doing," Mama said. "I didn't know."

Miss Wessie let out a crash of thunder. "Etta Mae's doing. You really think Etta Mae had anything to do with this?"

"I didn't mean to do it," Etta Mae wept into her hands, her fairy charm bracelet sliding down her skinny arm.

Mama hunched lower, pulling in closer to the steering wheel, shoulder blades sprouting from her back. "Didn't look like Analeise dragged her up on that stage."

Miss Wessie rolled her head from side to side, her neck cracking. I could feel the pressure building, the storm outside and the one percolating inside Miss Wessie.

I had to do something quick. Something to save Miss Wessie from murdering Mama and me. I took in a deep breath and shut my eyes.

"It was my fault. It was my doing."

The wipers raked across the windshield. The wind played the truck like a harmonica, whistling through gap and gape. Miss Wessie leaned against the seat, her neck lolling, her breathing measured. She sat up straight and looked down at me. "It ain't your fault, Miss Lady. Oh, what you did was awful. Yes, ma'am, plain awful. But I reckon you can't help yourself one bit. I reckon you got it honest from your deceitful Mama here."

Mama slammed on the brakes, all of us slinging forward and back again, the truck sliding off and ceasing on the side of the road. "How dare you."

Miss Wessie ignored Mama. "What you need to know, Miss Lady, for your own good and for all of ours, is that you is playing a dangerous game when you did what you done. Putting a colored child up on that stage in front of all them white folks. Putting her in a place they think she ought not be. That's the sort of thing that gets colored folks hung up in trees."

Etta Mae's crying stopped, her eyes filling with fear, her tiny body shifting and struggling to find her granny's face.

Mama yelled above the mayhem. "Shut up, Wessie. You're scaring the girls."

"Good," Miss Wessie yelled. "They need scaring if it's what's to keep them both safe. And alive."

"I'm warning you," Mama said.

"And I'm warning you. I'm warning all of you. When you mess with Cordelia Mayfield, you is playing with fire." Miss Wessie seemed to grow, to expand with each heaving breath. "You dare to put this here child in the same dress as Marlissa and have her parade around in front of God and everybody."

"Please be quiet," Etta Mae covered her ears with her hands.

"Have you forgot, Grace?"

"Leave it be," Mama said.

Etta Mae pressed her hands harder against her ears. "Please."

I wanted to know what Mama knew. What she failed to remember. "Forgot what?"

Mama revved the engine. "Enough."

"Only thinking of yourself, Grace. And poor Mercy. What about her? Cordelia Mayfield gonna eat her alive for bringing you that dress. And all the while, she think you her friend helping her, and all the time you is lying and scheming. You no better than that crazy Cordelia Mayfield."

Crazy.

Mama slammed her hands against the steering wheel. "Mind your words, Wessie."

I glanced down at my dress wadded up on the floor. A wingless, milky-white cicada nymph crept out of a fold, and then another. A cold crop of sweat beads popped up above my lip, the threat of vomit rising up right alongside.

"Hush," Etta Mae yelled, rivulets of tears at work again.

"So, I ask you again if you forgot? Forgot what I know. What I seen." Miss Wessie looked down at me when she spoke, Etta Mae's storm gaining force and churning in her words. "That I worked out there all them years at Mistletoe tending to them Mayfields. Holding Marlissa when she just a baby."

Holding Marlissa. Something close to terror took hold. "What did you say?" I swiped the back of my hand over my lip, smearing sweat across my cheek.

"You heard me, child."

Mama slammed her elbow into the door, sending a cicada nymph to skitter across her lap. "Dammit, Wessie."

"I reckon you forgot I was out there the day Patton Mayfield did what he did."

"Leave it be."

"When that wicked, beautiful boy burned up and fell out that window." She sucked in a big breath. When . . ."

Etta Mae opened up her dainty mouth and loose a howl. At first, it rang off key, but she held it, scaling it up one octave after another, transforming it into one perfect, ear-splitting, skin-prickling note.

I covered my ears and let loose my own shriek. "Make her stop." The taste of black licorice filled my mouth.

"Stop it, girl." Miss Wessie shook Etta Mae by the shoulders, not stopping until she rattled loose the note.

We sat there, chests heaving, Etta Mae's exquisite misery ringing in our ears.

"Do you hear that?" I said, aware something was different, that something changed.

"Hear what?" Mama said, sweat moistening the dried-up riverbeds of mascara trailing her cheeks.

"The storm. It stopped."

Etta Mae looked out through the foggy glass and into the gloom, the afternoon light preternaturally dim. "What is that?" she said, squinting and pointing, the charms from her bracelet hanging limp.

Movement. The fence, as far ahead as I could see and to our right squirmed. The whole place writhed.

"It can't be." Miss Wessie cranked down her window.

Mama squeezed the wheel again, her nails scratching at it. "What is it, Wessie?"

A smatter of raindrops fell across the top of the truck and across the windshield. "Dear Lord, Grace." Miss Wessie eased her head to the open window, just short of poking it through.

"It's cicadas," she whispered. A nymph crawled over the sill into the truck and down the door, its bulging eyes, red as rubies. Another followed and then another. Miss Wessie flicked at them with her middle finger.

"Roll it up, Wessie," Mama said.

Etta Mae panicked, leaning away from her granny, away from the window. "Close it, granny. Hurry."

Miss Wessie cranked at the window as hundreds of milky white, cicada nymphs spilled into the truck. Halfway up, the window stopped working.

"Hell fire," Miss Wessie said. "It ain't budging."

Etta Mae kicked and swatted. Everywhere were cicadas—all of them scurrying up and over us.

"Drive!" I hollered. Mama fiddled with the gears and stomped the gas, throwing us back against the seat.

"Get them off," Etta Mae yelled, another horrific scream growing in her throat, her body frantic and trembling, until the note broke loose, splitting our ears, ripping the sky back open again.

The rising gale shook the truck, blowing rain through the useless window. Pellets of ice fell and clattered, and still, Etta Mae held her stunning note. The hail grew larger and larger, lemon sized pieces pummeling the jalopy.

I covered my ears, staring straight into the storm. The bitter, smoky taste of black licorice swelled in my mouth. All the while, I stared at the glass, at the wandering crack. One fissure shot off from the other. The glass spun cobwebs, until at last it gave way. Thousands of jagged diamonds blew against us, catching in our hair. Spilling into our laps. All of us covered up and nicked with sparkle. Thousands of red, ruby eyes looking on.

Chapter 34

Hordes of nymphs clawed their way free from the deep down, all of them desperate for a place to molt. To every trunk, shrub, and post they clung, hail battered branches drooping from the weight. They clicked and skittered up the house, gambling on bowing shards of paint. No other place to claim, the cicadas relented, glittering beneath the light of a half-woke moon, accumulating quick and dangerous as fast falling snow.

The natural world had come undone, the delicate underpinnings unhinged and knocked loose by a song. Etta Mae, she had been the one to do it, to raze the place with hail—to unleash this plague of cicadas. But whose fault was it really? Had I not been the one to strike the blow, to set the plan?

There in the kitchen, by the light of a weeping candle, I dangled my legs over the side of the table.

"A miracle," Miss Wessie said, squinting in the gloom. "A sweet, hallelujah miracle we made it home alive." She dabbed the whiskey-soaked tail of a washrag against a tiny cut on my cheek. "We might have all been cut to ribbons." She took a swig of Old Crow and doused the rag again. "Do it hurt?"

The sting sent a thrill, a sensation I wanted to last, something to soothe and distract me, to temper or at least balance the teeter of panic and dread. The pleasure abandoned me all too quickly, numbed by the anesthetic property of spirits, leaving me unsatisfied and longing for other wounds. "No, ma'am. It doesn't."

"Looks like you got the worst of it. Just a nick here and there." Miss Wessie's breathing was a nervous tempo. "Altogether, I'd say we got off pretty good." She glanced at the window over the sink at the shadowy dance of nymphs scurrying across the panes. She took another swig of whiskey.

Passing over the top of the candle, the Old Crow sloshed and gleamed. To settle Etta Mae's nerves, Miss Wessie mixed her up a toddy with a splash of lemon and honey—the effect rendering the Queen of the Night unconscious and spooning against Mama in the parlor.

"Can I have a sip?"

She pressed the bottle against her bosom and looked down at me, her hair dusted and twinkling with glass. "Just a swallow." She leaned down, the candle flame playing eerie tricks upon her face.

I placed the lip of the bottle to my mouth, taking more than offered, enjoying the glorious scorch, the memory of Cordelia Mayfield's whisper swirling in my ear. *Some things in this world are meant to burn.* Warm and fresh with courage I asked my question.

"How come you never told me you worked for the Mayfields?"

Miss Wessie took the bottle. She stared down at me, her eyes gone darker and reflective in the puny light. We stayed that way, eyes locked and pulsing. The sound from the cicadas began to change. Amidst the *tick* and *clack*, there was a whisper of noise—a song. When my eyes drifted off to the window, Miss Wessie spoke, perhaps a kindness, a distraction from the rising calamity just beyond the walls.

"I reckon there was never a need for you to know."

"Was it a secret?"

"Wasn't no secret I suppose."

"Then why tell me now?"

Miss Wessie turned her head to the window, her hair glittery and glorious. Moments passed until she spoke again.

Miss Wessie turned back to face me. "You know what she say sometimes?"

I shook my head. "Who?"

"Miss Cordelia." She put the lip of the whiskey bottle just beneath her lip, blowing into it like a flute. "She say that this here world is a dangerous place for a beautiful thing."

I heard it before, spoken from Cordelia Mayfield's very lips that night at the gala. *Beautiful thing.*

"And she's right. There is danger in this world. That's why I'm scared for you and scared for Etta Mae. Two of the most beautiful things I know."

Why was she scared? Was she talking about what I did? About fooling Etta Mae up onto that stage. Making all the white folk angry.

"Are you mad at me? For what I did today."

"I'm not so much mad as I am disappointed." She reached out and touched my chin. "You is a smart girl. You ought to know better, and you ought to love Etta Mae better than you do."

Miss Wessie was right. I was a smart girl doing stupid things. Yes, I should do better by Etta Mae. I might have cried, the threat of tears working up from the knot growing in my throat.

The tin roof popped and contracted as it sometimes did in the throes of a powerful, summer heat. Only, it was fall, and the evening had turned off cool, chilled from the chunks of hail thrown down by the storm. Miss Wessie and I both looked to the ceiling. The cicadas grew louder.

Miss Wessie blew into the bottle again. "I looked after Patton before you was even a thought in your Mama's head. He was the most beautiful baby I ever lay eyes on. And quiet. So quiet." She placed one finger to her lips speaking in a hush. "People would carry on about what a good baby he was on account of it. From the very beginning, I knew something wasn't quite right, something unnatural about a baby never crying. Never making a peep."

"Was he sick?"

"I was worried something was wrong, that the child might be simple. He spoke nary a word long after children ought to be talking. Not so much as a jabber," she said, making a talking motion with her hand. "But Miss Cordelia, she wasn't a bit concerned. She just kept going on about Mayfield men and that's how it was with them. That she had it on good authority they spoke when they was good and ready."

"Was he mute?"

Miss Wessie took a step closer, the smell of whiskey strong on her breath. "He was near about four years old when he did up and talk. And when he did, it wasn't just some broken piece of a word or a single, proper one." She bit at her lip and shook her head. "No," she said, fanning out her arms, that bottle of Old Crow gripped tight in her hand. "It was a whole string of 'em."

"What was it he said?"

She cocked her head to the side, as if such an angle made remembering easy. "He called my name. And he stood there, not so much as a blink, staring a hole clean through me with those green Mayfield eyes, those long spider lashes, that angel hair curling at the ends. A face so pretty it almost hurt to look." She took another swig of whiskey. "And he say, 'Wessie. What was he doing, the great god Pan. Down in the reeds by the river? Spreading ruin and scattering ban.'"

My breathing turned quick and flimsy as Miss Wessie's. "What does it mean?"

"I'd heard it before. One of them poem's Miss Cordelia go about reciting on a whim. Written by a Miss Elizabeth Barrett Browning."

"Is that all he said?"

"Is that all?" Miss Wessie's was incredulous. "I reckon it was plenty at the time."

"Why you suppose he waited so long."

Miss Wessie nodded. "That's the point you see. He just sat back and watched those first few years, taking it all in." She dropped her voice to a whisper. "Looking and listening. Until he was ready. Ready to be a Mayfield. Ready to shine."

"Did he talk much after?"

"He had a way with words like his Daddy. He could be kind with them. He could be cruel."

Cruel.

"Those dark parts of Patton scared me—the parts hard to see through all that shine. Him telling a lie and making you believe it. Or

276

doing a terrible something and making you understand why it had to be done."

"Terrible things. What kind?"

Miss Wessie gave me a weak smile, her eyes shooting over to the window and back to me. "You sure ask a lot of questions."

"Go on. What kind of things?"

She took another swig of whiskey and wiped her mouth with the back of her hand. "He was always bothering Marlissa. Always toting her around when she was a baby, like she belonged to him only. And when she could walk and talk, he was always whispering things in her ear." She held up her finger to stop me from speaking, from asking another question. "That thing I worried over. That feeling I had. I was out there the day it happened. I was out there when that boy caught fire, when he went to jump out that window, doing anything to stop from burning up." Miss Wessie moved closer into the thrall of the candle's flicker, her hair all a dazzle. "Mr. Kingston, he did all he could, grabbing hold of that burning boy. Holding him up by the arm, trying to pull him back up through that window."

Mr. Mayfield's ruined hand. Right away, I knew; I knew how it happened. Just like Cordelia Mayfield said. *The time he tried to hold fire in his hand.*

"How did he catch fire?"

"Granny." Etta Mae stood at the door, her features dim in the shadows.

"I thought you was asleep," Miss Wessie said.

Etta Mae looked to the ceiling. "They woke me up."

I hopped down off the table. "Where's Mama?"

"Right here. I'm right here," she said, walking up behind Etta Mae.

"They're getting louder and louder." Etta Mae walked into the toss of candlelight. Her nightgown fell off one shoulder, wild strands of her hair sprouting from her ballerina bun. I thought of hateful Virginia Fenton all dressed up like Lady Macbeth, dead beneath a tree.

"Wessie, have you ever known such a thing?" Mama said. "So many cicadas all at once. This time of year."

"No," Miss Wessie said. "It ain't right, them coming back like they done."

A nymph scampered across my foot, lingering on my big toe. Another wriggled through a crack in the floor, another squeezing up right behind.

"They're coming up through the boards," Etta Mae whispered, as if any noise or sudden movement would send them flooding up through the floor to drown us.

"They ain't no harm to people," Miss Wessie said.

"It's just . . . they're so many." Mama hurried across the kitchen, taking Etta Mae by the shoulder and then me, moving us all over to stand with Miss Wessie.

"Will they be gone by morning?" Etta Mae took hold of my hand, lacing her fingers through mine, her fairy charm bracelet unpleasant against my wrist.

"Don't rightly know," Miss Wessie said.

Etta Mae squeezed my hand. "Well when? When will they be gone?"

Miss Wessie's eyes drifted upward. "I reckon when they done what they come to do."

The four of us moved in close, folding in together, weaving a knot. The song of the male cicada rose, the sound of millions of buckling tymbals. Vibrations passed through the walls with the rise of noise, agitating the floor, worrying our feet. Our heads jerked and strained in all directions, keeping check on the walls, spying all the dark corners. The light from the dwindling candle distorted our faces, having its way until we were no longer ourselves, all of us growing mad from the sound.

Chapter 35

Morning came, fallen hail chilling the air. A hungry choke of gray clouds gobbled the sun—the light turning dull as dusk. The whole night through, we held vigil there in the parlor, all of us undone by that never-ending noise. The windows granted but fragments of day, layers of cicadas clinging to all the screens, keeping us blind to what lay beyond.

In the quagmire of those sleepless hours before dawn, I languished, conjuring visions of the outside, painting terrifying landscapes in my mind. Miss Wessie was the one to suggest it, that we dare take a look.

"Stand back," Miss Wessie whispered, extending her arm. She pulled gently at the door, struggling at that familiar, warped spot on the floor. The cicada drone swelled in the room sending the keys of Daddy's old piano to tremble. With the front door open, we still could not see—the screen door, cicada infested and bowing.

"Sweet Jesus." Mama squeezed the collar of her nightgown.

Miss Wessie snapped her fingers. "Etta Mae, go fetch Granny the broom." Etta Mae ran to the kitchen and came back quick. Miss Wessie took to her knees and grabbed hold of the broom by the handle. She pushed the screen door slowly open with the stiff, straw bristles.

Mama stepped back, pulling Etta Mae and I with her, holding us in front, nervously kneading our necks.

Etta Mae gasped as the door yawned open, Mama's fingers digging into the soft tender of my shoulders. Miss Wessie wedged the handle against the leg of a side table to keep the door agape.

In the throes of my own imaginings, I failed to do it justice, failed to conjure the phantasmagoria of it all, the sheer numbers of the brood— an eternity of them dropped down like a drape to smother and suck all the xylem from the world, to shrivel every root and every leaf of every tree. Everywhere, Cicadas wrestled from their skin, gooey wings freshly sprung and crumpled, exoskeletons hardening, turning dark, growing resilient. Preparing.

Etta Mae tried to pull away, but Mama held her there with us.

"Wessie, Lord help us," Mama said.

Just look. Look at what we done.

"What do they want, Granny?"

Miss Wessie leaned back on the balls of her feet and shook her head. She reached for the broom handle, slowly sliding the door closed.

I thought of Halbert, his ear melting down his face. "They got secrets they keep," I said, softly. Perhaps he was right, perhaps they did keep our secrets, armies of nymphs buried in the deep down, nothing to do as the years pass but listen to the up above. Chewing and swallowing everything they hear. Bursting from secrets and lies.

Mama and Etta Mae turned to regard me, but I stared straight ahead, looking out into the yard. Miss Wessie eased the door a little at a time, the old rusty spring returning solemn. I watched until the door rested back in the frame, until the shabby parlor turned dim.

* * *

The phone lines were dead, a casualty of Etta Mae's tempest. Without a way of calling to check, for all we knew, we might very well have been the only four living souls left upon the sorry earth.

With it being Sunday and a cicada plague commencing, Miss Wessie took it upon herself to decide.

"We're going to church," she said. "If ever there was a time to pray, it's now, I reckon."

Mama and Miss Wessie set out to ready the truck, a ramshackle of rainwater, glass, and half-molted nymphs. They mopped, shooed, and brushed, doing their best to tend it—finally laying down towels upon which to sit.

Before heading out into the cicada drift, Miss Wessie maneuvered her feet into a pair of galoshes. She took turns toting Etta Mae and me to the truck. We wrapped our arms around her neck, legs scissoring about her waist. Affecting the high-stepping stride of a show horse, Miss Wessie tried her best, but there was no pleasant way around it, no way to lighten her step. All the while, she sang "Bringing in the Sheaves", but nothing could assuage that awful drone and the *squish* and *suck* of guts beneath her feet.

Mama drove slowly, a safe speed to keep the truck from fishtailing in the sludge.

"Poor Lucinda," Etta Mae said, looking up at her Granny's emergency wig, the one called upon when Lucinda needed tending.

"Don't fret none," Miss Wessie said, kissing the back of her head. "Some things ain't meant to last."

I glanced down at Miss Wessie's bug-caked shoes, thinking of Lucinda and the old oak that wore her—that monster tree that killed the Fentons.

"Can't we just all go to our church?" I said, talking out of my head, trying to distract myself from the calamity closing in around us.

Miss Wessie shook her head. "Lord, Miss Lady. Ain't you learned nothing? Ain't you heard a thing I said?"

"Please don't start up," Mama said, not even a twinkle of fight left in her voice. "My nerves can't take it."

"Pardon me. I'm don't mean to impose upon your delicate state. My apologies. Why don't we all do like Miss Lady here wants and go on down to that white church of yours and sit down on the front row, all of us side by side. I'm sure they won't mind one bit."

"I don't feel good," Etta Mae said, leaning her head back against her granny.

Miss Wessie put her arms around her. "Why don't you sing us a little something. That always perks you right up."

Sing? By my estimation, Etta Mae already sang a gracious plenty.

"Don't feel like it," she said.

That was a first, Etta Mae turning down a chance to shine. I was happy, relieved to know my sister had some sense.

Mama nudged me with her elbow. "Baby, why don't you turn on the radio." I fiddled with the knobs finding nothing but a flourish of static.

Miss Wessie hummed a few bars and sang. "Bringing in the sheaves, bringing in the sheaves. We shall come rejoicing bringing in the sheaves . . ."

Sheave. What in the heck was a sheave? Obliged to hear another something, a sound other than static and screech, I joined in, only I changed the lyric to something making better sense to me. "Bringing in the sheep, bringing in the sheep . . ."

Etta Mae giggled and bobbed her head along, a welcome sound whittling at the tension. Mama joined Miss Wessie and me, all of us abandoning the sheaves for sheep.

Mama pulled up close as she could to the colored church. The place was already filled up with folks, dozens spilling out onto the slanting porch. Hand in hand, men formed a chain, reaching out into the yard, fishing for congregants, grabbing hold, steadying them those last slippery steps up onto the stoop. *Come on now. You almost made it. Just a little more now.*

Miss Wessie eased out of the truck holding on best she could, her feet making that dreadful squishing noise. She leaned into the truck reaching in past Etta Mae and kissed me on the cheek. She extended her hand to Mama until she grabbed hold, the two of them fusing, their secret, silent language coursing between them—humming. Powerful as an electric line.

Miss Wessie turned around to face the church. "Etta Mae, hop up onto Granny."

Etta Mae took hold of my hand and kissed the front and back of it. She held it to her cheek and whispered, "A bushel and a peck."

I watched Etta Mae climb onto Miss Wessie's back, noticing her tiny frame, the smooth nape of her sweet smelling, honeysuckle neck. I felt it then, the ache of a powerful longing, the strangle of regret. What could be wrong with having a sister? A special someone who loved me? I fought against an urgent need to pull her back into the truck—to confess. To tell her I set out to harm her, that she was my sister. That we belonged to one another. That if she forgave me, it all could be okay. *A bushel and a peck.*

I sat still in the head-splitting cacophony, watching them trudge forward in the mush, the rope of men, handsome in their suits, their hopeful hands reaching. Taking hold of Miss Wessie and then my Etta Mae.

* * *

Broad Street was slick with bug guts and hail, making it difficult for Mama to stop the truck without careening. Ahead of us, the railroad crossing threw a fit. The cicada covered arms of the crossing gate rose and lowered repeatedly, bells chiming, lights flashing. The whole spectacle, a garish circus calliope.

Mama looked down the track. "See anything?"

I gave a look both ways, "No, ma'am." There was nothing coming from anywhere. Not a person in sight. Just Mama and me, and the beginning stench of decay.

"There's no other way except across those tracks."

I assessed the crossing gate, studied the tempo, grabbed hold of the beat. I counted to eight between the time the arm rose and held, until it lowered again.

"We can make it if you hurry," I said. "We've got eight beats at the top."

"I don't know. Maybe we should just turn back around."

The last thing I wanted was to go back home, to not know what lay ahead. If the end was upon us, just like Miss Wessie said, it seemed to me that church was the place to be. "We should at least drive by and check on Graceful Stitches."

"I guess you're right." Mama lowered her head to the steering wheel and lifted it back up again. She nodded. "Okay. You tell me when."

We both watched the arm retract and lift all the way to the top. *Click.* "Now, Mama!"

The back wheels spun hopelessly against the pavement, a desperate burn of rubber. At the count of four, the truck finally found traction.

"Go, Mama. Go." The truck bumped and rattled across the tracks just clear of the arm.

Mama stomped the brakes sending us into a spin, the world unraveling to a whir. It was the curb that stopped us spinning, sending us backwards, a rain of glass pelting the hood.

My breath caught in my throat. Mama turned and grabbed hold of my arms. "Baby." she hollered. "You all right?"

I nodded. The best I could tell I was still living. "I think so." I looked around in the darkened space, unable to gain my bearings. "Where we at?"

Mama thumped a cicada off her knee and then one off her shoulder. "Woolworth," she said.

I recognized what once had been Lady's Apparel. I looked back to Mama, her coiffure hardly bothered, a benefit of her Amani Wave hair setting lotion. "What now?"

Mama looked straight ahead through the empty windshield, beyond the shattered plate glass window. Cicadas scurried into the store over the jagged edges—swarms of them in awkward flight—puny, translucent wings barely supporting their girth. All of them clamoring for a place to light. "I reckon we walk," she said.

"What about the truck?"

Mama pushed at the dented truck door with her elbow. "Doesn't look like it's going anywhere anytime soon." With one final shove, the door rattled open.

Chapter 36

Providence was a freshly formed scab of cicadas. The town lay desolate beneath the burdened sky—all the wounded edges lifted and seeping. The premature twilight played tricks, fooling the streetlamps to life, casting glow upon the sidewalk. This queer enchantment tangled in newly sprung wings and twinkled in the larval goo, adorning the path with a gruesome shimmer.

Cicada guts collected around the edges, icing the tops of my daisy-yellow galoshes. The accumulation of gore weighed each step, slowing my pace. Halfway to church and already my back ached, my poor feet yowling for room to spread in those too-small, tight, rubber boots.

Mama and I chewed up pieces of Wrigley's Spearmint Gum, placing them in our ears, a futile attempt to guard our sanity and hearing from the ever-mounting din. Mama retrieved a handkerchief from her clutch and covered her nose.

"What's wrong?" I yelled.

"That awful smell," Mama hollered back. "I can hardly take it."

"Smells like stink bugs and collard greens."

We trudged along, the sludge sucking at our boots, waves of contemplation cresting and crashing. I thought of Etta Mae and Miss Wessie, hoping they were safe, that Etta Mae would not take it into her head to sing.

I glanced over at Mama. Daddy's fishing boots bothered the hem of her burgundy skirt. Would she and Miss Wessie ever tell me the truth—what Daddy had gone and done? That Etta Mae was my sister. "Do you miss Etta Mae's mama?"

She pulled the chewing gum earplug from her right ear. "Come again?"

"Do you miss Etta Mae's mama?" I followed behind her, fishing the Wrigley's out of my own ears, rolling it between my fingers.

Mama stopped walking and lowered the handkerchief. "Callie?" she said. "Why do you ask?"

"Just wondering is all."

"Of course, I miss her. I think about her every day." A look of curiosity came over Mama, her head tilting to the side.

"Did she ever make you mad?"

Mama tucked her clutch beneath her arm. "I can't recall a particular time off the top of my mind."

Certainly, Daddy taking up with another woman, especially Mama's very own friend would have been enough to cause an upset. "That's strange."

"How so?"

I shrugged my shoulders. "Don't know. Just is."

"Is there something in particular you'd like to ask?"

Perhaps Mama was innocent to it all. Perhaps it was only I who bore the burden of Marlissa's fairy secret. "Did you know Etta Mae's daddy?"

Mama took a step back to appraise me, her boots sinking in the muck. The sound, flatulent and off-putting. She discarded her earplug, tossing it to the street.

"I was acquainted . . . briefly."

"Etta Mae never talks about him. Is all she ever goes on about is her poor, dead, burned-up mama. I just wondered what happened." I pitched my gum alongside Mama's. "Where is he?"

A cicada landed on Mama's shoulder. She thumped it, sending the chunky thing to collide with the side of my head. It took hold, clinging to my hair, the weight surprisingly substantial. I stayed calm during the struggle. The cicada gave a good fight, thrashing like a riled-up rooster, pulling strands of hair loose from my ponytail. I slung it to the ground, pressing my heel into it, putting it to rest with the others.

Mama watched me, waiting until I finished my chore. She looked up into the gloomy sky. "He's about the place," she said. Right then, the noise subsided, the cicadas simmering to a hum, shifting the pressure in my ears.

"He's alive?"

Mama gave her head a quick, violent shake, as if she were also righting the sudden shift in barometric pressure. She looked all about, rubbing her old snakebite.

"He's a shadow. Always here. Always there." She bit her lip, wrapping her arms about herself, her eyes drifting off into the distance. The hum rose, the cicadas laying claim to the air, drowning all other sound.

I followed Mama's gaze, wondering how Daddy was a shadow. *Always here. Always there.* A good piece up ahead, the Sheriff's car turned from Washington Avenue onto Broad Street heading off into the opposite direction.

"Briar," Mama hollered. "Look-a-here." She waved her handkerchief in the air.

If anybody was a like a shadow, it was that Sheriff Dobbs. "He can't hear you," I said, snatching the rescue flag from Mama's hand, annoyed she called the Sheriff by his first name. Even without all the dreadful noise, we were still too far away to be heard.

"Mind yourself," Mama said, reaching out for her hanky.

I stepped back out of reach, scrunching it up, pressing it to my nose, inhaling so deeply I could taste the light floral notes of perfume. "Smells like Cordelia Mayfield."

The comment rattled Mama. "There are worse things," she said reaching out her hand.

Maybe I should have let sleeping dogs lie, but Mama's anger splintered, becoming my own, awakening all the ugly inside me. I stepped back just short of her reach. Oh, I was not angry she stole something from the Mayfields. They had plenty. No, I was furious she lied to me. That there were secrets between us—a distance.

"How is it you smell just like her?"

"I beg your pardon."

"Your perfume, you can't buy it at Woolworth. It's made special in Paris. Just for her."

"I don't care for your tone." She took a step forward. *Squish.* "And how would you know where Cordelia Mayfield's perfume comes from?"

"I know a lot of things. A plenty."

Mama took a step closer. "Just exactly what are you implying?"

"I know not saying a thing, an important thing, is bad as a lie." The cicadas began to stir—a low vibrating warble. I could feel the momentum, a thread pulling loose from a spool.

Mama grabbed hold of my wrist. "Is there something you think needs saying?"

"Turn me loose," I yelled, slapping her arm with my free hand.

"Don't you hit me, young lady." She gave my arm a jerk. The warble rose, the vibrations, tickling my ears. A cicada flew into Mama, knocking against her neck, another against her cheek, the force of the impact making an audible thud. She held tight, her grip growing angrier.

"Stop keeping secrets. Stop telling lies." A cicada flew into my collarbone and another against my ear.

"What's gotten into you? What secrets? What lies?"

Another barrage of cicadas smashed into me. The assault and rising drone knocking loose my senses. "About Etta Mae. About Daddy." I swatted my hands about my face. "Marlissa told me everything."

Mama froze, the artillery of insects thwacking against her. "Told you what?" Her clutch, tucked beneath the pit of her arm came loose and fell into the glop.

"That she's my sister." The insect chorus ascended, the vibrations so fierce my lips quivered.

"She said what?" Her words were quick and desperate. She remained still, cicadas knocking against her, angry welts blooming on her face and arms.

I shook my head, swatting. Deflecting. "I know everything, Mama."

"You know?" The chorus transformed—hideous and roaring. And then she yelled. "That Kingston Mayfield is your daddy."

The cacophony sucked quick from the air. Silence followed. *Kingston Mayfield. My daddy?* No, that could not be. It was a figment, a trick of sound. Another lie.

Mama and I stood, staring at the other in the hush. Dozens of cicadas clung to us, fluttering in our hair, latched to our shoulders, undulating on our hips. All of them--satisfied. Mama's mouth moved but I heard no sound. I was gone from the world. I was vapor.

Mama grabbed hold of my shoulders, anchoring me, giving me gravity. She spoke my name, the sound—a net cast to pull me back from the ether. An avalanche followed. A violent tumble of thoughts and questions. *Marlissa's my sister. Daddy's not my daddy. Did he know?* Mama shook me until her eyes caught mine. Upon Mama's shoulder, a cicada lit, sheer wings opening and closing lazy as a yawn.

"I'm a Mayfield."

A horn honked behind us, giving Mama and me a start. Eli was at the wheel, a lady at his side. From the bed of the red pickup, Abel Darlington stood waving at Mama and me, a camera dangling from his neck. "Analeise. Miss Grace. "Y'all okay?"

I'm a Mayfield. Analeise Mayfield.

"We were heading off to church," Mama squeezed my shoulder. "Isn't that right?"

"Mama ran the truck clean through Woolworth," I said.

Eli lowered his arm from the window and tapped his fingers against the door. "That was you, Miss Grace?"

"It wasn't intentional," Mama said, her voice distracted. "I prefer parking on the street."

Eli threw back his head and laughed. Abel joined in. Mama tried to laugh, her attempt slipping into an unnerving cackle. I stood there regarding them, finding it impossible to engage in the throes of a cataclysm.

Mama pulled me close, thumping off a cicada here and there. "What y'all doing out here?" she said.

"Daddy sent us out to take a look around. To snap some pictures," Abel said. "He's back at the paper trying to figure out what's going on, but he can't get through to anywhere."

"What does he make of all of this?" Mama said, her hands digging hard into the soft of my shoulders.

Abel adjusted the camera strap. "As long as he's been living, he said he hasn't ever encountered such a thing."

I was glad to see my Abel Darlington, glad to know he was alive and well in the world. But I wanted him to go away. I wanted to be alone there with Mama to sift through the lies.

"What about you, Eli?" Mama said.

"Can't rightly say, Miss Grace. It might be that nature is a bit riled up is all, a little off kilter." He drummed his fingers against the side of the truck again. "Or it could be something . . . bigger."

Bigger. I glanced the faces around me, all of them turning bleak.

Mama managed a smile, no doubt an effort to console. "Hello, I'm Grace Newell," she said, extending her hand through the window to the lady at Eli's side. "And this here is my daughter, Analeise."

Analeise Mayfield.

"Nice to meet you, Miss Grace. I'm Eli's sister, Zelda Clemons."

Abel moved to the far back of the truck, motioning for me. "Analeise, back here," he said, extending his hand to hoist me up from the glop.

The ground sucked at my shoes turning the whole ordeal into a game of tug of war. "Ups-a-daisy," he said, his warm smile beaming through the whole affair. Once I scaled the side, he hugged me, his chin pressing the top of my shoulder. "Sure glad you're okay."

I squeezed back, making use of the predicament, hoping to stay there as long as it took. Until I could make sense of it all, until I might be myself again. I imagined the two of us hugging for so long that cicadas came to molt. Both of us transfigured, intertwined, and rooting through the bottom of the truck. Anchored deep in the soil. Abel

Darlington and Analeise Newell—a glorious cicada tree growing up through the center of town.

Abel relaxed his grip, releasing me from his embrace. I pulled back slowly, letting my cheek slide against his, a new sensation sending tingles all the way down to my toes.

"I tried to call out to your place to check on you and your mama."

I was embarrassed, unable to look anywhere but down at my galoshes and the mess I made, gunk smeared across the bed of the truck.

"That was sweet of you."

"I'm sorry," Abel said. My body tensed. Oh God, did he know? That all was not what it seemed. That I was not who I thought I was. I managed to look up, meeting those chocolate drop eyes. "I know Jane was your best friend." He pulled a cicada from my hair and flicked it gingerly into the air.

Jane. Why did he have to bring her up? My emotional grip was already slipping. I had to hold on best I could. I nodded, knowing if I uttered a single word it would be my undoing.

"I can't get my head around it. That a body can be here one moment and gone the next. That death is forever, that a person won't come back," Abel said.

Please be quiet. Just hush.

"Have you ever tried to think about forever? How long it is?" I shook my head, trying to tamp down the urge to scream. "It's a sad rambling thing." Abel bit at his lower lip, blinking off into the distance. Forever and ever did not matter much to me, not when I could hardly cling to the moment, hold myself steady upon the titling world.

Mama called from the front of the truck. "Analeise, you all right back there?"

Somehow, I managed to speak. "Yes, ma'am." My voice sounded distant, the voice of another.

Abel's face brightened. "I have something for you," he said, reaching around to his back pocket, pulling out his notepad. He fiddled with it, carefully tearing a page from the seam. He folded the slip and pressed it into my hand. "A word. A pretty good one. Nine letters in all."

I was beyond tired; I was destitute. I just wanted to be alone with Mama. I had questions. I needed answers. I had no use for words.

"Where did you get it?"

"Mr. Kingston. He's got lots of them."

Kingston Mayfield.

"Go on, take a peek," he said, touching my elbow, urging me along.

I opened the gift, smoothing the seam. *Rapturous.* I looked up at Abel.

"Expressing great pleasure or expressing enthusiasm. That's what it means. Mr. Kingston used it the night of the talent show when you and Etta Mae were on stage. So, in a way, I guess it's a gift from him."

Mama hollered from the front of the truck. "Analeise, Mr. Eli is going to drive us down to the church. Isn't that nice?" Her tone was reticent, her words cracking in places. "You can sit back there with Abel or come sit up front with me." There was an urgency for the latter, a need to have me close.

I had to know more. "I'll ride back here, Mama." I turned to Abel. "What did he say?"

"He was grinning from ear to ear watching you and Etta Mae. And then he said it. 'Rapturous. Those two girls are absolutely rapturous.'"

"You sure you don't want to come up here with me?" Mama hollered.

Please just shut up. "I'm sure."

"Okay then. Go ahead and sit on down back there. Last thing we need is for the two of you falling out and breaking your necks."

Side by side, Abel and I lowered ourselves to the bed of the truck. I leaned against his shoulder, pressing Mama's handkerchief to my nose, taking in the smell of New Mama—of Cordelia Mayfield. *Cordelia Mayfield.* Did she know?

"Do you want to hear me spell it?" Abel said.

The truck woke, the engine joining the cantata. I nodded, holding the hanky to my nose, not wanting to turn loose the fragrance. Abel spelled the word, pausing a half note between each letter. When he was done, he spoke the word aloud.

* * *

Eli did his best to get us as close to the church as possible, but the drive and surrounding streets were mayhem, people parking anywhere they pleased, blocking the way. Some folks from the outskirts of the county drove tractors, pulling their families behind in trailers, hoping to make greater purchase against the slippery streets with sheer heft.

Mama held my hand, the two of us balancing the other the last fifty yards to the church. I turned around one last time and waved to my Abel. A terrible dread seized my stomach, tightening my joints. He waved back hollering something, his words censored—consumed by distance and the cicadas.

The church, a fluttery apparition, appeared to be held up by pillars of cicadas, the four white columns undetectable beneath layers of flittering wings. The sky turned darker—a sopping blanket drooping heavy on a clothesline. Moisture hung in the air, collecting on our faces like droplets of morning dew.

My head was a jumble, thoughts of Kingston Mayfield, of Etta Mae, and Marlissa. Of the nine-letter word. I had been wrong all along. Daddy was not the one who had done the hurting. No, it was Mama. She was the one who did the thing that broke us apart, banishing us all from her Thinking Spot.

"Did he know?"

"Who, baby?" Mama said.

"Daddy. Did he know what you did? That I'm not his?"

Mama stopped and turned to look down at me. "He knew."

"Does Mr. Mayfield know? Does Miss Cordelia?"

Mama reached out and touched my cheek. "They know," she said, shaking her head, her eyes tired—shadows creeping beneath.

"And Miss Wessie and Etta Mae?"

"Wessie knows," Mama said. "And you're not to say anything to Etta Mae about this." She took my face in her hands and kissed my forehead. She spied the handkerchief knotted in my hand, reached down and took it, tucking it back into her soiled clutch. Lightning flickered and then a distant roll of thunder. "We best get on to the church."

I did my best to keep pace with Mama, but burden and the ever-mounting weight of my shoes made lifting my legs a chore. My mind was a bramble patch—thoughts catching and snagging on the prickly parts. "Why did Marlissa tell me Etta Mae belonged to Daddy?"

Mama stopped and bent at the waist as if to catch her breath. She stood straight again, pressing the back of her hand to her forehead. "A cruel joke. A wicked game."

"But why? Why be cruel?"

Mama rolled her head from side to side, her neck crackling. "I reckon in some people it runs deep. As much a part of them as the color of their hair, or the color of their eyes."

I wondered then what ran through Mama and me, what awful thing cut through us both, slicing all the way down to the quick. "Why did you do it, Mama?"

This, of all the questions, stopped her, stole her breath. Brilliant glassy tears swelled in her eyes. "There are things I need to tell you, and I promise I will, but now is not the time for that."

I am Analeise Mayfield.

A heap of cicada-caked shoes flanked both sides of the church's double doors, shoes strewn across the boards. I thought of Mama's story, the night she danced with a rattlesnake.

"Look, Mama. Everybody's taken off their shoes."

"I'm not fooling with that." She scraped her instep against the sharp edge of the brick step. "I'll never get them back on again."

Holding onto Mama, I pressed toe to heel, finagling my feet out of those too-tight galoshes, the effort pulling off my socks, leaving my toes naked and wiggling in the damp October air. With not even a pocket in my dress to keep Abel's gift safe, I placed the folded sheet of paper into one of my rubber shoes.

Together, we walked through the vestibule into the frenetic murmurings of the congregation. I wondered if the Mayfields were off praying at their fancy church. If they were giving me so much as a thought.

"Guess the power is out here, too," I whispered.

Men folk stood at the back and along the outside aisles making room in the pews for women and children. Mama and I made our way down front, Walker Funeral Home fans stirring the pungent air with anxious tempo. People paid us little mind as we traveled the center aisle, panic rising in the place like stream from a roiling pot. Mama and I found a space to sit at the end of a pew.

Next to Mama, a red-haired woman held a baby to her shoulder. "The end is come," she said. "It is nigh."

"Hush up and stop talking nonsense," the woman next to her shot back. "You'll scare the young'ins."

"Don't you hush me up. There's plenty to be scared of. Plenty."

I felt unwell sitting there cramped in my seat—the air growing warm and turning sourer by the minute. To settle my stomach, I took deep breaths, staring ahead at the candelabra flanking the pulpit, focusing upon the lethargic sway of candle flame.

To the left of the pulpit, as was her custom, Miss Minnie Jean sat at the organ's bench, her instrument stricken impotent from the lack of electricity. Faint light seeped through the stained glass, tinting her in a patchwork of primary colors. This adornment was kind to her, suppressing the truth of her age. I watched her hands, her tight grip upon the lacquered edges of her seat, the tendons and muscles flexing and rippling. Her head swayed to some silent, legato tempo—something woeful playing within, a melody only she could hear.

I was the first to notice the darkening at the edge of the stained glass, the wriggling shadows creeping upon the windows.

"Where's the preacher?" someone behind me asked. "Ain't he coming?"

"He's a coming," the redheaded woman said, patting her sleeping baby's back harder than before.

Cicada legs clicked at the window, their proboscis searching for a place to feed. No one paid the noise any mind, no one but Miss Minnie Jean and me. She loosened her grip on the bench, turning to look up at the window behind her. She was on her feet quickly, the colors of light shifting across her face as she rose. "Look there," she said, pointing her bony finger at the puzzle-pieced window. The congregation quieted to a purr. "Look-a-here." She jabbed at the air. By the third poke of her finger, everyone looked upon her, every funeral fan stilled. Mama laced her fingers through mine.

"It's time to make right with the Lord," Miss Minnie Jean hollered. She looked about the congregation, her eyes feral and frightening. She sucked in a breath, holding her hand in the air above her head. "Blow a trumpet in Zion; sound an alarm on my holy mountain."

Mama tightened her grip, and I helped, pulling our hands into a single knot until it hurt. The shadows on the window flickered across Miss Minnie Jeans's torso. The *clickety-click* grew louder.

"Let all of the land tremble, for the day of the Lord is coming; it is near." Miss Minnie Jean tilted her head back until all that could be seen was her nostrils and gobble-neck. More cicadas assembled outside at the edges of the glass.

Murmurs rose in the church. "Have mercy," the redheaded woman said. "Have mercy."

Miss Minnie Jean walked to the pulpit. The cicadas left all but a circle of light that fell upon her face, brushing her in watercolor. She looked back to the window squeezing at her chest.

"Then from the smoke came locusts on the earth, and they were given the power of scorpions of the earth."

The click from the glass grew louder, the circle of light extinguishing from her face until there was nothing left of her but the truth, the ugly fissures of time and malevolence. It was then I heard the crack. The congregation paid it no mind—as if the world always had been loud with strange and awful noises. Miss Minnie Jean searched the crowd, her nose twitching, sniffing Mama and me out in gloom.

Mama pulled my hand into her lap. Miss Minnie Jean's head turned slowly from side to side. She lifted her crooked finger and waggled it at us, and when she spoke, she spoke loud and slow.

"For without dogs, and sorcerers, and whoremongers, and murderers, and idolaters, and whosoever loveth and maketh a lie."

A rumble made its way through the congregation. The next crack that followed was louder than before—more akin to a crunch. The church door flung open, slamming against the wall, giving us all a start, a bluster of cicadas following close behind.

Women screamed from the shock of it, waking the redheaded woman's baby, shaking loose an apoplexy of mewls.

"There's been a fire," a man yelled. "Out at the Mayfields . . . A fire."

Another *crack* and *crunch* filled the space until the man spoke again. "Kingston Mayfield," the man said. My senses grew keen, the dull colors of the chapel possessing a brightness. "Kingston Mayfield is dead."

Another *crackle* of glass and a long unnerving *rip*, the sound of ice cubes pried loose from a tray. The church followed the sound up to Miss Minnie Jean and beyond her to the window. I pushed close against Mama. In an instant, it was gone. Shattered. The window, an explosion of cicadas and shards of colored glass.

The sound was deafening, loud as a crop dusting plane. Hysteria spread fast, all of us covered in cicadas. Chaos. A stampede pushing toward the door. The room was thick, turned black with insects, glimpses of light escaping between.

A man screamed, pushing between Mama and me, breaking our hands apart. "Help me, Mama," I yelled, the distance between us growing wider. Flailing arms and kicking legs sent me to the floor. A foot landed heavy on my arm, just above my wrist. *Crack.* I knew from the sound it was broken. The pain was not immediate, but when it came, I howled, my mouth unhinging, allowing a cicada inside. My teeth clamped down, biting into the thing, stilling the fluttering wings, its insides spilling out like a jelly from a doughnut. I spit and spit until I pushed out all the oozing bits with my tongue.

Somewhere from within the swirling black, Mama hollered my name.

I'm here, I thought, too frightened to scream, too scared I might swallow one down. I held my good arm out. She found me, grabbing hold, dragging me across the worn, red carpet onto the vestibule floor. I pulled my hurt arm to my chest and rocked up onto my knees.

Mama yanked at my collar. I turned to look back into the church, squinting to see through the horde. At the pulpit, Miss Minnie Jean stood, her arms spread wide, her body, a cicada-covered cross—her gnarled, stocking feet, the only things not covered.

Mama snatched me through the door, pulling me forward, not stopping for my shoes. My bare feet slid easily through the sludge, gore collecting between my toes. I pulled my broken arm close to my chest— the pain, a quick climbing, flowering plant. I was overcome, my vision dimming, knees buckling. My body ceased, my weight too much for Mama's grasp. I toppled back. Up into gloaming I blinked, the agony blossoming, warming, turning euphoric. *Rapturous.* I understood it then, a good kind of hurt—a nine-letter word. Before all went dark, the last thing to be heard was a whisper. *Kingston Mayfield is dead.*

Chapter 37

I awoke at home in the glow of a kerosene lamp, an ornery sofa coil poking into my tailbone, bullying me back to consciousness. Outside the cicadas shrieked. Their hysteria rattled the sills, arousing the pain in my crippled arm.

At the opposite end of the sofa, Etta Mae sat, reading something aloud from a book, plucking stuffing from a rip in the armrest and poking it back in again.

"Do you think, because I am poor, obscure, plain, and little, I am soulless and heartless? You think wrong!" She squinted, lifting the book close to her face. "I have as much soul as you—and full as much heart!"

What she read was familiar, but there in my befuddlement, I struggled to place it. "How did I get here?"

Etta Mae jumped, dropping the book, grabbing hold of her chest. "You scared the feathers out of me."

Her beautiful face was strange in the lamp's glow, her eyes darker in the shadows—changed. Different. I remembered then. *Kingston Mayfield's my daddy.* "Where's Mama?"

"How're you feeling? Does it hurt?"

"Where's my Mama?"

"I think she's in the kitchen with Granny?" Etta Mae picked up the book from the floor. I recognized it—what she was reading, my copy of *Jane Eyre*, the one I stole from the library.

I shifted my weight, trying to maneuver myself to a seated position. At some point, my arm had been arranged and made tidy in a makeshift sling, a contraption contrived from a cut-up old bed sheet. In my pitiful hand, I held Marlissa's one-winged paper doll. "Where did that come from?"

Etta Mae stuttered, "You. You asked for it."

"No, I didn't."

"Yes, you did," she said, lowering her voice to a whisper. "You were talking out of your head." Etta Mae eased up from the sofa, lowering herself onto the floor to rest on her knees. "You told me to bring you everything from your keeping place. I brought everything but the whiskey," she whispered. She touched my good wrist, poking at the fairy charm bracelet I wore. "You told me to put that on you."

"Where's the locket?"

Etta Mae pulled it out from the collar of her blouse. "You said Marlissa gave it to you." She glanced down the hall and spoke in a hush. "I thought you gave it back to the Sheriff." She tucked it back in her blouse. "I'll keep it hidden here, so no one can see."

Etta Mae thought I was a thief, that she was wearing Marlissa's locket. I might have hated her for thinking ill of me, but in that moment I was touched, moved that she would protect me. What if I had taken Marlissa's stupid locket, the birthday gift from her daddy—my daddy? *Our daddy.* Would that have been stealing? No, more like borrowing from a sister. "The ribbon. Where's the ribbon?"

"It's pretty," she said, combing her tiny fingers through the length of my ponytail. "I tied it in a bow just like you said. Tight enough so it won't come loose."

I could remember none of it—arriving home, commanding Etta Mae to fetch my things. How was it a person could be living, awake and asleep all at once? I wriggled myself up into a seated position. "Did I say anything else?"

Etta Mae patted the neckline of her blouse where the locket lay beneath. She cast her eyes down, her face turned solemn. "You said Kingston Mayfield is dead."

Two dead daddies. One who did not love me. One who did not know me. My hands shook, the paper doll fluttering in the bad one. "I want Mama."

At the far edge of the parlor, short of the lamplight's reach, Miss Wessie spoke, her disembodied voice floating in the space. "Miss Lady, what's all this carrying on?"

300

"Come into the light," I said, desperate to see her. To know she was still herself.

The light caught beneath her chin, spreading up the sides of her face, narrowing its fullness. Her kerchief was gone. "You done slept the day away," she said, a queer crackle in her throat. She kneaded her hands into her apron.

"Where's Mama?"

"Best I can tell, your arm is a pretty clean break. Should heal up right nice. I did my best to tend it." She moved closer into the room. "We'll have the doctor take a look once things get on back to normal."

Normal. "What's she doing in there? Why won't Mama come when I call her?"

"Groceries all gone to ruin. All of it spoiled. Gas stove still works though. Nothing left but cabbage and neck bone. Ought to make up a nice enough soup."

Something was wrong. I pushed up from the sofa. "Mama." Etta Mae stood up alongside me, hooking her arm around mine.

"You need to lay on back down there," Miss Wessie said. "You've suffered a shock." Miss Wessie was heedful, uncharacteristically tempered. Mama must have told her I knew everything, that I knew who my daddy was.

"Lay on back down," Etta Mae said.

I jerked free, zigzagging across the floor like a drunkard, giving Miss Wessie a wide berth.

"Come on back here," Miss Wessie said. "Your Mama ain't in there. She gone."

Gone. I stumbled over to the table, grabbing hold to the back of a chair. Miss Wessie, hurried behind, carrying the lamp with her into the kitchen. "Where is she?"

"Calm yourself, Miss Lady."

Etta Mae followed behind her granny.

"Where's my Mama?" I could feel myself begin to spin. "If you don't tell me, I'm gonna tell. I'm gonna tell Etta Mae."

Etta Mae walked from behind her granny to stand in front. "Tell me what?"

Miss Wessie addressed Etta Mae, all the while staring at me. She held the lamp at her waist, the flame darkening the hollows of her face. "Sweet girl, there ain't nothing to tell. Miss Lady just be talking through a terrible pain is all." Miss Wessie's eyes were beseeching, the peculiar angle of light turning her unfamiliar.

The terrible pain in my arm sustained me, thrilling every nerve, bringing me fully to life. I looked away from Miss Wessie to Etta Mae, instantly moved by her lovely, expectant face. That Mayfield Shine. Did I have it too? We all had the same eyes, Marlissa, Patton, Etta Mae, and me. How had I not noticed before? Alive—awake and asleep all at once.

"I love you," I said, managing a smile.

"I love you, too," Etta Mae said, taking a step closer, her eyes drifting to the center of the table, filling with fear.

There it was, right in front of me, the thing frightening Etta Mae. I jumped back, pulling at the ladder-back chair, knocking it to the floor, *Flowers. Daddy's flowers.* Just like the bouquet from before, the one he sent to Mama.

"Mr. Claxton is dead," Etta Mae said.

"I want Mama." I turned around, kicking at the chair, sending it sliding and scraping the floor. "I want to know where she is. You tell me. Tell me now."

Miss Wessie hurried to the table and set down the lamp. "She's got business to tend."

"Business? What in the hell kind of business does Mama have tonight."

Etta Mae stared at the flowers. "Her daddy's dead. Gone away like poor, sweet Mama."

"And just how did she get there?" I said. "The truck's smack dab in the middle Woolworth."

Miss Wessie laced and unlaced her fingers. "Mr. Eli and that Abel Darlington. They was the ones that drove you and your Mama out here after you fell out at church. They was the ones who went back and hauled the truck out for your Mama."

"Where did she go?"

Miss Wessie put her thumbnail to her mouth but pulled it back out just as quick, resting her fidgeting hands at her sides. I followed her eyes to the table, to the cream-colored card at the side of cut-glass vase. She gave me a nod, and I reached for it with my good hand, angling it in the paltry light.

The River House. The words were written in an elegant hand. "She's at a river house?"

Miss Wessie let out a breath, her shoulders slumping a bit. "The Mayfield river house."

"Why would Mama go there?"

"It was Cordelia Mayfield that sent them flowers." Miss Wessie turned to look at Etta Mae and then at me. "Just like she done before."

Of course. I recognized those flowers, the kind Cordelia Mayfield grew in her Chrystal Palace of the South. "Why would she send Mama flowers?"

"A dangerous kind of game." Miss Wessie laced her fingers again, resting her hands at her chin. "I'm scared for your Mama, Miss Lady. Of what Cordelia might do."

"How did they get here?" Etta Mae said. "Who brought them?"

"They was just sitting here waiting. No sign of anyone coming or going."

Etta Mae wrapped her arms about herself and looked at the table. Miss Wessie and I followed her gaze, the three of us standing there staring at the flowers, none of us uttering a word, the layered scent of blooms mixing with the cabbage soup simmering on the stove. That is when I noticed something was different, that the cicadas had diminished to a hum.

"Do you hear?" I said. "They've gone quiet." Etta Mae began to speak, but I hushed her. "Be quiet."

"What is it?" Miss Wessie said.

"Shh . . . Listen. There's something else." I held my finger to my lips, my eyes darting about the room. *A piano.* Somewhere in the distance, a piano played.

Etta Mae cocked her head to the side, straining to listen. "I hear it," she whispered.

The kitchen grew brighter, a flickering light filling the space like sunrise. The music swelled, the chords growing frenetic. Miss Wessie squeezed at her neck. "Dear Lord Jesus, where's that coming from?"

"It's coming from outside," I hollered. Etta Mae hurried to me, knocking against my bad arm, sending another surge of good feeling hurt—a spinning pinwheel of color. Dear God, I knew the song. It was Cordelia Mayfield's wedding gift sonata. It was Mama's dream-fire song. I pulled away from Etta Mae, running to the kitchen's back door, yanked it open, and kicked at the screen. I stepped onto the back porch, cicadas squishing beneath my bare heels, the lucky ones tickling and scurrying over the tops of my feet.

Miss Wessie yelled after me. "Analeise, you get back on in here."

Great tongues of fire licked up the big oak tree in Mama's Thinking Spot. "Fire." I screamed. "The tree's on fire." Etta Mae ran out after me, grabbing hold of my hand.

Miss Wessie followed behind looking out into the yard. "It's coming for the house," she hollered.

Piano music played within the flame, spectacular, ascending arpeggios. The fire crested, lapping like ocean waves, moving in time with the music up the trunk of the tree, racing to the branches that rested upon the side of the house.

Cicadas, clinging to the old oak, *sizzled* and *popped,* bursting like kernels of corn in the heat. From all about, they commenced their shrieking, unleashing a ferocious, unmerciful sound. Etta Mae pressed her palms to her ears and shook her head.

Miss Wessie hollered again. "Get out into the yard. Get on away from here. I'll be right back." She turned and ran inside.

With my one good arm, I took hold of Etta Mae, doing my best to keep balanced on the slimy steps, not letting go until we made our way down into the yard. In time with the music, a waltz of heat swirled about us—whiffling the hems of our dresses, caressing our faces, flattering us to dance in the thrall of a firestorm.

Etta Mae let out a beautiful scream. "Somebody help us." Her words ran up a scale, frantic and melodious. The flame slowed, the music and cicadas turning mute to hear her. When the echo of her voice evaporated, the fire, music, and cicadas roared once more.

"Etta Mae." I pulled at her with my good arm. "Sing." Etta Mae stared at me, the fire reflecting in the shimmer of her eyes. "Sing."

"Why?" she yelled.

I gave her a jerk. "Just do it."

She snatched loose from me and looked up into the tree. "I don't know what to sing."

I gave her a push. "God, Etta Mae, sing anything. Sing lightning bug."

She composed herself best she could there in the billow of heat, shutting her eyes, lifting her chin to the fire. The firelight flickered down over her, turning her sweat to sparkle. She sang slowly and sweetly as a girl could manage in the throes of tribulation. "Lightning bug, lightning bug, light up the night." The fire grew sluggish under her spell, the cicadas simmering down to listen, all the world falling into a dreamy stupor.

The porch door slapped open, and Miss Wessie came running out, her black, patent leather purse swinging from her arm. "The phone still ain't working," she yelled. "Run on around to the front of the house." She took the first and second step. At the third, her bare feet skidded out in front of her, sending her to the ground—her head cracking against the bottom step.

"Miss Wessie." I screamed, shaking Etta Mae loose from her enchantment. It took only seconds and the world came to life again, the fire angrier than before, the cicadas provoked to hysteria.

Etta Mae and I ran to her granny. Miss Wessie lay motionless, her head resting against the step. We both took to the ground, cicadas flattening beneath our knees. "Wake up, Miss Wessie."

Etta Mae shook at her granny. "Please don't be dead."

"Be quiet." I grabbed hold of Etta Mae's collar and gave her a shake. I rested my head against Miss Wessie's chest, finding the slow rise of her bosom. "She's still breathing."

"The house is on fire, Granny. Please wake up." Above us the fire roared, eating its way up to the edge of the house, lapping at the tin roof making it buckle and *pop.*

"We got to move her away from here," I said. "I'll lift her head. You pull her feet." I cradled her head in my good arm. With some pull and drag, we managed to maneuver her across the yard with only three good arms between us.

"She's bleeding," Etta Mae said. Blood seeped from a gash at the back of her head spreading through her cropped white hair. "What are we going to do?"

I leaned back on my heels, wondering if Mama saw this coming, if this was her fire dream. The sonata played all around us, vibrant—presto agitato. I swatted my hurt arm, needing to give myself a start, to pry myself loose from panic. "I'll go for help." But who was there to help us? Our closest neighbor was more than two miles away.

"Don't leave me."

"I'll be back. I promise." I kissed Miss Wessie on the cheek and then Etta Mae. Before Etta Mae could speak, I was up and running beneath the big burning oak, around the corner to the front of the house, the ground squishing up between my toes.

It was the Mayfield car that stopped me in my tracks, a black alligator stretching across the lawn. I would have run right into it had it not been for the blaze behind me, the firelight dancing and reflecting on the hood.

From the fluttery shadows, a voice called my name. "Miss Analeise. It's me, Halbert. The gatekeep out at Mistletoe."

"Anybody come with you?" I glanced over at the car, unable to see through the darkened windows.

"No, ma'am. Just me." A strange laziness floated in his voice.

"Mr. Halbert, can you take me for help? Miss Wessie is hurt real bad." I was on the verge of spiraling into sobs.

Halbert moved from the shadows, his silhouette slowly materializing. "What's done is done, I reckon." He moved closer, his disfigurement more gruesome in the flickering light. A cicada nested on the rim of his melted ear. A few fluttered on the top of his head. "That there is Miss Cordelia's song playing."

"Mr. Halbert?"

"It's a pretty thing, that song Mr. Kingston give her. Aint' it?" He smiled, his scars pulling his lower lip down exposing his gums and sparkly white teeth. A long string of saliva dribbled down his chin.

"Are you gonna help me?" I tapped on my bad arm to keep the tears away.

He shook his head slowly. "Some things in this here world is meant to burn."

A wave of queasiness came over me. "Why are you here?"

Halbert tipped his head and opened the back door. "I come for you. I come to take you to your Mama."

From the back of the house came an explosion of breaking glass. Etta Mae screamed my name. Her lovely voice stirred my desperation—even distracted Halbert, causing his rheumy eyes to wander back toward the burning house. Another cicada perched on his good ear, opening and closing its wings.

Halbert nodded his head and smiled, his face pulling down to his slobbery chin. "Time to go," he said. "What's done is done."

Chapter 38

"What is this place?" I said, peering out from the rear window of the Mayfield car. Light flickered from inside the house on stilts, playing against the windows, spilling out into the darkness, falling in puddles upon the squirming earth.

"Where you is supposed to be," Halbert said, turning to look back at me, the profile of his spoiled face, a landscape of crackled, riverbed mud.

Caught in a thrill of fear and adrenaline, I could hardly breathe, worried for Etta Mae and Miss Wessie—desperate to know why Mama had come, and why Miss Cordelia sent those flowers. "So, my Mama's in there?"

Anchored in the short gray of his nap, a cicada clung to the back of Halbert's head, its translucent wings opening and closing. "I reckon she is," he said, an eerie chuckle following.

"And Miss Cordelia? She in there, too?"

"Umm-hmm," he said sleepily. "Best be getting on now, Miss Analeise." Halbert exited the car and came around to open my door. "Time's a slippin'."

I took hold of his hand, scooting myself across the seat. Cicadas tickled over my bare feet, fussing and knocking against my legs. *Slippin'.* I could feel it. That I was sliding toward the edge of something. Up close, I could smell Halbert, the familiar scent of whiskey seeping through pores. *Daddy.* Had I been the reason he drank? "Are you going with me?"

Halbert squeezed my shoulder and walked several steps ahead into the mottled light, lifting his arms above his waist in supplication. Cicadas clung to him, many more than before, as if the things grew from him, pairs of wings sprouting from his skin.

"They've gone quiet," he said. He sniffed the air, redolent with cicada smells—collard greens and freshly shelled peas.

"What are they doing, Mr. Halbert?"

"Listening," he said, placing his finger to his lower lip. "And waiting." He cast a glance over his shoulder, his frightful face mercifully darkened in the shadows. He turned back around staring up into the windows of the river house, the glass aglow from what appeared to be firelight.

"What do I do now?" Moments passed, a powerful storm of nerves brewing inside me, and all the while Halbert did not speak. "Mr. Halbert?" I moved past, regarding him cautiously, wondering if he might suddenly stir and lunge. "Should I go inside?"

He did not move or blink, his arms remaining lifted at his side. He stared up at the house, his wonky eye unable to open all the way.

The cicadas scurried away from my feet, parting—clearing the path for me to make my way to the long flight of stairs leading to the wrap around decking above. I hurried up the first few steps.

"Mr. Halbert, can you please go for help? Send someone to Miss Wessie."

"What's done is done."

In the stretch of quiet that followed, I heard the river—a bloated tizzy rushing behind me in the distance. Like the rest of the world, it spiraled loose from nature, broken apart by Etta Mae's tempest. Fueled by the urgency of that river, I took hold of the banister, hurrying up the steps. My good hand slid against the rail breaking loose the crumbling layers of cicada shells, my fairy charm bracelet *jangling* all the way. Broken bits of exoskeleton caught beneath my nails—desiccated appendages poking impotently between the soft of my fingers.

At the landing I was met with the scratch of a phonograph record. *A piano concerto? Chopin? Beethoven?* Aside from the crackling music, I heard nothing else, only the wild rush of river below.

I peeked into the sidelights, doing my best in the narrow span of pane to make out the place. In the sprawl of the candlelit room, it was Mama I saw. Primly in a chair she sat, the toss of fireplace light having its way, playing magic tricks with her profile, her features disappearing and reappearing. And Cordelia Mayfield, where was she?

Perhaps I would have rang the bell—pounded the door, but I was not the girl I used to be. Not the Analeise from yesterday or the one from the day before.

I crept around the corner of the wrap-around porch. French doors lined the length of the house, and I made busy, fiddling with the knobs until one rattled open. Without so much as a knock, I walked right through.

Inside an expansive hall, I was met with a rush of heat and Beethoven's "Moonlight Sonata". I leaned back against the doorframe, surveying the length of the space, regarding the shimmery, papered walls illuminated by an expanse of crystal, candlelit sconces. The flames did not relent, not giving so much as a quiver. I contemplated my predicament there in that long, elegant space. *Why did Mama call me here?* Did Cordelia Mayfield want me there, too?

Mama hollered out. "You're wrong, Cordelia. About Analeise. About Patton."

Which direction would lead me to Mama? To Cordelia Mayfield? *The music.* I would follow the music. I closed my eyes, turning my ears loose to roam, seeking out the gravelly phonograph recording.

Before I took even a step, I smelled her behind me, the unmistakable, floral intermingling of Cordelia Mayfield's perfume. And there was something I failed to notice before, the slightest hint of sage.

Heat rose from the floor, hot as a summer attic, scorching the lovely smell. It was then I was frightened, terrified of what was to come, of the woman lingering somewhere close behind me. I turned slowly, petting and scratching my sling.

A few feet away Cordelia Mayfield stood—her pink, enameled nails reaching and piercing the space between us. My glimpse of her was quick—a stingy glance of her stunning face.

"Patton," she whispered.

A weeping breeze swept the hall, one candle extinguishing after the other, smothering the place with darkness. I could taste the sadness in her voice—sharp citrus and raw cabbage leaf. It was the feel of those smoky tendrils, the spectral remains of candle flame curling about me that unmoored me from the place.

Holding my good arm in front of me, I hurried down the hall. Bumping and feeling my way to Mama, tasting my way to the music at the other end.

Beneath a door, light shimmied across the floor. This was the door I chose, the one that took me to Mama.

Everywhere, candles burned, the place radiant with flame. Across the room, tied up like a Christmas gift, Mama sat by the hearth, the fire wobbling in time to "Moonlight Sonata". Her arms and feet were bound to the chair with gold curtain ties—giant tassels dangling at the ends.

"Get on out of here, baby," she hollered. "Run."

And I did run. Only I ran to Mama yanking at the ropes with my working hand. "Who did this to you? Who tied you up?" Tributaries of sweat flowed from her temples, meandering down her face and neck beneath the collar of her dress.

Cordelia Mayfield spoke, giving me a start. "Come on away from there," she said. Across the room she stood, her slim figure sheathed in a strapless column of pale blue satin. A fan of fabric accentuated her tiny waist, falling into a train puddling behind her.

"I knew you would come. That you would make good on your promise," Miss Cordelia said. Her voice was lush—languorous consonants and seductive vowels. Like a camphor rub, the sound turned my skin to shivers, teasing and delighting every sweaty inch of me.

"Cordelia, I told you this is crazy talk. This here is Analeise. She's not who you think."

Cordelia Mayfield laughed, the lovely sound stirring a yearning inside me, enchanting the hearth, fluttering the firelight in time with each breath she took. "On a first name basis, are we? Taking liberties above your station, Grace?" She pressed her palm to her chest. "That old snake bite of yours. Does it speak to you even now? Does it tell you who is who? And what is what?"

"Let Analeise go."

The phonograph recording wound down, the notes slowing to a drunken slur. Cordelia Mayfield's eyes wandered the space, her face without a speckle of perspiration there in that terrarium heat. "There is no other place for us. Here is all there is."

"Your business is with me. Not her."

Cordelia Mayfield laughed, the sound delighting and whiffling the candlelight. "That you think this is about you. That you believe you bear some importance in all of this. Well, it is just sublime."

"It would be understandable. That you would be angry. I would. I would be a terrible kind of mad." Mama's skin, all that could be seen of it, was slick and dripping.

"But you are not me. And you should know that I am not angry with you." She looked over at me, a glisten blooming within her verdant eyes.

For a moment, I wondered if she might cry, and I was desperate for it, the splendor of a Cordelia Mayfield tear. But it did not come, and I was in that familiar place of want. Of needing more of her. I looked to Mama, and I knew I was not alone, that she felt it, too. That she was hungry like me.

"Then what are you, Cordelia?" If you're not angry, what are you then?"

The fireplace logs shifted tossing a handful of shooting stars. Cordelia Mayfield watched them fizzle, hugging herself, caressing her elbows. When her arms drifted back to her side, she spoke. "Bereft," she said. Drifting light as a dust mote, the word bore enchantment. Then, like a magnet, it seemed to quickly leech all the sorrow from the world, weighing the room, pressing into the floor. Tilting us all to the center.

"I know there is blame on my part. I know that." Mama fidgeted best she could within her confinement, trying to straighten herself in the fiddle-back chair. "But I did what I felt I needed to do. I did it to keep safe. The money—just enough to start the store. And the will? To protect Analeise."

"You do not seem to grasp the situation." Cordelia Mayfield laughed again, only with less intensity than before, the halfhearted effort causing the candle flames to sputter. "Of course, you would think this is about money. There is so much of that, you know. And you foolishly think your efforts could thwart anything he had a mind to do? That he would crumble beneath your paltry attempts at extortion. That anyone would take your word over his."

"Paltry?" The word riled Mama, bringing life back to her listless eyes.

Cordelia Mayfield smiled and pointed at Mama. "That. Right there. Just then. That is the sort of fight he liked. I mean no offense, but yours is of the common variety. But none the less, it set a thrill within him. It always did. Women with gifts. With resourcefulness." She moved a few steps across the room, collecting a half-full martini glass from a side table. Her gait, an effortless movement, gave the impression she floated above the floor, and when she returned, she stood at the side of the black, baby grand piano.

She took a slow sip, the diamond bracelet sliding down her tiny wrist. The taste seemed to please her, relaxing her face, softening her lovely angles. Standing there in the heat, close to Mama, I wondered if what she drank burned like whiskey. If I reached out and took a gulp, might it melt away my nerves?

"Kingston." Mama dropped her head and chewed her bottom lip. "You know there is no resisting. No saying no."

"His charms." Cordelia Mayfield took another sip, the liquid sloshing and glinting. "I know them." She looked over at me when she spoke. "I know the perils of the Mayfield charm. How hard it is for others to look away. To be caught in the glare. And I can only imagine how his attention must flatter a woman like yourself."

That Mayfield Shine. Yes, I knew it. And what of Cordelia Mayfield? She was a Mayfield by marriage. How was it she shone as bright?

"A woman like myself?" Mama was riled, wriggling in the confines of the elegant curtain cords, doing her best to sit straight.

"Grace, I do not say these things to hurt you." Cordelia Mayfield rested her glass on the piano next to a bouquet of flowers, an arrangement like the one Daddy sent Mama, like the one in our kitchen just that very night. She leaned back against the piano, her long neck curving to the side, the soft wave of her blond hair teasing her shoulders. "I only speak the truth. And should that not be our business? Here in this circumstance." The logs shifted again—another burst of stars. A churning of embers. "Amongst the ashes, at least let truth remain."

Mama took in a breath of that hothouse air. "The truth? The truth is that you're not so very different from me. The truth? The truth is that Kingston Mayfield was unkind. The truth is that you aren't an innocent in all of this."

Cordelia Mayfield sighed, tilting her head to the other side. Her diamond, teardrop earrings swayed, taunting the room's meager light. Shifting her gaze from Mama to me, she lingered, both of us regarding the other. Best I could, I took her in, memorizing the length of her. How was it that there in the dense heat, Cordelia Mayfield flourished? A rare and spectacular orchid. I wanted to look away from her and to ogle her all at once. Sadness, a sense of longing pooled in her iridescent eyes. I knew the look of it, or at least the weight of an amalgam of such emotion. The way my insides curled and splintered at the edges when I looked upon a Mayfield. I was desperate, praying she would look away, that she would release me.

Mercifully, her eyes drifted back to Mama, her mascaraed lashes blinking away all the wistful, rescuing me from sweltering into the sweet, hot forever.

At last, she spoke, the suddenness of her voice startling all the fire in the room. "Innocent." She offered the word like a question—as if it were curious and new to her. "There are so very few of those." Cordelia Mayfield took another sip of her drink. "I'll accept my part. But you, Grace. What are you in all of this?" She loosened an elaborate orange and blue petaled flower from the bouquet. "Bird of paradise," she said, holding the bloom out, looking upon it with admiration. "Faithfulness, love, and . . . thoughtfulness. All the things this flower represents." The smile slowly left her face; the sadness that remained, wielded an unnerving beauty. "All things I never knew with Kingston."

I knew the flower, seen its kind before—preening like a peacock in the bouquet at home on the kitchen table and then behind Etta Mae's ear. "I know that flower," I said.

"Of course, you do, dearest. It was always amongst your favorites."

Amongst my favorites? What was she talking about? Was this the kind of crazy Miss Wessie told me about?

"Cordelia, enough of that foolishness. I told you. She's not . . . She's my Analeise. That's all. No one else."

Cordelia Mayfield placed her finger to her lips. "Shh." The sound flustered the candles, causing the flames to skip. She looked away from Mama and directly at me. "You remember, do you not? The family to which the bird of paradise belongs." She took a step forward, holding out the bloom.

"No, ma'am," I said. However, there was something. *Bird of paradise.* A fragment. A toss of letters. Mrs. Lawrence had mentioned the flower once before in class. What had she called it? "Paradisaeidae?"

"There, you see? You remember." A smile delighted her face, changing all but the sadness in her eyes. "Forever and always a clever boy."

My stomach went sour, that awful feeling before a body catches and heaves. "Miss Cordelia, I beg your pardon, ma'am." Soaked through with perspiration, my dress clung to my legs like a fraidy cat. I fussed with the skirt best I could, needing to be busy, to shift the awkwardness. "But I'm not a boy."

Mama finagled her way back straight into her seat. "She's not . . ."

"No," Cordelia Mayfield said, silencing Mama—a finger to her coral lips. "No, my dearest one. You were never just a boy. More like your father than ever imagined. So many things you are . . . were." She reached out to me, a look of longing and then fear, the bird of paradise sprouting from her pretty hand.

The fireplace caught a draft, a *whoosh* of flames rolling up into the chimney. A surge of heat billowed in the space, warming my cheeks, drying the fringe of my sweat-soaked hair. *Patton Mayfield.* That is who she thought I was.

"Dead. That boy is dead," Mama said.

Cordelia Mayfield was quick, the bird of paradise falling to the floor. She grabbed hold of Mama's chin, pinching it between her shellacked nails. "Dead? You disappoint me, Grace." She leaned down toward Mama, so close I thought she might kiss her.

Paradisaeidae. I longed for it to happen, for Mama to know the glory of a Cordelia Mayfield kiss. For Mama to speak of what I knew must be warm, soft places. The sweet tasting, waxy remnants of her lipstick lingering upon Mama's lips.

Cordelia Mayfield turned loose and backed away, the train of her dress curling like a cat's tail, the bird of paradise disappearing beneath it. "A woman with your insight. A woman who can see beyond today." She drifted backwards, her hand caressing her throat until she rested against the piano. "And you believe the dead leave us. That the boy is not right here in this very room. That he doesn't stand there deceiving us, dressed up and pretending to be another." She finished the last of her drink, closing her eyes as she swallowed it down. "And you did not see this coming in the quaint things you sew?"

"I can't see what lives in another's imaginings. Only the truth."

"I knew this day would come," Cordelia Mayfield said. "No god. No devil. No whatever it is that speaks to you whispering into my ear to tell me. And do you know how it is I know this thing?"

"How, Miss Cordelia? How did you know?" I said, my throat dry as cornhusk.

The room stilled, candle flames standing at attention. Cordelia Mayfield's eyes shifted, the movement so quick I thought I heard a *click*. "My dearest." She returned her hand to the soft of her throat. She held her breath. Upon the hearth, the fire slowed, flames taking long, lollipop licks at the air. "It was you." A smile nearly crested, but she reneged, disappointing the room, returning it to chaos.

A rush of heat took my breath. *Paradisaeidae.*

"You told me you would find your way back. Make me regret harming you. And I suspected from that first moment I saw you." Cordelia looked at Mama and pointed at her. "The day Grace brought you back to me. Back to Mistletoe."

Mama struggled and wiggled in her chair. "There aren't any dead children in this place. No ghosts."

Fantômé.

Moments passed before Cordelia Mayfield spoke, the fire upon the hearth biding time—licking the air from the room. She unmoored herself from beside the piano, taking several steps toward me. "Indeed, Grace. There are no dead children here." For another pass of time she was quiet, her eyes locked to mine, her arms twitching to reach and touch. "The eyes. Greener than my own. Greener than Marlissa's. You know you have your father's eyes, and even his cannot compare. Never was there a more vibrant and alluring eye than your own, my dearest boy."

Dearest boy. I was desperate to be close, to be adored by Cordelia Mayfield, to be her dearest boy. But I knew she meant to harm me.

"The music, it brought you here," she said. "All along, it was meant to be the charm that kept you from us—the thing to keep our Marlissa safe."

"You're talking out of your head," Mama said. "Making no sense."

"You remember, do you not?" Cordelia said. "The piece I was playing that day you came back. You detested it. The way I would make you play it over and over."

"Yes, ma'am." I pulled at my fraidy cat skirt. "I remember." Of course, I remembered. I could never forget such a lovely sound. But she was confused. Never had she made me play it. There in the heat, in the room with Cordelia Mayfield, I knew she must be crazy.

"Analeise." Mama spoke my name like a reprimand.

The corners of Cordelia Mayfield's lips twitched. First, a promise, then the full glory of her smile, brightening the place and nearly snuffing the candles. "An engagement gift from Kingston," she said, looking at Mama. "'Cordelia's Sonata', the whimsy of a German composer. A technically challenging piece, and you detested it."

She was wrong. I could never detest a sonata lovely as her own. "I can play it with my eyes closed."

Mama yelled from the chair. "Analeise, you stop this. This is no time for games."

Cordelia Mayfield touched her own cheek. "True. There is very little time for anything but reckoning. And for truth." She hurried across the room to the Victrola, the train of her gown rustling and scraping the floor. "There are things that need saying. There are things to be done."

"Exactly what needs saying?" Mama's breathing was heavy, her head starting to droop. "And doing?"

Cordelia Mayfield removed the record from the Victrola, replacing it with another. "It was not Claxton or you I intended to harm when I sent the flowers. Of course, I knew there would be trouble. But in the end, it was Kingston I hoped would suffer most."

"I've wondered exactly how that night came to be." Mama blinked away the sweat trails tricking into her eyes. "Why you sent those damn flowers."

"Perhaps you thought it jealousy. Or that it was a punishment of sorts for you bringing your bastard child into my home. A woman of your ilk would knit together such mundane imaginings."

Mama was riled again, a circus bear poked in its cage. "Of course, you could never be jealous of a woman like me."

"Yes, that is true. But it does not mean that I do not . . ." Cordelia Mayfield searched the ceiling. "It does not mean that I do not hold a particular kind of admiration for you. For how you handled Kingston after he tossed poor dead Claxton off into that river."

Mama shifted best she could in the chair to look at me, straining her neck to search my eyes. I was desperate to call out. To ask what it all meant. *Poor dead Claxton off into the river.*

"Why?" Mama said.

The candles and fire in the hearth turned sad, burning low, darkening the room. "Marlissa," she said. Cordelia Mayfield turned loose the Victrola's crank, leaving the phonograph silent. She fiddled with her diamond bracelet, unfastening the catch, removing it from her wrist. She laid it down on the console and exhaled, as if her action made her lighter. "To keep her good." Mama and I watched her drift back to the piano. "To keep her safe."

"Safe from what?" Mama said.

Cordelia Mayfield's eyes clicked in my direction. "From Kingston. And from my dearest boy." Upon the piano, a candelabra taper spilled wax upon the black, shiny lacquer, releasing the faintest *hiss.*

Dearest boy. What a glory to be Cordelia Mayfield's dearest boy. To be her dearest anything.

"Kingston told me I was out of my head again. That I had confused things. The girl is just a girl. An indiscretion, just like the colored one. And you are to do her no harm." Cordelia shook her head, those magnificent, teardrop earrings wobbling and spilling shimmer. "That is what he said." She reached up and removed one earring and then the other, setting them both down next to the crystal vase of flowers. "You were your father's pride, his black heart. His legacy. And he never forgave me the first time I sent you from this world. And why would he

319

help me do it again?" All the fire in the room stirred, shaking off its stupor. "Even if it meant saving our Marlissa."

The room seemed to tilt, pushing us all to the center, closer to some truth. And I would nudge it along with a lie. "Father loved me best."

"Analeise," Mama yelled.

"Your father would do anything to keep you safe." Cordelia released me from her stare and turned to Mama. "That is why I did it, Grace. Why I sent those flowers to you pretending they were from Kingston. Writing that note insisting you meet him here." She pressed her hand into the bodice of her gown. "I knew you could not refuse. And of course, I knew that when I sent the note to Kingston pretending to be you, his . . . dark passions would swell."

"None of this makes any sense," Mama said.

"All it took was a call to Claxton down at that Bait and Tackle, and the slightest suggestion you and Kingston were reacquainting." Cordelia smoothed her hands against her bodice. "You and I are both women, Grace. This is one thing we share, that and our understanding of men. And tolerance."

"Dear Lord, if you wanted Kingston dead, why didn't you just do it yourself?"

With those long, pale fingers, Cordelia serpentined her earrings atop the piano. "A drunk, angry cuckold was the most prudent choice."

Cordelia Mayfield, she had been the one to send the flowers to Mama. She had meant to kill Kingston Mayfield. To have Daddy kill him. "It didn't work," I said. The fireplace woke. Logs shifted, tossing embers, singeing the rug.

"When Kingston came home that night with not so much as a scratch, I was afraid." Cordelia reached her hand out to Mama. "I could have told Marlissa about her brother, that he had returned. But that would have only terrified her. So, I told her Analeise and that colored girl were her bastard sisters. That she needed to be cautious, to keep a distance. That they only would ever mean to harm her, to try and take what was hers." She pressed her lovely hand to the small of her throat. "Of course, it was the truth. But not the whole of it,"

"Enough," Mama said. "Of all this crazy talk. It doesn't make sense. If you wanted to keep Marlissa away from Analeise, and you believed she was your dead boy, then why'd you invite her to that damn-fool party?"

"That was Kingston's doing. He wanted an opportunity to see his son, to begin to make his way back to Patton. To pick up where he left off," she said. "Do not think for one moment, I would have allowed my Marlissa to attend the same school with my Patton masked and pretending to be your girl. That I would have had him back in my home a second time if I had any say in the matter." Her eyes drifted to the fireplace. "Kingston meant to punish me. Make me suffer." Sadness fluoresced about Cordelia Mayfield, softening her.

"You're right, Cordelia. He meant to make you suffer. Not because he believed in ghosts. Not because he thought your boy had come back. Only because he was cruel."

Mama, she was taking all of Cordelia's attention. "And why should you not be punished, Mother," I said, speaking to both women in the room. "Help me understand. Finish the story."

"Is that what you want, my dearest, beautiful boy? To hear me say the disgusting thing?"

"Maybe we can move on from here," I said. "If you tell the rest."

The fire strobed, tossing shadows about the room, playing beautifully against Cordelia's eyes. "You were next to Marlissa on the piano bench while she played my sonata, your lips pressed to her ear. Your hands sliding to forbidden places. Are these the vile things you wish me to speak?" Cordelia Mayfield's eyes broke free from mine, wandering the walls, taking in the dance of light. Her body stilled. Her shoulders tensed. "When did it stop?"

Mama looked raptly upon Cordelia, mesmerized by the look of her there in the waltz of fire light. "When did what stop?" I knew at once from the look upon Mama's face we shared the same powerful kind of

321

yearning. How could I blame Mama for not resisting Kingston Mayfield? Any Mayfield.

"The music. It is all played out." She turned, gliding back to the Victrola. She wound the crank, looking to Mama and then to me. "There is just this one recording. Of your father playing my song." She lifted the arm and set down the needle. The phonograph crackled.

I felt faint in the heat, my mind comprehending the terrible thing Cordelia was suggesting. "It's a lie," I said, but deep down inside me, in that place the music played, I knew she spoke the truth.

"And do you know what he said? What my dearest, beautiful boy told me when I found them. When I snatched him from that bench?"

Mama shook her head, tributaries of perspiration converging in her eyes.

"Maybe next time you'll knock." Cordelia pressed the back of her hand to her cheek.

"Surely you aren't saying that . . ." Mama's words melted with the candle tapers.

"She's saying I did a terrible thing. That I hurt Marlissa."

Click. Cordelia Mayfield's eyes grabbed hold of me. She moved back quickly across the room, the train of her dress, a grounded kite desperate to lift. She stood at the hearth, her pale bosom rising and falling. "In your heart, Grace, you know the vile thing of which I speak."

"That's enough of this, Cordelia." Mama said, once again wriggling in the chair, struggling to be free.

"Say it, Mother," I yelled, pretending to be Patton, her beautiful boy. "Tell her."

"The vile thing I speak, Grace. The dreadful thing my son wants you to know with certainty is that even a Mayfield can not resist a Mayfield."

"Don't say another word. Analeise is a child. She doesn't need to know these ugly things."

"But we are not finished here. There is more to tell."

I knew Cordelia was right. I could sense it; I could feel the red-hot of it. The place to where we were slipping."

"I only remember the end," Cordelia said. "The very end."

"Liar. Of course, you remember," I said, not knowing if she did—but hoping.

"Only the end," Cordelia Mayfield said. "You running for the window. Your father right behind you. The awful smell of burning flesh."

"You remember all of it," I said, hoping and hedging she remembered. "Only you don't want to tell it."

Cordelia covered her ears. "Be quiet." She turned away from us, moving in a circle. When she was still, and the train of her gown was straightened and made tidy behind her, she spoke. "You are devoid of shame just like your father. That you could want me to speak it aloud. That you would want anyone to hear."

I glanced at Mama tied there in the chair and nodded, beseeching with my eyes for her to follow along. "Mrs. Newell, here. She wants to know. Don't you, ma'am?"

Mama leaned forward. "I want to know."

"Of course, you do. And why should it not be told before we finish our business here? Why should you not understand what must be done? Before you are gone from this world."

"Go on," I said. "Tell it."

Cordelia turned at an angle to Mama, her breathing once again quick. "I pulled Patton from Marlissa and dragged him best I could across the floor and from the room. In both my children's faces, I knew it happened before. That it would happen again. The way a mother knows a dreadful thing." She glanced from Mama to me and back again. "I screamed for Kingston. To tell him what our son had done. And that is when it happened." Cordelia turned to face me. "That is when you said it. The thing that took me to the edge." Cordelia's eyes drifted lovely and mad about the room. "Would you like to tell it, Patton? Would you care to say the thing?"

323

"You do it," I said, desperate to know and terrified all at once. "You say it."

Those lovely, mad eyes of hers, at last they found me again. "What would Father care, you said. You are all dirty cunts."

A hush tumbled into the room, pressing down upon us, nearly putting out the fire. Only the scratch and wobble of the sonata filled the void, keeping the silence from flattening us, from killing the flame. "That is when I did it. When the match was struck."

Cordelia Mayfield's hands traveled to her naked, pink lobes, the place from which her diamond teardrops had hung. Her hands drifted back to rest at her tiny waist.

Halbert appeared from the hall, startling us all. "Miss Cordelia," he said. The ailing candlelight found its way to his scars, shadows settling into the creases. Dozens of cicadas clung to him, flitting in the heat of the room, their tymbals tuning and preparing to sing. "Came back like you said. To help with the rest of it." He lowered his head at Mama and then at me, those broken baby doll eyes *clacking*.

The candle flames grew taller. The fireplace noticed, shifting the logs. Cordelia Mayfield took a few steps away from the fireplace, moving close to Mama. The surge of light delighted and played upon the sheen of her pale blue gown.

"For as long as I can remember. As long as ever was, a fire has burned deep down inside me," she said, her look of stunning sorrow replaced with a far-off dreaminess.

"Perhaps you should tell them, Mother," I said, "Why you brought us all here."

Cordelia Mayfield cupped her face with her hands. "To end you, of course, my dearest boy."

The awful thing grew heavy again, rolling to the middle, tilting us all to the center of the room. Mama rocked, nearly toppling the chair. "That boy is dead. Dead and buried."

"That dead boy has business." Cordelia turned her marvelous face to me. "Please tell this woman why you are here."

And just why might a beautiful, burned-up boy come back from the dead to visit? Overcome with sadness and beauty, a tear spilled from my right eye and then the left. Then I remembered Miss Wessie's words. *He was always bothering Marlissa. Always toting her around when she was a baby, like she belonged to him only.* Patton, he wanted what I wanted. He wanted our sister.

"To take what is mine," I said.

Moving quickly, Cordelia was fast upon me, those elegant fingers squeezing my bad wrist. "Then we are here for the same thing." She snatched Marlissa's ribbon from my hair.

"You killed me," I said, not wanting to pull away, but not wanting to die.

Mama screamed. "Stop this, Analeise. Stop it now."

"I told you I would do it. I told you to be quiet, to stop talking filth. And all the time you taunted me. Dared me to do it. Telling me you would come back when I threatened to end you." Cordelia went quiet, her sonata *crackling* and *popping* until she spoke. "And look. You are here."

"A promise is a promise," I whispered.

A tease of tears found their way to Cordelia Mayfield's eyes. Her grip loosened. The phonograph skipped and scratched to the sonata's third movement, the turn of the table growing tired and spoiling the music. "Dearest boy. Did I ever tell you of the time your father tried to hold fire in his hand?"

The fireplace fumed. Logs disintegrated and toppled, collapsing onto one another, pushing one to roll onto the train of Cordelia Mayfield's gown. She looked back, regarding it with affection. She lingered, giving it time to catch before she stepped forward pulling me with her, sending the log gyrating across the room toward Mama and into the drapes.

The fire was slow moving, creeping up Cordelia Mayfield's train as if it were another of us in the room taking time to ogle her.

Mama screamed. "Cordelia."

From behind, Halbert yanked me free pulling me up against him and away from her. "Behold, Miss Cordelia," Halbert cried. "The bible—it say children are a heritage from the Lord." He kept pulling me, the heels of my naked feet dragging across the rug, the cicadas and my broken arm wild and screaming. "The fruit of the womb a reward."

"A reward?" Cordelia laughed, bending gracefully at the waist, covering her coral-waxed lips with her hands. "Then what is to be my punishment?" She stood erect, laughing, her supple shoulders pitching forward. When those perfect shoulders stilled, she was quick upon us.

Halbert held fast, pulling me against him, his back to the paneled wall. Cicadas fluttered and fussed, escaping him—tangling in my hair.

Cordelia Mayfield leaned close, fire-blooms billowing up her waist. My good fist found its way to her chest sending her stumbling back a step. Above the cacophony of yowling, burning things, I yelled, "You can't kill me."

Flames rode the drapes, licking and catching the ceiling on fire. Cordelia glanced up to watch the embers—the shower of falling stars. "You are right, dearest one," she said. Moisture pooled again in her eyes, the droplets of fire reflecting and flickering. "Bad always finds its way back to good."

Cordelia looked at Mama. "You asked me if I was angry, and I told you I am not." Holding her hand to her breast, she shook her head. "Bereft . . . That is what I am. This is what I shall always be." She turned from Mama and back to me. A final time she spoke my brother's name as she first spoke it to me that day at Mistletoe. And when she spoke it, only then did the flame take speed, a spectacular blossom of fire petals closing around Cordelia Mayfield.

Holding out her burning arms, she admired her hands, gazing down her torso and then behind herself, exploring the length of her gown. She spun and flailed across the space, the hem and train of her Christian Dior waltzing and scorching the parquet, exciting the fire burning in all the corners of the room. Against the French doors she collided, twirling out onto the porch.

Halbert took hold of me, pushing and pulling me across the burning room to Mama. Both of us yanked and finagled the ropes until she was free.

Mama and I hurried to the doors to watch Cordelia descend the stairs, to glide across the slanting earth and down the riverbank, the train of her gown turning the earth to char.

Behind us, Halbert caught fire. We paid no mind to his shrieks. How impossible it was to look away from such a wonder, to set one's eyes adrift from Cordelia Mayfield.

We spied best we could, the trail of brilliant footsteps she left behind. Mama squeezed my shoulder. "We have to go."

"Do you hear it?" I whispered. "Your dream-fire song. Do you hear how it plays through the flame?"

"It's time, baby."

"Just another minute."

Mama kissed the back of my head, and I knew she heard what I heard. That she wanted what I wanted—the same thing desired by anyone in the thrall of that Mayfield Shine. To be close and blinded—a good kind of hurt burning all the way down to the bone.

I leaned back against Mama, inviting the creeping thing, allowing its runners to take liberties, to slither and curl, making its way to intimate places.

To where all the bad runs deep.

1957 Providence Georgia
Epilogue

Cordelia's sonata vibrated up through the floorboards, rattling the bottle of Old Crow in the keeping place beneath my bed, beguiling Etta Mae and me from sleep.

Etta Mae sang pianissimo to the water stain keeping watch above. "Beautiful, beautiful boy."

I hummed along, the two of us shimmying barefoot through the window into a chorus of cricket and phantasm howling in the night. Etta Mae on one side and I on the other, we wrapped our sapling arms far as they could reach about the oak tree in Mama's Thinking Spot. Rhapsodic, the sonata undulated through the charred bark, sending thrills through our nightgowns. Ravishing our skin. Only at night did the sonata play, a feverish memory of a gone away lover the tree could not forget.

Thunder roused the earth, a low roll tickling the bottom of my bare feet. "A bee in her bonnet," I whispered.

Careful of storms as I of prayers, Etta Mae sang, seducing the clouds to undress the moon, baptizing us in a puddle of celestial glory. "Hush-a-bye, hush-a-bye. You there in the sky."

Tendrils of smokey smells crept the air, bleeding into the spectral scent of Cordelia Mayfield's perfume. *The smell of New Mama.*

"Is she coming back?" Etta Mae said.

If she spoke of Cordelia, I might have told her she never left. That her fire burned deep and for always. That if she cared to listen, off in the distance, she might know the sizzle of earth. The drag of leaf beneath the train of her Christian Dior gown.

Etta Mae, like all of Providence, believed Cordelia Mayfield burned clean through, calcine and final. Not a gleam of tooth or shard of bone treasure to be plundered. How lovely they spoke of her ashes gathered in evening flurry. Pixie dust sprinkled upon the river to dazzle the current and scorch the fishes.

Only Mama and I knew the truth. A secret meant for keeping. *Another lie.* I pushed myself free from the tree, from damnation and bliss.

"Who?" I said, taking my sister's tiny hand, prying her loose from the bark.

Etta Mae took notice of the *jangle* of my fairy charm bracelet, stroking it with the tips of her fingers. "Marlissa," she said. "Our sister." Etta Mae's long lashes blinked moon shadows against her cheeks.

Our sister. She had been stolen away to Charleston by her grandmother to live on an island, in a palace, by the sea. How desperate I was for Marlissa to return, and how terrified I was that she would.

"One day," I whispered. *One day.*

"Analeise. Guess what?"

"What?"

"I love you a bushel and a peck."

"Is that all?" I said. "That's just a bitty little ole scrap of nothing."

Etta Mae giggled, the sound of a flute thrilling the air. The taste— peppermint and chess pie filling.

Against the soft pillow of Etta Mae's lips, I placed my index finger. I looked back toward the house where Mama slept with Sheriff Briar Dobbs by her side. *New Daddy.*

"He'll keep us safe," Mama had said.

And who will keep New Daddy safe? I wondered.

Etta Mae cupped her hands about my finger, the cradling of the last of a dogwood's bloom. "How much do you love me?"

"A gracious plenty." No one could resist a Mayfield, not even a Mayfield, that much I knew as truth. Etta Mae was mine, and I was hers.

Etta Mae stood taller than yesterday, taller even than the moments just before. She grabbed hold, pulling me close, her chin near about level with mine. From beneath her nightgown, I felt the rise of fever from her fast-growing legs. For weeks, change crept upon my Etta Mae. The inevitable dawning of that Mayfield Shine. Her hand found my shoulder, setting the frame. Forward, she stepped, taking lead, setting us off into the dip and spin of a midnight, garden waltz.

Accompanying the oak tree, Etta Mae hummed. Adagio at first, the tempo building to a frenzy, steps so quick I could hardly keep time. We were ardent. A ghostly, hummingbird whir of nightgown in the ashen-blue light of a covetous moon.

Faster and faster we reeled. Into oblivion, Etta Mae might have spun us had I not grabbed hold of my wits. Remembered our chore.

Velocity slung and slurred my words, turning them to gobbledygook. *"Avez-vous,"* I gasped. *"Peur des fantôme?"*

Etta Mae heard, slowing our reel, turning our dance maudlin, the last tremulous moments of a carnival Tilt-A-Whirl ride. She pressed the warm slick of her cheek against mine.

"Fantôme," she murmured, then pulled away.

To the ramshackle bench, she made her way, abandoning me in moonglow's wake. The final steps, she leapt, the thud of her naked feet turned gentle by the cushion of mushrooms creeping the seat's rotting wounds. Through the thin fabric of her gown, that jealous moon shone, glorifying the umber floret of bosom beneath. Loose, her sleeves hung. She spread her arms, and in the blue-gray light conjured the impression she sprouted wings.

A fairy meant for keeping, to stow safe beneath the boards.

The first notes of Etta Mae's lullaby astonished the night, consoling the oak tree's thrum to a newborn's mewl. A flourish of vanilla, peppermint breath blew through the garden. The sweep of confectionery breeze sugared sword fern fronds, tantalizing the rabbit-eared leaves of Mama's neglected cast iron plants.

Quick, the fireflies came. Then the *clack* of the click beetle. Worms followed, slithering to the surface, glowing blue and wriggling slimy between my toes.

"Lightning bug, lightning bug," Etta sang, her notes chromatic, ascending a preternatural scale.

A lonesome firefly found the rhythm of another, and then another, until the constellation of lanterns glowed synchronous. The spectacular beacon pulsed slow and sultry, the singular yellow-green light turning mutinous to throb bright poppy red. My own heart took notice, stretching the beat. Turning me woozy.

Lightning bug. Lightning bug.

A veil of mist crept, turning the febrile air cool. From the poppy red brume came Jane Fenton to stand beyond the garden's gate. Always was she first, her eyes wide with wonder, aglow from Etta Mae's singing.

Virginia took shape, the edges of her Lady Macbeth wig fluttering in the breeze. Close as a whisker, she stood next to her sister, their fingers threading. The pulse of firefly light flirted with Virginia's white tunic, turning her festive as a Christmas tree bulb.

I waved to the gossamer twins, only they paid no mind—both a prisoner to Etta Mae's refrain.

Halbert came next. All about he looked, searching for Cordelia, his candle wax ear bending and listening for the cicada song. Many times, I told him Cordelia wandered the path alongside the riverbank—cicada nymphs dug deep beneath our feet. Some ghosts are forgetful, their memories slippery as deviled eggs.

"What's done is done," I said. A little something perhaps to comfort my gatekeep friend.

Lightning bug. Lightning bug.

The smell of Old Crow whiskey and river water conspired with the heart notes of Cordelia's perfume to threaten the acrid air. Daddy Claxton had come, standing yonder beyond the gate, a stretch far enough only spectral edges could be seen. I wanted to call out. To apologize for what Mama and Kingston Mayfield had done. To tell him I never meant him any harm. Only, it would do me no good. Some dead bear grudges you see.

Etta Mae trilled, conjuring another sugary breeze, the swell of chocolate and peppermint growing stronger in my mouth. Above the chorus of click beetle came the percussion of Miss Wessie's *boom boom* hips. Her cropped hair fluoresced, brightening the lonesome faces of the Fenton twins. Behind Jane and Virginia, she stood, placing her hands upon their shoulders. Too long had it been since the last moon. Since we last saw Miss Wessie. I longed to run to her, to tangle myself into her apron. To smell the flesh of sweet acre pea beneath her fingernails. But there is no hugging ghosts. There is only loving them from a distance.

"A bushel and a peck," I cried out to my Miss Wessie.

Fireflies flirted, adoring and tracing Etta Mae's fast-growing silhouette. I knew the truth of the thing; Etta Mae loved singing for dead folks even more than she loved me.

My sister looked beyond, her face growing dim. A sparkle of tear found her eye, and I knew to whom she truly sang. The one who had never and might never come.

From the bench, mushrooms blossomed, curling about Etta Mae's ankles to swaddle and comfort her feet. I hopped up aside Etta Mae, wrapping my arm around her.

Lightning bug. Lightning bug.

Miss Wessie joined the chorus. Then Jane. Then Virginia and me. Off in the distance, Daddy Claxton conceded, singing along. For in that deep down place, I knew—we all knew that when Etta Mae sang, she sang for her poor, sweet mama.

CPSIA information can be obtained
at www.ICGtesting.com
Printed in the USA
LVHW090748190222
710939LV00003BA/15